Triorion: Reborn

Part II
Book Four

by L. J. Hachmeister

Copyright © 2014 by Source 7 Productions, LLC
www.triorion.com

First Edition*

This is a work of fiction. All names, characters, events and situations portrayed in this book are products of the author's imagination. Any resemblance to actual persons or events is purely coincidental.

All rights reserved. No part of this book may be used or reproduced in any manner whatsoever without written permission, except in the case of brief quotations embodied in critical articles or reviews. Please do not participate in or encourage the piracy of copyrighted materials in violation of the author's rights. Purchase only authorized editions.

Cover art and design by L. J. Hachmeister and Nicole Peschel
Illustrations by Melissa Erickson and Jeremy Aaron Moore

Source 7 Productions, LLC
Lakewood, CO

Novels by L. J. Hachmeister

Triorion: Awakening (Book One)
Triorion: Abomination (Book Two)
Triorion: Reborn - part I (Book Three)
Triorion: Reborn - part II (Book Four)

Forthcoming

Triorion: Nemesis (Book Five)

Short Stories

"The Gift," from *Triorion: The Series*
"Heart of the Dragon," from *Dragon Writers*

A Note from the Author

Thank you for taking this journey with me across the Starways. Although the series continues with book five, *Triorion: Nemesis*, I consider book four to be the best reflection of my hopes, dreams, and imaginings as a young kid (that was supposed to be paying attention in class), as well as some of the tougher trials I had growing up... with a few Toorks, Liikers, Scabbers, and extraordinary telepathic powers thrown into the mix.

Thank you for sharing this with me. I hope you enjoy book four, *Triorion: Reborn   Part II.*

For Gail Radcliffe
with all my love

Triorion: Reborn

Part II
Book Four

PROLOGUE

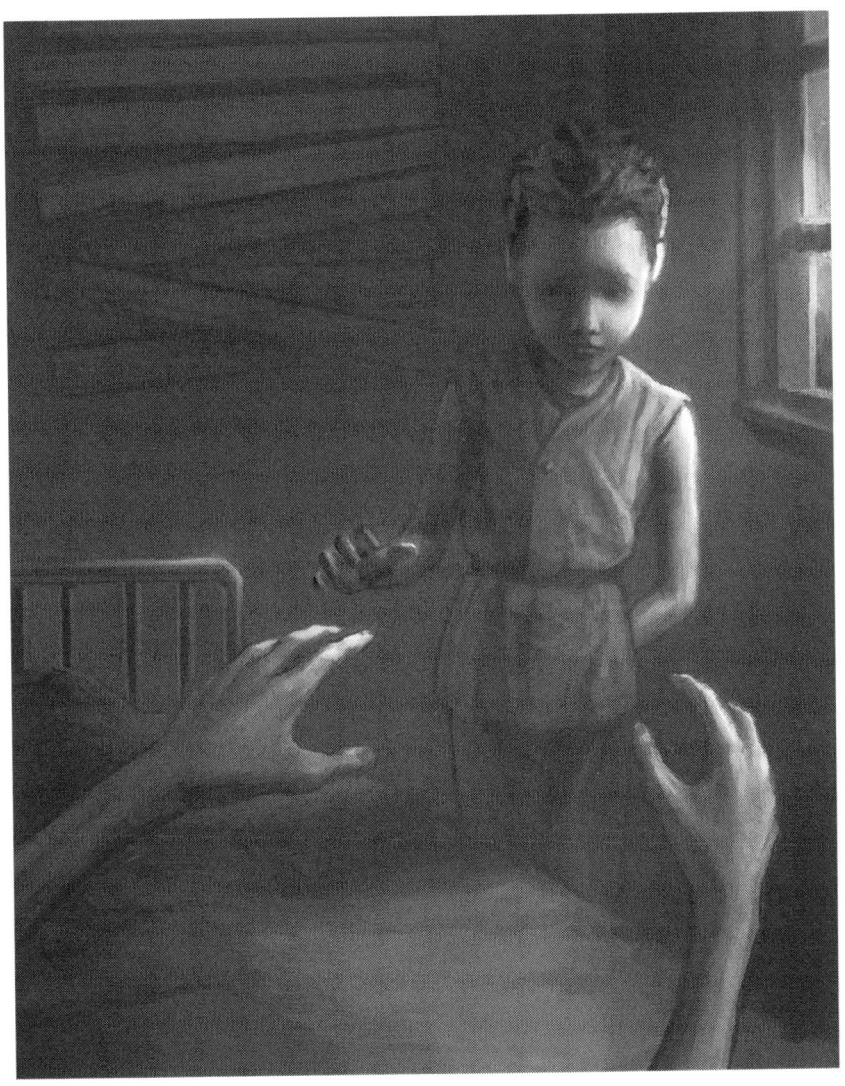

Fiorah: Year 3180

Jahx never told his sisters about his secret trips to room 311. If circumstances had been better, Jaeia might have understood, but Jetta would have only given him grief. Sneaking off became exceedingly difficult, and as often as wanted to go, his family, particularly his sisters, kept a close watch on him. And no unattended four-year-old went unnoticed, especially on Fiorah.

He chanced upon room 311 the day they moved into community housing. While Galm comforted Lohien in their squalid new apartment, promising her their situation was only temporary, Jaeia covered for her siblings so that Jetta and Jahx could explore the housing project and look for vending machines and discarded air conditioning units that they could possibly fix.

"Hey, look," Jetta said, nudging him.

Putting down his collection of plastic bottles, Jahx followed Jetta to the last apartment on the third floor.

"Do you feel that?" Jetta said, her hand hovering above the doorknob.

Jahx didn't have to say anything.

"Are you scared?" she asked. She hadn't intended to sound so peevish, but she, like the rest of them, suffered the hunger pangs of three bellies.

"Jetta... Maybe not this apartment."

But arguing with his survivalist sister got him nowhere.

"It wouldn't be right," he emphasized.

Jetta ignored him, testing the lock. Nimble fingers and safety pins did the trick in seconds.

Please, Jetta.

With a quick glance over her shoulder, his sister checked the hallway to make sure they wouldn't be seen. Aside from the screams of the arguing couple two doors down, the rest of the place felt like a tomb.

Everyone else is either sleeping off benders or making back alley deals, Jetta reassured him.

Driven by need and disgusted by his own poverty, Jahx followed her in. *(Stealing is wrong,)* his conscience whispered, *(especially from 311.)*

The place was cobwebbed and blanketed in dust. Cockroaches, surprised by their appearance, skittered toward their hiding places as they tiptoed to the kitchen.

Check the pantry. I'll check the fridge, Jetta spoke across their connection.

Jahx wavered, feeling the heavy pull in the adjacent room. *(This is wrong. We will only find death here.)*

Jahx! Jetta emphasized, making his brain rattle.

Careful not to disturb the nesting spiders, Jahx searched through empty tin cans and food boxes. The place had already been picked clean, probably by some other launnies or scavengers in the same situation.

"*Skucheka,*" Jetta whispered, despondent at their failed mission.

They both jumped as a growling croak came from the next room, rising in pitch. Grabbing her brother, Jetta yanked him toward the door.

"Jetta, wait—"

His sister, stronger and determined, dragged him out into the hallway and back to their new place, not listening to his protests, knowing only the fear that charged her reaction.

"Hey—what was that?" Jaeia asked as Jetta and Jahx caught their breath in the entryway.

"Don't know. Waste of a trip. Nothing in there but crumbs," Jetta said, opening her hands to reveal a few stale cracker bits.

The three of them stared at Jetta's open hands, salivating at the laughable prize. Jetta's anger and embarrassment throbbed in Jahx's chest as she divided the cracker bits and distributed them to her siblings.

"Things will get better—I promise," Jetta said, closing her hand into a fist. "I won't let Yahmen destroy this family."

That night Jahx couldn't sleep. Maybe it was the new apartment, the itchiness of the cots, the sonorous snoring of his uncle or the rats scurrying inside the walls. Or maybe it was something else. Something he had escaped in apartment 311.

I have to go back.

Without disturbing them, Jahx looked inside his sisters' dreams. Jaeia travelled to somewhere unfamiliar, a green and yellow landscape with only one sun. It wasn't the first time he had seen such a place in her mind, and he delighted in taking an observer's viewpoint when he had the chance. But now was not the time.

Jahx turned to Jetta. Curled up in a fetal position against the wall, Jetta slept fitfully as usual. Jahx put a hand on her shoulder, trying to draw his sister away from the pain and terror that plagued her sleeping mind. Unable to soothe her without waking her up, he withdrew, giving her one last look before slipping out the front door.

He waited until the underhanders were done with their hallway drug deals before making his way to the last door on the third floor. The drunk wadded up in the corner gave him a confused once-over but fell back into his bottle, singing a maudlin drinking song.

Walking on his tip-toes, Jahx let himself inside 311. Even in the middle of the night, the Fiorahian sunlight streamed through the shredded drapes, giving rise to new shadows and creeps. He noticed the smell this time, probably because his sister's will was not stifling his senses. *Sour and dewy—like decomposing waste.*

A desiccated whisper tickled his thoughts. *Who are you?*

The moan that followed stripped the gumption right out of him. He turned on his heels to flee when a bony hand, reaching up into the thin rays of light in the adjacent room, caught his eye.

Jahx held his breath. One of the long-nailed fingers curled at him. *Come here.*

Stronger stenches touched his nose; a smothering rot of old bed sores, body fluids soaking through unwashed sheets. Gagging, his animal instincts bade him to run, but the psionic pull from the bedroom drew him to put one foot in front of the other until he stood at the end of a bed.

An open mouth keened at the ceiling. Quavering hands with paper-thin skin held tightly to the bed sheets. Red-veined eyes, inflamed and blind, hollow cheeks; a face ravaged by time and disease. Jahx could not look away.

Frail and agonized noises came from the old woman, but what whispered across the unseen dimensions felt unfettered by corporeal confines.

Hello.

Hello, Jahx whispered back, surprised he could hear the woman so clearly.

She grunted and sighed, dry tongue caught across stained teeth. *Who are you?*

Jahx didn't know what to say. Who was this woman, and why did he feel compelled to seek her out? Death was nothing new to him or his sisters, nor was suffering.

Do not be scared. I am not going to hurt you.

"I am Jahx," he said out loud.

I am Sister Gailia.

A nun?

Yes. I was part of a missionary group, but most of us were driven away. I am alone now.

Jahx thought to take her hand but hesitated, imagining it crumbling and turning to dust.

The sister released the sheets and extended her fingers to him. *Please... I need to see you.*

Gently, Jahx touched the tip of his fingers to hers. Light exploded across his inner landscape. He gasped for breath as a shimmering star emerged from her dried out husk.

I see you now. Thank you, Jahx. You are so magnificent.

You see me? Jahx said, still reeling from the sight of her.

Two eyes, pellucid as washed-out glass, connected with his. *For all time.*

He tried to tell his sisters about the encounter with the dying telepath, but they both agreed it was dangerous. With the Dominion hunting telepaths, it would put them at even greater risk to associate with one. Besides, it didn't take long before Yahmen posted guards to keep a tighter rein on Galm. Even Jaeia agreed with Jetta—*"If she can't help get us food or off this planet, we can't afford the risk."*

But something told Jahx otherwise.

The day came when he knew it would be his last visit. He was getting slower, weaker, as sickness made his belly grow and starvation ate away his muscles. There was only so much energy he could expend slipping past the guards and evading his sisters' detection. Yahmen was beating them every day now. Soon, there wouldn't be anything left of him.

I have enjoyed our talks, Jahx. Thank you for telling me of your family, of your life, the sister whispered. Her breathing was audible now, rasping and thick with mucus. Her hands hung at her sides, gray and stiff. *Now I must go.*

Are you afraid? Jahx asked.

The nun's chest rose and fell erratically. The air changed in the room, as if even the shadows held their breath.

No. You shouldn't be either.

Jahx could feel her eyes inside him, seeing his fear, knowing his infirmity.

Is that why you've come here, Jahx? To know what death is? she asked.

When I see death, Jahx said, thinking of the countless bodies laid to waste in the alleyways. *I feel only emptiness.*

But you do not see beyond the vessel, the old nun whispered. *Look into my eyes. Look into all that ever was and shall be.*

Leaning forward, Jahx looked into membranous, unseeing eyes. He tried to stop himself, but he pitched forward, beyond the limitations of his own perceptions.

I see... Jahx said, standing over the well.

An old man with Jahx's face sat against a tree wearing a bearded smile. Children laughed somewhere ahead. His name was spoken by many voices. Old eyes filled with joy. He rested his head against the tree trunk, relaxing into the warm summer's embrace.

Do not be afraid of death, Jahx, the nun called as the last of her breath sighed out of her lungs. Something in the room with them exhaled with satisfaction.

Jahx saw himself one last time from within her sight, drowsing in the sun.

"Now I know." He drew the bed sheet over her head. "There is no such thing."

CHAPTER VII

Agracia felt much better around Bossy. No more strange headaches, no more inner conflict. Back to her old self, she bantered with her companion and harassed passersby that gave them any sort of look as they made their way to the center marketplace in the Spillway.

"This place gets more boring each time," Bossy lamented, thumbing her weapons belt.

"It's 'cause you've already hustled half the city."

Bossy snorted. "Well, 'scuse me for wantin' a little action now and then."

"Whaddaya lookin' at, sucker?" Agracia flipped up her middle finger at a sour-faced vendor before returning her attention to her friend. "See, this is why we gotta get out of here. Not a single Scab has an ounce of common courtesy."

This is the real me, she decided, taking in the dank smells of the underground city. Whatever memories Jetta Kyron had uncovered were in the past, something that *used* to be her but was no longer relevant. Getting off Earth was relevant. Making money was relevant. Old starships, uptight Skirts, and somebody else's war games were no longer a part of her life, and as far as she was concerned, she was better off without those half-remembered truths floating around her head.

"Hey, you got one hour."

A beefy hand slapped down on her shoulder. Agracia had almost forgotten the two thugs escorting them to the edge of the marketplace. With Bossy at her side, she didn't take anything too seriously, even a job for a snake like Victor.

"Don't miss me too much while I'm gone," Bossy said, batting her eyes at Shandin's men.

"Go chak yourself," one of them muttered.

Bossy licked her lollipop and stroked a grenade, baiting them to step up, but they walked away. "Pussies!"

"So anyways, we'd pro'lly best to ask Tiny," Agracia mused, standing at the crossroads. Old sewage treatment pipework and the mish-mash parts of tanker trucks gave the subterranean city its own distinct, ramshackle ambiance. "He always knows where to find the best juices."

The flow of people moved around them indifferently as they decided which direction to go. Slightly east was the Hexers district where practitioners of European paganism and Prodgy fundamentalists performed their magic tricks. Agracia hated going there. All the old witches, dressed in a gloomy amalgamation of nineteenth-century clothing and modern gothic, flicked their nails in her direction, spouting off strange chants until she passed by their stalls. Bossy loved it, always dragging her down to see what unfortunate animal was boiling in their pots or what strange smell was coming from the backs of their shops. Potions, herbs, and anything weird and unorthodox could be found down that street, but nothing practical.

North of their location were the black market avenues where most of what she needed could be found, but they didn't dare venture down there unless absolutely necessary. The Scabbers that dealt on the north side were notoriously vicious, and even with her dark horse she didn't feel comfortable even setting foot on the unpaved roads.

"So, you get things straightened out in your head?" Bossy asked as they headed down an unmarked alleyway between shops.

"Yeah. It was all a bunch of *gorsh-shit*," Agracia said, keeping her eyes trained ahead. *Don't say nothin' else,* she told herself. *Feels like even the walls are watching.*

"Good," Bossy said, counting the 20-20 grenades on her belt. "Didn't want things to get messy."

The alleyway was deserted, an unusual find in an underground city that utilized every centimeter of space. But Agracia and everyone else knew better than to loiter in this place. At the very end of the bricked up alley lurked a Scabber with the face of a pit bull and the build of a tank, strapped down with more ammo and firearms than a munitions warehouse. There, under a rusted flood lamp, he guarded one of Earth's best-kept secrets.

The Cathedral, she thought, imagining the legendary palace decked out in white gold and expensive playthings. Accessible only by invitation and a ride in the city's lone working elevator, the high-stakes retreat held little interest or investment for Agracia, though part of her wondered what really went on in the most secluded area on Earth.

"'Sup, Tiny. How's business?"

The man with the pit bull face snorted and looked away from her.

"Hey, that's no way to treat a lady," Agracia said, crossing her arms and leaning against the wall. "Thought we was friends."

"You have no friends, Agracia Waychild," Tiny replied, still avoiding her gaze.

"You're right. Just enemies and allies. What are you, Tiny?"

Sucking noisily on her lollipop, Bossy moved in front of her, playing with her pigtails while stroking the pins on her 20-20s.

"Get your lapdog out of my face." Tiny shoved the butt of his gun at Bossy, but her companion sidestepped his strike and disarmed him with a quick pull and thrust.

"You bigger, but she's better," Agracia said, nodding at the petite little girl aiming Tiny's own gun at him.

Tiny chuckled and blew a kiss at Bossy. "Just give me one night, little missy."

Face souring, the dark horse clicked off the safety to the gun.

"Don't got much time," Agracia interjected. "I need a drop on a good juice shop."

"Where you headed?" Tiny said. "Don't tell me you're going east."

Agracia smiled.

"Jeezus, Gracie," he said, pulling a smoke from behind his ear. He never smoked it, just chewed on the end. "No one goes there anymore. Necros really have a foothold."

"Hey man—what's that?" Agracia pointed to the silver lozenge sticking out of Tiny's left ear. Deeply embedded in the canal, the inflamed, red tissue that surrounded the device hinted that it had been freshly implanted.

"Nuthin'. Forget you saw it," he growled.

"What the hell, man? You getting into some crazy business or what?"

Tiny shielded his ear from her. "I said, *forget it*, okay?"

Bossy finally lowered her weapon and gave it back to Tiny. "Look, forget you, alright? Just tell us where to find the juice, man—we ain't little kids. We professionals."

Tiny's smirk came back. "Just one night."

"Go to hell," Bossy said, licking her lollipop slowly with the very tip of her tongue.

"Come on, man. We need this. I'll throw in five hundred for ya when I make the purse," Agracia said.

Tiny rolled his eyes. "Yeah, yeah."

"Seven fifty. Final offer. Just tell us who's selling."

Agracia hated having to pay to know where to find good anti-radiation meds, but the crime lords that ran the cities always sequestered the best stuff. Everything else was contaminated, partial doses, or completely ineffective. At least guys like Tiny knew where the shipments from the Alliance came through and how their bosses redistributed the goods.

Tiny's eyes flitted to the left. Making sure not to let her gaze drift that way, Agracia caught the edge of something black and shiny hidden under a corroded sign. *Bastards. We're being watched.*

"Things ain't the same anymore, Gracie. With the Alliance gone, we're under new government aid."

Aware of the unwelcome eyes monitoring their exchange, Agracia held her tongue, unsure if she should ask anything more to clarify what he meant.

The man with the pit bull face saw her confusion and bit the scar that bisected his lower lip. "Gotta new boss," he whispered. "Things have changed."

Agracia looked again at the device embedded in his ear. "New boss? Who? Two Time Rex? Fat Yai? Wait—not Little Cho?"

Tiny's eyes widened with every whispered syllable. "Victor Paulstine."

Agracia's gut dropped to her knees. "Thanks, Tiny. Be cool, alright?"

"Give me a hug, Gracie. For old times' sake."

Not one for physical contact but picking up on his Scabber code, Agracia grudgingly gave him a hug. Tiny held on tightly and for many uncomfortable seconds beyond standard etiquette. When he released her, Agracia had all she needed.

"Wait!" Bossy shouted, trying to catch up as Agracia hurried back down the alleyway. "What the hell just happened back there?"

Agracia waited until they were out of the alley and back on the streets before answering.

"Victor spooks him," Agracia said, showing Bossy her palm.

The dark horse blinked, taking a second to realize how Tiny got his message across. One of the oldest forms of back-alley communication, signing on someone else's hand had practically become a Scabber custom, a quick way to deal under tables and away from prying eyes.

"So?"

"*So*, there's a big shipment of some new fancy stuff. He said Shady Tom had a cut of it."

"I *hate* Shady Tom," Bossy said, crossing her arms.

Agracia chuckled. "I know you do."

Shady Tom was one of the few people still living that had confused Bossy for a Puppet. In truth, Agracia couldn't fault anyone who did. Unusually young-looking, the dark horse didn't look a minute older than the day Agracia met her years ago. On top of that, she held a certain sexual air, from the way she swung her hips to the perfect roundness of her breasts.

But no Puppet has an appetite for violence like my Bossy, Agracia thought, falling back on old arguments. *Or the strength of ten men.*

The few genetically-designed call-girls Agracia had encountered had been void of superior intelligence and lacked any sense of dignity or self-preservation. If nothing else, Bossy was an expert at self-protection, especially for a carnage-loving Jock.

"He's just a few blocks up on the North Side. Come on; don't have much time left."

Sticking together, they made their way up to the North side. Despite the danger, Bossy didn't deny herself the pleasure of giving the finger to as many whistlers and catcallers as she could.

"Come on, lay off, will ya? I don't want to get canned up here."

"A lady's reputation is everything," Bossy said, flipping her pigtails.

They stopped at the end of the line. Sandwiched between an all-night juke joint and a brothel, Shady Tom's shop used to be the prime stop-off for Jocks about to make a surface run. One of the back exits to the Pit sat behind his business, and until one of the fighting ring operators carved a better access near the dome on the south side of town, he saw most of the action in town.

Agracia muttered several expletives and a prayer as she pushed open the barred door to the shop. A little bell jingled, alerting the man sitting with his feet propped up on the service counter. With most of his attention still glued to the black-and-white hologram of a nude dancer, he afforded them a glance.

"Oh *sycha*—look what the cat dragged in."

With Bossy following in behind her, she stepped into one of the many disorganized rows. Biosuit parts, radiation and plague meds, miscellaneous tools, weapons, and a few outdated rations that were more dust than food lined the shelves. In the back of her mind she remembered his reputation for having maps of the wastelands—real ones, dating back before the Last Great War—but none of her persuasions ever got him to admit whether or not he really possessed them.

Imagining a chance to loot the last of Earth's treasures, she sucked on her lower lip. *Something like that is worth more than gold.*

Bossy tugged on her sleeve. "Make this quick."

Agracia didn't argue. She almost hated him more than Bossy did. There was something seedy and underhanded about him, more than the other dealers in town. If it meant screwing over his own mother to make a profit, Shady Tom would do it. Even the lowest of Scabbers knew that survival on the dead planet meant some kind universal cooperation, but Tom wasn't interested in such sentiments.

"I need your best juice, Tom. Not the *gorsh-shit* stuff on the shelves, either." Agracia threw down some of the cash that Shandin had advanced her. "That's more than fair."

The sight of the green and grey stack peeled him away from the holographic nude dancer. Greed lit his eyes, and he took the cash in hand, an ugly grin cutting into his face.

"No deal," he said, setting the stack back down and massaging his chin with scraggly fingers. His gaze shifted to her companion. "Not what I want."

Agracia couldn't believe an aging man like him—a waste of bones, pocked skin, and half a mouthful of teeth—could be so brazen. "What then? 'Cause she's more than you'll ever be able to handle. Unless you like pain."

Bossy picked up her cue and hopped up on a countertop, lifting her skirt a little while palming her 20-20s.

Shady Tom wiped his hands on his jacket. "Things are changing 'round here. Rules aren't the same. Cash don't seem to have the same value no more."

"What's more valuable than cash?" Agracia laughed.

"People. Flesh. Life," Tom replied.

Agracia didn't like the way he said those words, or the hungry expression in his eyes.

"Got me a side business going. Good profits—no, *unimaginable* profits. But I don't have the legs for it," Tom said, rapping his knuckles on knobby, deformed knees. "At least not right now. Need some help gettin' started. Interested?"

Agracia instinctively took a step backward. "I got a big job right now, man. Maybe some other time."

"Gonna get me some new legs—gonna get me a new life," he said, licking his lips. "What say you? Ain't no money hockin' junk for Tourists. There's so much more than this *chakking* life."

Agracia didn't know why, but Tom's eagerness for her to ask him more made her very nervous. Even Bossy sensed the odd shift, and returned to her side. "What you up to, Shady Tom?"

He leaned over the counter, his eyes wide as he whispered the most terrible word she knew: "Roundups."

Roundups. A word used in the time of the Eeclian Dominion when their military, the Core, seduced young children into joining their armies. She had also heard it used to describe the mass arrests of telepaths during that same time period. *But this is different—something much bigger,* she sensed.

"Who are you rounding up?"

"Deadskins. Traitors to our people. Those who left us behind."

Agracia felt the blood leaving her fingertips. "Who's your Joe?"

Even in the otherwise empty shop, Shady Tom looked left and right. "Some Tourist. Some man calling himself Shandin. A real *assino*."

The memory of the trafficking port hit her full force, jarring her senses. She heard Shandin's voice—

—*"I run a butchery and packaging plant. We distribute survival rations to the poor across the Greatlands."*

It couldn't be.

Just a coincidence, she told herself. No way could they be killing that many humans right underneath the noses of their own kind.

"The Deadskins didn't leave us behind," Agracia started, but Shady Tom slammed his fist on the counter. Bossy jumped back, reaching for a pin on her 20-20, but Agracia stopped her.

"They sure as hell did. Only those with real money could board those ships, and the rest of us scum were left behind. The war's forgotten children left to rot in this godforsaken place. Who's ever come back to save us?"

"There were plenty of times that—" But he wouldn't let Agracia remind him of the old United Starways Coalition's many attempts to relocate the Earth-bound humans. Instead, he continued on his rant.

"Now's our chance to get even. I get two weeks every month to scout out new encampments where the Deadskins hide out. I give Shandin the location, and he pays me more in one job than the lifetime I've wasted in this store. See? So simple, right?"

"Then why do you need us?"

"My legs are too bad," he said, gripping the brace that held together the remnants of his left leg. "Hurts too much. Can't travel farther than Saturn's moons. I just need a few more scores to afford the surgery and get off this *chakking* rock!"

"You can take that job and shove it."

He moved to grab Agracia by the collar, but Bossy batted his hands away and held out a 20-20. "Back off, *ratchak!*"

"Just give me some juice for the road," Agracia replied evenly. "And we'll be on our way."

Shady Tom's eyes burned with rage. "Get out of my store, you *chakking* Scab!"

Then she felt it. Something that wasn't her—or was it? Normally she would have cold-cocked the bastard and ransacked the store. She didn't need anything else from him, and she certainly didn't care who was profiting off of whom for whatever reasons. But an unforeseen compulsion kept her grounded.

"Hey," Bossy whispered, shifting foot-to-foot as she hesitated. "What gives?"

An unstoppable force rose within her like a tidal wave in her throat until she spoke the words that formed before she could think them through.

"You sick *chakker*. You're throwing me out of your store when I'm trying to make an honest living? Yeah, I'm a garbage picker, but at least I'm not selling out my brothers and sisters to a Tourist. You think our own abandoned us? You wanna know the truth?"

Tom backed up against the wall as Agracia crawled over the counter and got in his face. The spit flew from her mouth as she screamed every word. *"We abandoned our own humanity!"*

That isn't me, she thought, breaking out in a cold sweat. The back of her neck stiffened, and the base of her skull throbbed. *Someone else said those things.*

"Who's your Joe, then?" Shady Tom whispered. "Huh? Who is it? 'Cause everyone 'round here works for the *assino.*"

Agracia said nothing, too afraid of what would come out of her mouth, but didn't back down.

Shady Tom pulled out a safe from under the counter with Bossy watching his every move, 20-20 in hand, as he turned the lock.

"Here," he said, throwing a pill bottle at her before replacing the safe in its hiding place. "Take this."

As Agracia turned to go he gave her a long, hoarse laugh. "Stupid Jocks. I hope the Necros eat your faces."

Agracia dragged Bossy out screaming, denying her the kill she thought completely justified.

"What the hell, Gracie? You gonna let him lip off at you like that?"

"What good would killing him do? He's working for our Joe now—it'd be bad business."

"You never thought twice about a good time before," Bossy said, kicking the side of the building. "I want the old Gracie back!"

(I'm not me—)

Staggering into a pile of trash, Agracia fell to her knees.

"Gracie!"

"I'm okay," she mumbled, rubbing her temples furiously. "Just another *chakking* headache."

She squeezed her eyes shut and saw her family crowded in a one-room apartment, but an image of a uniformed man shouting orders at her overlapped the memory.

"Wasting your time evacuating the ground teams? You needed to drop your missiles!"

"God—" Agracia cried, rocking back and forth as the voice drilled into her skull in an auger of unrelenting pain.

"What's wrong? What do I do?" Bossy said, running back and forth in a panic. Onlookers stopped and pointed in their direction. The last thing they needed was unwanted attention, but Agracia could do nothing to quell the agony.

In her mind's eye she saw her mother, shouting at her after she hit one of her sisters—*"You are without God's grace!"*

At the same time, a Tarkn man with thinning hair and a freshly pressed uniform barked harsh words in her face—*"You're a disgrace, candidate!*

Know when you're defeated!"

"You can't help her."

Agracia peeked open one eye. Standing in the shadows between the buildings, a familiar figure vibrated in the confusion of her senses.

"You again!" Bossy shouted, taking out a fistful of 20-20s.

"I can help her—or you can let her stay that way. It's your choice."

"I oughta—"

"What?" the voice in the shadows contended. "You don't have a collar for me now. Put your weapons away and bring her back here before it's too late."

Several more curses left Bossy's mouth before she complied. The dark horse wrapped Agracia's arm over her shoulder and hoisted her to her feet, dragging her into the dark passageway between stores. That's when Agracia recognized the speaker.

"Doctor Death... God, you look like hell," she said, giving her the once-over.

Even though Jetta's appeared sallow and sickly, the intensity in her eyes hadn't waned. "I told you I'd return."

Bossy wrinkled her nose. "Who are you?"

A tall, dark-haired woman stood next to Jetta, watching the exchange with a careful eye. She gave Bossy an equally disgusted look. "Triel."

"Triel of Algardrien—the last Healer?" Agracia said, pressing her thumbs into her temples. "I thought you was a legend."

"Fortunately she's not," Jetta replied.

Succumbing to the hammering pain, Agracia slumped against the composite siding of the brothel.

"Gracie!"

She wasn't sure who was talking anymore. Her mother continued screeching at her as the uniformed man yelled in her face. The faces of her siblings, freckled with dirt and disease, passed before her eyes like mournful ghosts in a forgotten dream. Other children, dressed in uniforms and hunched over consoles, shouted commands and racked up points on a holographic scoreboard.

"Make it stop... please..." she whispered, rolling onto her side.

"Do you remember our agreement?" Jetta crouched besides her. "You were supposed to find out more about my tattoo."

"I couldn't.... New job. Had to take it..." Agracia said between the hammer strikes to her head. "Save Bossy."

"Fine then. Let me all the way in and I'll take what I need," Jetta said, offering her hand. "And I'll give you back your freedom."

"No!" Bossy jammed herself between the two of them. "Don't *chak* with her anymore! She was never like this until you leeched her brain!"

Tension sizzled through the air, but Agracia didn't want to open her eyes. The few rays of simulated skyline that peeked between the buildings sent bolts of pain through her skull. Still, even if she couldn't see, she could *feel* Jetta's anger.

It's getting hotter, she thought, wiping her forehead as invisible cords wrapped around her intestines.

"I'm trying to help her." With each word Jetta spoke, Agracia could feel the phantom cords tightening around her gut.

I'll be choked from the inside out, she thought, digging at her stomach. From the heavy sounds of Bossy's breathing, her companion felt it too.

"Bossy—move. Let her through," Agracia said.

Bossy grudgingly moved. The strangulation stopped.

"Please, don't hurt me," Agracia said between breaths.

Jetta rested a hand on her shoulder. "Then don't fight me, and this will all be over quickly."

Before she could protest, Agracia felt shoved outside her own body. Looking down from above, she watched Jetta pick her apart, sifting through layer after layer of reconstructed memories.

Images of her mother rippled like agitated water until the hatchet-faced old woman washed away and a man in uniform settled in her place. Their dirty flat, crowded with a half-dozen of her siblings, wobbled and whined and fell away, only to be replaced with a sterile classroom. No more cobwebs and grime. No more screaming babies with unknown fathers and empty bellies. This was a controlled environment, one with a video feed that tracked and recorded everything she did. Rows of children in gray uniforms sat straight-backed in their chair with fixed, robotic gazes.

"Cadet Leone."

Someone called her to the front of the classroom. If she hesitated, punishment would be swift. She hurriedly made her way to the front and saluted her teacher. "Yes, Sir!"

"Please outline the specific energy requirements necessary for a starclass ship to make the minimum jump during a battle."

Dissecting her every move, the man in uniform stepped aside so that she could use the holosim.

The calculation is easy, she thought. *After all, she had mastered advanced mathematics in her second year.* But I know what he's going to ask me to do next...

"Now cadet, tell me what you would do if your radiation shielding was deactivated in your forward decks and your damage status was critical."

A dark-haired boy with slanted eyes and a cold, calculating gaze studied her with smug satisfaction from one of the front-row seats.

She stared at the diagnostic readout of the ship. There aren't just soldiers on board, but families—

I know what he's asking me to do...

I can't do it.

Her hands worked quickly as she recalculated new parameters for the ship and executed the sequence. The holosim chirped and displayed her results.

"Congratulations, cadet. You made the jump, but at the expense of your weapons systems. Now you're as good as dead when the enemy finds you," *the teacher said, circling her.* "Explain what you did wrong to the rest of the class."

Shame speared her as she faced the classroom. "I chose to save my entire crew."

"And?"

"And... in doing so, I gave up my arms."

"Which would lead to the death of your crew."

Agracia's cheeks felt as hot as embers. "I thought—"

"Cadet Li!" *the teacher barked.* "What was the correct course of action?"

"Disable life support on forward decks and reroute all energy to the jump systems," *the dark-haired boy said.* "Save the deck crew and the ship."

25

Urusous Li. That was his name. Her enemy; the boy who wanted her dead.

The memory changed form. Blue-paneled walls above her, with a soft-glowing light illuminating the sign near the foot of her bed: Bunk 6, Barrack 12. Stiff sheets and a coarse blanket rubbed up against her skin when she shifted. No way to fall asleep with a full, aching bladder, but leaving the warm protection of her bed would be equally miserable.

Can't sleep.

Go quickly, and maybe nothing will happen.

Dangling her feet off the bunk, she paused for a moment, listening to the snores and sleep sounds of her other barrack mates before dropping quietly to the floor. She tiptoed around the other beds to the lavatories, counting each step to keep herself calm.

In the mirror above one of the sinks, her reflection caught her attention. Agracia couldn't believe her eyes. She had never seen herself without heavy eyeliner, a streak of color in her hair, and a scowl. This was someone different. This was—

"Tarsha," a voice whispered.

She looked ahead. A scream started in the tips of her toes and skyrocketed its way to her throat.

The splayed-open body of Sarrie Dhox, a fellow cadet, hung from a stall door, her blood and viscera collecting around the drain in the floor. Whoever had done this had performed the gruesome act with clinical precision, applying tourniquets to her limbs to keep her alive after slicing them off.

"Sarrie!" she cried, trying to loosen the bindings holding her up, "who did this to you?"

"Tarsha," the girl said with her last breath, "it's you he's after."

She dropped down, cracking her knees against the cold bathroom tiles. "Why?!" she screamed.

The military police showed up only seconds later. She was shoved aside as medics, teachers, officers, and other cadets flooded the lavatories.

Sarrie wasn't the first, she remembered. There had been Henderson, though the teachers had been quicker about covering that one up. More would follow.

(Li...) *Agracia realized.* (He's going to kill me.)

She felt Jetta tugging at the buried layers of her psyche, burrowing into her deepest secrets. Without her consent, Agracia tumbled backward and inward into a long-suppressed memory.

"You are without God's grace!" *her mother shouted, holding a frying pan above her head.*

That frying pan came down with brutal force, smacking her in the face and sending her spiraling to the ground.

But that wasn't real. What Jetta uncovered was.

Agracia saw herself as Tarsha again, this time standing before a massive holosim with innumerable game pieces.

(The Endgame,) she remembered.

"You're a disgrace to that uniform, candidate, and to all the people that have wasted their time and money training you. Why did you evacuate the ground teams? You needed to drop your missiles! What the hell were you thinking?" a man in uniform screamed in her face. "Know when you're defeated!"

Damon Unipoesa. That was his name. He was the Program's proctor. At one time he had been her idol, a father figure that she looked up to, but now he was her tormentor, pushing her beyond her limits, beyond any reason, to a point from which she didn't think she could return.

Horror-struck, Agracia watched herself scratch at the raw patches of skin under her uniform. No matter how many times she showered, she always felt grubby and vile. There was something about her, some kind of phantom stink leaking through her pores.

Sickening—

Can't get clean, can't get off this grime, *she thought, digging her nails into the red-ring of angry skin around the opposite wrist.*

A dark voice inside her played into her fears: (What can Unipoesa do to me now? I've lost the last thirty-eight straight battles; there's nothing he can do to bring me any lower.)

But impossible assignments and unwinnable simulations didn't stop him from delivering swift and harsh punishments for her failure. (It's as if he wants to ice me out...)

And then Li walked in.

"But Sir, we're not scheduled to battle for seven more months—" Tarsha said as Li sat opposite her on the game console.

She and Li were both leagues ahead of any other student, and for a long time Tarsha held the top rank, but their score differential had slowly diminished as Unipoesa pushed her to the brink.

"Your final is now. I'd suggest you pay better attention to your front lines this time."

Unipoesa leaned over and whispered into her ear: "You're weak. You're pathetic. You're no match for Li. Let's get this over with."

She froze. The moments seemed to pass in some distant dreamlike realness, even in the memory. There had once been a purpose in her training, though now it seemed impossible to recall. Now only confusion and disappointment dominated, and a terrible, pitting shame that hollowed out her stomach

I can't do this. *She tried to hide her shaking hands, but her entire body trembled. Catching a glimpse of her reflection on the chrome plates below the holosim projector, she cringed.* I don't belong in this uniform.

Anger percolated through. The strategist in her saw the underpinnings of Unipoesa's manipulations, and hated herself for letting him get to her. But somehow, despite this, she still cared about what he thought.

You made me love you, *she thought, remembering better times; the lilt in his voice when he spoke with her, and the ways his eyes were always careful not to linger too long when he approved of her strategies.* Even after all these years of trying to strip me of any type of humanity, putting me through hell—I know why you did it. You wanted to make me a better commander, you want to save the Starways.

The game started, but she couldn't bring herself to take the controls, not even when Li began pulverizing her forces. Tears streamed down her cheeks. Everybody saw it—the other teachers, cadets, Li, and Unipoesa. It didn't matter anymore. The only person in the galaxy that meant anything to her was in her face and threatening her termination.

"Know when you're defeated," Unipoesa spat in her ear.

The memory vanished, only to be replaced by something even more disturbing.

"Candidate 0113 has failed personality trials. We will have to terminate her from the program."

Masked faces came into view beneath the bright ceiling lights. "Now count backward from a hundred..."

Something stung her hand and traveled up her arm, spreading a blanket of drowsiness across her body. A familiar tune played in the background—

(My music!) *Agracia thought, thinking of the industrial tune that constantly cycled in her headphones.*

"Relax, Agracia Waychild," someone said.

(That's not my name!) she tried to say, but her lips felt numb and unresponsive to her commands.

"I hate that godich *noise,*" said a gruff voice above her.

"This is that gorsh-shit *the Scabbers listen to. It'll blend right in,*" a different voice replied.

A red-haired man slipped the headphones over her head. She struggled at first, but as the music repeated over and over, she found herself soothed.

"She's our toughest agent; her training made her resistant to our standard conditioning. She'll have to wear these things almost continuously to keep her sensitized to our control. It also means we'll only be able to trigger her with visual stimuli."

"Whatever it takes, Lieutenant," the gruff voice said, sounding unusually irritated. "I want her stationed as soon as possible. Keep this quiet."

"What about the Commander, Sir? He's been inquiring about her status."

"Get this through your head, Shelby—this is Agracia Waychild, the Scabber. Tarsha Leone is dead."

No, I'm not dead.

I'M NOT DEAD!

Agracia opened her eyes to a circle of curious and concerned onlookers.

"Gracie!" Bossy said as she scrambled to her side. "You okay?"

"Are you alright?" the Healer asked, offering her hand.

Agracia scooted up against the wall of the brothel. "I'm not dead!"

Bracing her by the shoulders, Jetta got in her face. "No, you're not. You're just remembering."

Tears squeezed through closed eyelids. Bossy had never seen her cry—she couldn't remember ever crying, at least not as Agracia. "Who... who am I?"

Empathy softened Jetta's face. "You are Tarsha Leone."

"No," Bossy shouted. "She's my Gracie!"

Her little sidekick reached for a ball of 20-20, but Jetta seemed to anticipate the move and disarmed her before she had a chance to remove the pin.

"Stop it," Agracia said, covering her eyes with her hand. "Please. I'm neither. I'm not Tarsha Leone, but I'm not Agracia Waychild. I'm…"

Slender fingers touched her wrist, sending a comfort warmer than any alcohol flowing through her body. She looked up to see the Healer, whose eyes sparkled with a glittery sheen. "You have been reborn."

She relaxed a little and took in a slow breath. The pulse thundering in her temples receded to a dull roar, and the headache faded to a low but steady drum.

Huh. Leeches ain't that bad, an old voice whispered in her head. She half-smiled. *Well, that's the Scabber personality shining through.*

"You're still my Gracie," Bossy insisted, taking her hand.

Agracia made sure to appear confident for her companion, even though she didn't feel the least bit certain. *Tarsha Leone is a remembered dream, something that happened in a different lifetime on the other side of the galaxy. And Agracia—she isn't real either. She's some half-baked idea of the United Starways Coalition, a freakjob they thought could blend in with Old Earth's underworld.*

But as Agracia looked at her young friend, she realized an important truth. "You're right, kid. I'm still Agracia. After all, she's the one that kept me alive all these years."

"Don't call me kid!" Bossy said, sounding more relieved than irritated.

Jetta shrugged her shoulders. "Agracia it is."

The Alliance officer offered her a hand up. "I got what I needed out of that gummed up head of yours. And I saw that you're traveling to the Deadzone."

"Yeah," Agracia said, adjusting her belt and gear with unsteady hands. "It's weird 'cause it's where I woulda taken you. You know that, though."

"Yes. It can't be coincidence that Victor's job and my tattoo are located in the same area. We'll travel together for safety."

"*Gorsh-shit!*" Bossy exclaimed.

Agracia pulled her aside. "We need all the help we can get in Necroland."

"There will be more than Necros to worry about," Jetta commented.

"No kidding. I've got tails," Agracia said, pointing to a few shifty-eyed men hovering around a food vendor across the street. "Guess our Tourist friend doesn't trust us so much."

Jetta peeked around the corner, her keen eyes sweeping the block before returning.

"We'll meet up with you near the border. Don't be late."

"Hey, wait," Agracia said. Something hitched in her throat when Jetta turned around, and she found herself unable to say everything she wanted to. "That... that was something else. What other magic tricks you got up your sleeve?"

"Was that your idea of a thank you?"

Agracia squirmed nervously in her boots. "Yeah. Yeah, it is."

After a pause, Jetta nodded and disappeared into the shadows with the Healer.

"Thanks for what?" Bossy rapped her friend's forehead with her knuckles. "Implanting dumb ideas in your skull?"

"Quit it," Agracia said, shoving her away. "She kept her end of the bargain. She showed me the truth."

Bossy's face soured. "Bunch of *chakking* mind games if you ask me. You've always been Agracia Waychild."

"Just like you've always been Bossy?"

It was a low blow, and it hit her companion hard. If anything, Bossy's past was more perplexing and muddled than her own.

"*Assino*," Bossy muttered, her eyes filling with tears.

"Hey, wait!" Agracia said as Bossy took off down the street toward the warehouse.

But Bossy didn't slow her stride. Agracia jogged along, weaving in and out of the crowd, shouting for Bossy to slow down as elbows and legs connected with her face and legs.

Someone shoved her off the street, and she collided with a mobile cart of raccoon meat. The vendor held tightly to his stock of dried skins and cursed at her. "*Chakking* watch it, kid!"

Agracia steadied herself against the barred window of a liquor shop. She saw her reflection in the glass next to the flashing ads for Redfly. From the depths of her mind came that same gruff voice: *"Tarsha Leone is dead..."*

"I'm not dead," she whispered back.

As she sank back into the flow of human traffic, she no longer saw herself as one of the countless dregs of a forgotten world, but as an unknowing player in an intricate lie.

Thinking of Unipoesa, she made herself a promise.

Never again.

***

The only way to placate Bossy was through booze, sex, or action, none of which she had immediate access to. *I guess the only thing left is to tell her everything...*

"So... don't you wanna know?" Agracia asked over the grind of pistons as their flat car ascended the railway to the Pit exit.

Bossy faced away from her, arms crossed and spine rigid, next to the headlamp mounted on the front of the car. While chomping loudly on her lollipop, she said, "Go to hell, Gracie."

This ain't gonna be easy. After all, their bond was rooted in a shared past—two throwaways who paired up and beaten the odds on a dead world. But something told Agracia that Bossy had to know. "My ma wasn't a boozer, and I didn't have a house full of half-brothers and -sisters. I was sent here because I failed out of the United Starways Coalition's Command Development Program."

Bossy thought about it for a minute. "Never heard any *gorsh-shit* that thick."

"It was a hush-hush thing."

"You're a *chakking* Skirt then?" Bossy said, whipping around. They both ducked simultaneously as they passed under a support beam, but it didn't break Bossy's thought. "I should slit your throat."

"Whadda 'bout you then? Don't you think it's more than coincidence that you and me met? If I was some pet of the government, they'd probably invest in someone to keep me safe. You're the best fighter around these parts. Don't you think that means something?"

Bossy's eyes narrowed and her hands twitched above her grenades. "Just what are you trying to say?"

"That you're important too, *assino*. That maybe the holes in your memory were put there for a reason."

"You think I'm a Skirt?" Bossy said, tackling her. Agracia smacked her head on the wooden frame of the flat car, and stars exploded across her eyes.

She had to be careful. Bossy was her best friend—but first and foremost a fighting-ring dark horse.

"I think that we need to find out the truth about your past."

Bossy's hold on her slackened just slightly, but the anger remained in her eyes.

"You're my best mate," Agracia continued, minding the tone of her voice. "No matter what, you and I survived this stink of a world together, against Meatheads, Jocks, Joes, Johnnies, Tourists—the worst of 'em. It don't matter what happened in the past except that if someone is using us, we need to set them straight. We *both* need to remember."

The flame in Bossy's eyes fizzled to a smolder. She rolled her lollipop to the other side of her mouth before popping it out and holding it near Agracia's face. "How can you trust Dr. Death? How can you think she doesn't want to *chak* us over? What if your memories aren't real?"

"They're real," Agracia said. "Or I'd be dead. Dr. Death got all she needed about the location of the tattoo; I felt her suck it right out of my head. The reason I'm still alive is because she knows that it wasn't *me* that captured her—it was Agracia the Scabber."

"Not Agracia 'reborn,'" Bossy said, mocking the Healer and sticking the lollipop back in her mouth. "Come on, Gracie—you better than that."

Agracia rolled out of the way as another low-hanging beam passed over them. In the distance she could see the glow of the portal light up ahead. *We're nearly there.*

"Suits on," Agracia said.

Both of them smacked on their helmets and zipped up their hazard suits.

Not bad, she thought. Shandin's biosuits seemed top of the line, at least for Old Earth. They didn't smell like a fat man's armpit, didn't have any patches or leaks, and the readouts on her visor were clear, accurate, and continually processing. Most of the time she just guessed the level of radiation and plague by the wreckage of her surroundings—now she had detailed maps and limited sensor sweeps of the area.

"Fancy schmancy," Bossy remarked, knocking on her helmet.

The weapons and other gear she'd pulled from Shandin's warehouse didn't seem too shoddy either. Not state-of-the-art, but not busted out and overused. It made her even more leery about the true nature of the job. *And how badly we're gonna get screwed over.*

"Okay, fine," Agracia said, holding onto the railing as the flat car slowed and they approached the end of the line. "I don't know why, but Jetta still needs me for something."

"Duh," Bossy snorted. "With her rep, I can't imagine her not wanting revenge. If I didn't hate her guts, I'd probably ditch you and be her best mate."

Agracia grinned, although Bossy wouldn't see it behind her helmet. "Jerk."

They opened the magnetic Pit doors to relatively calm skies. The clouds looked like churning pools of mud, and the wind came steadily from the north. If her helmet's filters hadn't been so efficient, she would taste the sulfur in the air.

"Up ahead." Agracia pointed toward the mountainous west. The sun was just rising in the east, but, like most days, it was banished behind a dark curtain of clouds, keeping the daytime world in the grim heart of twilight.

"Jeezus," Bossy exclaimed when she spotted the Rover parked behind the safehouse.

Shandin had loaned them the six-wheeler for their trek into the heart of the wasteland. Fresh paint decorated the body, and the rims and mirrors appeared intact.

"This just keeps getting fishier," Bossy mumbled as she circled the Rover before hopping in through the passenger side. "No one has this kinda coin."

"Yeah," Agracia said, revving the engine. It turned over easily and purred like a giant cat, waiting for her to put it in gear. "Good thing I got us an insurance policy."

She heard Bossy sucking on her lollipop through the mike. "Whaddya talking about?"

Agracia rummaged around in her suit to find the pocket where she had stashed her prize.

"Wheredja get that?" Bossy exclaimed as Agracia produced an extra datawand.

Agracia tossed it to her companion for inspection. Unlike the high-tech one packed with intuitive functions and fluid modifiers that Shandin had given them, the extra datawand had an adaptor at the tip to interface with ancient computer modules from the Last Great War.

"It's pretty old and beat-up."

"Yeah, well, I lifted it off Jade."

"That old prune!" Bossy snorted.

"So...?" Agracia said, prompting her to think of the next step.

Bossy smacked on her lollipop as she thought about it. "We make a copy of whatever information we find on Jade's datawand. Nice insurance policy—it'll keep our Tourist bosses honest."

"Yup!" Agracia said brightly.

As their vehicle rumbled across the wasteland and into the boundaries of Ground Zero, Agracia watched the dashboard computer's radiation and plague monitor tick upward.

Bossy fiddled nervously in her seat. "Been a while, yeah?"

"Yeah... At least a few." Memories of the Deadzone made her heart beat faster. *And we were lucky to come out alive.*

The Necros had established a strong foothold in the Deadzone since the Last Great War, and no Jock with any sense had taken a job on the inside, not even for all the booze and hard cash in the galaxy. But the rumors of viable cryotubes still running deep in private underground vaults baited her in her younger years. She figured if they could find war survivors still frozen in tubes of prototype cryon, then maybe she'd garner a name for herself. Well, at least that was back when she thought she had a legitimate shot at getting off Earth, back when—

No.

She gripped the steering wheel with all her might. *Wait... that job came off of a telegram from an unnamed Tourist. It read just like that stupid letter I got several weeks ago, right before I met Jetta Kyron.*

"*Dichit*," Agracia said, slamming her fist against her wheel.

"What's your problem?"

"*Chakking* Skirts," Agracia muttered. She explained to Bossy the connection between their first treacherous job in the Deadzone and the recent letter hiring them to dig around the surrounding wastelands for the passenger lists. "Those Alliance *ratchakkers* orchestrated all of it!"

"Mother *chakkers!*" Bossy shrieked into her headset and sprang up on her seat. She rolled her window down and blasted away at decaying structures with her sidearm until Agracia yelled at her to conserve ammunition.

For some reason Agracia's thoughts drifted to Commander Unipoesa. *Were you a part of it?* she thought.

No, he couldn't have been. He was her idol. He was her closest thing to a father—

The rolling wasteland disintegrated into rows of desks and a teacher's board at the head of the class.

"Cadet Leone," Commander Unipoesa said, checking over her battle plan on her datapad. Her heart lodged itself in her throat as she waited for what seemed like days for him to finish his thought. "Excellent work."

He returned her datapad and continued his inspection down the rows.

This was a special day, she remembered. A visit from the commander was a major event, and every cadet rallied for his arrival. Even Li had seemed more animated, and he had stepped up his efforts on his homework.

"Marginal work, Cadet Li," the Commander remarked, giving Urusous back his datapad.

She could feel Li's eyes shooting daggers into the back of her skull as Unipoesa moved on to other students.

Something warm and wet touched the base of her neck, and her left hand reflexively went to the site. "I will kill you..." he said just loud enough for her to hear.

She slowly brought her fingers back, finding them smeared with blood.

"Gracie, watch out!"

"*Sycha!*" Agracia screamed as they banked off the lip of a wrecked superstructure.

The sky became indistinguishable from the ground as the Rover flipped and rolled until it came to a wobbly rest near the foot of a partially collapsed billboard.

"Holy jeez..." Bossy braced herself against the dashboard. "I think I'm gonna vom."

"Hey, no puking in here!" Agracia said, reaching over her and cranking on the door handle. The passenger door flipped open and Bossy spilled out, whipping off her helmet and emptying her stomach onto the cracked pavement.

As her companion continued to retch, Agracia tried to restart the engine, but she paused when she saw the billboard. Whatever advertisement had once graced its canvas had long since faded, replaced by centuries of graffiti and drifter art. The main theme, as it had been for the last five hundred years, remained the same: *The End of the World*.

"Welcome to Paradise," Agracia said as Bossy crawled back inside.

"What the hell happened back there?" Bossy asked, putting her helmet back on and checking her exposure levels. "Ya fall asleep?"

"No," Agracia whispered.

She looked back and saw Li's shattered datapad in pieces on his desk. Embedded in his hands were the neo-plastic splinter casings from the rim of the device. He didn't seem to register the pain as he made tight fists, squeezing the shards even deeper into his own flesh.

He mouthed the words again. I will kill you.

"Just thought I saw something."

I'm still not right, she realized, but she tucked the thought away.

"Well, you ain't drivin' no more, so shove over," Bossy said, trying to fight her for the keys.

Agracia pulled them out of the ignition and stuffed them down her suit. "I ain't. And neither are you. We're walking."

"Walking?!"

Agracia pointed to the billboard.

"*Chak*," Bossy muttered.

Traveling in Necro land was too dangerous in a Rover. Loud noises attracted the undead predators, and in the tangled jungle of steel and urban ruin, navigation was only possible by foot.

"I *hate* walking," Bossy reminded her.

"Awhh, buck up," Agracia said, punching her in the shoulder. "You need the exercise. A girl your age is liable to get a beer gut."

Agracia was stunned that her partner did not have a retort. Instead, she picked at the ribbed knee guards on her suit.

"Gracie… how old do you think I am—really?"

Never in all their years together had Agracia heard that tone in her voice, or such an old sound, one that came from far beyond her pigtailed, youthful figure.

"I dunno," she said stupidly. But she knew better. There wasn't anything natural about her friend's appearance or supposed age, and they both knew it.

Bossy stopped sucking on her lollipop. "You happier now that you know?"

Agracia didn't respond right away. "At least I know, right? No one can *chak* with me anymore. I'm not happy about what I was or what I was made to believe… but it doesn't matter now. I *am* Agracia. I'm a survivor. And I plan on making the rest of my life *mine*."

Bossy nodded. "Yeah." Then, after a moment of consideration, she added a more emphatic, "Yeah! *Chak* 'em all!"

Springing out of the Rover, gear bag and weapons in hand, Bossy made for the nearest shelter. Agracia raced after her, the wind whipping savagely against her suit as she headed toward the safety of the fallen beams of the old elevated railroad about four hundred meters from their location.

Agracia leapt over a pile of debris to find Bossy already hunkered down with a holographic map of the area. Skeins of ash swirled over their heads as they studied their surroundings.

"We didn't have a map the last time we came here," Agracia said, keeping her voice low, even though the helmet muffled much of the sound.

"Yeah, this is *gorsh-shit* anyway. Scale is whack, and half these buildings are dust now."

Agracia took the hologram from Bossy. Shandin had given them all the information he had on the area, but the map he had provided was one from the first century post-war, when a band of humans had returned to Earth for the first of many failed recolonization efforts.

Shaking her head, Agracia turned the hologram over in her hands. The landscape had changed so drastically in 1,100 years that most of it would be unrecognizable to any pre-war human. Only buildings designed or reinforced with synthetic steels had survived the holocaust; the rest had become heaps of indiscernible rubble. Worse yet, bioweapons and radiation had destroyed nature's usual methods of reclamation, but somehow a strain of mutated flora blossomed in the heart of the wasteland.

Red Polyps. Even the thought made her nose wrinkle. The Scabbers named the strange vegetation after the pungent plant's crimson tinge, but Agracia thought they should have named it after the smell. *What name did*

Bossy come up with? 'Fart Factories?' Heh. That's much more accurate.

Smelling like rotten eggs, the plant-like creature grew in gnarled clumps in the cracked patches of poisoned Earth. Deeper in the Deadzone, closer to Ground Zero, it was widely whispered that the Red Polyps had stalks bigger than six-story buildings with massive, bloated heads the size of domed stadiums. Though they flourished around sites with heavy Necro activity, rumor had it that they were spreading beyond undead territory, fouling the air with their sulfuric stink.

Agracia hated them more than anything. Stepping on one was worse than getting stuffed in a dumpster for a week. The Polyps exploded on contact, befouling everything with their toxic stench, and their mushy purple insides didn't scrub off easily. Even worse was breathing in the spores. Agracia had only seen a few cases of Redder Lung, but it was enough to keep her from ever risking exposure.

"Well, does that thick head of yours remember our old route?" Agracia said quietly, tossing the hologram into the blackened ash.

Bossy muffled her belch. "Yup. Betcha you forgot."

"Ha, you wish, smartass."

Lips curling up in an unsure half-smile, Agracia remembered the truth behind the lie. Her Scabber mother always told her she was a worthless imbecile, and she had a distinct memory of failing out of her pitiful dump of an Old Earth school. But after years of surviving the streets, she figured out she was smart enough to beat the odds and learned to believe in her own abilities.

Conversely, the Alliance had selected her because of her superior intelligence, and expectations were high from the start. After scoring leagues ahead of the other cadets in the CDP, the pressure was even greater. If it hadn't been for her eidetic memory, the same one that helped her navigate the treacherous Pits of Old Earth, she would never have survived as long as she did.

A military genius in one life, a lucky bastard in another. The thought made her uncomfortable, and she immediately shifted her attention.

"We'd better get going," Agracia said. She took back the gear, surprised at its weight. "What the hell did you add?"

"Some snacks."

Agracia unzipped the main pouch and found the survival gear she had packed. It wasn't until she unzipped the side pockets that she found Bossy's stash of booze.

"Really?" Agracia said, holding up the bottle labeled *Mississippi Diesel 999*. Bossy must have really liked the booze brewed by Shandin's thugs to lift an entire case of it.

Snatching it from her, Bossy stuffed it back in the bag. "For celebratin' later. It's *good*."

Agracia could hear her licking her lips. "God, Bossy; it reeks like gasoline and witch hazel."

"It was the purest *sycha* this side of the universe," she said, hardly able to keep her voice down. "I was pissin' *fire!*"

Agracia rolled her eyes. She considered tossing it out to lighten the load, but something stopped her. A memory, locked away somewhere deep, bubbled just beneath her grasp. *Keep it*, an unseen force urged her. She saw a flash of blue fire and heard an alarm wailing in the distance.

Unsure of what she remembered, but heeding the call of her instincts, she picked up a flat rock with a discoloration on one side. "Heads or tails for carrying the gear bag then, lush-head?" she said, turning over the rock for her to inspect.

Bossy pointed to the discolored side. "Tails. And loser buys all after this crap job is over."

"Remember, you're just a kid, okay?" Agracia jibed, flipping it up in the air.

"I'm *not* a kid!"

As they both waited for the rock to come back down from the mud-colored sky, an uncommon hush passed over, pricking Agracia's senses. *Something's not right.*

The rock clattered to the ground, rolling off into the tangle of railroad spikes and baseplates as both Agracia and Bossy instinctively dove for cover.

Agracia caught the sound of exploding Red Polyps and lifted her head.

"Four of 'em. Big *chakkers*," Bossy whispered, pointing to the north.

Up ahead, four lumbering Necros huddled over what looked like a freshly killed dog. She hated seeing anything or anybody get killed in the wasteland, but the critter population in the Pits was out of control, and if an animal wasn't someone's pet, meal, or fighting ring property, then they were usually released onto the surface. Even rats, the skilled survivors of mankind, didn't stand a chance against the Necros and the wastelands.

She used to think it was stupid to continue to provide sustenance for the Necros, but many a whispered bar conversation suggested that the Necros survived on something other than animal scraps and the occasional unfortunate Jock. It made sense, too; the undead population remained strong, even after the post-war efforts to douse the cities with chemical fire.

"We can get around them while they feed," Agracia said, grabbing the gear bag. Waves of disgust rippled up her throat. She swallowed hard, trying to keep her dinner of cat meal from filling her helmet. Watching Necros eat reminded her of the gore-fest horror movies Jade used to show them on something called a "DVD player."

"Jeezus..." Bossy whispered.

Feeding like crazed animals, the undead tore into the dog, flinging chunks of hair and skin in every direction. Purulent fluid dripped from their porous, flexible mandibles.

Gross, she thought as the dog's flesh sizzled. She didn't see how the deranged skeletons with elongated limbs and translucent yellow skin could have possibly ever been human. If it wasn't for the fine, bristled hair covering their bodies, their ugly mass of decomposing internal organs would be clearly visible.

One of the Necros bit a competitor, causing him to slink back and circle the group, waiting for his chance to feed.

That bastard looks like he's in the advanced stages of decay.

His red eyes glistened wetly in deep sockets as he got down on all fours.

God I hate when they do that, she thought. *Reminds me of spiders.*

Old thoughts crossed her mind: *How could it have come to this? What drove Josef Stein to unleash a scourge upon his own people?*

Even when she was Agracia Waychild, uninterested in anything but booze and a good time, the same question somehow nettled its way under her skin. *What could drive a man to destroy the world?*

She thought about her experiences in the Command Development Program, but came up answerless. They wanted her to be a razor, a soulless, lethal tool of the military, but even as a lowly Scabber who killed often in the name of survival, she never crossed certain boundaries.

Her thoughts came around to Urusous Li. It happened a long time ago, but Li was weak and wounded once—

And that's when Unipoesa struck.

Maybe that's what happened to Joseph Stein, she thought. *Maybe that's how monsters are made.*

"Come on, let's go," Bossy said, interrupting her thoughts.

Agracia crouched down and followed her along the broken railroad track. Busy feeding, the Necros didn't pick up their scent amidst the carnage.

We're going to make it—

One of the Necros shrieked.

Oh chak—

Agracia poked her head over the lip of a baseplate. "What the hell?"

"Where'd they go?" Bossy said. The Necros had scattered, leaving the gutted carcass of the dog flapping in the breeze.

"Dunno," Agracia said, lowering herself back down. "It's like something scared them off—"

The words died at her lips as a massive shadow fell over her and her companion.

"Holy *chak*," Bossy said, backing up against the wall. "That's no four-legger."

Agracia reached desperately for her sidearm as the hulking monster came into view. Not a regular Necro, the massive creature came straight out of her worst nightmares.

"It can't be…" Bossy gulped.

A long-held Jock legend of the Deadzone spoke of Necros that congealed together to form massive, symbiotic creatures. The Scabbers called them Behemoths, but Agracia thought it was only a stupid rumor concocted by deadbeat Jocks who needed an excuse to avoid the tougher areas of the wastelands.

"Run!" Agracia shouted, grabbing the gear, but Bossy had already bolted for the next superstructure, leaping over the dog carcass while unslinging her 20-20s and whipping them at the monster.

Agracia shielded herself from the blasts as Bossy detonated her grenades. The Behemoth reared back on its hind legs, its roar like a peal of thunder.

Daring a quick look over her shoulder, Agracia picked up her pace. "Oh *sycha—*"

An unearthly beast with shimmering black skin, the Behemoth had opaque eyes set inside the deep recesses of its skull. She saw no teeth, only prickly nubs lining the pink gash that must have been its mouth. It spanned the size of a small building, with a collection of mangled arms and legs hanging from its bulky midsection.

As it smashed its way through the debris of fallen buildings, its heavy accessory limbs dragged behind, leaving a soggy brown trail in the dirty asphalt. Agracia fired off a few rounds, but that did nothing to slow its progress. The monster's skin divided and reconstituted where the shots hit, impervious to her assault.

"*Chak*," Agracia said, taking a breather behind a building. Bossy continued to throw 20-20s and curse words at the thing, not having any better luck.

She looked around at the heaps of fallen buildings and broken superstructures. *We're not too far from our destination.* The Behemoth shrieked, making her wince. *But that won't matter if we can't shake this thing.*

Agracia considered going underground, through the old subway station, but there was no telling how much the landscape had changed over the years, and she didn't want to try digging for access with that thing on their backs.

After firing a few more rounds, she took off running again. *Whatever that thing is made of, it isn't going to be destroyed by regulation bullets or 20-20s.*

The Behemoth bellowed, striking down the crumbling tower of an old church, and hunkered down on all of its arms and legs. It slowed its pace, advancing carefully, as if sensing it had run down its prey.

Bossy stooped behind a pylon a few meters away, struggling for air. With its decreased oxygen levels and high levels of pollution, the surface was no place to run. Inside her hazard suit, steaming with sweat, Agracia wasn't doing much better, especially carrying a heavy gear. She needed to come up with something, fast.

Gods, I'd kill for a smoke right now.

Agracia shook her head. That was the Scabber talking, not her—or was it? Tarsha Leone understood the value of function over more destructive pleasures. But still, her body craved the caustic flavor of her favorite cigarettes. No, not just her body—

—Agracia fell to her knees as a headache cut her in two.

"I will kill you..."

She looked up and saw Li standing in front of the women's locker room door. Caught off guard, her fright carried in her voice. "Urusous, what are you doing in here?" she said, wrapping her towel around her shoulders.

He didn't say anything as he regarded her with the cold gaze of a learned clinician.

"Get out, Li!" she shouted. *Instead, he clicked over the lock on the door.*

The maintenance access, she thought, *but when she saw the grate secured to the wall with tiny bolts desperate fingers could not pry free, her heart sank. And she couldn't hope that another girl might want to use the facilities and figure out his scheme. Only two other female candidates remained, and both had showered and returned to their bunks.*

Nowhere to go, all alone.

No one will hear me scream.

Her strategist mind assessed the situation: Li is bigger than me, and his hand-to-hand combat skills are unmatched in the CDP. I can't fight him.

"Stay back—I'm warning you!" she said, posturing for strike.

Sensing her empty threat, Li approached her unhurriedly, his boots lightly tapping the tiled floor. The object he carried behind his back glinted in the reflection off the locker doors.

Li is no amateur. *She thought of Henderson, Li's first victim, who he had slaughtered and tortured in the boy's bathroom. The teachers tried to hide the murder from the other candidates, but Agracia remembered peeking out of the bunks and seeing the soldiers steer his lifeless body down the hall in a freezer case.* He is not an impulsive killer; he's prepared for this moment.

The military-trained part of her recognized his strategy: He had waited for her to be finished with her combat training, knowing she would be exhausted and take her time cleaning up during the guards' shift change.

"Tell me why," she said, backing up into the sinks. She lost her towel *under her feet and wobbled, but managed to keep her balance.*

He said nothing, though his eyes dipped briefly below her neckline. A smile wavered on his lips as she stood there naked, her hair dripping wet, with nowhere to run. All that's left is spilling my blood.

Something inside her bucked and resisted. (Don't let him win.)

Her eye caught sight of her only chance—the body dryers next to the shower stalls. Lunging for her towel, she rolled onto her shoulder, and sprang up next to the sinks. He easily readjusted his position, withdrawing the blade he had fashioned out of stolen utensils from the mess hall.

Wrapping her towel around her hand, she bashed the top of the faucet with all her strength. The pain was incredible, shooting up her arm and into her shoulder, but the piece broke free. She grabbed it out of the sink as water sprayed everywhere.

It did nothing to slow Li down. The smile on his lips grew in size. Only a few meters from her now, he held the blade in front of him, his eyes transforming into dark pools of rage.

She slipped behind the translucent partition in the body dryer and hit the switch. In a flash she was dry, along with her towel.

"Li... why?" she said behind the partition.

"Because I can," he whispered, knife firmly his grip.

He jabbed at her, but she dodged as best she could inside the dryer tube. The blade nicked her right side, slicing the skin below her rib cage. With her hand still wrapped in the towel and gripping the faucet head, she plunged the metal piece into the interface, sending sparks flying. The towel, dry as a bone, quickly caught fire.

Li stumbled backward as the body dryer crackled and fizzed. A flash of blue fire exploded from the interface, singeing her back and shoulders. She dove out of the tube and underneath the protection of the sinks while the body dryer continued to belch angry blue flames.

I'm safe now, *she told herself.* The soldiers will come. He can't kill me now.

Smoke quickly filled the locker room as the fire alarms wailed.

She crawled around on her hands and knees, blood spilling from the knife wound, disoriented in the black haze of smoke.

Hard to breathe—

Black fire filled her lungs, choking the air from her chest.

"Help me!" she shouted, but to no avail.

She collapsed in a heap. Somewhere, in the confusion of fire and smoke, she felt two hands grasp her wrists and drag her along the floor.

"Gracie!"

Agracia saw her pigtailed companion bent over her, desperately trying to drag her across the wasteland away from the charging beast. "What's wrong with you? We have to run—"

No time. Death opened its maw, eager to finish her off in one sweet bite.

Why, Urusous?

That's when she appeared. Doctor Death, Jetta Kyron. The destroyer of worlds, the savior of the Starways. Even dressed in some rag of a hazard suit, Agracia knew it was her by the way she moved. Her inhumanly fast, swift movements confused the Behemoth, and in one motion she flung their gear bag into the beast's mouth and fired off a single round.

The resulting thunderclap shattered the world into mushy black gobs and inhuman shrieking. She careened backward, stars wheeling across her sight as she slammed into something hard and unforgiving.

With a groan and considerable effort, she lifted her head, only to find herself covered in black sludge from head to toe. Jetta Kyron stood over her, concealed behind the gold tint of her visor. "Are you okay?" she asked through their radio frequency.

"Ughhh," she mumbled, shaking her head. As her senses realigned, Agracia found her voice. "Yeah, sure. Where's Bossy?"

The dark horse popped up beside her hooting and hollering, also covered in the black slime. "Holy *chak*, that was awesome!"

Agracia slowly pieced together what had happened. The gear bag. The *Mississippi Diesel 999—(No smoking!)* —crammed inside.

"Jeezus, you bastard," she chuckled, marveling at the scattered, fiery remains of the Behemoth. "You read my mind."

Jetta cocked her head to the side. "I thought you'd like that."

Agracia accepted her hand up.

Realizing who it was, Bossy changed her tune. "Hey—back off, *chakker!*"

"She's a tough one to win over," Agracia said to Jetta. She turned to Bossy. "Hey, kid, she just saved our lives—no need for swearin'!"

Bossy huffed and kicked what looked like part of a necrotized leg into the soupy black mix of charred Behemoth parts.

"Jetta," a concerned voice said.

The Healer, Agracia thought, recognizing her calm inflection. She spotted Triel of Algardrien rising up from behind the wreckage of an old train car. "We should keep moving."

"She's right." Agracia scanned their surroundings. "The four-leggers will get curious and come see what we cooked up."

"Smells horrible," Jetta commented, inspecting the heap of smoldering remains. "Even through the filters."

"Watch out!" Agracia pulled Jetta back before she stepped on a small cluster of Red Polyps. "That's the only thing that stinks worse."

Agracia felt Jetta's mind applying pressure to her own, exploring her knowledge on Red Polyps. At first she bristled, but realizing it was far better to keep Jetta informed, she relented.

"Thanks," Jetta commented as she withdrew.

"Just warn me, okay?" Agracia said quietly, trying not to tip off Bossy that Jetta had used her telepathic abilities.

"Hey wait." Jetta stopped her and took her by the shoulders. This time Agracia felt a different kind of pressure in the back of her mind. Curiosity and concern, not her own, slid down her spine and through her limbs. "You're not okay, are you?"

Agracia shrugged away. "I'm fine."

"She's fine! Back off, Skirt!" Bossy said, muscling her way in.

"No, you're not," Jetta whispered.

Agracia shied away from the truth. *I've got it together,* she told herself, but the memory of dazing out while driving the Rover and running from the Behemoth burned in the back of her mind.

"Let's just get going," Agracia said. "We can't stay out like this."

Nobody argued her point. The city block had become terribly quiet as the fires from the *Mississippi Diesel 999* died down.

Agracia kept her eyes peeled for any kind of movement. A loose plastic bag danced in the wind, rolling by them, but it otherwise felt as quiet as a cemetery.

As they passed the skeletal remains of an old high-rise, Jetta opened a private conversation with her over the headsets. "Why did Li pull you from the fire?"

Agracia didn't know what to say. Keeping her eyes trained on the capital skyscraper as their landmark, she focused on navigating their way through a maze of abandoned cars.

"Agracia?"

Realizing Jetta wouldn't let her off the hook, she said the first thing that came to mind. "He saved my life."

Jetta didn't respond immediately. "Why didn't you tell Unipoesa about it?"

Why is she asking me all these stupid questions? she thought angrily. *That* assino *knows just about as much as I do anyway.*

But Jetta's questions got in her head. Agracia's mind fell back, drudging up the truth.

Li had a solid alibi—he had three other students attest to his presence in the gaming room at the time of the fire. And somehow he had scared the Program's psychiatrist into reporting that she had started the fire in order to get out of finals that week. At that point telling Unipoesa didn't matter. Besides, he was trying to destroy her, too.

"That *ratchakker*," Agracia muttered to herself. She decided she hated Unipoesa.

"Up ahead!" Bossy said, cutting into their conversation.

The four of them knelt behind a collapsed bridge.

"Jeezus," Bossy said, sucking loudly on her lollipop. "What, is that like fifty of 'em?"

"At least." Agracia cursed under her breath and tried to better assess the numbers. An enormous polyp had sprouted up from the subway access tunnel, attracting a huge cluster of Necros. The undead milled around the smaller polypoids growing off the main stalk, making it hard to get an accurate headcount.

"That thing is mostly underground; I bet it spans the entire city block," Jetta said.

"Uck," Agracia said. "I hate Polyps."

As Jetta checked her weapon, Agracia looked on with shock. *Wait a sec—that's just a laser bolt gun.* Firing those things with accuracy was next to impossible. She couldn't help but feel a little more grateful for her skin.

"There has to be some sort of relationship between Red Polyps and Necros. The two couldn't otherwise exist on a dead planet," Jetta commented.

"No duh, Skirt," Bossy said, smacking her lips.

"Quit it, Bossy," Agracia said.

Bossy crawled over and took her aside. "You can't be serious about letting her follow us. She threw our gear away!"

"She saved our lives, *assino*," Agracia said. "Just give it up. She's coming with us, and that's that!"

Bossy growled at her but didn't protest further.

"Any ideas?" Agracia asked the group. "Never dealt with this many."

Jetta pointed to the subway tunnel. "That's our entrance, right?"

"Yup," Agracia confirmed.

"And you wasted all our booze already," Bossy reminded her.

Unperturbed by the dark horse, Jetta searched through the sack that she and the Healer had brought with them. Agracia caught sight of a socket lugger, a flashlight, and a feather grinder, but nothing immediately useful.

The Healer made an unusual observation. "They're human. Well, formerly. I can feel them—there's something left."

Agracia couldn't believe it, and neither could Bossy. The kid snorted and pointed at one of the Necros with missing limbs and half of a face. "That ain't human."

The response of her Scabber personality perched on Agracia's lips: *They just zombies!* Instead, she asked in a tentative voice: "What do you feel?"

She could see the Healer's brow pinch behind her translucent green visor. "They're... like Liikers."

The Healer's words startled her. Bossy nearly choked on her lollipop. "What?! No way! They're not tin cans!"

Jetta seemed equally distraught. "No, not quite the same, but I... I see it, too. Discordant minds. Decaying bodies. Not alive—

"—but not dead," Triel said, completing the thought. "It's not a normal biorhythm, but there is one. And there's... emotion. It's not like normal. Almost like a—"

"—repeating thought," Jetta finished.

Both telepaths seemed to be stuck in some sort of trance, swaying back and forth as they bridged unseen planes into the psyches of the undead.

"So," Agracia said, unsure if she should try and snap them out of their daze. "What do we do?"

Triel and Jetta seemed to communicate silently before Jetta finally offered an idea. "You stay here. And stay back. Whatever you do, whatever you see—*don't* interfere."

Agracia looked at Bossy, but her companion just shrugged.

"Oh God, you're not gonna do some leech—I mean telepath—thing, are you?" Agracia said as Jetta sat cross-legged on the ground, her back against their cover.

"Your Scabber side will love this."

"Oh snap!" Bossy exclaimed, animated at the prospect of action. "You gonna pull some Doctor Death *sycha*, arntcha?"

"I'm here for you," Triel whispered, taking Jetta's hands in hers.

For a moment Agracia thought she saw something more than friendship pass through their touch, but she set aside the idea as soon as it formed; something much more interesting was starting to happen to the walking corpses.

"You know what you're doing?" Agracia asked, spying the activity below them through the hole in the collapsed bridge. The entire lot of Necros froze in place. Some of them made strange grunting noises, twisting their heads toward their position.

"You wanted to know what other magic tricks I have," Jetta said, tipping her head back. In seconds, the temperature inside Agracia's suit dropped. Blisteringly cold, she curled up into herself, squeezing her knees to her chest.

"Oh *chak*—" Bossy cried out.

She barely heard Jetta's voice above the din of screeching Necros. "Get ready for my best trick."

***

Jaeia had been on her way to see the Spinner named Aesis when she got a notification on her sleeve.

Please return to the bridge. [Priority level 2]

"*Dichit*," she whispered, rerouting her destination.

Jaeia had never cared for military life, even after she accepted rank in the Starways Alliance. She didn't like the uniforms, the salutes, the training—any of it. But an unexpected longing hit as she rode the lift down vacant corridors and empty barracks. Would there be any more early morning drills or artificial-tasting instant meals? Monthly field training? Flight classes with her sister so she could tease her about her piloting skills?

Oh, Jetta, Jaeia thought. *I wish you were here. If only you could see what Victor has done to the Homeworlds.*

She arrived at the bridge of the Central Starbase, meeting the gazes of overworked crewmen and a deck officer who had worked three straight shifts.

"Captain," the deck officer saluted weakly. Sleep deprivation had carved large bags under her eyes and rounded her shoulders.

"Lieutenant Roca," Jaeia acknowledged. "Report?"

The Lieutenant handed her a datapad and led her to the holosim in the middle of the bridge. "You wanted me to let you know when the Taurians arrived."

"Yes, thank you, lieutenant."

Leaning over the display, Jaeia analyzed the positions of the Galactic Republic Fleet around Trigos. *This isn't good,* she thought, noting the increase in enemy starships. *Victor must have commissioned warliners from the neighboring planet of Tauros Prime.* It was a smart move, and a particularly demoralizing one, using the Alliance's own ships to move in on the last remaining Homeworld not submitting to Victor's control.

His last broadcast played out in the back of her head: *"We need a unified front to survive these attacks; we cannot be divided in these times. One Starways, one banner. Together we will stand against any threat to liberty, peace, and freedom!"*

"How long do you think we can hold out, Captain?" Roca asked, her eyes searching Jaeia's face for any indication of hope.

Jaeia studied the holosim again, wanting to find something to give them an edge over Victor's Fleet. As she ran through her cache of grafted strategies and wartime speeches, she couldn't help but notice the steady flow of little red enemy starships going to and from the surface to a massive cargo ship.

Li's transporting the dissenters off-world. She pressed her knuckles into the rim of the projector. *...And probably carting them off to Victor's reprogramming facilities.*

Despair touched her thoughts. As much as she wanted to reassure the last remaining troops that they could counterattack, that they still had a chance, she feared the critical state of their situation.

With the Motti's weapon getting closer to Trigos, we can't afford to resist. Worse yet, they were no closer to figuring out the Republic Fleet's weapon against the Deadwalkers, and revealing that Kurt Stein was alive was a bluff, a chance to stall—but for what? Once the veil was lifted, they had no working plan. *The only reasonable choice is to relinquish arms.*

Jaeia pressed her knuckles even harder into the projector. *No. I can't give up. With all the minds I've stolen from, there has to be something.*

"For my troops," she whispered, closing her eyes and reaching farther within.

She slalomed through a thousand years of military experience, but found little that could help. In her time of need, the things that usually upset her became only a pale distraction.

Please, she thought as steel air beasts congested skies pulsing with flash fire. *I need this.*

"Kill them all!" someone shouted.

To her left, armored tanks crunched over countless bodies scattered across open fields.

"Send in two squadrons," another voice called.

The landscape shifted. As different memories competed for her attention, she saw masked troops with thermal explosives storm into a civilian outpost.

"Mow them down like weeds," someone laughed.

Another memory surfaced. Gun turrets took aim at unarmed soldiers. Horrified, she watched the scene play out as a disembodied voice whispered in her ear: "Leave no one alive."

Keep going, she told herself, pressing forward.

She passed through war after war behind many eyes and many voices. Battlefields, both on the ground and in the dark matter of space, became a strange amalgam of strangulated light and sound, until she was left facing a bloodied horizon and the tortured skies of unimaginable suffering. Even after all that, it wasn't enough.

"Don't give up, Jaeia."

Jaeia snapped her head toward the voice. Jahx hovered beside her, most of his body translucent against the dark tides of stolen memories.

(What? Jahx?! How did you find me here?)

"Trust yourself. Follow your instincts. It is our only chance."

Before she could ask why, her brother disintegrated into a faint mist that dispersed as she reached out to him.

A new landscape of ash formed around her, with an unforgiving sun peeking out behind dark, swollen clouds. Jaeia shielded her face from the sun's harsh rays falling onto the cracked ground beneath her. The weight of the dead world sank into her bones, and the scars of a struggle long forgotten cut into her marrow.

Her brother's voice fell from the rumbling skies. *"Follow your instincts."*

Jaeia could barely lift her head as a crippling grief seized her by the throat, but the torment stopped when something caught her eye. At her feet trembled the tiniest green leaf, a seedling growing out of the wounded earth. A miracle, an impossibility in the face of certain death.

Jaeia cupped it gently as tears fell from her cheeks. So beautiful…

A low growl caught her attention. Jaeia whirled around on her heels, coming face-to-face with a gray-masked, colossal lupine animal. Glowing yellow eyes watched as she scrambled backward, narrowly avoiding the budding plant.

Why isn't he pursuing? She tore herself away from his gleaming teeth for a second to spot the chains binding his feet.

A polluted wind carried the stink of sulfur and her brother's whispered words: *"Follow your instincts."*

Jaeia's heart boomed in her ears as she stared at the wolf-like animal. The predator's gaze never left hers, his ears pricked to her every sound and movement. Fear, ripe in her belly and mind, bade her to run, but her brother's words kept her grounded.

Follow my instincts, *she thought.* What does he mean?

She looked again at the animal's bindings, this time spotting the Alliance insignia stamped on the metal plating. But the marking changed in the blink of an eye. In next moment, it formed the same design as her tattoo, and a second later, Victor's crest.

The shifting marks didn't make sense to her, but when she saw the *shock-wand injuries that lashed the animal's chest and back, she heard her own voice come up from the depths:* Free him.

Carefully, she made her way over to the bound animal, speaking softly to him. (I don't want to hurt you. If you let me, I will help you.)

He continued to growl, showing her the glistening whites of his teeth, but made no move to harm her as she unpinned the locking device on his chains. Once freed, he snapped his teeth in her face, and she leapt backwards, readying her defense.

Somebody laughed. Jaeia reared around to see a man, terribly burned from head to toe, standing over the tiny seedling. His eyes, two flames in their sockets, betrayed any earthly origins. As he continued to cackle, she fixated on his teeth, black nubs set in a jaw stripped of flesh.

Not real not real not real— she thought as the sun hid behind the protection of the clouds. The land beneath her feet quaked. Her senses deepened her fright, painting an overlapping picture of a thing devoured by hate and misery, carved from the dark matter of nightmares.

He raised his gnarled foot up over the plant and screeched in a voice that set her skin on fire. "With eyes open, they burn!"

She screamed, throwing herself forward to protect the fragile seedling, with the terrible knowing that it wouldn't be enough to withstand the incoming blow from such a menacing creature. But as death came crashing down, a gray shadow streaked up beside her, claws outstretched, teeth sinking into the charred flesh.

The burned man and the lupine beast disappeared before her eyes, vanishing with the howl of the wind. As her fears lifted, the sun broke through the clouds, and the ground settled beneath her.

Jaeia bent down to inspect the plant. Instead, she found herself and her siblings sleeping in a bed of flowers.

"Follow your instincts. It is our only chance."

"Captain!" Lieutenant Roca was bracing her against the holosim. "Captain—are you okay?"

Jaeia reflexively wiped her nose, smearing blood on her sleeve. "Gods…"

Jahx. His words still resonated in her mind: *"Follow your instincts. It is our only chance."*

It couldn't have been. From Dr. DeAnders's last report, the Grand Oblin's body had severely deteriorated; his cellular decay was at critical levels, and his brain showed minimal activity. And when she had last tried to contact Jahx, she could barely sense his tune, as if it were trapped at the bottom of an infinitely long well.

It couldn't have been Jahx.

But the blood on her sleeve was real.

"Shall I call a medical team, Captain?"

"No, Lieutenant, I'm fine," Jaeia said, trying to shake her brother's words from her head. *What did he mean, to follow my instincts?*

Jaeia ran her hand through her hair. *I can't stay here.* Every part of her screamed to go to the lab and see her brother, even if she had to use her second voice on DeAnders. *There's too much at stake for me not to understand his message—*

(if it was him at all.)

She looked at her reflection in the silver rim of the holographic display. Except for the spotty patches and red-rings around her eyes, the color of her skin matched the blanched white of her uniform sleeve.

It's not just sleep deprivation and stress...

(I'm dying.)

There isn't much time. I have to see Jahx. I have to understand—

A voice, distant and fading into oblivion, rose up to her ears. *"Trust yourself..."*

"Captain!" the lieutenant shouted as she bolted to the lift, "Captain, what should we do?"

Jaeia sped down the corridors, not knowing her destination, but knowing she had to go faster and faster. As she whipped around the deck exchange, a vision hit her like a head-on collision with a starclass freighter.

"Come on, Jaeia, we're gonna get in trouble!"

Jetta's voice. Air, hot and unbreathable, filled her lungs. The entire place stank like the inside of a rotted pipe.

As the vision settled, she saw herself back aboard their first mining ship, stuck in the lower decks doing grunt work alongside the other child laborers. Everything felt new and scary.

I remember this time, *she thought.* Jetta wanted us to stay away from the other kids and avoid the gangs.

"No, Jetta, we can't just leave him," her younger self whispered.

A dimwitted, eleven-year-old Reptili-humanoid boy named Vinnie lay near a grinder after being beaten by the other kids. Though as big as some adults, he didn't know how to conceal his winnings in the daily food scramble, and had foolishly sported his success in front of the other starving children, most of whom were in gangs.

Jetta, impatient to reunite with Jahx to share what they had secretly won, left her sister to worry over Vinnie. To Jetta he was useless anyway: The kid was severely injured and had proved himself to be a liability. Given their lowly reputations as humans from the slums, Jetta didn't want to affiliate herself with any other hard cases, nor did she want to be reprimanded by the laborminders for taking a break.

But Jaeia couldn't help herself.

One of the kids had used a driver gun to nail Vinnie's hands to the floor so his companions could steal his bakken. Vinnie wailed pitifully as he tugged at his hands. Blood oozed from the sites, but the nails remained solidly fixed into the floor.

"*I can help you,*" *Jaeia said, scooting her way closer to him.*

Vinnie spat at her, and she shielded her eyes against the spray. "*Ay batc!*"

His words were hard to understand, impaired by the birth defect that divided his palate and tongue, but his body language made it clear that he didn't want her anywhere near him.

(He just doesn't understand,) *her instincts told her.* (He's afraid.)

No, *she thought, stopping herself.* Why am I doing this? Why can't I just leave him here like Jetta said?

Again and again he lunged at her as she tried to remove the nail with an electro-plyer she had stolen from a tool closet.

Jaeia considered using her second voice, but there were others just around the corner, and she couldn't risk getting caught.

"*Vinnie, there are laborminders coming. They will toss you out if they find you like this. You don't want to end up as dinner for the rats, do you?*"

This seemed to make some kind of sense to him, and he stopped trying to bite at her hands.

"*I just want to get these nails out, okay?*"

He didn't make a sound as she pried the nails out of each hand. Instead, he stared at her with mustard-colored eyes, the scales on his forehead pinching together as he tried to understand her actions.

When she released the last nail, she didn't move fast enough to avoid the back of his hand. It connected with her temple and sent her crashing into the grinder. Her shoulder hit the corner of one of the grinder teeth, splitting her skin and bloodying her clothes.

Jaeia turned just in time to see him gearing up to come after her when the familiar footfalls of the laborminders froze them both in place.

Vinnie growled at her through brown, chipped teeth before hobbling off down a service shaft.

Back at home she got what she expected from her sister: a long, drawn-out lecture about keeping to themselves and staying out of other kids' fights. Jaeia nodded when she was supposed to and acted beaten-down enough to make Jetta stop after about an hour, but it never truly changed her mind.

After Jetta left to go collect water from the broken pipes outside their apartment, Jahx approached her.

"So... Why did you help him?"

Jaeia couldn't find a way to rationalize what she had done other than it seemed liked the right thing to do, even though Vinnie had attacked her afterward. Jahx only smiled and said, "You need to trust yourself more, Jaeia. Jetta's right about a lot of things, but she doesn't see all that can be."

The incident didn't come full-circle until three months later when she was lugging a load of topitrate into the grinder. Exhausted, she had forgotten to keep an eye on who was filtering in and out of the dump room. Before she knew it, she was alone with four kids from one of the most notorious labor gangs.

The one that stepped forward went by the name Hericio. Even at nine, he was one of the most brutal children she had ever met. It was whispered that he had once spooned out another kid's eyes for cutting in line at the food pantry, and his unpalatable psionic emanations suggested it wasn't far from the truth. She had seen him order the beatings of small children and organize hits on older children that threatened his reign over their convoluted world.

"Launnie," Hericio hissed, "give me your bakken. I saw your rat sister steal three!"

He was right. Well, partially. Jetta had actually grabbed five, but gave two away in a failed attempt at an alliance with some other humanoid kids their age. With only one piece of bakken to last her the rest of her fourteen-hour shift, Jaeia couldn't possibly afford to lose her share.

No way out, she thought, *eyes searching the dump room for an unguarded exit. Three kids blocked the door, and dropping through the back end of the grinder seemed like a bad idea, even in a panic. And with Jetta tending to Jahx in the coolant room, nursing their wounds from another one of Yahmen's drunken fits, she had no one in position to come to her rescue.*

Hericio removed a shiv from his tunic and waved it at her face. "Rumors are true, launnie, so give up them breads!"

Terrified, she screamed out to her siblings for help across their psionic connection.

I'm coming! *Jetta cried back.*

But given the way Hericio advanced with his blade, she would be too late. Jaeia sensed his cold-blooded plan: kill her, take her bakken, and dump her body in the grinder.

The edge of the shiv bit into her cheek. Warm blood trickled down her chin.

I don't want to die.

Jaeia despaired. She would have to chance using her second voice, even if it meant freezer cases, shock collars, or the labor locks.

"Rotten launnie!" Hericio said, kicking her in the stomach. The blow took the wind right out of her, and she fell flat on her back, her head only centimeters from the crushing teeth of the grinder. Hericio grabbed her neck, and his imaginings manifested in gory detail: her head slowly grinding away, brains and blood mixing with topitrate. "Let's see what your insides look like."

Intoxicated with violence, his companions left their post at the door and crowded around her, hungry to see more.

Jaeia bucked against his grip, but he was stronger and had the help of his companions. But as he reared back to drive the shiv into her face, someone caught his hand mid-strike and slammed it into the teeth of the grinder. Hericio shrieked as his hand disappeared into the mouth of the grinder, which continued to gobble him up to the elbow.

"Help me!" he wailed, reaching out to his fellow thugs, but shock had driven them from their skin. His minions looked upon him with ghostly faces as the rock grinder swallowed him past the shoulder. "Help me! HELP MEEEEEEEEEEEE!"

Jaeia tried to grab onto his hand, but the rock grinder was determined *to consume him, crunching bones and mashing intestines along with topitrate into an unrecognizable pulp.*

One of the other kids tried to pick up the shiv that Hericio had dropped, but her rescuer beat them to it.

Jaeia couldn't believe her eyes. "Vinnie?"

Vinnie yelled something unintelligible as he threatened the other kids with the shiv. They bolted, leaving her to fend for herself.

"Here," Jaeia said, uncovering the bakken in her pocket and offering it to him. Vinnie looked at it with starving eyes but made no move to pluck it from her outstretched hand. Instead, he grunted, hid the shiv in the lining of his jacket, and hobbled out of the dump room.

It wasn't more than a few minutes before another round of kids came along to unload their carts of topitrate, oblivious to her struggle or the person that had just been fed through the grinder. Jetta arrived too, congested with fear and aggression, ready to take out the entire ship if necessary.

"Are you okay?" Jetta asked, looking around for evidence of the fight. The smell of blood lingered, but was hardly noticeable against the stench of topitrate.

"Hey! Get back to work!" one of the laborminders shouted to the kids outside the dump room. In their condition they couldn't risk a beating at work, so they skipped the verbal conversation as they scrambled back to their duties.

Even though Jaeia allowed Jetta an unfiltered, firsthand glimpse into what had transpired, she received only a gruff reminder to be more careful.

Jaeia, you need to stay away from the gangs and watch yourself!

Her brother's voice returned in her mind, whispering with the same fervency: Trust yourself.

"Captain Kyron?"

Jaeia shook her head. How long had she been standing there?

"Sir, can I help you?" one of the soldiers said, increasingly concerned at her unresponsiveness.

Jaeia found herself in front of the security and interrogation wing, her original destination before she had gotten a call from Lieutenant Roca.

Aesis. The Spinner that donned a costume of fair skin and violet eyes. She knew that deep down inside he was nothing more than a little green worm, but through his eyes she had seen something more than his physical reality.

"I want to see the Spinner called Aesis. This is an urgent matter, soldier."

"Sir, the Minister ordered—"

Jaeia didn't bother arguing this time. Sidestepping the soldier, she spouted off her priority codes as he fumbled to input and verify them in his interfaced uniform sleeve. Heads turned as she searched the interrogation cells for the Spinner's familiar tune.

The soldier guarding the entrance caught up to her. Expecting resistance, Jaeia instead found him holding the key to Aesis's cell.

"Cell B. He's in the final stage of metamorphosis."

"Why is he in lockdown?"

The soldier seemed confused by her question. "All Spinners are kept in lockdown until they complete their metamorphosis. It's for protection."

It's not his fault, she reminded herself. *That's a lie propagated by Razar.*

Years ago, the Military Minister had created the secret program to use Spinners in interrogations and kept the wing off-limits from most of the Starbase staff, including the senior officers. *If it wasn't for this crisis situation, I probably wouldn't even be allowed in the cell blocks.*

"Thank you," she said as the soldier unlocked the door.

Jaeia stepped into the dimly lit cell. Drab, brown walls enclosed a spartan living space. She eyed the wash basin, toilet, locker, and bed. Only the Alliance mission statement, tacked in the center of an otherwise empty wall, broke up the monochromatic scheme. *Even the lower deck cabins have more character.*

Letting out her disgust in a huff, Jaeia turned her attention to the semi-cocooned body lying on the bed. Viscous fluid saturated the dark sheets and dribbled onto the floor. The air smelled heavy and sharp, with a strange alkaline tang.

"Aesis?" she said.

A reflective film covered the white body. No movement could be seen.

"I'm sorry," she stuttered, her cheeks turning red.

She turned to go, but stopped in her tracks when she heard a crack. More snaps and pops followed. She backed up into the door as a pink hand slid out from underneath the protective white casing.

"I—I came to ask you..." Jaeia started, but then stopped at the sight of something wiggling beneath the white covering. "No, I can't do this. I'm sorry," she said, shaking her head. "You're free. I'm setting your people free."

She hurried out, heart hammering in her chest, afraid and uncertain of her own actions.

"Soldier, I order you to set the Spinners free," she said, this time using a psionic push to her words. "*Now.*"

The chief of the security deck popped out of the monitoring station. "What's this about, Captain?" He turned to the soldier with a scowl on his face: "And why the hell didn't she go through decontamination?"

The soldier mumbled to himself as Jaeia continued her conversation with the chief. "I want the Spinners set free on my orders."

The chief looked at her through the narrow scopes of his optic implants. A few weeks ago Jaeia overhead that he had lost his eyes in a battle against the Dominion. Now, every time she saw him, she secretly wondered if it had been an assault that she had led. "We're under direct orders from the Minister."

"I'm aware of that."

In one quick motion he plucked a loose strand of hair off her shoulder. "You have to be careful around here, Captain."

"What do you mean?"

"Your DNA. All it takes is a strand of hair, or just the right touch, and they have you."

"You mean they can replicate me," Jaeia clarified.

"Yes," the Chief said, not hiding his contempt very well. "And forgive me, *Sir*, but every time you have an unauthorized interaction with one of them, I have a lot more paperwork to do."

Jaeia thought about when she first met Aesis and brought him before the senior military council. She had innocently put her hand on his shoulder. *Does he have my DNA now? Can I be replicated?*

"Those *worms* are best kept under lock and key, Captain," the chief added, his eyes retracting with a whir into their metal sockets. "We don't want to compromise your safety."

His tone sparked her anger, but she kept herself in check. By the way his psionic rhythm rang in her ears, she afforded him some empathy. *He's a victim of his own ignorance.*

"I gave an order, Chief. I expect it to be executed," she said.

Their minds drifted in a cloudy air of confusion. She was glad they didn't press her for a reason, because she didn't think she could offer them a rational answer.

As she walked back to her quarters to change for her shift, she grimly thought, *After all, what's left?* Setting the Spinners free was radical, but in light of Victor's imminent takeover of the Starways, something so relatively minor would not register the attention of her superiors.

The Spinners could be dangerous. They might replicate me or my sister—maybe even Wren or the Minister. It's an unnecessary risk—

(Trust yourself.)

"But it's the right thing to do," she whispered as she changed into her formal uniform.

She ran her finger along the contour of her face, watching her reflection in the mirror do the same.

"At least I hope it is."

***

Long, delicate fingers found their way under Jetta's suit and helmet to the notch underneath her jawline, feeling for a pulse. Someone with a high-pitched, squealing voice shouted and screamed. A young voice with burdened tones.

Two arms grabbed underneath her armpits. The ground raced underneath her. Jetta tried to pick up her feet, but they felt like blocks of cement dragging in the ash.

"Hey," she mumbled through numb lips.

She lifted her head and opened her eyes. A field of decimated corpses littered the street. Breathing in sharply, she tasted blood in the back of her throat.

What happened?

Memory fragments slowly refitted into a larger picture. The Necros milling around the entrance to the subway tunnel. Running out of time. The sickness spreading in her chest. Had to know—the tattoo—the Steins—*why?*

My talent... She remembered her awful deed, reaching into the corroded minds of the deceased and pulling out the only nightmare they could know. *Their last moment...*

Jetta jerked her head up, her helmet rearing to the sky as the clouds rumbled angrily.

I made them remember their last moment they were alive.

"Stop!" Jetta cried, wrestling against the forces dragging her along.

Agracia and Triel slowed their pace, but didn't stop. "We have to reach the tunnel—it isn't safe!" Agracia shouted.

"No," Jetta said, freeing her arms and crawling over to the nearest Necro. Twitching, it sputtered black juices from its oral cavity, eyes open but blind to her presence.

"I saw." Jetta stroked the stringy crescent of hair that lay across the Necro's mottled brow. "I know who you were. Who you all were."

"Jeezus, Doc," Agracia said, trying to grab her, but the Healer cautioned her against touching Jetta.

"Just give her a minute."

"It's not your fault," Jetta whispered as her mind returned to the mangled recesses of its necrotizing heart, and the collective nightmare that shook her from ignorant slumber.

The skies were still, the entire city silent in the last breath before the bombs fell. Before the poisons leaked from their biocapsules. Before death consumed the world.

"You were on your way home," Jetta said.

She no longer saw the mummified man before her, but a middle-aged father of three dressed in a tailored gray suit, a briefcase in one hand as he signaled for a taxi with the other. He smelled like aftershave and perspiration, and his palms were sweaty from nerves.

Jetta's eyes drifted to another Necro nearby. This one was missing two limbs and possessed no recognizable ears or nose. "You were riding a bicycle, on a delivery."

When Jetta looked around, the street was no longer a part of a greater wasteland, but a busy avenue bustling with people, bicycles, hovercars, and airbuses. Birds flew across a blue sky in a V, and the smell of hot dogs and fresh pretzels tempted her nose. It wasn't Red Polyps that pierced the sky but massive skyscrapers, powerful and indomitable. The collective energy—the synergy—of all the life in the city, in the country and well beyond, filled her like an infinite number of shining stars until she felt like she would burst.

Life.

Earth.

"Home..."

"Jetta," Triel said gently, touching her arm. "We need to go. Now."

Still caught between the past and present, Jetta was only faintly aware of the new horde of Necros creeping over the hill.

"They're all human," she mumbled as Agracia and Triel helped her to her feet.

"Can you walk?" Triel asked.

Jetta's legs felt like slabs of cement, but Agracia and Triel helped her limp to the subway entrance where Bossy was furiously trying to dig a hole through the wall of fallen debris.

"*Chakking* thing won't budge!" Bossy said, straining against a studded beam. Triel and Agracia joined her as the Necros began to hoot and holler, alerted to their presence.

"Move," Jetta said, shoving them aside.

Sick, exhausted, and still wobbly from overexerting her talents, Jetta pressed into the beam and lifted it with a groan. Bossy quietly cursed her out as she passed underneath.

"Freak show..." the dark horse muttered.

Jetta held it together until they were safely through the clogged trap of fallen archways and impassable rail lines and inside a barricaded office at the farthest end of the station.

"We're safe," Agracia assured them, using the flashlight attached to the arm of her suit to illuminate their dust-covered surroundings.

Jetta thought otherwise. *The Necros might not have been able to make it past this blockade a few years ago, but the station has changed.* With a careful eye, she scanned the erosions and cracks on some of the vertical support beams. *That Polyp is butting up against some of the main structures of this facility. There could be new entrances—*

The station quaked, and debris rained down from the ceiling.

Or the whole thing could just collapse.

"Uh, we need to keep moving," Agracia said. "This *sycha* ain't stable."

"Give us a moment," Triel said, putting her arm around Jetta.

"Whatever," Agracia said as she her companion wandered off into an old storage closet and rummaged around for parts. Bossy cursed up a storm about something, but Jetta didn't care.

Triel clicked on her flashlight and set it next to them.

"What was that? What just happened?" Jetta said, as Triel lightly rubbed her back. Jetta sensed that she wanted to connect to her, but it was still too dangerous to take off the hazard suits.

"You're pushing yourself too hard, Jetta." Triel took her hand and squeezed. "You need to look out for yourself, too."

Exhausted, Jetta didn't have it in her to fight the Healer's grip. Not that she really wanted to. Part of her relished the touch, even as another bristled.

"You're in no condition to use your powers that extensively, even with my help," Triel added.

I'm dying.

She angrily pushed the thought from her head. *No. I won't let what the Deadwalkers did to my body stop me. And I won't let Victor, or the monster inside me, get in my head. Nothing will keep me from finding the truth—and a solution.*

Old promises solidified her resolve. *I will save the Starways, if only to protect my brother and sister.* She turned her hands into fists. *And I will rescue Galm and Lohien, and find my mother. I won't let anything bad happen to anyone I love.*

But anger wouldn't serve her now, not with Triel's concerns pricking her mind. Jetta hated doing it, but she knew she had no choice if she wanted to quell the Healer's anxieties.

"I'm sorry," Jetta said, putting her other hand on Triel's. "You're right. I'll be more careful."

Triel pulled her in close. "Please, Jetta. For me."

Eyeing the Scabber Jocks, Jetta pushed back and got to her feet. "We need to get going."

"Jetta, wait—just take a second—"

Although the aftershock of her talents had finally worn off, the exhaustion remained. Still, they couldn't afford to wait. "We don't have time."

"What's wrong?" Jetta said, joining Agracia and Bossy as they fussed near the supply closet. One of them had opened the hidden trapdoor inside the closet.

"Gonna be a tight squeeze." Agracia stepped aside to expose the stairwell. Peering down, Jetta saw that the stairwell had partially caved in. "The kid here hates small spaces."

Bossy let loose another string of cuss words and slammed her fist into a dust-covered desk. A name tag sitting on the edge fell off. Jetta reached down and grabbed it, rubbing away the dirt to reveal the name. *Ms. Ariya Ohakn.*

"Ariya Ohakn…" she said aloud.

When she looked up, her companions were gone. A woman with auburn hair and pale green eyes sat typing away at her desk on an electronic tablet. Her brows pinched in a familiar way, reminding her of somebody. Somebody important.

What's happening?

Barricades and debris vanished, replaced by mid-twenty-first century décor and design. A faded black-and-white modernist print hung in the middle of the far wall beside an uninspired arrangement of fake flowers on a side-table. Eco-friendly lights with nature-themed trimmings hung from the ceiling.

This can't be real—

Jetta caught sight of something discontinuous with the minimalistic décor. On the desk, tucked away from customer sight, lay a series of designs scribbled on a piece of paper—intricate patterns woven together like Japanese kanji, but in an esoteric language that struck a chord within Jetta.

She leaned forward, trying to get a better view. It almost looks like… my tattoo.

The woman chewed on the inside of her cheek before hitting the send *button on her tablet.*

"Please God, tell me I'm doing the right thing," she whispered.

"Hey!"

A hard-hitting punch landed smack against the meat of her shoulder. Jetta reared her fist back before realizing she was back in her own time.

Bossy stood in front of her, audibly slurping on her lollipop. "Are you pulling one of your tricks again?"

"Back off!" Jetta said sharply. Bossy stumbled backward in surprise.

What just happened? she thought as she found herself holding tightly to the name tag.

"Jetta?" Triel whispered.

Jetta opened a private channel between the two of them. "I saw that woman again—the one from the memory stain you got off of Reht. The one that Jaeia thinks is our birth mother."

"What?" Triel exclaimed.

"It's impossible, but I know I saw her. She was here—centuries ago. She was some kind of secretary."

Tilting her head to the side, the Healer studied the name tag in Jetta's hand. "I can't read English."

Jetta translated the words for her as best she could. "It says this was just a service station for the subway, but that's not the feeling I got when I was there, especially in light of the fact that there's a laboratory underneath. This place was a front, and this woman—Ariya Ohakn—guarded its secret."

"Hey, kids—let's keep it among friends," Agracia said, butting in on their channel.

"We should get moving," Jetta said as the station gave another ominous rumble.

Leading the way through the tangle of pipework and fallen construction, Jetta brought them far enough beneath the Earth that she felt confident they could remove their helmets. However, the thin air and lack of active filters made her wait.

This feels like something out of a long forgotten dream, she thought, entering the laboratory. An eerie feeling crawled into her belly as they passed dried-out stasis cylinders and ancient testing equipment. She felt as if she should know the place, as if she had been here before, apart from the memories she had grafted from Agracia. *Or maybe it's something else.*

"Same weird *sycha* as before," Agracia said, clicking the switch back and forth on a dysfunctional Bunsen burner. "Nuthin's changed."

"Yeah..." Jetta said.

Triel touched the back of her hand.

"It's okay," Jetta whispered to her through their private channel. "Just strange to be here."

The Healer put her hand out in front of her as if to steady herself. "No, it's more than that. These walls contain memories."

"*Chakking* leeches," Bossy mumbled, kicking over a chair.

"Shut it, kid," Agracia said. She turned her attention to Jetta. "Keep me in the loop, Doc. Is this place haunted or what?"

"In a sense," Triel said, running her fingers along the control board on a thermostatic biosphere regulator.

Jetta froze mid-step. "It kind of feels like the Temple of Exxuthus."

"Wha?" Agracia said.

The ground shifted, and debris showered down from the ceiling. *No time to figure that out—we have to get in and out as quickly as possible.*

"Let's get to where you found my tattoo," Jetta said.

Agracia led them down a series of steel-plated stairs hidden behind a bookshelf to another dusty subbasement. Aside from the portion of ceiling that had caved in, the structure of the laboratory appeared relatively intact. Most of the internal destruction, from smashed smartservers to broken stasis cylinders, looked like it had happened centuries ago.

"Gods," Triel said, holding her helmet with both hands as she stumbled into a workbench. "Something terrible happened here."

All the hair on Jetta's arms and the back of her neck stood on end. *There's something alive in this place, just like in the Temple of Exxuthus,* she thought. *Something with tethers in this world and the next.*

Sweat filled the inside of her hazard suit, and her heart boomed inside her chest. She went over the room with her flashlight but found nothing abnormal or out of place; it looked like a bombed-out laboratory with ancient equipment she didn't recognize.

"Jetta—we need to leave this place," Triel whispered across their headsets. She backed against the wall, frightened, and moved back to the center of the lab.

Not wasting any more time, Jetta shoved the desk away with her foot. With the force of her movement, a hidden drawer popped open, revealing an old revolver inside.

"Cool!" Bossy exclaimed as she pulled out the gun. "And it's loaded!"

"Gimme that," Agracia tried, but Bossy whipped around and protected her find.

"It's mine!"

"Hey—there it is," Agracia said, removing the protective cover and pointing to the safe hidden under the desk. Jetta noted the scorch marks around the exterior. Someone had tried multiple times, without success, to get inside. "Exactly as I found it. Could never get it open. Just saw your mark."

And there was her tattoo, scrawled in blood across the safe door. Her inner voice screamed as she took off her glove, extended her fingers, and touched the past.

Catapulted into another time, Jetta watched as the walls of realities shattered and the rules of physics and reason broke.

"Please forgive me for all that I have done..." someone whispered as pieces of the world reformed. The only light came from the emergency systems, casting the laboratory in shades of blood.

Another voice came from the sightless, impenetrable shadows. (You were useless, blind, inhibited—but I showed you your power. I destroyed that which was unnecessary inside you. Now, Josef, and you can help me end this war.)

"Stay away from me!" the first speaker screamed, stumbling forward and swinging blindly at the dark.

Jetta saw his face in the red light. Josef Stein. Doctor Death. The man with the immeasurable second shadow. Dark brown eyes had transformed into black wells of fury. Something possessed him, something unearthly and inhuman, turning his skin into a mottled canvas stretched over prominent bones.

A dark form slithered in the shadows. (Now is the time to be reborn.)

That voice—so familiar. The inflection, the way each syllable was enunciated with a venom she could never understand.

(Victor.)

"No!" Jetta screamed as three sets of hands tore her from the safe. Hugging her tightly, the Healer tried to keep her from flailing about. "He was here! Victor was here!"

"Jeezus," Bossy said, backing away as Jetta broke free and smashed her fist into a wall, taking out a chunk of siding.

"Calm down." Triel raised her hands. "Tell us what you saw."

Jetta fell to her knees, gripping her head. It wasn't Victor. Not exactly, at least. Someone else—

Something else.

"I saw... Josef Stein. He was—" Jetta wanted to say *murdered*, but that didn't feel like the right word. "He was taken here."

Jetta shined her light into the far corner of the room and spotted a splintered, dusty cylinder labeled: *Smart Cell Technology Series #117.*

"This is it—the lab where he created the Smart Cells. This is where the world ended."

"And where we will find a new beginning," Triel said, helping her stand.

Crossing over and running her fingers along the cylinder, Jetta hoped to glean something, but nothing came to her.

"We have to get inside that safe," Jetta concluded. "Something was hunting him, so he hid the most crucial elements of his work."

"Believe me, I've tried." Agracia kicked the dial on the safe. "But this thing is bulletproof, explosive-proof—Jock-proof."

"You've just never had the right tools," Jetta said, running over to rummage through their gear sack. She withdrew the feather grinder, socket lugger, and laser bolt gun. "Now we do."

"Pshhh," Bossy sputtered, "a feather grinder? That ain't gonna work."

Not bothering to explain her intent, Jetta picked apart each piece of equipment to fashion something more useful from their components. Outside of the knowledge she'd stolen, making new tools out of old ones was the one thing she had always been naturally good at, and her days on the mining ships had given her plenty of practice.

Jetta went to the safe and ran her newly fashioned splicer along the edge of the dial until it came off neatly. After inspecting the inside wiring, she fried the remaining locking device.

"I'm impressed," Agracia said.

"So am I," Triel added.

Jetta pulled open the safe door. Grumbling, Bossy kicked the side of the desk.

"Whoa," Agracia said, bending over and aiming her flashlight inside. "Not exactly what I expected."

Bossy stuck her helmeted head between the two of them to have a look. "What a load of crap!"

Jetta withdrew a blood-stained envelope. Inside she found a photograph of a smiling young man with golden-brown hair and warm eyes. Someone had written on the backside: *Kurt Stein. 29 years old. May, 2049.*

Wisps of emotion touched her senses. Smelling cologne, she felt the soft press of a knitted sweater in a tight embrace. Her fingers ran through fine hair, and her lips kissed a stubbled cheek. As grief knotted her chest, tears wet her face. "This can't be goodbye."

"Kurt Stein," Agracia marveled, snatching the photo from Jetta's hand. "Wow. This'll fetch a price."

"Be careful," Jetta said, taking it back.

She searched for more in the envelope and came up with an ancient, battery-driven video-recorder module. Turning it over in her hands, she saw the flecks of dried blood in the cradle.

"It's dead. It needs power," Jetta said as she flipped open the battery cartridge and inspected the housing. "*Skucheka.*"

Jetta shook out the rest of the envelope's contents. A wedding ring and billfold dumped out onto the desktop, as well as a flattened origami crane.

"Weird," Bossy said, pulling the dollars from the billfold and discarding the rest.

Picking up what Bossy tossed aside, Jetta sifted through the assortment of licenses and pictures. Her attention snagged on a picture of a blonde-haired woman that had been torn to pieces and carefully taped back together. A susurrus passed through her, carrying with it a dank chill. *Edina. Wife. Dead.*

Jetta shivered and dropped the photo. It landed on its face. Scrawled on the back was a note in German, followed by *love always, your Dina.*

"What's this?" Triel said, picking up a plastic card from the billfold.

Jetta took it from her. "It looks like a keycard."

Agracia shone her light directly on it. "That's an access pass, alright. Look at the numbers! Let me see—" Her excitement only increased as she inspected the keycard more closely. "This is it! This is it!"

Agracia and Bossy jumped around in a frenzy, puzzling Jetta and Triel with their over exuberance. "*Chak* yeah!" they expressed in unison.

"What is it?" Triel asked.

Jetta tasted the nature of Agracia's thoughts before she spoke. *The keycard is evidence that there are still 'treasures' left on Earth.* She also sensed the conflict inside the Jock mount as her opposing personalities warred for control. *Will Tarsha Leone stand for Agracia the Scabber's goals?*

"*Sycha,*" Agracia said, falling to her knees.

"Grab her," Jetta directed. Bossy helped her stand up as Jetta pressed her consciousness inside Agracia's head, trying to help her sort through reality and illusion.

I don't understand this, Jetta thought, unable to make distinctions between the Scabber and CDP candidate. Clarifying her true past should have fixed the problem, not exacerbated her confusion.

"She's getting worse," Triel whispered to her on the private channel. "I don't know how help her."

"Neither do I," Jetta admitted. "We might have to take her back to Alliance grounds. They're the only ones that will know how to undo what they've done to her."

Jetta flipped back over to the group channel as Agracia came to. For whatever reason, the Scabber personality won the latest round.

"I'm alright, jeezus!" she said, shoving everyone off. "Just winded."

Bending over a broken canister, Agracia caught her breath. "Alright, here's how it is: Me and Bossy gonna explore a little," she said, trying to take the keycard.

Knowing better, Jetta held the keycard away. Agracia the Scabber wouldn't be as cooperative as Tarsha Leone, and she was still stupid enough to try and hide her ultimate agenda.

"I see right through you, Agracia," Jetta said. "I see the cryotubes you're after. We have to complete this mission first. That's our priority."

"Scoring is our only mission," Bossy said, muscling her way through.

Agracia held her companion back. "You're getting what you want, right Doc? All this junk? I need more than a payout from Victor. I need an insurance policy—a *real* score. If me and Bossy were to find a private, subterranean cryovault, then hell, we'd be set for life. That keycard is proof. I know those numerics—I spent years studyin' all the particulars."

Jetta didn't want to waste time arguing with the Scabber. After all, she already knew what she wanted to do. *She'll sell the tubes of centuries-old, frozen humans to the highest bidder, regardless of whether they are humanitarians, flesh collectors, or farmers.*

Tarsha would have thought differently, and Jetta could sense her opposition rubbing up against Agracia's conditioned logic.

But then it kicked in. Maybe it was the original, Alliance-driven mission that had made Agracia obsess over cryotubes and brought the Scabber personality back to the forefront. If it was a covertly planned mission, it was possible that allowing her to complete her assignment would put to rest the ugliness that was Agracia Waychild.

The building above them quaked. A plume of dust sprinkled her visor. As she wiped it off, she reassessed their situation. *The only way to extract the material on the module is to find a compatible host or energy source.* It would be tough to find anything on Earth that had survived eleven centuries and the hands of Scabbers. *Our only other option is the research labs on Alliance grounds, or possibly the Hub.*

"*Mugarruthepeta*," Jetta muttered, stuffing everything back in the envelope and shoving it inside her suit. Her questions about the Steins and her tattoo would have to wait. For now, they needed to resume the assignment Victor gave to Agracia. "We still have to find a smartserver."

"This way," Agracia said, leading them through a cluster of cubicles to an elevator at very back of the room. The doors had been pried open, but the car was missing.

"You did that?" Jetta shined her light down the shaft, illuminating the car at the bottom of the shaft with the hatch flipped open.

"Yup," Agracia said. She brought up a wad of mucus, opened her visor, and spat down the empty shaft.

Laughing hysterically, Bossy followed suit. Jetta felt Triel's disgust echo in her own mind.

"It's a few hundred meters down. Can you slide down on the cables?" Jetta asked.

The Healer nodded, but Jetta couldn't tell if she was lying.

(Not that I'm doing much better.)

She flexed her arms, trying to increase the blood flow to rubbery muscles. *No, can't think that. Still so much farther to go.*

"Last one down is a rotten egg!" Agracia proclaimed, jumping into the empty shaft and grabbing hold of a cable. She whizzed down with Bossy at her heels, howling. A loud *thump* reverberated off the plated walls as they hit the top of the car, as well as the subsequent sounds of play fighting.

Taking Triel by the waist, Jetta leaned over and grabbed a cable. "Hold onto me, okay?"

"Thanks," Triel whispered as she wrapped herself around Jetta.

Don't let go, she told herself. Every meter of cable that passed through her gloved hand threatened to strip away her control, but she couldn't adjust her grip, not with Triel's life in her hands.

A new, surprising feeling bubbled through to her awareness. Despite exhaustion, sickness, and hunger, holding Triel during their descent into the unknown sublevels of Stein's laboratories filled her with a strange, tingly warmth that lifted her from pain. It felt just as strong as when she was with her siblings, but on an entirely different level.

(I love her. I really love her.)

Jetta reflexively bit her lip. Although she couldn't deny her drive to protect and support her friend, she could still resist her other more uncomfortable feelings for the Healer. *Can't do this. Not now.*

She pushed on, embracing the pain that seared her hand as the material on her glove eroded down to flesh. When she finally touched down, she looked at the gaping hole in her glove and the deep abrasion underneath.

As Triel moved to remove her own gloves and heal her, Jetta stopped her. "It can wait. We can't risk your exposure, too."

"Come on!" Agracia called insistently from below. The two Scabbers had already dropped to the floor of the car and were crawling through the gap in the doors.

Jetta helped Triel down as gently as she could. When it came to her turn, she narrowly landed on her feet.

The thought crept into her head before she had time to censor it: *(It won't be too much longer for me.)*

"Skucheka," she mumbled to herself.

"Oh my Gods," Triel said as they popped through the doors into a new arena. "This is a launch site!"

Jetta couldn't contain her surprise. She had seen the videos of the lifeboat launch site sweeps when the United Starways Coalition briefly resumed interest in the dead planet, but it was a grafted memory, and an old one at that. None of the sites the USC had located were as structurally intact as this one, nor as well preserved. Ancient orbiter schematics hung on the far walls, while backup rocket boosters lay dormant in carefully arranged stacks. Verdigris copper rings were still piled high in hunchback loaders. Best of all, no one had looted the area for any of its invaluable electronic or mechanical parts.

"This must be a private site or someone would have already found it," Jetta said.

Popping her head out of a hunchback loader, Agracia chimed in. "Lots of rich bastards paid for private lifeboats. This one is definitely off the map."

"You found this a few years ago?" Jetta asked while circling beneath the control tower.

"Yeah, but we had to turn back. Ran out of juice. Didn't have fancy suits like this last time."

Jetta came to Triel's side near the launch pad, where old scorch marks still scarred the foundation. "What is it?"

"This isn't right..."

Stooping down for a closer inspection, Jetta took off her torn glove and tracing the burn marks with her fingers. "These patterns are strange. This isn't like the old rocket boosters of the twenty-first century. This is more like..."

No. Impossible.

Jetta shined her light into the infinitum darkness above, but she already knew the truth without having to see it. *The bay doors are still locked.* Whatever launched from the site could not and did not pass through locked doors.

"Something happened here that broke the laws of physics," Triel said, coming to the same conclusion. "That is why this entire place feels so... haunted. This is where two sides of the mirror became one."

"Whatever lifeboat launched here wasn't like the others, was it?" Jetta said.

Triel shook her head. "This is a place of crossing."

"A what?" Bossy interjected.

As she stood back up, Jetta kicked something out of the dust, sending it skidding across the room toward a computer terminal. She retrieved it, shaking away the debris.

Huh, a bracelet, she thought, running her fingers along the intertwined silver and wood. She turned it over, reading the inscription on the inside. *"My dearest Ariya, my heart has always been yours. Kovan Kyron."*

"Sycha!" she screamed as an invisible force ripped her mind from reality.

"Please, we can't leave her here," the woman with auburn hair pled, holding her swollen belly with both hands. Ample hips and thighs, thick with extra weight, struggled to keep her upright in the last stages of

pregnancy. She waddled away from the docking bay toward a door with a red-painted symbol, reaching out as if she could somehow cross the super-steel barrier.

A man with fair skin and tall stature wrapped his thick arms around her and pulled her back. "We have to respect your mother's choice. Come on—we don't have much time. He's coming for us."

The foundation quaked as the bombs rained down on the surface.

This is the launch site, *Jetta realized,* but centuries ago, back when it was up and running.

A lifeboat cycled in the bay, but it looked different than the ones she had seen in the videos. Someone had modified it, fitting it with the same transphasic modulators she had seen Victor crafting in his video.

That's Victor's design!

Jetta also noted the logo painted across the lifeboat's broadside: a blue and green world cradled by human hands. Black letters beneath the image spelled out Cause For Earth.

"I can't leave my mom," the woman said tearfully, resisting the man as he tried to drag her inside the modified lifeboat.

"You have to. This is what she wanted," the man said firmly.

Those eyes, *Jetta said, seeing the familiar blue.* He has my brother's eyes.

"Come on!" another man said, running down the lifeboat's ramp and helping the first man. "We have to go—now!"

Jetta recognized his golden-brown hair. Kurt Stein!

"Jetta!" Triel said.

Jetta came to with the three of them huddled over her, still clutching the bracelet.

"Gods," Jetta said, in shock from the abrupt transition.

Bossy rolled her eyes. "What happened this time, freak job?"

Too stunned to answer, she looked at the bracelet in her open hand. *I just saw my mother and father. And Kurt Stein. They were traveling together on that ship, Victor's lifeboat.*

"They bent space-time," Jetta whispered, putting the pieces together. "That's why they didn't have to go through the bay doors."

"Like jumpin'?" Agracia said. "But then this whole place would be blasted!"

"No," Jetta said. "They didn't jump. They passed through dimensions."

Triel sucked in her breath. "Just like Saol of Gangras."

"Yes," Jetta whispered. "Just like Rion."

I know how it all started...

But something inside her bristled at the idea, and she threw away the thought as quickly as it came.

Nothing's for sure, she told herself. A part of her needed to believe it was all in her head; some unfulfilled wish for a real mother and father to be somewhere out there. *And there's no time for guessing and nonsense.*

"Let's see if this smartserver works," Jetta said, putting the bracelet inside her suit pocket and trying to get back on her feet. Getting up too quickly, she nearly collapsed. Agracia stuck out her hand and held her steady. "Whoa, Doc. Careful now."

Bossy sniggered.

Jetta's temper flared, but she was too exhausted to put much fire into her reaction. Seeing her frustration, the Healer squeezed her arm as she helped her over to the terminal. "You've got this."

"How the hell are we gonna download this information?" Bossy said, kicking the inert unit with her foot. "This thing ain't gonna have any juice left after a million years."

"Just eleven hundred some, kid," Agracia corrected.

"Stop calling me kid!"

Jetta continued her inspection as the two Scabbers bickered. "This should have an emergency backup somewhere," she said, feeling around underneath the hood of the monitor with her ungloved hand. Finding a few buttons wither her fingertips, she tried them all. Nothing happened.

"*Skucheka,*" she muttered. But just as she retracted her hand, the screen flickered, and a green question mark appeared in the upper left corner.

Agracia and Bossy stopped fighting and ran over. "Sweet," Agracia said, digging out the two datawands and jacking them into the ports. "Ummm... now what?"

"Didn't Victor give you a code to get in here?" Jetta said as she tried to bypass the lock screen.

Agracia shrugged her shoulders. "No. Why?"

Closing her eyes, Jetta dug deep into her bank of stolen memories.

There's got to be something on interfacing and hacking ancient computers...

"It's going to be intuitive, don't you think?" she said out loud, mostly to herself. "Just an older programming language."

She typed in a few override command codes, but nothing came up.

"Oh *sycha*," Agracia said, backing into the terminal.

As Jetta turned, her stomach dropped to her knees. Drooping, inhuman faces dipped in and out of the beams of their flashlights. Molten eyes flashed in the shadows, coils of gray viscera dragging through the rubble. Moaning, gurgling. The sounds of the undead creeping towards them.

The Healer gasped. "There must be another way in."

"Work faster, Doc," Agracia said, withdrawing her gun from its holster as Bossy unslung a handful of 20-20s.

Returning to the terminal, Jetta sensed more Necros than the four of them could fend off.

(My father. I saw my father. I know it was him!)

The thought slammed relentlessly against her focus as she pushed herself to crack the smartserver.

"Jetta," Triel whispered, nudging her from behind. "Hurry, please!"

Think. Think. Must think.

(Victor was here. I know he was here.)

(My father!)

(Pregnant mother—)

(—with us?)

(Victor couldn't have been here. He lies.)

(Cause For Earth?)

(Transphasic modulator. Dimensional travel. Rion.)

Think, Jetta. THINK.

(It wasn't Victor's launch site or he would have had the passcode. He must have been working for Josef Stein.)

Suddenly the bracelet inside her suit pocket felt as hot as a burning coal. She withdrew it and held it tightly in her hand, allowing the phantom heat pass to through her. A sweet, elderly voice slipped into her mind: *"Redemption. Reparation. Deliverance. There is still hope, my dearest daughter."*

"Jetta!" Triel said, squeezing her shoulder as a Necro hissed, slowing its pace and approaching them on all fours.

Do something, anything—

A wild guess, a prayer uttered between gritted teeth. With Triel's fingers still digging into her shoulder, she typed in the numerical equivalent of *hope*.

"Got it!" Jetta exclaimed as the green screen dissolved into lines of alphanumeric code. She didn't waste a second, dumping the contents of the smartserver into the two datawands.

Bossy flung a 20-20 into the mass of undulating Necros. "Suck on that!"

"No!" Jetta screamed, yanking out the datawands. "No explosions or it will—"

The blast launched the four of them off their feet and slammed them against the far wall. In the midst of havoc, Jetta saw yellow and orange flames billowing outward from the point of contact, carrying the screams of the undead. The bay shuddered and shook violently as the effect cascaded throughout the sublevels.

Rolling over, Jetta checked on Triel first. "Are you okay?"

"Fine," she winced, sitting up. "But we can't go back the way we came."

Jetta shined her flashlight toward the elevator shaft. Waves of Necros spilled out between the broken doors and trampled through the blazing remains of their kin. *No, definitely not that way.*

"Oh, my head!" Bossy complained as she brushed herself off and tipsily stood up.

Behind the pint-sized dark horse, Jetta's eye caught an edge of the red-painted symbol she had seen in her vision. The rest of it hid behind a fallen beam, covered in a thick layer of black grime. Seeing all of their other options exhausted, Jetta took the chance.

"Help me move this beam," Jetta said, helping Agracia to her feet.

The Necros drew nearer, advancing on deformed limbs, faces caved in and dripping with mucoid fluid. Their sour, rank smell preceded them, making her stomach twist. Through the garbled noises that emanated from their many orifices, she thought she heard whisperings, like frail voices trying to rise above the ferocious din of the undead.

The four of them shoved with all their might, but the beam wouldn't give way. Finally, exhaustion triumphed.

Panting and holding herself up with one arm against the wall, Agracia flipped off the beam. "*Chakking* thing won't even budge."

"Look!" Bossy said, pointing to the slatted opening above the door. From what Jetta could tell, it appeared to be a vent shaft for keeping the circulation intact in launch sites. *And big enough for a full-grown adult to fit inside.*

Jetta didn't hesitate. "On my shoulders!"

For the first time since she met her, Bossy complied without a fight or crass remark. She hoisted the tiny Scabber up with shaky limbs while she unscrewed the ventilation shaft cover.

"Hurry!" Bossy said, crawling back around and reaching down for Agracia's hand.

The launch site trembled again, this time enough to knock Jetta off her feet. She scrambled up quickly, as Agracia popped off a few rounds at the Necros nearest their group.

"You next," Jetta said, helping Triel up.

"Jetta!" the Healer tried to protest, but Jetta wouldn't hear it. She helped boost her up, allowing Agracia to pull her the rest of the way.

Cold, slimy hands groped at her shoulder. Jetta reared around and kicked the nearest Necro in the sternum, her boot crunching against its hollow and pitted chest. Something wet sprayed her suit, but she didn't have time to investigate.

"Give me your hand!" Agracia shouted.

But when Jetta reached for her, Agracia froze in place.

"*Skucheka*, no!" Jetta screamed as the Jock's mind arrested and her body went flaccid. "Not now! Agracia, snap the hell out of it!"

Agracia didn't move, her arm dangling over the lip of the vent shaft.

Hands reached out for her in the dark. Jetta used the splicer she had created to shear off any fingers that managed to grab onto her suit, but their numbers overwhelmed her ability to stave off each attack. Moans and gurgles grew more excited as they smelled her sweet flesh, living and full of warm, rich blood.

"Tarsha," Jetta screamed through the headset. "Tarsha Leone, I need you! What you're seeing isn't real! This is real! You're on Earth battling the Necros. Come back!"

Jetta could see Agracia's nightmare uncoil from the depths of her, winding around her mind and suffocating her waking eye.

Li's voice came whispering up from the blackness of her worst fears: "I will kill you."

Standing above her, Unipoesa reviewed her failed test scores, belittling her in front of the class. "You have disappointed me, cadet."

Alone. So alone.

The same dream over and over, poisoning her sleep. Her and Li, in the showers again, but this time there was no escape, no means of delay as she lie naked, immobilized, and unable to scream. Unipoesa watched alongside the other faceless teachers and students as her enemy vivisected her slowly and methodically.

"Oh Gods!" Jetta yelled, tearing herself away from Agracia's memories.

Something like wet intestines wrapped around her leg, pulling it out from under her. Within the span of a choked breath, the hoard clawed and crawled on top of her. She flailed out, her fists and feet connecting with jaws and faces, but nothing slowed the assault. Their stench, rotting flesh and gangrenous bone, swamped her nose and lungs while their joyous howls assailed her ears.

I'm not going to die, she thought as they tore into her suit. *Not like this.*

Jetta was prepared to dig into her talent, to sacrifice the last of herself, when a blinding blue light illuminated the entire launch pad. The Necros shrieked and backed away, scurrying behind equipment and machinery to protect themselves from the startling light source.

Anticipating pain, Jetta shielded her eyes, but then gradually brought her arm down when she realized it didn't hurt. Instead, the light felt inviting, intoxicating.

Just like the halo created by the Dissembler weapon, only...

(...beautiful. Safe.)

Slowly, Jetta stood up. The ethereal light source was coming from the vent shaft. As she drew nearer, she could see the outline of a face.

"Agracia?" Jetta saw the Scabber crumpled up on the floor beneath the shaft. Someone or something had shoved her out.

Jetta looked back toward the source, reaching for it, extending her fingertips into the light until she touched the contour of the face. A kiss of sunlight started at the base of her fingers and spread to her toes until her entire being felt illuminated from the inside out. The most sublime feeling pervaded her soul, kindling her heart with songs she had never sung.

The Great Mother.

"*Amaroka...,*" Jetta, dazed and unaware of her words, whispered. "Take me."

CHAPTER VIII

In the privacy of her quarters, Jaeia watched an older newsreel questioning the reports released by Victor's campaign team. The same buzz played on all the news channels. *The highly controversial Kyron twins. Powerful telepaths. Unstable. Volatile. Dangerous. More dangerous than Dissemblers.*

Jaeia didn't think it would be long before Victor played his next hand. Even as Trigos buckled under the pressure of his political and military agenda, a few outlying colonies and stray bands of loyalists remained under the Alliance banner. But he didn't just want the Starways to pledge to his Galactic Republic.

He wants to seize the minds of the citizens, she realized, finally appreciating the breadth of Victor's goals. *As if the fear of the Motti's Dissembler device isn't enough, he's now aggressively pushing the impotency of the Alliance and slandering me and my sister.*

She ran her fingers along the interface module, anchoring herself with the smooth feel of the plastic keys.

I'm so glad Jetta isn't here to see this, Jaeia thought, muting the newscaster's voice. At first the videos bothered her, but as time passed, she grew numb to the slanted portrayal of her and her sister. Most of the videos were taken right after they had killed their brother, exposing their mental and physical breakdowns.

What else could anyone expect of us? Besides, she had forgiven herself long ago for what happened.

But as the thought passed through her, she made another connection: *Jetta's been struggling with her self-image...*

Maybe the broadcasts weren't geared toward dismantling the Alliance's influence through fear, but at unhinging Jetta herself. *Victor's tricked her before; my sister is susceptible to his manipulations.*

Shaken by the thought, Jaeia walked over to the food dispenser. As she ordered herself a jasmine tea, she heard the volume to her terminal click back on.

"Jaeia Kyron. It's been far too long since we've last spoken."

Her hand stopped halfway to the steaming cup of tea. *That voice.* Leaving her tea in the dispenser, she slowly turned around to face him. "Victor."

He smiled, deeply carved lines bracketing his mouth. "I hear you've been promoted to captain now. Congratulations."

"How did you get on this secured line, Victor?" she said, typing in commands to trace the call. She knew better. Victor was only traceable when he deemed it necessary.

"You still don't believe that I designed the Alliance defense network system, do you?"

Jaeia sent a manual text to Wren on her uniform sleeve, alerting him to the breach. The defense network patch that had been mysteriously sent to her had saved a few of the starbases and ships from Victor's attacks, but not many. *How did Victor make an unauthorized connection?*

"This is a secured station. Tell me how you got on this line."

Victor lifted a martini glass to her. "Not the time, my young friend. This is a moment of celebration!"

He's going to provoke me, she thought. Even as she steeled herself, she couldn't have prepared for what appeared on the projectors.

"*Pao!*" Jaeia whispered. Walking back over to her desk, she touched the edge of the hologram, bending the blue image. Galm and Lohien smiled back at her, waving and calling out, but she couldn't understand what they were saying.

This isn't live, she realized. No, it was the same short, recorded segment he had shown her once before, continuously replaying in the background as Victor resumed his communication.

"After Fiorah joined the Galactic Republic, I've made it my mission to clean up the planet."

Jaeia couldn't find the words or take her eyes off the images of her aunt and uncle. She leaned in closer, her face only centimeters from the dancing array of projected light.

"One of my relief teams reported finding your adoptive parents in an abandoned apartment building. I assume it was your old residence; nearly burned down in some sort of electrical fire. Apparently your uncle refused to leave. Claimed you were going to come back for him. Well, fortunately, I found him."

Jaeia knew better. She pulled herself away. "From your treatment of me and my sister in the media, I highly doubt you'd do anything so kind as to help our parents."

"On the contrary—I have immense desire to help you. My contention is with the Alliance, not with you. It was wrong for Minister Razar to keep you in service after what happened to your brother."

"It was our choice."

Victor chuckled. "I think family is what will give you and your sister stability. The Alliance has not been forthright with you about your origins or your adoptive family."

"Meaning?"

After flashing her another smile, Victor took an exaggerated sip of his drink. "Meaning that your adoptive parents have been on Fiorah all along. The Alliance kept you from finding them because the moment Jetta found them, she would have insisted that the two of you discharge from the service."

Not entirely true, but close, Jaeia thought. Jahx was Jetta's biggest grounding force now.

"What do you want?" Jaeia asked, surreptitiously checking her sleeve. A message from Wren flashed in red: *"We have a lock on the signal."*

"Come to Jue Hexron. Reunite with your family. See that I only want what's best for you and your sister. I want to give you a second chance."

The communications feed bleeped out, but the image of her aunt and uncle froze on the hologram.

Time passed without her noticing as she stood there, too stunned to move. *Reunite with family—is that possible?*

When the door chimed, and a visitor stepped in, she barely noticed.

"May I come in, Sir?"

Jaeia spun around. Aesis stood nervously in the doorway, accompanied by two guards with their weapons thrust into his back. Assuming the same body she had first seen him in, he looked upon her with warm, violet eyes, his blonde hair standing out against his light skin. *It must be his choice host.*

She found herself happy to see him.

"Yes, please," she said, dismissing the guards. Regrouping herself, she straightened up and fiddled with the ends of her uniform sleeves. "What can I help you with?"

Aesis's eyes drifted toward the image of her aunt and uncle, locking onto their faces.

"What is it?" she said, alerted to his heightened curiosity.

"I—I just came here to thank you for setting us free."

"Of course," Jaeia said. She got up and went back for her tea. It had cooled considerably, but she still took a sip.

"Something else is on your mind, isn't it?" As she waited for him to continue, she watched his eyes repeatedly return to the image. "Those are my adoptive parents. I haven't seen them in a long time."

Aesis took a few steps toward the projector and bent forward into the light field. His violet eyes grew wide and his chest bulged, as if the worm inside him had become unsettled. "You know those are Spinners, don't you?"

Jaeia set the cup of tea down too hard on the desk, splashing the synthetic mahogany finish. "No, I was not aware. How do you know?"

"I know my own kind, Captain."

Sucking on her lower lip, Jaeia tried to decide whether or not to accept his statement. "Thank you, Aesis; I appreciate your help."

"I know I have no right to ask, but are your parents okay?" he asked. "I—I watched your biography on the post-war broadcasts. They're on Fiorah, aren't they?"

There was no reason to trust him, but then again, there hadn't been a good reason to set him free other than that it was the right thing to do. Jaeia sighed. "I haven't seen them since I was recruited by the Dominion. I don't know how or where they are. I was... hopeful... when I got this transmission of the two of them, but I'm glad you told me the truth. I would have done just about anything to see them again. Maybe even something foolish."

"Now you see why my kind is dangerous," he said quietly, lowering his eyes.

Jaeia lifted a brow. "You realize who you're saying this to, right?"

A smile ticked at the corner of his mouth. Aesis allowed himself a hesitant chuckle. "Okay, fair enough."

"Look," he added. "I will find your parents. Your *real* parents. I will go to Fiorah myself. I can blend in."

Jaeia shook her head. "The Alliance contracted a few Spinners for that kind of mission long ago. On Fiorah it's not that easy. You can't just wear someone else's skin—you have to know who to talk to, how to travel, what not to eat—"

"I *will* find them. I'm resourceful—you have to trust me."

Jaeia paused, letting the words she intended to say go unspoken. For a moment, everything stopped. The entire universe suddenly fit inside her quarters, in the slender space between them. He held the same look, the same expression in his eyes, that had first captivated her attention.

"Why?" she said, her words hushed.

Aesis fumbled with his hands. "I want to repay you."

Wait...what is that? For the first time she could remember, Jaeia sensed the inner workings of a Spinner mind. One lifetime, a thousand different faces. The confinement of a single body, of one station, fell away as endless possibilities unfolded before her. *He's opening himself up to me.*

(He's... attracted to me.)

"You didn't have to save us, but you did," he finished, blushing. "I don't have to help you find your parents, but I will."

She found herself reaching for his hand. Warm and soft, his skin felt as smooth as a newborn's. "Can I be honest with you?"

"You know I'm being honest with you," he said with a faint smile on his lips.

It was now Jaeia's turn to blush. "My first intention was to see if you can help me save my brother. He's in a kind of coma. He needs a new body or he'll die."

He withdrew his hand. "Oh."

"But there's no pure source of his DNA. It's hopeless," she said, dropping her arms by her side.

Aesis didn't respond right away. "There is a legend among my people, that if you can spin someone a new body right as they die, their spirit will possess the new body."

"I know," she said, smiling wanly. "I studied your people's culture and history extensively on our databases. That's why I sought you out. It was selfish."

"Not selfish." Aesis took her hand back. "But it's never been done before. It's only a legend."

"I know. I'm just trying to find a way not to lose him again."

Aesis fell quiet for a long time. Jaeia didn't understand the conflict of emotion brewing inside of him. Discomfited, she went back to her desk and faced away from him, pretending to study a report on a datapad.

"I could find something of Jahx's and bring it back, too."

Jaeia stopped what she was doing. "Everything that was ours was destroyed in the apartment fire."

Silence, then the feel of him behind her. Only centimeters away, the heat of their bodies mingled in the space between.

"Then they weren't looking in the right places."

Standing so close, Jaeia detected a hint of his natural scent. Her body reacted before she could stop herself, inhaling sharply and breathing him in.

Turning around, she found his violet eyes looking down on her, intent but unobtrusive. "My senses are far better than any scanner or machine. I can find traces of DNA in the most unlikely places. I will find your parents, and I will find your brother's DNA."

Jaeia considered telling him to find hers and Jetta's too, given their declining conditions, but decided against it. *How can I be so trusting? I've gone too far already.*

A message alert beeped on her desk.

"I have to get back to work," Jaeia said, seeing it was Wren's response to Victor's latest maneuver.

Aesis cast his eyes downward. "Please, give me a chance. I will prove to you that I can do this."

He left before she could say anything. As the doors to her quarters closed behind him, she cursed herself for believing any of it. *Where's Jetta to set me straight on all of this nonsense?*

"Jahx," she whispered, closing her eyes and resting her head against the wall. "I'm trying. I'm really trying. But everyone keeps leaving me. It's all so impossible. Please, give me a sign that you're still out there… that I'm doing the right thing."

A message alert chirped insistently on her desk, breaking her thought. Unnerved, Jaeia scraped her knuckles along the edge of the keyboard interface until it hurt.

Jahx—where are you?

She felt nothing, nor did her senses pick up any aberrations in the psionic fields around her.

(I don't want to be alone.)

Finally, she signed in to accept the transmission.

"Please," she whispered as Wren's message played across her screen. She no longer knew who she was asking. Certainly not the haggard stranger in the reflection. "Please, tell me I'm doing the right thing."

***

"Just tell me where to find them, and this can all be over," Shandin whispered into his ear.

Reht fell to his knees, pain spiking through his kneecaps. Blood dripped from his father's fingers onto the wooden floor. His mother's eyes, sightless and fixed, stayed open and unblinking as her body grew rigid.

A cold-blooded murder. Heartless. Cowardly. Killed eating breakfast, unarmed and unprepared for attack. Not that his missionary parents would have expected the natives to attack. And it was the natives, after all. Who else would bury their razored featherhawks in his parents' backs?

"I will tell you everything," Reht whispered back.

Flash forward. Shaking with pain, he removed his hands from the acid vats. Tears streamed from his eyes as he carved the words into his hands with his father's wood-cutter.

Can't forget. Can't forget what I am. I am—
The words bled down the backs of his hands. Mukrunger
(Traitor.)
(Weakling.)

Reht screamed himself awake. No longer in his father's workshop, he found himself in his den, Femi curled up beside him. Somehow, she was still fast asleep, undisturbed by his terror.

Reht looked at his hands. The bandages were frayed and wet from gnawing on them in his sleep, but otherwise intact.

"*Mukrunger...*"

He bit his forearm as hard as he could stand, holding back the tears with rage.

Not like this. He would not allow himself to be undone now. Not when it was still possible to get revenge against the man who destroyed his world.

Slowly, so as not to disturb his companion, Reht untangled himself from the bedsheets. Femi snorted and mumbled in her sleep as he tip-toed through the sea of garbage, pulling bottles of Redfly and vodka off his shelf before stepping out of his den.

The empty corridor welcomed him with cold tiles and the droning sound of the ship's engines. Except for Mom who rarely slept and took most of the night shifts on the bridge, the rest of the crew was asleep—not that he would have cared if anyone saw him naked.

But he did want to be alone.

A couple shots'll take care of it, he thought, plodding his way into the galley. He rummaged around disorganized cupboards until he found a smudged glass and topped it off with Redfly. As he grabbed his drink and tilted back his head, he spotted movement within in the shadows.

Reht slammed down his drink in a single gulp, welcoming the fire that lit his stomach. "How did it come to this, Sebbs?"

Seated on the remains of a couch that Ro and Cray had dragged onto their ship from some rave a few years ago, the Joliak regarded him in silence.

"Do you know where that thing has been?" Reht said, nodding his head toward the couch. Aside from the ugly stains and half-chewed cushions, the damn thing had a rancid smell that he *hoped* was just cumulative body odors. But he had once bedded a Felciccan princess on it, so it had stay.

The old Sebbs would have made some self-pitying remark by now or been comically uncomfortable with his nudity, but this Sebbs—the one that claimed to have been altered by the Alliance—said nothing. And he should have been smoking, drinking, or taking hits. This one only stared back at him with quiet indignation.

"I liked the old you better, ya know," Reht said, taking another drink. He didn't recognize the cold look in Sebbs' eyes.

"Nobody liked the old me."

Something about the way Sebbs said it put Reht's guard up. He felt himself wishing he had at least worn his holster. "What are you doing up this late?"

"Can't sleep. Haven't slept in a long time."

"Bad dreams?" Reht chuckled, refilling his glass.

"You know what I'm talking about," Sebbs replied quietly, his face still hidden in the shadows.

Reht rolled the drink back and forth between his hands, not looking at the man in the shadows. "What's your nightmare?"

Shifting on the couch, Sebbs finally turned away. "How long until we reach Old Earth?"

Reht looked out the window. The ship was mid-jump, cycling near a blue-gray planet with three orbiting moons.

"We're halfway there."

Sebbs got up and faced the window. Reht had always perceived him as a smaller man with unremarkable features. Now the light played sharply against the bony ridges of his cheekbones, and cast the rest of his body in strange, alien shadows.

"You're lucky, Jagger. Pancar is a man of his word," Sebbs said.

Reht wasn't so sure of that, but his instincts told him Sebbs was right. The Nagoorian was a good man, and had agreed to asylum and privileges for him and his crew in exchange for the information Minister Razar was seeking on his former crewmember, Diawn Arkiam. It was a good deal, and a fair one.

"Pancar will find a way to deprogram the Alliance out of your head. Me, I'm not so lucky."

"What are you talking about? He's going to help you, too, *assino*."

In a creepy silence, Sebbs watched as Reht took a pull directly from the bottle of Redfly.

"He can't help me. No one can. What I am now is soulless. But what I was before was pathetic."

Reht traced the rim of his glass with his fingers. "You were always a bugger, Sebbs, but you weren't—"

Sebbs turned and faced him, his eyes flat, opaque. In that moment Reht saw something he had never cared to recognize. Sebbs had never been more than a shoal of Sentient detritus to him, a means to an end, but whatever had driven the Joliak before, whatever infinitesimal spark of life had sputtered beneath the haze of chemicals, was lost in the dead eyes of the man that now wore his skin.

Growls came from the galley entrance. Reht didn't realize how tense he had become until he saw his first mate and finally let his grip on the bottle of Redfly relax. "Hey, Mom. Things are cool. Right, Sebbs?"

Sebbs' mouth pinched at the corners. "Yes. I was just going."

Mom continued to growl at Sebbs until he left the galley, letting the claws on his forearms protrude through his skin as a reminder.

"Don't be too mad at him," Reht said, offering Mom a drink, but the Talian shook his head. "He's just afraid. Can't blame him."

Reht took a long pull from the bottle of vodka this time. "I'm not who I was, but I remember enough of what I was, what I hated about myself…"

Carefully, Mom pried the bottles away from him as tears formed in his eyes. His first mate had only seen him cry once, many years ago, when he vowed to avenge the death of his parents. But he was just a kid then, not a veteran dog-soldier captain.

"You know more about me than anyone, Mom," Reht said, unwrapping his hands. Mom tried to stop him, but Reht pulled away and continued to unravel the bandages until the raw, angry flesh of his hands was unveiled. The plum-red scarred letters stared him in the face, angrier than he had remembered them. "And yet you've always been my best mate. You've always stood by me."

A low rumble rose in Mom's throat as he tilted his head to the side. His first mate wasn't sure where any of this was going, and neither was he. The booze was making his head buzz, and the room float by in his peripherals.

"I can't be weak. I can't," Reht said, balling his hands into fists, making his scars blanch. Mom grabbed his left hand and pried it open. Shocked by his first mate's sudden action, Reht allowed him to re-bandage his hands.

"Promise me you'll help me kill that *jingoga* Shandin," Reht said after Mom had finished. "Promise me!" he said, grabbing his forearms.

Mom gently removed his captain's hands from his forearms.

The booze hit him hard now. He tried to stand up, but his legs felt like wet noodles. Giant arms wrapped around him and hoisted him onto broad shoulders.

"Promise me, Mom," he whispered drunkenly. "Don't let me go back to what I was…"

***

No longer in the launch site, Triel found herself lying atop soft grass and flowers in full bloom. Towering stone sculptures framed her inside the heart of the garden.

The old Seer's face appeared above her, shrouded by celestial light. "She is not ready for what she must do. She will try and stop you…"

Jetta—

"She will not let you fulfill your destiny," Arpethea whispered. "Do not hesitate to end her life to save your own."

She could hear Jetta calling to her, voice distant and frantic. "Give me your arm!"

There were other voices, recognizable but indistinguishable, and the remote sense of someone yanking on her legs.

Is this real?

She felt a distinctive warmth press against her, and when she rolled over, Jetta lay beneath her, naked, fair skin shining with a light of its own. Green eyes wet with tears, she reached up and cupped the Healer's face. "Take me."

Arpethea's voice boomed like thunder. "Kill the Apparax!"

Triel screamed. Against her will, the Healer's arms rooted themselves inside of Jetta's stomach through the self-inflicted gash she had made in the Temple of Exxuthus. Jetta resisted, crying out her name and trying to get away while blood spilled from her abdomen and spoiled the surrounding vegetation. Flowers wilted and stone sculptures crumbled as Triel burrowed deeper and deeper inside her—

"Triel!"

The Healer came to, helmet off and suit halfway unzipped under the beam of a flashlight. Jetta was on top of her, helmet discarded, worried eyes searching the Healer's face. "You're okay—you're okay."

Triel wasn't sure who she was trying to reassure. A terrible headache throbbed in the back of her skull, making it hard to put the pieces back together. "What happened?"

Agracia and Bossy dipped their heads into the light. The two Scabbers looked at her with dangerous uncertainty. "You started glowin'," Bossy said, twirling her lollipop in her mouth with her tongue, keeping her hands on the last of her 20-20s.

"Yeah, what's up with that?" Agracia said.

Jetta shot the other two an angry glare.

"It's okay," Triel said, putting her hand on the commander's.

Returning her attention back to the Healer, Jetta helped her zip up her suit. "What happened?"

Triel sat up slowly, regaining her senses as the headache receded. It felt bitterly cold, and she could see her breath in the frigid air. "I... helped you. That's all I remember. The Necros were going to kill you. I went back."

"You *chakking* pushed Gracie out of the vent!" Bossy said.

By the aggravated look on Jetta's face, Triel could tell they had already been through the argument.

"Agracia blacked out," she said, putting herself between the Healer and the pint-sized dark horse. "Back off—*now*."

Agracia spat on the floor. "Give it up, kid. We're all here now, right?"

"Right," Bossy said sarcastically. "Bunch of *chakking* psychos!"

Bossy went off, cursing and knocking things off shelves as her partner tried to calm her down.

"Where are we?" Triel said, accepting Jetta's hand. "Why is it so cold in here?"

Jetta lead her to a railing. "We're in a cryobank." Sweeping the area with her flashlight, the commander illuminated a vault filled with thousands of cylindrical cryotubes covered in blue ice crystals. "Agracia and Bossy are already planning their retirement."

"How is this possible?" Triel asked. "How are they still alive?"

Jetta pointed her light at the energy source. Triel didn't recognize the writing on the pipeline, but she inferred the meaning of the orange warning signal. "It's a type of nuclear energy they discovered before the Last Great War," Jetta said. "It can last a few thousand years if run on its lowest levels. The Scabbers use a modified version of it to power their cities."

Triel gripped the railing. "Jetta—what happened to me? Did I Fall?"

"No," Jetta said, shaking her head. Her forehead pinched as she tried to describe the experience. "It was the opposite. It was *beautiful*. Whatever happened to you—I felt…"

Jetta didn't finish the sentence right away, instead making a circular motion over her heart. "I've never felt so at peace."

Triel thought back. *I remember hearing Jetta call out to Agracia for help, and Agracia's mind locking…* Retracing her steps in her mind, she saw herself going back and shoving Agracia out of the ventilation shaft. *I found Jetta swarmed by Necros. I had to save her—*

The same desperation and confusion that seized her in that moment returned. *What do I do?*

Triel gasped. "I had to save you, so I…"

But she couldn't put words to her thoughts. She recalled allowing herself to be overcome by her feelings, much the way she had when she would Fall, but this time she shifted her focus.

"Jetta, was I really glowing?"

The commander nodded. "It was so beautiful," she whispered.

"But that would mean…"

"Check this out," Agracia yelled. "Working terminals!"

Bossy and Agracia whooped as they recharged the stasis cells and initiated a primary diagnostic cycle.

"No!" Jetta yelled across the catwalk. "That will cause a massive power drain! You'll kill them!"

Agracia shrugged her shoulders. "Oops."

"*Skucheka.* We don't have time for this," Jetta said through gritted teeth, pointing to the vent shaft where they had descended into the cryobank. Triel could see the three of them had made the effort to blockade the entrance with furniture and lab equipment. "Bossy discharged a few 20-20s, but they'll sniff us out and find a new way in. We need to keep moving."

Jetta grabbed the helmets off the floor and tossed Triel hers.

"We don't need protection in here?" Triel asked.

"No," Jetta said, putting hers on. "There's enough radiation shielding in here to protect against direct nuclear strikes. That's one of the reasons these people are still alive. But we have to get going."

Jetta saw her hesitation. "What is it?"

Tentatively, Triel reached out and touched Jetta's stomach. Even through Jetta's biosuit she could feel the inflammation of Jetta's unhealing wound. Flashbacks of her vision clouded her waking eye, and she retracted her hand.

"Nothing."

Jetta squared her shoulders to her. "Don't lie."

"I just..." she started, unsure of what she was going to say. "I don't know what I'd do without you, Jetta."

Even with the helmet blocking her facial expressions, Triel could feel the warmth radiate from her friend.

"I'm not going anywhere," Jetta said, taking her hand. She held onto the Healer for a moment longer before releasing her and grabbing what was left of their gear. "Come on, we have to find a way out."

"Jetta," Triel said as the commander lead her down an aisle of cryotubes. People of all ages, races, and genders stood erect in frozen slumber, their dreams sinuous chords of foreign tunes. "Can you hear them?"

Jetta picked up her pace at the question. "Yes. Come on, Agracia! Bossy!"

The two Scabbers shouted profanities at her, but as the lab quaked, they quickly caught up.

"These people," Triel said between breaths, following Jetta to the back of the cryobank where a red-hashed pressure door marked their only promise of exit. "They might know something that could help us."

Jetta stopped abruptly. "What do you mean?"

"What if they knew something about what happened to Earth?"

Jetta turned around and took off her helmet. A look of fear and excitement widened her eyes. "Maybe... no. Impossible."

"What?" Triel said as Bossy and Agracia came up behind them.

Jetta's brow furrowed as she debated something in her head. "I know it sounds crazy, but I might have family in here. I saw something in my last vision. My mother saying her mother—my grandmother—was in here."

Agracia swung her flashlight back and forth. "There's hundreds of human popsicles in here. Good luck finding Granny, Doc."

The structure rumbled violently, sending the four of them to the floor.

"Come on," Jetta said, ramming her helmet back on. The rest of them followed suit as they sprinted towards the red-hashed door.

Jetta shouted at the top of her lungs while the structure continued to quake. "Hurry," she said, cranking open the valve-release to the door. "Get inside!"

The four of them crowded inside the emergency elevator, but all of the backup functions and controls remained dark. Without waiting for the Jetta or Triel, Agracia and Bossy pushed open the top hatch and began their ascent.

Jetta secured her flashlight and her gear bag on the back of her belt before helping the Healer to the top of the car.

"Jetta, I can't..." Triel said, seeing the endless ascent. The access ladder and a web of cables would prove difficult to ascend under normal circumstances, but impossible given the extent of her fatigue.

Jetta took her hand firmly. "You can do this. You will do this. I will help you."

"No, Jetta," Triel said, pulling away as the commander tried to wrap her arm around her. "You can't carry me. I know how much you hurt, how tired you are. I can't ask that of you."

The walls shook, and the surrounding structure groaned from the stress.

"There is no time!" Jetta ripped off her helmet and held her by the shoulders. "Listen to me—I know you don't believe it, but you are no ordinary Prodgy. You are phenomenally special. Whoever or whatever the Great Mother is, I saw her inside you. Now please—for me, for your people—climb!"

Jetta tried to hoist her up, but the Healer's arms couldn't support her weight. "I'm so sorry, Jetta."

Ever since she first awakened from cryostasis she had been denying the gravity of her fatigue, and compounding it with their restless journey across the stars. Furthermore, she couldn't believe what Jetta was saying, or what she had witnessed inside the Temple of Exxuthus. If it was true, if what her ghostly visions of Arpethea were authentic, then it meant she would have to harm the one she loved.

"Let me go, Jetta!" Triel said, trying to wrestle away from her grip.

"No!" Jetta tackled her and held her against the wall. "I will not let you die here."

Before she had a chance to protest, Jetta removed Triel's helmet, and pressed her forehead into the Healer's. Triel breathed her in, feeling their heartbeats synchronize and her catecholamine levels drop. Jetta drew closer, allowing their lips to touch.

"Please, Triel—"

"Jetta—"

"I can't do this without you."

Jetta's moved quicker than she expected. In one swoop, she shouldered the Healer and began the climb.

"Oh, Jetta...," Triel said, finally relinquishing control.

As the structure quaked, debris rained down on them from above. Metal sheeting broke off from the interior wall, narrowly missing them before clattering to the bottom of the shaft.

With every movement, Triel could feel the extreme exhaustion consuming her companion, and the stubborn resolve that refused to give in.

If I can't climb, I can at least help her.

Triel removed her gloves and placed her hands inside Jetta's suit.

"What are you doing?" Jetta shouted above the commotion. Her ungloved hand slipped, slicing the pink tissue of her palm neatly against metal wires. Blood painted the cables and her suit, jeopardizing her hold.

"Helping the only way I can," Triel said, clinging tightly.

She closed her eyes and allowed herself to fall inside her friend. The same black iron construct of Jetta's will obstructed her complete passage, but Triel sensed a change.

There might be way in, *she thought, testing the surface. Cracks and fissures compromised the integrity of the barrier, worn by time and pressure. The Healer gently wiggled her way through a larger split until she came out on the other side. Assaulted with the suffocating whirlwind that Jetta locked away, it took everything she had not to retract.*

(Doubt. Loathing. Disgust.)

She didn't know if it would work; she had never heard of anything like what she was about to attempt, but the action felt natural, and she had to do something.

Oh Jetta, *Triel thought*, I am here. Feel me inside you.

Triel let go.

***

Jahx found himself on a grassy knoll overlooking rows of headstones. Not a single animal scurried about, or bird took to the twilight sky, save the shadowy wisps reminiscent of a tail or feather. Even the rolling breeze, or sway of the Japanese maples, did not disturb the quiet of the cemetery.

Half-forgotten memories shuddered and faded all around him pulsating motes, too grave to be remembered by the one who created this perdition. As much as he wanted to see them reactualized, Jahx kept his focus on the man facing away from him, toward the amber horizon.

"I've been looking for you for a long time," Jahx said, approaching him cautiously.

The man didn't acknowledge him, still hypnotized by his own delusion.

Curious, Jahx followed the man's line of sight. In the distance Jahx saw a crowd of mourners surrounding two fresh gravesites. A priest conducted the ceremony, but his words came as empty sounds in a lifeless world.

"Please, you must hear me," Jahx said, trying to capture his attention.

He didn't have much time. Somewhere, off in the physical world, his life dangled by a thread inside the Grand Oblin's body. Without knowing how much longer the old man could survive his inhabitance, he had to act now, make the connection before it was too late.

"My name is Jahx Kyron. I have come to help you."

The man turned to him, eyes swollen with tears. "You can't help me. No one can help me."

"Josef, there is still hope. Not all is lost."

The crowd around the headstones disappeared and the landscape changed, pulling them forward to the gravesite. Rain fell from the somber, gray sky in icy sheets.

The man kneeled down in front of the gravesites, hands and fingers extended but hanging in the air, unsure and frightened.

Jahx read the headstones. Edina Jägerhon Stein. Kurt Josef Stein. Wife. Son.

"You were deceived," Jahx said, trying to be as soothing as possible, especially at such a dangerous juncture. "You were made to believe they were dead. It was a lie."

The man smashed his fists against the headstones. "I will have my revenge." He screamed, tearing at the skin on his face.

The sky turned black, and the horizon blazed with an ominous white light.

"Listen to me!" Jahx shouted, the world shrinking down around them. "You were deceived. Ramak was out to destroy you!"

The man stumbled to his feet, his skin crisping under an unseen heat source. He shrieked, his voice garbled and shredded. "With eyes open they burn!"

Jahx shielded his eyes against the flash of light that preceded the thunderous explosion. With a heavy heart he lowered his arm, seeing the white mushroom cloud growing in the distance.

Jahx turned away. The man continued to hiss and scream, despairing at his failure as he transformed into something hideous and unrecognizable.

I have to reach him, *Jahx thought.* It is our only hope.

Withdrawing from the sphere of memory, he promised himself to return as he faded back into the lonely interstice of limbo.

But how? *he realized, sensing the faint tether that kept him from transitioning to the next plane.*

My sisters, *he called.* You must save Josef Stein.

***

As uncomfortable as it was for both of them to have the Healer draped over her shoulder, Jetta couldn't figure any other way to carry her weary friend up the long ascent to the top of the elevator shaft.

(So tired.)

Not that she had much stamina left herself. Running on the fumes of desperation, Jetta forced her ragged body into labor, but with each centimeter gained, her arms and legs felt less responsive to her demands. She poured everything she had to keep each hand reaching above the other, pulling them up the canopy of broken cables and ladders toward the faint light at the end of the shaft.

(Infinitely far away.)

Gentle hands slipped inside her suit, jarring her concentration.

What's she doing?

"Come on, Doc!" Agracia yelled down.

Jetta spotted the Scabber pair about fifty meters above, dodging falling debris and ascending via the emergency brake track system.

(We're not going to make it.)

Gritting her teeth, Jetta bit back the thought. *No. I have to get back to Jaeia—and Jahx. I have the answers we need on the datawand, I'm sure of it.*

Triel's warm hands pressed against her skin.

Don't waste your energy trying to heal me, Jetta thought. But this felt different than when she managed her wounds. The Healer went deeper, traveling farther into her viscera, much like what she did in the safe house.

Triel's voice called out from within: *...feel me inside you...*

The tingling started in her belly and flowed like rushing water throughout her limbs. Jetta saw herself as an empty vessel, being filled with a seismic energy source.

"Triel, what are you doing?" Jetta shouted above the quake.

The Healer's essence stretched across their two beings, a wonderful electricity that charged her senses and her muscles.

She's draining herself to help me! Jetta thought. Panicked, she could do nothing to stop the Healer. *—Unless I risk letting go of the cables.*

Even then, blood ran down her exposed palm, drenching her biosuit and making the ascent slippery. If she lost hold now, they would plunge to their deaths.

No, not for me, she thought. "Please, Triel—stop—don't do this!"

Tears slid down Jetta's cheeks as she pulled them up meter after meter while opposing forces fought for control. She felt revitalized, complete, and yet she resisted, not allowing herself to relish the feeling for fear of consuming her friend.

"Here!" Agracia shouted. Part of a semi-conduit scraped down the interior wall, sending sparks flying into the shaft. The Scabber ducked out of the way and then extended her arm. "Give me your hand!"

Hurry! Jetta screamed at herself.

Adjusting her body weight, Jetta tried to swing them to the right so that Agracia could reach their cable and pull them the rest of the way to the upper platform.

"No!" Bossy shouted, wrenching Agracia away. "They're gonna screw us!"

Jetta couldn't hear the rest of the argument above the rattling and groans of reinforced steel splitting apart. As she grappled with the cables with the last of their shared strength, Agracia and Bossy came to blows. Agracia was no match for Bossy, but it wasn't a contest meant to be settled by force.

Sweat poured down her forehead, and her arms and legs shook, a terrible knowing eating away at her consciousness; every second that passed dragged them closer and closer to death.

Can't hold on any longer—

Only one way to survive; she had to accept the last of Triel's strength.

I will not hurt her.

Jetta's hands began to give, and the two of them slid down the cable. Her exposed hand screamed in pain as the twisted wires cut deeper into the raw wound.

I will not let go.

Squeezing her eyes shut, Jetta forced every last ounce of her strength into holding tight, but the added weight of her friend and the fatigue of her body proved insurmountable.

Soft lips pressed against hers, breaking her from her pain. Jetta tasted Triel on her tongue and felt long fingers tracing the jagged scars on her stomach.

"Let me inside you..." Triel whispered.

(No,) *Jetta replied.* (I will not let go.)

"Then we will both die..."

Blue eyes, the color of a steely winter sky, connected with hers. She felt the Healer's voice inside her chest. "Save yourself, for me, for your brother and sister."

"No!" Jetta shouted, commanding failing limbs to hold tight.

But it was no use. She had pushed too hard for too long, and her strength was sapped.

No. Not now—not when I have the answers!

Her arms and legs spasmed.

She let go.

***

Agracia deflected Bossy's attacks. "Stop it! Quit!"

Her pint-sized companion wouldn't take it and slapped her across the chest. "They're going to screw us. Don't you get it? She's the Slaythe—the *chakking* destroyer of the universe! There's no way in hell that she's going to let us go. We got what we needed—let's get outta here!"

Agracia rolled away and kicked Bossy squarely in the hip. "I said *lay off*!"

"*Chak* you, Gracie!" Bossy said, slamming her fist into the wall just shy of her head. "This isn't you. You would never *chak* over your best friend for a *chakking* Skirt!"

Agracia removed her helmet and cradled her head in her hands. *No, this isn't me—*

(Tarsha Leone?)

—She would never help a Skirt, never risk their safety for someone with a reputation like Jetta's, even if she had helped her.

A lean girl with red highlights in her brown hair stood before her, a fragile smile trembling on her lips. "Thanks, Tarsha."

She popped open the collar of her uniform, still damp and ringed with sweat from the last Endgame match. "I just can't keep these numbers straight anymore," *she whispered, half-heartedly retying her hair back in place. Loose strands fell out, but she did nothing to collect them.*

"Me too," *she heard herself say, mouthing the words more than speaking them so that her friend could understand her over the hum of the bathroom dryers.*

Syra. That's her name, *she thought, remembering the brilliant tactician.*

One of the few other female cadets left, Syra proved to be a cunning rival on the practice mats. However, just like Tarsha, Unipoesa drilled her hard, and it was beginning to show in her schoolwork.

An old longing pulled at her heart. As much as she wanted to be friendly with other students, the Command Development Program's design pitted them against each other at every opportunity. Helping each other with schoolwork or lessons was strictly forbidden, and since all contact was monitored, no relationships, even platonic ones, ever developed.

Except for ours.

Tarsha had always liked Syra, and the two of them had kept their friendship secret since they were little. To an outsider it would have seemed strange and nothing like a normal relationship, but in the Command Development Program it was the best they could do. A passing glance in study hall or a disguised high-five during drills. Lingering around each other's bunks before lights-out and pretending to exchange class schedules. They were supposed to be rivals, and even though Tarsha was the top student in the program, after Li, Syra was next in line.

In the limited sanctuary of the bathroom, Tarsha comforted her friend as best she could. After she hit the dryers a second time to keep up the noise and prevent the recorders from picking up their conversation, they entered adjacent stalls. Tarsha slid her notes from gaming strategy underneath the gap.

They had less than a minute for the exchange.

Syra poked her head out from underneath the divider. Reddish-orange eyes, peppered with dark flecks, regarded her with both gratitude and something unnamable.

Tarsha couldn't help but envy her exotic looks, and the intensity that came with the unique coloring of her eyes. Syra intimidated other students and teachers, and she sometimes wished she had that quality. Then maybe Li would leave her alone.

"You don't have to help me."

Tarsha shrugged her shoulders.

"But you do," Syra said, her eyes searching her face. "You're not like *the other cadets."*

A warm, curious feeling blossomed in her chest. "What do you mean?"

The dryers clicked off. Time to go.

Syra flushed the toilet and pretended to rearrange her clothes.

Tarsha went to open the stall door but caught Syra's eye peeking through the partition. "No matter what they do to us," *Syra whispered,* "hold on to that."

"Come on, Gracie!"

Agracia snapped to in the quaking elevator shaft platform with Bossy dragging her down the hallway.

"No!" Agracia shouted, breaking from her grasp. Running to the edge of the platform, she found Jetta clinging to the cable wires, hands covered in blood, the Healer hanging limply off her shoulders. The commander shook violently, a heartbeat away from losing her grip.

Bossy flipped open her visor. "Gracie, no!" she shouted as Agracia leapt off the platform.

In the shifting light of the elevator shaft Agracia fell headfirst, grasping wildly at the cables until she snagged a handhold. Her shoulder screamed and popped, but she held fast, tangling her feet in the web below for added support.

Agracia swung herself next to Jetta and grabbed onto her suit just as she let go. "Hold on, Doc!" she shouted as another fixture came loose from the interior wall and skidded by them.

But Jetta couldn't, not with her arms and legs shaking violently.

There's no way I can support the three of us—

"Bossy!" Agracia called. "I need you. *Please!*"

Bossy hesitated, wavering on the edge of the platform.

"Do it for me—you have to trust me!"

"*Chak* you, Gracie!" Bossy said, flipping her off. But the dark horse jumped, sliding down the cables until she aligned with Jetta and Triel.

A string of curse words flew out of Bossy's mouth, but the tiny fighter grabbed the Healer off Jetta's back and hoisted her upward. Agracia got below Jetta, helping boost her the rest of the way until the four of them landed safely on the platform.

"We gotta go," Agracia shouted, helping Jetta to her feet as the elevator shaft collapsed.

Keeping the commander at her side, Agracia followed Bossy's lead around and over the overgrown Red Polyps in the hallways while the rest of the underground structure caved in behind them. Bossy never slowed down, even with the Healer slung across her shoulders, nor did she stop cursing to save her breath.

Don't look back, Agracia told herself as the mouth of destruction gained on their position.

"*Sycha!*" Agracia shouted, covering her eyes.

Bossy rammed feet first through the back entrance to the labs. The four of them spilled out on the broken asphalt, followed by plumes of smoke and debris.

As the adrenaline began to wane, the pain of her shoulder forced Agracia to the ground. "My shoulder... *chak.*"

The Healer, dazed but conscious, sat up and motioned her closer. "Let me help you."

"No way," Bossy said, removing her helmet. "Don't let that leech touch you, Gracie—she'll fry your guts!"

Jetta rolled over, coughing to clear the smoke from her lungs. "Her shoulder's dislocated. Triel can easily heal that. Stop being a *Mugarruthepeta* and let her help your friend!"

"What the hell is a *Mugga*—whatever? I don't speak launnie!"

Agracia put herself between the commander and the dark horse before it got really ugly. "Quit it, all ya'll!"

Bossy grumbled and muttered but took no further action. Seeing the tiny warrior stand down, Jetta redirected her attention to their whereabouts.

Agracia followed suit, scanning their surroundings, looking for movement, but the area appeared vacant. From what she could tell, they were in an empty lot in some sort of warehouse district, with the back door to the labs disguised as part of an intake/output portal for pneumonic trucks.

"God," Agracia winced. The hammering pain in her shoulder would not be ignored any longer, wiping away all other considerations. *This ain't the time to get injured, 'specially if we gotta soon deal with that* assino, Shandin, she thought. The survivalist in her broke through the thumping agony: *Get this fixed, or it's just gonna get worse.*

Muttering under her breath, Agracia kneeled before the Healer. A crass remark butted up against her lips, but she thought better with Jetta standing so close. "Please...help me."

Even before Triel made contact, she could feel the energy and warmth radiating from her being.

"I've never done this before."

"Don't be scared," Triel said, smiling weakly.

Jetta scooted over and wrapped her arms around the Healer. She whispered softly into her ear, "I'm here. I'll help you. Use me."

The Healer placed her hands inside of her suit. Reflexively, Agracia closed her eyes. Fireflies filled her chest, tickling her sternum with fluttering wings before gathering around her injury. The pain melted away as tissue fibers repaired and joints settled back into place.

"Holy..." she mumbled.

"Get away from it!" Bossy said, shoving Agracia.

Agracia fell flat on her back, knocking the wind out of her. If she could have, she would have screamed.

No, don't—

Jetta slammed into Bossy with uncommon speed, throwing her to the ground.

"That's it," the commander shouted, driving her knee into the dark horse's belly. Bossy doubled up, but Jetta pushed her head back down into the asphalt.

"Jetta!" Triel cried.

"Doc," Agracia choked out. "No!"

Nothing could stop her now. The Slaythe's eyes narrowed, alight with absolute focus and something dark and indescribable that Agracia could only understand by the panic carving into her stomach.

Jetta was going to kill Bossy.

***

Jetta held Bossy down by the throat, delighting in her desperate attempts to break free. *You shouldn't underestimate me.*

The dark horse hadn't anticipated her strength or her speed, especially given her failure in the elevator shaft. *You don't know about the abomination inside me—and the power it gives me.*

Squeezing her neck a little tighter, Jetta reached down and in to Bossy's head.

So easy to kill you... She sensed her divisible mind, the way her fragile gray matter would disintegrate with a single thought. *But that won't be enough—not with what I can do.*

As her excitement mounted, the world around them dissolved into a singular desire for pain. Jetta quickly rooted through the trivial malaise of Bossy's life until she uncovered the deepest, most unsettling wounds.

Grinning, Jetta delved in further, greedily indulging the pleasures of the unmentionable thing inside her.

I see you...

But something didn't feel right, and her greater instincts snagged her attention.

This isn't real. She isn't human. She's—

(manufactured)

The differences were subtle, easily missed by a casual eye, but Jetta's intent, cruel and vicious, uprooted every detail that would elicit the most pain.

Pushing past the years of booze and action, Jetta experienced many of the same memories she had once seen in Agracia's head through a different set of eyes. But just as she reached the end of the reel, an unexpected obstruction kept her from pursuing any further.

What's this?

Jetta felt her way around the barrier, sensing its size and shape. She found precisely laid neurons and nerve pathways interwoven in repeating patterns, too perfect to have been formulated by a human mind, even one that had purposely repressed a secret.

Backtracking, Jetta reexamined the memories from a different perspective, threading herself inside the body of the pint-sized warrior, with arms and legs that were disproportionately strong for her frame, and a brilliant, cunning mind belied by a foul mouth and rude manners.

Anger still fueling her search, Jetta abandoned caution and smashed headfirst into the barrier. Somewhere in the distance of her temporal being she heard Bossy screaming for mercy, and Agracia and Triel tugging at her to let go, but the thing inside her hungered for her nightmare.

What she found, unexpected and surprising, stole away her rage.

She couldn't move. Straps held her down across her chest, arms, and legs, pinning her back to a cold, metal table. At the foot of the table she could make out rows of stasis cylinders housing naked, identical female youths with perfectly crafted features. But a man in a dirty green gown and microscopic ocular implants leaned over her, cutting off her view as he inspected her with flashing instruments.

"You are the next generation. You are far superior to any other model," he whispered. "You are perfection."

Jetta watched helplessly as the man in green gown tattooed a barcode on the inside of her left wrist. She experienced Bossy resisting, spewing profanities and spitting at his face, but it did no good. A narcotizing cocktail dripped into the line running through her forearm, and she drifted into a state of semi-conscious bliss.

Images shifted and reformed. Jetta found herself in the midst of a blazing fire, lighter in one hand and fuel in the other. Dead girls, mirror images, were sprawled at her feet, removed prematurely from stasis and drowning in their sleep. The man in green gown staggered toward her, trying desperately to dislodge the scalpel that had been driven into his back.

"You were... perfection!"

Walking over to him, she ripped out the scalpel and plunged it into his neck. "I am not yours!"

The man in green gown fell at her feet, blood sputtering from his lips. The disbelief in his eyes, the denial and fear of death, made the kill that much sweeter.

In the growing intensity of the fire, Jetta turned over her wrist and sliced away the barcode. "I am not a puppet."

Jetta opened her eyes. Her fury was gone, but her hands still gripped Bossy's neck.

Did I...?

Eyes vacant and mind disengaged, Bossy didn't move, her coveted orange lollipop dangling from her lip.

"Is she dead?" Agracia asked.

"No." Triel looked cautiously at Jetta before placing her hand on Bossy's forehead. "She's just in shock."

"What did you do?" Agracia asked, fear and anger evident in her eyes.

The truth hit her hard: *If she wasn't so afraid of me, she'd probably attack.*

Jetta leaned back on her heels, unable to reconcile her actions with the unexpected discovery. She chose to avoid the uncomfortable reality. "I know what she is now."

"What?" Agracia said, holding Bossy's hand tightly.

Triel gave her a sidelong look before resuming her attempts to restore the tiny dark horse.

"She's genetically engineered to look like a young teenage girl, but she's really a custom-order puppet," Jetta said. "She's one of hundreds, maybe thousands of new-model puppets designed with augmented strength and a heightened sense of self-preservation to protect them against aggressive customers. Except Bossy's different. Her maker decided not to circulate her among the Scabbers."

Jetta saw the man in the green gown bending over her again, smoothing down her hair, whispering a song in her ear as he injected a red serum into her shoulder. Something wiggled and squirmed beneath her skin, and she struggled to get away from the tickling sensation, but to no avail. It crawled and slithered inside her, burrowing through tissue and nestling into her viscera.

"She was to be his. But he didn't want any ordinary thoughtless puppet—he wanted a real girl. So he gave her autonomy."

She gave once last glance at the flames rising from the building before disappearing into the subterranean crowd. No matter how far she ran, she could still hear the screams of the other puppets, the other girls that bore her likeness, as the fires consumed them.

"But he miscalculated how much he could grant her, and she rebelled."

"Well, how did she end up like this?" Agracia asked. "How come she couldn't remember?"

Jetta turned over Bossy's wrist and removed her glove, exposing the self-inflicted scar. A few black dots of ink hinted at the barcode once embedded in her skin. "She didn't mean to kill her sisters. It wasn't something her programming could handle."

"Wait—she's not human?" Agracia asked.

Jetta shook her head. "Not entirely. She's engineered. Some of her makeup was designed by nanites."

"Like the same ones that Josef Stein used?" Triel said, making the connection.

Jetta looked to the horizon. *It's getting late.* The pale disc of the sun, still hiding behind the smear of dark brown clouds, sunk lower toward the western mountains. "Could be. I can't say for certain."

"*Chak...*" Agracia whispered.

"She's coming around," Triel said, helping to hold Bossy's head up. Her lollipop threatened to fall, but before Jetta could move to rescue it, Bossy shoved her away.

"*Godich ratchak!*" Bossy shrieked, lunging for Jetta.

Jetta sidestepped her and pinned her arm behind her back. "Stop struggling or I'll break your arm."

"Jetta," the Healer said, her eyes full of concern.

Her cheeks flushed. *Triel thinks I'm going to lose it again.* Still, she didn't let go until Bossy submitted.

The dark horse stormed away, Agracia chasing after for a second before realizing the futility.

Agracia jogged back to Jetta. "Nice work, Doc. You sure know how to make friends."

Jetta didn't back down, instead offering the only peace she could. She broke the primary routers first and then handed Agracia Victor's datawand. "Here. Take this back to Shandin. Say it got busted in a battle against the Necros; they'll believe that. It will give me time to decode the other."

"Why not just corrupt the data?" Triel asked.

"He'd expect that," Jetta and Agracia answered in unison.

Agracia shook her head. "Well, what about her?" she said, jacking her thumb toward Bossy as she smashed anything and everything in her path.

Jetta flexed her fists. *How stupid can she be? She's going to attract every Necro in the area.*

(You have fault in this,) a small voice inside her whispered. She ignored it.

"Jetta," Triel said, pulling her aside. "This is your chance to see what else you can do with your talent. Remember what I said in the Temple after you hurt Amargo? Your powers are limitless. But right now you draw your talent from your fear."

"What?" Jetta said, surprised at her own defensiveness.

Triel turned over her hands to display the intricate swirl of her people's markings that decorated her palms. "Look at my people, Jetta. We are capable of healing—or dissembling."

Averting her gaze, Jetta thought otherwise. *Triel doesn't understand what's inside me.*

"Listen to me," the Healer said, her tone firmer and her grip strong on her hand. "I believe in you."

Still unconvinced, Jetta turned back to Bossy, ready to silence her by any means necessary before she alerted every Necro on the continent. *Oh no...*

"Bossy!" Agracia cried, running back to her friend as the rampage turned into self-harm.

The voice inside her called again, this time with force as the dark horse repeatedly smacked her head against an apron of asphalt that had pushed up against the side of a leveled building. *(You did this.)*

"Stop, jeezus," Agracia said. With tears in her eyes, the Scabber Jock tried to stop her friend as red smear painted the asphalt. "Kid, please! Stop, Bossy, *please!*"

"*Skucheka,*" Jetta muttered.

As she ran toward Bossy, her mind recreated some of the many scenes of her disgrace: The late-shift foundation worker she injured on Trigos. Hurting Jaeia. Nearly submitting to Victor. Slaughtering the soldiers in the museum. Murdering the man with the artificial limb near the Narrus cluster. Slaying Amargo. Trying to destroy Bossy.

Killing Jahx.

I am an abomination.

"It's impossible," she whispered to herself as she cautiously approached the dark horse. *I'm not strong enough...*

Though slow to catch up, Triel approached from behind and whispered softly in her ear. "Jetta, feel my faith. I believe in you."

Two arms wrapped around her waist and held her close for a second before releasing her. Taking a deep breath in, Jetta knelt down beside Bossy.

"Bossy, I—"

"*Ratchak!*" the dark horse screamed. Grabbing Jetta by the neck, Bossy thrust against the ground. Jetta shielded her eyes from the spray of blood as she screeched and howled in her face.

Nothing could have suppressed her reaction. The heat in her arms and legs built to a feverish peak, inflaming her desires. *She's no match, not with the powers inside me.*

It would be so easy to—

I believe in you.

Jetta heard Triel's voice through her touch, flowing out and through her like an effervescent wave. With the Healer's aid, she held herself in check and plunged back into Bossy's head.

(I killed them all I killed them all I killed them all I killed them—)

Jetta's consciousness reformed inside a place she hadn't seen the first time she invaded Bossy's mind. Behind a chainlink fence she viewed a gray seaside harbor, washed of color and frozen in time; waves poised to crash, gulls halted in mid-air turns. Bossy stood near the dark water, naked, her smooth, ivory skin offset by a menagerie of burns and bruises.

This isn't a real memory, *she thought, sensing the discord rippling through the images. A long time ago she encountered something like this in Galm; a parallel truth, something a mind created in the wake of horrific trauma.*

Bossy's voice sounded all around her, inside her, thrusting her against the chainlink. (I killed them all I killed them all I killed them all I killed them—)

Time sped forward, gulls crying out in unison, and then came to an abrupt stop. She saw Bossy waist-deep in the water, towering waves curled above her head, ready to swallow her whole.

Jetta remembered Triel's words: "Your powers are limitless. But right now you draw your talent from your fear."

Which she had already done. She had seen Bossy's darkest secret: In a fit of confusion and rage against their maker, she had accidentally murdered her like models, her sisters, but the programming written into her systems wouldn't allow for her to be companionless. Without her maker or her sisters, she would be alone in a foreign, uninviting world, and that terrified her more than anything.

Then it dawned on Jetta. That's why Bossy latched on so hard to Agracia.

With her adaptive design, she had adopted traits and personality quirks that made her Agracia's perfect companion, evolving her into the foul-mouthed, crass dark horse that dominated the fighting rings, loved one-night stands and getting sloshed in the bars.

Agracia. She's the key.

She felt Triel's hands slide into hers as she reached back and fell into the memories she had grafted from Agracia. With the Healer beside her, she slalomed through countless drunken binges and raw battles in which

Agracia and Bossy took on hoards of Necros in the wastelands. There were cold, painful nights spent together in safehouses, nursing wounds and staving off radiation sickness, and many more spent hungry and looking desperately for work on this dead, forgotten world. But always, through it all, Jetta felt the constant pull of their friendship, an unspoken bond between kindred spirits. Even though both of their personas had been artificially created, Jetta couldn't deny the reality of the loyalty they shared, or their dedication to each other. As she focused on the essence of that memory, she wove her energies into the tapestry of Bossy's mind.

Sunlight glinted in the backdrop of overcast skies. The gulls fluttered in place.

Something's happening.

Other memories competed for her attention. Jetta saw herself bruised and cuffed, lying in the corner atop a mattress of cardboard boxes. Her capture. Bossy's delight. Rage swelled to a conflagration in her chest.

Jetta clamped down on Triel's hand and ground her teeth together. Opposing desires fought for supremacy in her mind. It's just as easy to destroy Bossy as it is to save her. *And every second she spent in the psionic plane, she taxed her already drained and beaten body, putting herself—and her mission—at risk.* Is a crazy, Scabber puppet really worth it?

From the depths of her fear, Victor's voice whispered, "…there are some people that don't deserve their skin…"

Reality split in two. She saw behind Bossy's eyes as she got between her best friend and a Johnnie with a knife. At the same time, she remembered Bossy laughing and goading her from the stands as she fought Rigger Mortis in the fighting ring.

Why am I risking myself for her?

And then she heard Jahx's voice, clear and steady, as if he were right next to her.

"Jetta," *he said. A hand pulled her away from the chainlink. Blue eyes drifted to her right hand.* "It's your turn."

Confused, Jetta opened her hand, and rock dice clattered onto the broken cement. She watched them roll away until they reached the edge of the chainlink where the sand from the beach had sifted through.

(How did you—what do you mean?) *she said, but when she looked up, he had disappeared.*

Crouching down, she inspected the dice. She had rolled a crescent-

double, a tricky score. Equal chances of losing and winning...

The skies shuddered, and the gulls shrieked. Waves came crashing down on Bossy, rolling her under in a thunderous collapse.

(No!) *Jetta screamed.*

Focus.

Loyalty. Friendship. Dedication. Jetta conjured these memories from both Agracia and Bossy, inadvertently pouring her own sentiments into the mix as she bombarded the dark horse's mind.

The waves broke against the beach with ferocity, rattling the entire world. Jetta fell to her knees, looking up at the muggy sky where the gulls morphed into midnight creatures with membranous, webbed wings. She covered her ears as their cries escalated.

Something emerged from the sea.

(Bossy?)

A glaucous mass, not remotely human-looking, pulled itself through the sand on elongated legs. The thing wore a saurian crown on a featureless head. Blood trickled from tiny slits in its slick skin.

(*Demei Uo!*) *Jetta whispered in her native tongue.*

She would have to go deeper. It wouldn't be enough to give Bossy good memories, it had to be more. It has to be real.

Jetta opened her eyes in both worlds, grabbing for Agracia's hand. In the echo of the two realities she heard Agracia swear and resist, but Triel calmed her as Jetta held fast and pulled her inside the celestial limbo of worlds.

(This is real...)

In the vast expanse of the in-between, Jetta saw the radiant light of their beings, pulsating and shimmering in an infinite universe of living stars. She reached out into the prism, gathering their soul material, and brought them together into a state of dual existence, where one pattern could not be distinguished from the other. Jetta didn't know how or why she did it, or how it was possible. Everything she had ever learned or grafted spoke to the universal understanding that two objects could not occupy the same space, but in this place, the rules of physics had no application.

In the back of her mind she could hear Triel's anguished thoughts, and saw a terrible vision of a stone garden and an old woman's weather-worn face.

Oh Gods, *she sensed the Healer think,* does she know what she's done?

***

Agracia couldn't believe what she felt. Somehow, Jetta Kyron made her part of Bossy, knitting her into the very fabric of her being.

I've never experienced—

—couldn't imagine anything like this—

The war within her paused as the two sides pulled together to witness the truth she felt in the very marrow of her bones: Bossy loved her. Unequivocally. Unconditionally. Her friendship was a real, tangible thing in a fluctuating, torrential universe. That's why the imposter, Tarsha Leone, was an unwelcome and threatening discovery.

I can never embrace my past, or I will lose my best friend, *Agracia concluded. With renewed spirit, she whispered across the stars:* (You are my friend, forever and always, you stupid kid. I love you.)

Hands let go, and she fell onto the hard, unyielding earth. Agracia opened her eyes to the dirty sky. The air, still and frigid, tasted like rotten eggs.

"What just happened?" she said, her words hushed.

"Jetta did the impossible," Triel answered.

Rolling over, Agracia found the Healer cradling Jetta's head in her lap.

"I told you, you could do it," Triel whispered, stroking the commander's hair.

She doesn't look good, Agracia thought, looking over the unconscious Jetta Kyron. Although she had seen her in bad shape before, her chalky face and her limp body worried her more than her injuries after crash-landing on Earth.

Agracia crawled up beside her. "Is she okay?"

"No," Triel said, feeling her neck for something. "I need to get her to a medical facility. I'm not strong enough to heal her on my own."

As she debated what to do, Bossy came around, her body wobbling and eyes dancing in their sockets. "Whoa, that was some trip."

Too excited for words, Agracia leapt over to her friend and hugged her with all her strength. For the first time since she could remember,

Bossy hugged her back with the same intensity. It only lasted a brief moment, and within seconds Bossy shoved her away and pretended to dry-heave. "Get off, sicko!"

"Forever and ever, kid," Agracia mumbled under her breath.

"God," Bossy said, gathering herself. She did a double-take at Jetta, her face contorting in odd expressions before settling on uncertainty. "You *chakking* leeches and your magic tricks."

Agracia got up cautiously. "Hey now…"

Bossy's confusion only worsened, and she took one step forward and two steps back, fists flexing and relaxing. As she readjusted the belt holding her 20-20s several times, her lips formed words that never came.

"We need to get going," Agracia said, surveying their surroundings. Quiet streets, no wind. A feeling of dread burgeoning in her stomach. *We've made a lot of noise and stayed in one place far too long.*

Besides the Necros, their exposure to the poisons on the surface would reach critical levels in less than an hour. *If we don't take meds soon, the other Scabbers won't allow us to re-enter the Pits.*

Triel shook her head. "We're in no condition to travel."

"The Rover can't be far from here," Agracia said. "I can take Jetta, and Bossy can help you."

Bossy made a hissing noise between her teeth, but Agracia ignored her.

"We can't afford to wander around and—"

"Oh *sycha*," Agracia said, backing up. Two Necros hunkered in the shadows between an old firehouse and bus depot, too large to be ordinary walkers.

"Gracie…" Bossy tapped the last of her 20-20s, "I only got one left."

Frantically, Agracia searched for anything that would pass as a weapon as one of the creatures emerged from the shadows.

"No, don't!" the Healer cried as Bossy cocked back with the last of her grenades.

"What the hell is that?!" Agracia said as scarlet eyes locked onto her position.

"Wolves."

Not like any Scab wolf I've seen. The two gigantic animals stood taller than her, with fur blacker than a starless night. One had a distinguishing gray paw, the other a half-moon of white fur encircling its neck.

"Kiyiyo... Cano..." Triel extended an arm. The wolves' ears perked up and they trotted over.

"You know these two?" Agracia said, taking a few more steps back.

The Healer smiled hesitantly as the white neck buried his nose in her chest. "They traveled with us from Algar."

The one with the gray paw went directly to Jetta, while the white-necked wolf inspected Bossy and Agracia.

"It's okay, Kiyiyo," Triel said, scratching his ears. The gray-pawed wolf whined and licked Jetta's face. "You'll help us get back to the Pits, okay?"

"Wait, wait, wait," Agracia said, waving her hands. "You can *chakking* ride these things?"

Gently, Triel laid Jetta down and got up with the help of the wolf. "It wasn't my first choice back on Algar, but it got us here. And hopefully they're going to get us back to safety."

Agracia balked until she saw something else moving in the shadows. "Well, okay. Just as long as they don't bite."

"Help me with Jetta, quickly," Triel said, spotting the figures emerging from the bus depot.

"*Chak*, we got lots of dead-heads!" Bossy shouted, tossing the last of her 20-20s. The explosion sent fragments of asphalt, dirt, and body parts into the air, but more of them poured out from the firehouse and over the top of their liquefied brethren.

"Agracia!" Triel snapped.

Scrambling to the Healer's side, Agracia helped lift Jetta on top of the crouching wolf before sliding in behind her.

"Come on, Doc," she whispered as Jetta slowly came around. Mumbling incoherently, the commander still couldn't hold herself up. Agracia braced Jetta between her arms and clung to the fur around the wolf's neck. "How the hell do you ride this thing?"

With a pained expression, the Healer crawled onto the back of the white-necked wolf. "Just hold on."

"Bossy!" Agracia shouted as the tiny dark horse screamed obscenities at the swarming Necros. Her wolf, with hackles raised and ears flattened against his dark fur, edged away from the approaching undead. If Bossy didn't get on now, the wolves weren't going to stick around. "Get on!"

The tiny fighter swore up and down, but in the end gave in as the

Necros closed in, springing onto Triel's wolf.

Unprepared for the jolt, or the speed at which the animal ran, Agracia yelped, and hung on to the wolf's fur with all her might. As massive as it was, it glided effortlessly over the twisted terrain, making hairpin turns with ease. Within minutes they lost sight of the Necros and the inner city.

She was just getting used to the bounce and sway of the animal's body, the way its muscles flexed and rippled with each stride, when the Rover came into view. Or at least what was left of it.

"*Sycha*," Agracia said as they approached the dismantled vehicle. Her rivals had trashed and raided it, rendering it inoperable. Unsurprised, Agracia half-grinned. *I woulda done the same.*

Carefully, she eased off the wolf, leaving Jetta on top, slumped over on its shoulders, and inspected the site.

The second wolf came trotting up beside her. "Guess we're riding the rest of the way to the Pits," Triel commented.

"You shouldn't," Agracia said, barely keeping the greed out of her voice, "at least not real close. Wolves like those would be prime for the fighting rings."

"But I have to make contact with the Alliance and help Jetta."

"Ain't nothin' in the Pits like that. Well, nothin' reliable or accessible. Don't you have a communicator or somethin'?"

Triel slid down off her wolf and teetered over to Jetta. The commander seemed more conscious, but not by much. "Yes and no. We have the ship we came in on. It's badly damaged, but I'm sure Jetta can rig something up with what is left over. Or even contact her sister through their bond."

By the way Jetta looked, Agracia didn't think would happen anytime soon. She would need to get somewhere safe for medical supplies and recuperation.

Too bad for them, Agracia thought, sniggering. *These wolves will make a sweet trade.*

But as the thought passed through her, so did echoes from the past.

"You don't have to help me," Syra said. Reddish-orange eyes seemed to find the weak points in her carefully laid armor. "You're not like the other cadets."

(But you are my friend.)

"No matter what they do to us," Syra's voice called to her, *"hold onto that."*

"Agracia?" the Healer asked.

The Scabber Jock found herself hunched over, her face wet with tears, and heart pressed heavily against her sternum. *What is that name?*

"It's nothing," Agracia said, collecting herself.

Bossy jumped down and punched her in the shoulder. "You okay?"

She wasn't sure. "Yeah."

"No, you're not."

Whoa—

Jetta, still pale and sickly, sat straight up on the back of her wolf, shocking all three of them. "We need to get you back to the Alliance Central Starbase."

"*Chak* that!" Bossy exclaimed.

"Why do you even care about me?" Agracia spat. "What's one ex-military project—or a *godich* Scabber—to you, anyway?"

Green eyes, as vibrant and intense as she had ever seen, struck down her anger. "We're going to need all the commanders we can get when the time comes. And all the fighters," she said, shifting her gaze to Bossy.

Bossy snorted. "Fat chance, *ratchak*."

"Yeah—get the hell out of here," Agracia said, waving her off.

Tilting her head, Jetta looked at Agracia in a way that made her uncomfortable in her own skin. "You and I aren't as different as I first thought. I know that your soul won't rest until you've faced Li, just as mine won't until I've confronted Victor. I can't make you come with me, but sooner or later you're going to have to decide which life to master."

Before Agracia could formulate a retort, Jetta's gaze drifted down to her wolf. Swaying from side to side, Agracia intuited that she communicated something that only the wolves and Triel could understand.

"Cano will take you two as close to the Pits as he can," Jetta said as the Healer slid off her own wolf and joined her. "Don't try anything stupid—he's onto your games."

"Psshhh," Agracia huffed, mumbling expletives under her breath.

The Alliance commander looked at her through hard-set eyes. "You know how to get a hold of me. That mind of yours won't let you forget." She didn't wait for her response, spurring her wolf and taking off.

"*Chakkers!*" Agracia yelled, throwing a handful of dirt in their direction as they sped off.

The white-necked wolf growled at her, and she took a step back.

"Well, it's getting late," Agracia said, trying to decide their next move.

Bossy backed into her, pointing at the fallen archway of a bridge where shadowy figures slithered out of hidden crevices.

Can't stay here; have to get out, fast, before the next wave of Necros.

"*Sycha*," Agracia muttered, taking a hard look at the wolf. His red eyes saw right through her, and any scheme to take advantage of his hide. "Alright, wolfy—I'll be nice to you if you be nice to me, okay?"

The wolf showed her his teeth but crouched down low enough for her to hoist herself up.

As she offered Bossy a hand up, Jetta's words recirculated in her head: *"That mind of yours won't let you forget."*

Totally weird, she thought, brushing the statement off.

But another part of her couldn't dismiss the commander's words as easily. *Wait...Jetta Kyron doesn't do or say anything without calculation.*

"Get out of here," Bossy said, slapping her outstretched hand away and jumping up behind her.

Retracting her hand, Agracia realized a frightening possibility: *Jetta knows that I'm too smart to forget her signature—*

—or to let go of the idea that there was more dimension to her character than a wayward Scabber.

"*Godich*," Agracia whispered.

"What?" Bossy asked.

"Nothing," Agracia shouted back as the wolf took off into the lonely expanse of the wasteland.

***

Triel held on tightly to Jetta as Kiyiyo sprinted back to their crash site. The winds picked up, flinging dust and debris, and stirring up the swollen, brown clouds along the horizon.

Oh Gods, she thought as lightning zig-zagged across the sky. *Hearing Jetta talk about the hellish firestorms on Old Earth was bad enough.*

As her muscles ached for reprieve, she readjusted her hold on both the wolf and her friend. The commander faded in and out of consciousness, her speech muddled and disjointed. "Please, Jetta, stay with me. We're almost there."

Kiyiyo approached the crash site slowly, circling twice before deciding to approach the bay door. With alert ears and eyes, he stooped down low enough for his riders to dismount.

"Hey," Triel said, rubbing Jetta's sternum with her knuckles. "We're here."

The commander opened her eyes just a crack, enough to see where to tumble.

Just get to shelter, Triel thought, helping Jetta back up on her feet and slinging the commander's arm around her. Half-holding up her friend, the Healer stumbled her way inside the old freight cruiser, the cold, wet nose of the wolf nudging them along. Triel coaxed the wolf inside the bay door, but he wouldn't stray any further inside.

With a grunt, the Healer managed to shut the door against the rapacious winds. When she turned around, she found the wolf sitting on his haunches and panting heavily.

"What's wrong?" she said. He wouldn't relax, even after Triel cleared them a place to rest in a pile of insulation that had been dislodged from the interior walls on their initial impact. "Take care of yourself then."

Returning her attention to Jetta, Triel untied the gear bag from the commander's belt and rummaged for the last of their supplies.

"Here," she said, putting one of the pills to Jetta's lips. "You have to swallow this. We've been exposed for too long."

Jetta pointed back to the bag. "You too."

"I know," Triel said, swallowing another black and red striped pill. It tasted terrible, like battery acid, but she washed it down quickly with a packet of water.

"We have to find a way to contact the Alliance, Jetta." She brushed back the commander's hair from her forehead, feeling for more than her temperature. "We can't stay here any longer."

"I'll try to reach Jaeia," Jetta offered.

That's too dangerous. Through her fingertips, the Healer sensed a growing, distorted energy collecting around all of Jetta's vital organs. *The last encounter with Bossy nearly killed her. If she extends herself into the psionic plane again, she'll die.*

"No," Triel said, massaging her hand. "Don't. Just stay here with me a minute. Let me try and manage your wounds."

"Absolutely not," Jetta protested. With a grunt, she rolled over just enough to look Triel dead in the eye. "You need your strength, too. Don't think I can't still read your thoughts."

Triel said nothing, allowing a moment to pass between them as the wind beat against their fallen starcraft. The wolf yawned, his long, red tongue curling in his mouth, and settled down on all fours as close to the exit as possible.

"I knew they'd come back," Jetta whispered. She reached out to stroke Kiyiyo's fur, but the wolf still refused to come inside any further. "I wonder what they got into..."

Uncertain of her own feelings, the Healer said nothing, but politely smiled.

Jetta's eyes drifted back to her. "Hey—what was that place?" she said, scooting back against the bulkhead.

"What place?"

"When I was in Bossy's head. I looked back into you, and I saw... a place of stones. And an old woman's face."

She saw Arpethea...

Her chest tightened. She couldn't tell her about the old Seer. *"She is not ready for what she must do. She will try and stop you. She will not let you fulfill your destiny."*

Or that Arpethea had demanded Jetta's death.

"Kill the Apparax!"

And she certainly could not tell Jetta that she had done something unprecedented, unfathomable—and legendary—among the Prodgy when she had knitted Bossy and Agracia's souls together. It made the reality of her fate more certain and visceral, and she couldn't stand the thought. When she looked at Jetta, even in her darkest moments, she couldn't believe anything more than what she felt in her heart.

"It was nothing. Just an old memory."

Jetta's face soured. "You shouldn't lie to me."

"You worry too much." The Healer stroked Jetta's arm, lacing her fingers around her own. "Jetta, I love you," she whispered, laying beside her and resting her arm across her chest.

But Jetta stiffened and tried to roll away.

Retracting her arm, the Healer tried to withstand the crush of rejection. "What is it?" she said. "Please, talk to me. Don't shut me out again…"

"You shouldn't say things like that," Jetta said through stiff lips. "I'm not right for you."

Why is she doing this? Is it me? she wondered. "Jetta, I don't understand."

"Just, please…" Jetta said, brushing her off. "I don't want you to get hurt."

Triel rolled onto her back, away from Jetta, confused and heartbroken. *Why does she push me away? She's loving and compassionate one minute, then cold and aloof the next.*

"Just let me rest," Jetta whispered, her voice catching. "And then I'll get us out of here, okay?"

The Healer, too exhausted to argue, reluctantly agreed. "Okay, Jetta."

Despite her tumult of emotions, Triel found herself submitting to her own fatigue, unaware of the wolf's agitation or the figure approaching in the windswept wasteland. Thunder tore open the skies, and lightning and fire descended from the heavens, leaving only the unfortunate and those with murderous intent on the surface of Old Earth.

CHAPTER IX

It was a dream, or so she hoped. The wreckage of an ancient spaceship and the charred remains of its passengers smoldered in the sodium-yellow light of the horizon.

(Who are you?) *she whispered.*

The thing standing before her wore human skin loosely around a reptilian frame. His eyes were the color of molten terror, his voice the sound of immeasurable suffering.

(Apparax...)

Jetta catapulted to her feet from their nest of pink insulation, heart thudding violently against her sternum. As she caught her breath, she spotted Kiyiyo pacing near the door, ears pinned to his head, hackles raised and teeth gleaming.

Something's outside.

Still dazed and disoriented, Jetta looked back and saw Triel sleeping restlessly. *Maybe it was just a dream...?*

No, she concluded, seeing the wolf's agitation. *Something—someone—is out there.*

As Jetta debated waking Triel, she reached for the bay doors.

What am I doing?

The wolf barked at her, but she couldn't stop herself. When he tried to get in her way, he bounced back, as if deflected by an invisible wall.

"Kiyiyo!" Jetta cried. The wolf bowed to an unseen attacker, whining and whimpering against its blows.

Before she knew it she was outside, her body whipped around like a loose kite. Someone whispered her name, the sound rising above the crackling skies and slithering its way under her skin.

Apparax...

No, impossible, she thought. Intoxicating and unbearable, the call guided her feet through the blinding storm. *Just like my sister's second voice.*

Fear, more severe than she had ever known, seized her heart. *And this feeling,* she realized as her entire body screamed with unseen terrors. *This is my talent—*

When she looked with her inner eye, she saw the distinct glow of a telepathic aura before her, growing in magnitude with every step she took. *Not Jaeia or Jahx—*

No, this was something malevolent, an entity seething with ancient rage that she could not being to comprehend.

Thief...

Without recourse, Jetta reached within herself. *Get away from me!* she screamed across the psionic expanse, drawing forth her own fury and slamming it against the unknown entity.

Harsh yellow light exploded outward from the horizon, blasting the howling wasteland. Jetta shielded her eyes, but when she looked again, a humanoid figure stood before her, unaffected by her attack.

(I'm just fighting fire with fire—)

"Who are you?" she shouted into the storm as cyclonic serpents of fire danced around her.

Murderer!

Invisible hands grasped her neck and squeezed. She felt the tips of her boots leave the ground as she was lifted off her feet. The silhouette of her assailant stayed fixed in the distance, unreachable, enshrouded in glowing saffron light.

I can't fight it— Jetta pawed at her neck, desperate to relieve the pressure crushing her throat. A deeper recognition worsened her panic: *(It's stronger than me and my siblings combined.)*

In the back of her head, horrors she could have never conceived played out across waking dreamscapes.

Peeling flesh, the raw pulp of bloody marrow spewed across the gulfs—

Complete separation, total darkness.

Only terror, and pain—

Torments wrung her body and mind until she only desired the relief that death would bring.

Then something happened. Cerulean light filtered in through invisible slats. A bestial roar bellowed out from the humanoid form, wavering like an interrupted signal. The pressure slackened on her throat as her boots touched the ground, and she drew in a strangled breath.

Jetta coughed violently, but something still constricted her windpipe, and she could not regulate her breathing. Bright flashes of light exploded around her, and she fell to her knees, assaulted by opposing forces. A woman's voice rose above the din of the storm, and the beast roared in a language that withered the last of her strength.

She closed her eyes and fell into darkness.

***

Jetta woke with a start, flinging off the insulation and scrambling to the other side of the entryway ramp. As she braced for an attack, she saw Triel, undisturbed, still passed out atop their makeshift bed.

With shaking fingers she checked her throat and looked for her wolf. *Must have been a dream.*

"No, it was not."

Jetta reared her head towards the engineering compartment. With his hackles raised, Kiyiyo stood over a body of a man who lay on his side, facing away from her. Even unconscious, such incredible power radiated from his being that she could feel the psionic oscillations bouncing off her skin.

That's the thing that attacked me! she thought, recognizing the electric charge in the air. For some reason she expected it to be Victor, but this man was much too young, his skin too fair and natural.

Kiyiyo whined and moved to the side, revealing another person hidden in the shadows.

"Who are you?" Jetta couldn't make out their figure, only the power, much like her own, that tore through the overlapping planes like a scream in an empty room.

"I am Ariya Ohakn. I am your mother."

All the air left her lungs. Still injured and weak, Jetta tried to stand, but her limbs refused to hold her weight.

Kiyiyo bounded over and sniffed her, licking her wounds and offering his help, but Jetta shooed him off to one side.

"Step out where I can see you," she demanded.

"I'm not in much better shape than you, I'm afraid," the woman said, unmoving. "It took everything I had to stop him."

Jetta lurched to her feet, gritting her teeth against the wall of pain that slammed into her with every step.

The woman gave a weak laugh. "You've always been a fighter, haven't you?"

Jetta stepped into the engineering compartment, and her eyes adjusted to the light. Propped up against a control tower was a human woman in her late twenties, dressed in the ragged remains of a green and gray civilian jumpsuit. Her hair, braided to the middle of her back, stood out in a wild mess around her shoulders. Jetta couldn't see any injuries, but by the protective way she guarded her stomach, she had been dealt a severe blow.

"Who are you?" Jetta repeated.

Lightning struck dangerously close to their craft, illuminating their compartment. Jetta immediately recognized the woman's pale green eyes.

"I am your mother," she replied softly, her voice tinged with pain. "I lost you, but I have finally found you."

"Impossible. I don't believe you," Jetta said, fighting the queer feeling that built in her chest.

The woman closed her eyes and rested her head against the tower. "You do. I can sense it. You have always fought your feelings, but you can't deny this."

Rigid and shaking, Jetta refused to give in. "It's not possible."

The woman sighed. "I put a message in your friend's head. The obnoxious dog-soldier with fire-dyed hair. I'm sorry I couldn't be more direct, but *he* was following me," she said, tilting her head toward the unconscious man.

Jetta looked closely at the man at her feet, trying to assimilate what she was seeing. The golden-brown hair. Familiar laugh-lines etched into a kind face. "No. *This isn't possible.*"

"I know I have a lot to explain," the woman said, trying to move, but she winced and acquiesced to her previous position.

Stumbling backward, Jetta looked for the exit. *Have to run, get away, far away from—*

(Kurt Stein.)

"No!" she screamed, reeling and falling to her knees.

It isn't possible...

***

Where am I?

Jetta opened her eyes to a different world, one that bustled with city life. People whizzed past her in hovercars and bicycles, unaware or unconcerned about her presence. The smell of processed meat and condiments hung in the air. A man with a funny hat and a stained apron touted his fare to fast-moving pedestrians in the daunting shadow of silver high-rises.

Home.

Ariya appeared beside her, no longer so disheveled, but tired and faded. (I don't have much time, so you must listen.)

The scene dissolved into a smeared sepia glaze. As Ariya spoke, her memories blossomed across the background, buildings, objects, and people appearing and disappearing as her thoughts played out. (By the middle of the twenty-first century, another world war had broken out. During this time, the United People's Republic conducted secret experiments to create more sophisticated weapons of mass destruction after the devastating effects of 2045's nuclear war on the world's ecosystems.)

Jetta watched the fertile landscape shrivel into desiccated heaps as entire cities crumbled to ashes.

(With unrest building, the UPR pulled the most prominent researcher in the field of nanotechnology for their new biological warfare division.)

(Let me guess,) *Jetta interrupted.* (Josef Stein.)

(Yes,) *Ariya said as the memory shifted to a white-walled laboratory.* (He was in the midst of developing nanites that could revitalize and regenerate tissue for war victims. The UPR commissioned him to modify his work for combat purposes.)

Josef Stein, hunched in a lab coat over a grayish, severed leg, carefully applied a droplet of red serum to the base of the stump. The faceless onlookers murmured with excitement as the leg began to twitch.

(He brought the dead back to life?)

(Not exactly. The military wanted him to create a "programmable, indestructible soldier.")

Rows of stiff-backed soldiers stood at attention as they received injections of red serum in one arm and a tattooed barcode on the other.

(Such a thing wasn't possible, but Josef came close. He made nanites that could repair injured soldiers in the field. The military wanted more, though; they wanted to keep their grunts focused on their mission. No fear, no pain, no sense of consequence—no psychological liabilities. Worst of all, they wanted to make sure that if a soldier was fatally wounded in combat, the nanites' programming would keep them "alive" until the objective was completed.)

(But they're not alive,) *Jetta said, observing a mortally wounded soldier charge through fire to reach a rival battalion.*

(No, they weren't. They were soulless, morally absent creatures. Josef was mortified. He originally created the nanites to help war victims, not create them.) *Ariya's lips pinched at the corners as they watched Josef pore over schematics and argue with military heads.*

(I knew Josef for years,) *Ariya continued.* (He was a good man. He had always believed in the kindness and potential of the human spirit, but by the end of the war, he was growing bitter and resentful toward his employers and disillusioned about the human race surviving itself.)

(How did you know him?)

(Your father, Kovan, and I were part of a secret environmental group called "Cause For Earth." Josef and his son, Kurt, were our biggest scientific contributors, and while the government was making Josef use his nanites for the war, we gave him the facilities and means to develop his Smart Cells for a better use.)

(Like what?) *Jetta asked as the background changed again. She was now in the same underground lab where they had found the hidden vault. Red stasis cylinders lined the walls, and animated monitors projected graphs and numerical codes for white-coated technicians.*

(A project we called "The Ark." Kurt helped us catalog and store all the genetic information of life on this planet, and Josef designed a whole host of nanites that could do everything from reconstruct living organisms to modify the toxins in the environment. We hoped that once things settled, we'd use the Smart Cells to restore Earth's ecosystems. But the Doomsdayers had other plans.)

Jetta witnessed Kurt and Josef entering lines of code into an enormous machine. At the center of the room, a miniature golden globe rotated on a suspended axis. Latticed steel pylons, arranged circumferentially around the globe, housed vast storage cells while boxed compensators grounded the dancing bolts of electricity flying from the immense energy field.

The Ark, *Jetta realized.*

The world fluctuated, and the scene faded from view. (God...) *Ariya whispered, her image torquing.*

(What's wrong?)

(It took everything I had to lock Kurt into sleep. I don't have time to tell you everything, so I will tell you the most important thing: Josef Stein did not destroy the Earth. It was Ramak Yakarvoah, leader of the Doomsdayers.)

The gears of time reversed, flinging her backward until a severely disfigured man came into view. Jetta could barely look at him. Extensive burn scars mangled his face and crippled his stature. However, she did not cringe at his deformity, but his eyes, deep wells of hatred, and his hands that shook with unmitigated rage.

(He was right there, all along, right beside Josef, but your father and I were too blind to see it. Something happened to him a few months before the end of the world, and he went into hiding. That's when he somehow tricked Josef into thinking his wife and son were murdered by the UPR and coerced him into unleashing his nanites to infect the world.)

Another image tried to form, but Ariya winced outside their psionic connection.

(Are you okay?)

(Yes—please—I can't stop,) *she said, her eyes alight with fear.* (Your father and I were the only ones left on Earth from our group, and even though I was at the end of my pregnancy, we followed a hunch and broke into Ramak's private lab. We found Kurt, but by that time, it was too late. Josef was mad, and the world was burning. So we stole Ramak's ship to try and escape with the rest of the Exodus, but we didn't know it was some sort of experimental trans-dimensional ship. I can't even describe to you what happened next...)

Jerky images ripped through her sight at incredible speed. Jetta caught only fragments of objects and sensations. The white outline of a face. Wheels of impossible colors arching across the sky, voices whispering in an unfamiliar tongue.

(We went to a place outside our universe, outside time. But before we could get our bearings, the three of us were seized by these ghostly entities.)

Jetta saw through Ariya's eyes as a faint silhouette appeared before the starcraft dashboard and hovered above her for a fraction of a second, long enough for her to throw her arms up against the attack. It was a violation unlike anything she had ever experienced. Hungry fingers raked at her soul, trying to carve out a place in her mind for its new home, but her body was already host to those that lay unborn in her womb.

(I'm not sure why—maybe it was because I was pregnant—but

somehow we were spared the insanity that took Kurt and your father. Still, I was changed. Even though that thing never managed to take control of my mind, it left something inside me—inside each one of us. I could read people's thoughts; I had a heightened awareness. I was so frightened...)

In the memory, Jetta witnessed Ariya holding up her hands, seeing through their fleshy confinement and the flux of time into other realms, other places of existence beyond conception.

(The others saw that I wasn't overtaken and attacked me. In the struggle I went into labor. That's when your father came back to me, if only for a moment.)

Kovan lifted his hand for the killing blow, but paused when he heard the anguish of her labor cry. Sweat poured from his brow and he bit back a scream, the veins on his forehead popping out from beneath colorless skin.

"You will not have them!" he screamed, blood streaming from his nose.

Kurt lunged at him, but Kovan, a bigger and stronger man, knocked him out with the back of his fist and stuffed him a storage compartment.

Terrified, Ariya scooted back into a corner, unsure of the man that approached her.

"It's me, it's me," her husband whispered, his voice strained as he clutched the back of the console chair.

The labor pains intensified, demanding all of her strength. She had no choice but to allow him near. Moments later, three squirming babies with squishy red faces took their first breaths. Two girls and a boy, heads full of curly black hair.

(He and I both knew we had to protect you from the entities, so we did the only thing we could—we put you in an escape pod and prayed for your safety. But not before I gave you this.)

Kovan and Ariya bent over the three tiny bodies, hurriedly marking the insides of their right arms with a pen-like device.

What the hell is that? Jetta didn't recognize the instrument until Ariya turned over her own wrist, and with a quick press of a button, embedded in her skin the graceful strokes of her like tattoo.

That's a graffiti laser! Jetta thought, drawing from her stolen knowledge of twenty-first century Earth. The anti-government groups used them all the time.

(The emblem of our conviction, our hope, our love.)

Jetta's breath hitched in her chest as she traced the outline of the tattoo on the inside of her right arm. Not a mark of shame. Not a symbol of her abandonment.

(Somehow Kurt came back around and broke free,) *Ariya said as the scientist freed himself from the compartment.* (Kovan knew he was no match for the thing inside Kurt—or inside himself—so he forced me into the aft lifeboat. I wanted to help him fight, try and save him—both of them—but he set the jump coordinates back to Earth before I could stop him. I don't know what happened to him. All I know is that in the short time that passed in that place, centuries had passed on Earth. I expected you to be dead, but instead I saw you on the newsreels after you defeated the Motti. Somehow, against all odds, you survived. I didn't even need to see my tattoo to know it was you. You have your father's face, his intensity.)

Through Ariya's eyes, she watched herself on the newsreels, reluctant and camera-shy, trying to act tough in front of countless viewers across the Starways. She felt the woman's pain as Admiral Unipoesa gave his infamous speech revealing the twins' involvement in the defeat of the Motti.

(I couldn't contact you, at least not right away; I knew the others would be hunting me, and I didn't want to lead them to you. I tried to send you a message through the dog-soldier, but that failed.)

(You tried to contact Jaeia, too, didn't you?) *Jetta realized, remembering the strange messages her sister had received via encrypted piggyback.*

(Yes. The Alliance defense network wasn't hard to hack. It utilized the same base programs as when your father and I first worked for the government's defense net.)

(Your patch saved our Fleet from being crushed by Li,) *Jetta said.*

Ariya gave a sad smile as her appearance lost some of its opacity. (Please—you must understand. Ramak and Josef... they're not dead. I see their masked faces in my dreams.)

Jetta whipped around, coming face-to-face with griddled steel and truncated flesh. A porcelain veneer hid his expression, all except the reddened eyes seething behind narrow slits. Another man, consumed by flames, stood behind the first. He wore a mask dotted with crimson dewdrops, and his breath came out as white smoke through the jagged cut for his mouth.

(But above all else, you must help Kurt—you must find a way to save him.)

The young scientist appeared before her, palms up, the golden globe of the Ark floating above his hands.

(He is the key to unlocking the Ark. If you kill him, you will destroy our last hope of saving our world.)

A vague shadow congealed into a smiling human face. Despite the resemblance to Kurt Stein, Jetta saw the entity dwelling within him, outlined underneath the gray ruin of his flesh.

Barely visible now, Ariya drifted into view. (The accident—our survival—must be made to mean something.)

Jetta reached out to her, but her hand passed through her wispy form.

(Find Charlie. He was a present from your grandmother…)

Another memory unfolded around her. Three sobbing babies swaddled in jackets and shirts, still wet from birth fluids, placed carefully inside the escape pod. Ariya holding back tears as she placed her gold cross necklace and an old, stuffed bear beside their tiny bodies.

(Behind his eyes lies our salvation…)

The scene changed, morphing into the store that she had grafted from Jaeia's interaction with Triel, its air stuffy with mothballs, old paper, and wood stain. The same white-haired man with dark-rimmed glasses sat behind a counter, counting round, copper disks. Stacks of books and ancient-looking contraptions clogged the aisles and threatened to tumble off the shelves, collecting dust and insect husks.

(And most importantly—do not think for one second that I didn't love you,) *Ariya whispered, reaching out to her.* (That I abandoned you—that I wouldn't have given anything to hold you in my arms for just one more moment…)

***

When Jetta opened her eyes, she found herself breathing heavily, flat on her back, the dark-haired woman slumped next to her.

Sitting up with a grunt, she took the woman's hand, feeling the luminous edge of a familial soul lingering on its last tethers to life.

"Mother..." Jetta said, finally allowing herself to believe her own words. "I have so many questions. I have so many things that I need to tell you—"

Jetta looked to Triel and calculated the risk of a restoration in her debilitated state.

"Don't wake the Healer," Ariya said, interlacing her fingers with Jetta's. "She needs her strength, and you'll need yours for what's to come."

"No," Jetta said, feeling the unbearable crush press down on her soul. "Not now. Not after I've found you. Not after you made me believe."

"My daughter," Ariya said, cupping her cheek. "Not all is lost."

With a trembling hand, her mother pulled a rose-embroidered handkerchief from her jumpsuit. It smelled faintly of a sweet perfume. "I will always be with you. *Always,* my little Ashya."

"Ashya..." Jetta said, feeling something beyond herself realized, as if a door she had never known existed suddenly unlocked.

Her hand closed tightly around the handkerchief, ready to extract the memory stain, but Ariya stopped her. "You must wait."

"It's not meant for me?" Jetta said, sensing her unspoken intentions.

"No, not just you." Her eyelids grew heavy, and her breath came in gulps. "Wait for the time... you need... to feel..."

Cradling her mother's head in her arms, Jetta tried to hold onto the ethereal cords of her being.

"No!" she cried, shaking her by the shoulders. Her mother's head bobbed limply as Jetta searched for her presence. "You can't just die!"

Jetta opened her mouth for a scream that never came as Ariya's body went flaccid in her arms.

It was real— her mind cried. *She was real and I allowed her to die!*

Overcome by anger and grief, Jetta's attention went to the unconscious man in the opposing compartment, slumbering in a dreamless psionic state.

"You *Mugarruthepeta!*" she said through gritted teeth. She leapt up to attack when white teeth pinched the back of her suit.

"Let me go," Jetta said, swatting at Kiyiyo's muzzle.

The wolf held fast, sending her impressions of the psionic conversation she had held with her mother.

Don't interfere, Jetta warned, but the wolf would not have it.

"...you must help Kurt—you must find a way to save him..."

The memory of her mother's words soothed her fury until she saw nothing but little black motes buzzing before her eyes.

"It was real," she whispered, acquiescing to defeat and allowing herself to fall back against the wolf.

Kiyiyo licked her face with his long, wet tongue until she finally put her hand up to shield herself from the loving onslaught. Curling up around her, he comforted her with his thick black coat and soft tail.

Jetta buried her face in the wolf's fur. "I just lost my mother…"

***

Old Earth stank. It was worse than the piss-washed Underground of Fiorah, or the grimy backrooms in Guli's old place. The place reeked of human ills, of bad memories, of things too vile to comprehend. On some level Reht recognized things his eyes refused to see as he chewed on the mangled quick of his fingernails.

"I hate this place," Reht muttered, spitting out more flesh than nail.

"And I thought Ro and Cray's bunks were bad," Bacthar commented as he passed a man puking in a trash barrel. He wore only scraps of clothing across thin, jaundiced skin and peered up at them long enough for Reht to catch a glimpse of his hollow eyes. He knew the look, and it hit him harder than he expected.

"*Chak*," he said, tearing away a larger chunk of his thumbnail than he intended.

Kids with dirty, outstretched hands ran along beside them, begging for anything of value, but Reht kept his eyes trained on the signs leading to the processing district. Since he and his crew were unwilling to part with any of their possessions, the tone of the streets changed. As people accumulated along their pathway, he kept hearing a strange word—*Tourist*—muttered and grumbled his direction.

Not like I'm worried, he thought. His off-worlder crew could manage anything a weakling human could throw down, and it showed. Even the most aggressive Scabbers kept a respectable distance, especially from the Talian.

"There it is," Reht said, pointing to the carved sign reading *Berish and Mau Imports and Exports.*

From what little word-of-mouth he had managed to collect on the west side of the Spillway, this was a dangerous section of the Pit, and the "Johnnies" that worked here were no ordinary thugs. They were the worst of the worst, the most violent offenders in the galaxy, kept in line by the profit and addictive need their "Joe" generously provided.

"Ugly lot," Ro muttered, licking the edge of his knife. "Let me pretty up their faces."

Reht couldn't disagree. Both of the thugs that guarded *Berish and Mau* had lost their left ears and sported other body modifications that were taboo in most other cultures. Filed teeth, scarification, amputations, implants—alterations that were almost heraldic in their ugliness. Only the red bandana tied around their right arms indicated their affiliation.

So typical of Shandin's flunkies.

Bacthar surveyed the subterranean architecture with his flecked red eyes, following the archways patched together with random scrap metal parts to the barricaded structure up ahead. "It's an old subway station. There will be a few back entrances for sure."

"Yeah, we ain't gonna walk right into this one," Reht said, spying the derailed and gutted subway cars that had been refurbished with weaponry and riot control mechanisms.

As he considered his options, he looked over his crew. He had elected to take Mom, Bacthar, Ro, and Cray with him, leaving Vaughn, Tech, and Billy Don't to watch Femi and the ship. Since Tech was too shy, Billy a glorified tin can, and Vaughn sterilized by the prison system, he didn't have to worry about the safety of his prize.

And Sebbs went out to peruse the streets, probably to satisfy his new "appetites," he thought, shuddering.

Femi. He caught a whiff of her on his hands and grinned. There was something about her, something pure and untainted that made him want more, despite the sickening feeling he got now when he made love.

"Let's break up," Reht directed. "Ro and Cray, take the north sweep, Bacthar and Mom the south. I'll try and get above the warehouse to see if we can drop down. Keep an open channel and no *chakking* around," he said, giving Ro and Cray the eye.

Mom growled at him, but he put up his hand. For whatever reason, he needed to scout this out on his own.

As they split off in their teams, Reht backtracked down the walkway and took a hard right into a secluded alley. Climbing up on the dumpster and hoisting himself onto the rooftop of the housing unit, he managed to get a direct eye on the warehouse. He watched as his crew went their separate ways, trying to appear as inconspicuous as possible as they searched for an easy backdoor into the warehouse. Ro pretended to be drunk and Cray assisted him. Mom and Bacthar blended into the shadows, keeping as low a profile as possible for two giant outerworlders on a human world.

Reht tested the plated ceiling of the Pit with his hands, feeling the hum of electricity. Old Earth was completely dependent on fuel and food donations from the Alliance and other sympathetic governments, but like many unregulated colonies, it wasn't long before criminal minds devised ways to take advantage of the underprivileged.

After a few minutes of studying the routing ducts that fed into the warehouse, he didn't even need to see the substation to figure out Shandin's game. *That bastard's controlling all the electricity to the Pit.* How else could he keep his illegal activities off the radar and attract Johnnies for work?

"*Etaho benieho,*" he said, bending the safety latch off the running panel with the butt of his gun. It would be a tight squeeze, but there would be enough room in the primary router shaft for him to crawl his way into Shandin's warehouse.

"Hey mister—don't go in there," a kid said in broken Common. Dressed in patched food sacks, the little girl stared up at him from the alley with wide brown eyes and a ratted tangle of hair. She held a doll's head by its hair and sucked on the tip of her thumb with her free hand.

"Why?"

Twisting her shoeless feet on the ground, she mumbled something in English and then pointed ahead of him.

Reht almost stepped off the roof when he spotted the shriveled, blackened body hanging from the opposite edge by a few remaining shreds of tissue.

Small enough to be a child—

He looked back, but the little girl was gone.

"*Chak,*" he muttered to himself. No time to reconsider. He had to go, no matter what the cost. *I have to find Shandin.*

"*Why son—why would you betray your family?*"

Reht squeezed his eyes shut. Those weren't his father's words, just the ones he imagined him saying. Through bloodied, lifeless lips.

(I didn't know, I DIDN'T KNOW!)

Reht thrust himself up and into the electrical conduit, careful to keep away from the black cords that snaked their way down boxed channels. The glow from the grounding lights showed the hairs on his forearms standing at attention as he grazed past the charged housing units.

Voices came from up ahead. He crawled on his hands and knees until he could hear them more clearly.

"*Chak* you, you *godich assino!*" a young female voice shouted.

"This datawand is damaged. You're lucky enough I paid you ten percent."

Cold indifference to the girl's rage, a hint of arrogance.

Shandin.

"Hey man, we risked our necks out there," a second girl said. This voice, deeper but still young, tried to mask her fear with a cool attitude. "You got what you wanted—now give us our payment."

Reht scooted underneath a deck-divider and positioned himself above a slatted vent. A terrible smell wafted up, but he could see Shandin clearly, and the backs of the two girls talking to him. The shorter one had her hair in pigtails and her hands on her hips in a provocative manner. In stark contrast, the other slouched, her body language bored and lax.

Touching the tip of his right contact with his finger, Reht initiated the recording device embedded in the lens and secured the direct upload to the Nagoorian. As much as he hated wearing Pancar's recording tech, he had no other choice if he wanted to keep his end of the bargain.

The implant in his ear vibrated as soon as the taller girl turned around and spat on the floor, giving him a full face-shot. "Reht—is this really what you're seeing?"

"Yeah," Reht whispered. "What the hell, man? I thought we were keeping this channel closed unless there was an emergency?"

Silence over the com.

This is something serious, he thought as the residual static buzzed in his ears.

"That is Agracia Waychild. She is a high-priority retrieval," Pancar said.

From what Sebbs told him about the Nagoorian, he seemed like an honest chump who wouldn't deal well with bartering. *All the more reason to push when the stakes are high.*

"A high-priority retrieval, huh?" he said, licking his lips. "Sounds like you're going to up my payment."

"Ten thousand, my only offer. But she has to be alive and *unharmed.*"

Reht took umbrage to the Nagoorian's emphasis on keeping his package intact. The girl was cute, with a tomboyish, punk look, but her friend, at least from the backside, seemed much more his style.

As the younger one turned around to flip off a Johnny, he caught a glimpse of her face.

"What the—?"

Where have I seen that face before? he thought as the girl sucked on a lollipop and twirled her hair with her fingers.

Ash's puppet.

Nah. They look alike, but this one is too surly and crass to be in the same serial as the others.

A Meathead snuck up behind her, and she proceeded to defy all the rules he knew about puppets. Wielding sharpened fingernails, she attacked at the thug's face, stabbing him in the eye. He screamed and fell to the floor as he tried to scoop back the clear goo that oozed between his fingers.

"Sucker!" the little girl shouted.

More Johnnies descended upon the duo, but the puppet moved quicker than any of them, tearing arms from sockets and gouging eyes faster than Reht could register.

If Shandin's gonna double-cross them, it's gonna take a hell of a lot more Johnnies.

Oncoming gunfire rattled him inside the conduit. With new urgency he shimmied ahead, unconfident that the thin metal housing could protect him from a stray bullet. He heard the girls' shouts as the battle unfolded, catching only brief flashes of their ordeal through the slatted breaks in the conduit. Pigtailed ire. White bone splintering through tattooed flesh. Skin yielding to sharp, pearly teeth. Spurts of blood. Thumbs locked over a windpipe, crushing down. An abraded leg corkscrewed backwards.

His stomach lurched as his mind tried to reconcile what he saw. *Puppets are programmed for blind compliance, not merciless aggression.*

"Better make it twenty thousand," Reht said above the racket. "He friend is a real brat."

The Nagoorian grunted. "That's Bossy. I don't have to tell you to be careful."

"What is she?" Reht asked, watching her decapitate a Johnny with her bare hands.

"An inventor's failed attempt at a personalized companion. No synthetics, no artificial parts. She was genetically programmed, grown in a vat with the rest of her lot of puppets. The only switch she has is the one in her head."

"How do you know so much about her?" Reht said as the tiny girl overturned and threw a full-sized table at two gunmen.

Pancar paused. "She was sought out to keep Agracia safe."

Reaching a junction, Reht assessed the drop to the ground level. "Ohh, Panny-boy, you know more, dontcha? You and Unipoesa, always got your *penjehtos* in everyone's business."

"Just tell Agracia when you see her that you're a friend of Jetta's. Do not mention any affiliation with the Alliance or you'll be killed."

"Okay, okay," Reht said, sliding carefully down the tube.

Once on the ground, he crouched down and peeked through a slit in the access panel into the warehouse where the fight had taken an even bloodier turn. Bossy and Agracia were trapped in the far corner behind a barricade of furniture, as Shandin's men fanned out to descend upon them from almost all directions.

"You guys nearby?" Reht called over the com.

"Yeah. Guards ditched their posts," Cray said.

"We got in easy, too," Bacthar added.

"Can you find me? I'm in a storage room or somethin'. Smells like a dumpster. Just follow the gunfire."

"Sure, Cappy. Are we crashin' this party?" Cray asked giddily.

"Have at it boys. Just spare the girls."

"Girls?!" Cray repeated excitedly. Reht could hear Ro hooting in the background.

The hot, steely outline of the Cobra pressed into Reht's hip. In his mind he could see the gun uncoiling like a living thing, chrome scales glimmering as it snaked up Shandin's body and wrapped around his neck. Fangs, dripping with venom, sank into the meat of Shandin's neck. He tasted blood and the sweet tang of poison against serpentine lips.

Reht snapped himself out of it. Gritting his teeth, he pressed his fists against the panel and shoved. As he broke through, he unslung his gun and fired at the thugs' backs.

Don't you run, ratchakker! he thought, losing Shandin in the fray.

Smoke and gun flashes added to the confusion as his crew joined in on the surprise attack. Mom bellowed as he sliced open Johnny after Johnny from stem to stern. Something hot and wet sprayed the dog-soldier captain's face, and the room filled with the smell of copper and sparks.

As the smoke finally dissipated, Reht did a body count. Fifteen Johnnies dead, all crew of the *Wraith* unscathed, and two girls still huddling behind barricaded furniture.

"It's safe now, lil' britches," Reht called, lighting a cigarette.

Agracia peeked her head out from behind the leg of a chair. "Who the hell are you?"

"Reht Jagger. Captain of the *Wraith*."

"And why the hell are you getting in our business?"

Reht blew out a puff of smoke. He liked her already. "Seems as if we have a common enemy. Thought you may be interested in a little cooperative venture between our two parties."

"We don't play with Tourists!" Bossy said, popping on top of the furniture pile. Still sucking on her lollipop, she rolled it from side to side in her mouth as she flipped them off.

Ro snickered, and Cray made lewd gestures with his hands. "I'll put that mouth to better use!"

Reht could tell that the little puppet would have made a move, but she correctly assessed that Mom, with claws fully dropped, outmatched even the likes of her. Instead, she hawked a wad of spit at Cray. The frothy, sugar-laden mess splattered his face, sending him into a fit, but Reht warned him to stay back.

"How's that for ya?" Bossy laughed.

Amused, Reht gave Agracia a wink. She didn't react. Instead, she studied him with the intensity not found in a wayward young woman, but an experienced hunter.

She's no ordinary Scabber.

Agracia held Bossy back with her arm. "I'm listening, chump."

"I want Shandin's head on a plate. I suspect you want something similar. How 'bout we give you a lift off this rock when we're done? Anywhere you choose."

Dark eyes narrowed with suspicion.

Act confident, and a bit stupid. Reht flicked away his cigarette, and looked down the barrel of his Cobra.

"Alright. But one bad move, Tourist, and I'll let Bossy have her way with you. And she don't play nice," Agracia said, pointing to the headless Johnny lying in a pool of blood.

Reht snorted. "Yeah. Some puppet you got."

"What did you call me?" Bossy shrieked, her eyes blazing, held back only by the will of her companion.

"Yeah, I know what you are, lil' britches. Saw the likes of you on Aeternyx. Twice."

He didn't get the reaction he expected. Instead of a slew of obscenities, little puppet wavered, fighting back unwelcome tears. "They're not all dead?"

"Huh?" Ro said, confounded by the derailment of the conversation.

Agracia shuffled her companion behind her. "Yeah, well, let's get going. Shandin will have plenty of reinforcements in here if we keep dickin' around."

"She's right," Pancar said to Reht through the aural implant. "Follow her lead."

Popping her lollipop out of her mouth, Bossy went straight to Mom and looked up at him, her neck craning back at the level of his waist. "I ain't afraid of you, wolfman," she declared, thrusting her lollipop at his face.

Mom growled, but the dog-soldier captain heard the slight difference in his vocalization. Reht stifled a chuckle. *Awh, Mom made a friend.*

"Why you want his head?" Agracia said, pulling Reht down by the collar of his jacket to her eye level.

He flashed his incisors. "He broke my heart."

And then he saw it. A strange duality he had seen before in another precocious little girl, a glimpse of a dark secret that boiled underneath a veneer of control. "Whatever, freakshow. Just stay out of my way, and if you double-cross me, I'll let my friend do whatever—*whatever*—she wants with your ugly hide."

Reht smiled. *This is going to be great.*

***

With the Alliance's fragile grip on Trigos, one less starship guarding the planet weakened their already dismal chances of maintaining authority. Despite this risk, Jaeia commissioned the only working vessel Wren would allow her to have.

I know what I saw. She recalled Jetta's distress, and the visions of another world, one that seemed frighteningly familiar and desperate to reclaim her. *And what I felt. I have to go to Old Earth.*

"Take us to mark 764-293-44-31 with a descent to eight-thousand meters, ensign," she ordered her helmsman.

Rechecking the statistical holographics on the command chair armrest, she couldn't help but look back at the center viewscreen. The brown planet, congested with soupy clouds and lightning, offered no welcome.

This is no use, she thought, shutting off her armrest. *As soon as we enter the upper atmosphere, the storms will disrupt all of our instrumentation.*

Glancing around, she sensed the heightened tensions of her crew. *And they know it, too.*

She stopped herself before doubt could gain a stronger foothold. *Most of this crew has served in Jetta's SMT; they have confidence in her powers, so they must have faith in me.*

(Trust yourself.)

"Beginning descent," the helmsman intoned. "Thrusters only. Twenty-thousand meters and holding steady at three by five."

Jaeia held fast as the medical frigate slammed into Earth's upper atmosphere, hitting every air pocket and pressure change. Anything not bolted into the bridge came loose within seconds, batting around the deck.

Gods, I hate flying, she thought, swallowing hard against the urge to vomit. Under most circumstances she could calm herself by focusing on her mission, but not necessarily when the objective was to survive the rough descent through a polluted, unsafe atmosphere. *I swear Jetta does this on purpose.*

"Forward thrusters offline. Switching to secondary," one of the ensigns called above the noise.

Jaeia wrapped both her arms and legs around her chair as they hit a bump that sent one of her deck officers flying into the command console, breaking his leg. The whine of the struggling engines drowned out his screams as the ship's stabilizers fought against the turbulence.

We'll be blown apart!

Blue lightning zigzagged across the screen. A thundering gust knocked them hard to port, triggering an old memory as her ensign announced the loss of their secondary thrusters.

"In an atmospheric firestorm, it is unwise to engage your drives," the man standing beside her said. Ranked as a lieutenant commander in the Dominion Core, he sagged at the shoulders and barely made eye contact with her as he flipped through the views of a firestorm on the holographic display. "Instead, allow your gravitational adjusters to stabilize your orientation and gravity sails to guide you to the surface."

As she watched him work the display and listened to his instruction, Jaeia absorbed something more. Even a humanoid in his mid-thirties shouldn't be prematurely graying—

—or look so sad.

"Why?" she asked, standing on her tiptoes to touch the yellow light of the holograms. She cringed and pulled back to attention, expecting vituperation for questioning an officer. Instead, he bent over to meet her eyes and pointed to the tiny ship bouncing around in the blaze of a simulated storm.

"Look closer, cadet."

Despite what he really meant, Jaeia sensed an opportunity. She hesitated at first, but when she felt little resistance, she allowed herself to sneak inside his head, beyond his immediate front. Along with some of his knowledge, she took in two little girls playing in an open field while a woman in a red-and-white apron called them in for supper. She caught glimpses of the man regarding himself in the mirror. The full head of hair and youthful eyes surprised her, as did his doubt about everything he would become.

As she withdrew, she saw papers in his hand, demanding his expertise in aerospace engineering in service of the Sovereign.

"Simply put, you can't fight fire with fire," he said, turning away from her. "Sometimes, you have to surrender yourself to the unknown."

"Cut thrusters!" Jaeia shouted. Internal alarms shrieked and red warning lights lit up all sides of the command console as the ship slammed hard to starboard. "Now!"

(Trust yourself.)

The helmsmen punched the console, killing the engines. Within seconds, the ship stopped quaking as the gravitational thrusters adjusted to the varying atmospheric densities. Even though the dangers to the structural integrity decreased, it didn't quell the see-sawing of the ship.

Well, she thought, still holding tight to the armrests, *at least we won't break apart.*

"Ensign, I want you to slowly decrease gravitational adjusters in two percent intervals," she said, as the ship tipped onto its side and then rolled back on its belly. "Don't adjust for orientation; maintain fixed descent."

Waves of nausea made their way up the back of her throat, but she flexed the muscles of her stomach, willing herself not to lose it in front of the crew.

"Come on, come on," Jaeia said, waiting for a break in the storm. Violent bursts of red and orange streaked across the viewscreen as they pitched hard against a hot spot.

"Shields down to 12%," the helmsmen announced.

Terror undammed all the fear she had held inside for years. *I don't want to die like this!*

"I surrender," she whispered, letting go of her iron grips on the armrest, "to the unknown."

The internal sirens went silent. Jaeia checked her registry: *offline.*

"All nav stations down," the helmsman said.

Jaeia looked up at the primary viewscreen. The air, still thick with a brown and yellow haze, was no longer on fire. *We broke through.*

"Reengage thrusters at fifteen percent and hold position," she said, wiping the sweat from her forehead. She gave herself a moment to collect herself, wringing her trembling hands and adjusting her uniform.

Okay, Jetta... where are you? she said, falling back into their connection.

Luminescent images of Earth unfurled, its vastness reaching beyond her field of vision. With all the thousands of glimmering lights dotting the gray mists of the psionic landscape, how would she find her sister?

(I'm here. Tell me where you are.)

Even with their bond, she could only perceive her sister's signature as a faint, almost indistinguishable thrum in the commotion of psionic noise.

(Tell me where you are!)

Panic leaked in, dominating her senses. She whipped around without any real direction, flinging herself at any visible light. I can't find her like this—there are too many people!

A woman with pale green eyes and a sad smile surfaced at the forefront of her panic. My Gods! That's the woman I saw inside Triel's mind, in that memory stain—

"My sweet Ryen.... You are so beautiful."

Ryen. The name sent shockwaves through her body.

My name...

The dark-haired woman reached out for her, translucent fingers combing tenderly through her cheek. "I am so sorry I could not hold on. I wanted nothing more than to see you with my own eyes."

(Mother?)

"Your sister is too weak to answer your call," *she said, her voice distant, receding into the gray.* "You must follow my light..."

(Mother, wait!) *Jaeia shouted, trying desperately to hold onto her, cool mist slipping through her fingers*

"Never forget my love for you. I will be with you, always."

White light, as brilliant as a star, formed from the woman's aura and eclipsed her figure. Jaeia extended herself, expecting to find some tangibility, but found herself being drawn forward, just out of reach. The world rushed past in a blur, but Jaeia hardly noticed.

If I can reach her—

A voice wrapped around her, filling her soul. "Find Ashya. Help Kurt. Come home..."

***

Jaeia opened her eyes and found herself standing over the helm controls, the ensign awkwardly bent over sideways, allowing the captain to manually navigate the ship. At her fingertips flashed coordinates that put them in the western part of the northern hemisphere.

"Sir, I'm detecting a freight crusher, beta-class, with activated distress beacons at position 39-104," one of the deck hands said over the hushed bridge crew.

"Enhance view by two hundred percent," Jaeia said, moving to the center of the bridge.

The tell-tale pattern of wreckage made her shake her head. "Oh, Jetta…"

No matter what the circumstances, her sister always seemed to crash her starcraft in the same way. A smile crossed her lips; a small part of her wanted to point out to her sister that she was zero for two on her terrestrial landings, but she quickly doused the thought with the sobering truth of her sister's recent behavior.

"Ready an evac team," she said, signaling her ground crew.

"Captain—I'm not sure if my instrumentation is reading correctly, but it appears as if there are other life forms present in their cargo hold."

"Species?"

The officer hesitated, a puzzled look furrowing his brow. "Not human."

"Let's move," Jaeia commanded, checking the biostat on her uniform sleeve. Her numbers showed another low-grade fever and a decreased white blood cell count, but she couldn't imagine how Jetta felt—sleep deprived, hungry, and most likely injured. Maybe even—

No. She wouldn't think that.

Jetta, she called through their silent connection. *Hold on—I'm coming.*

***

(You don't know where you're going,) an inner voice whispered as Reht ran down another empty hallway in Shandin's warehouse. Wild need spurred him on, suppressing his instincts. *(This isn't you.)*

In some remote corner of his mind he recognized that control had been lost to him long before he touched down on the dead world.

(Disowning Triel, taking that stupid, much too coincidental bounty board on Diawn—) When he heard Shandin's voice rise from the grave. *(It's wrong—all wrong.)*

And he couldn't stop himself.

"You check down that way," Reht said, fanning his crew out around the maze of the warehouse. Mom stayed at his side, not heeding his order to check the upper stairwell.

"What are you worried about, old friend? Half his Johnnies are already down. Nothin' we can't handle."

His gut told him otherwise. *(It's a setup.)*

It was too easy getting in, too easy defeating the Johnnies threatening the two Scabber girls.

"*Mom, Dad—*"

His young, unscarred hands reached out, tugging at his father's hair. The dead man's mouth fell open, spilling gobs of coagulated blood.

Reht flexed his hands, nerve memory recreating the burn of the acid.

"*Chak,*" he whispered, pushing the feeling aside. Focus; can't think of the past. *This is my chance—the only chance to make things right.*

"Gods, what is that smell?" he exclaimed, covering his nose. The smell of decay got worse and worse the farther they traveled into the warehouse. It reminded him of—

Two hands emerged from the shadows, pulling him behind a hidden door. Mom roared when his captain disappeared behind the partition, slamming his fists against the barrier.

A cloth that smelled like sour cabbage and ether clamped down over his nose and mouth. After one breath, all the energy sapped from his body. His eyelids grew heavy, his muscles relaxing without his consent as strong arms dragged down an unlit passageway.

"You... *jingoga...*" he muttered.

His attacker threw him into a chair. A caged fluorescent bulb shined down on him from above, illuminating only a small radius in an otherwise dark room. As his struggled to keep his head upright, someone tied his hands and feet to the legs of the chair.

Is that... blood? He smelled a fresh kill, and the tinge of bile and digestive fluids from an opened gut. The peculiar dampness to the air made his stomach turn.

"Reht Jagger. Little *Keedai.*" A cold voice, with inflections of vicious delight. Shandin's face dipped into view. "I didn't think you were still alive, *mukrunger*. I thought you would have killed yourself after I raped your world."

Reht picked up his infinitely heavy head, trying to look Shandin in the face. Somewhere in the distance he could hear his Talian warrior beating on the walls, howling in agony for his captain.

"Who... how... did you...?" Reht said through thick lips.

(Mom, Dad—I'm so sorry—)

Shandin's face remained emotionless, his voice even and unaffected.

"You've always been so useful to me, Jagger. First, you give me the fertile and profitable planet of Elia. If it wasn't for you I would never have been able to get rid of those *godich* natives. You knew all their secrets."

"*Etaho benieho!*" Reht managed to sputter.

What did they drug me with? He panicked, his heart going into overdrive as tried to move his arms and legs. Numbed limbs responded sluggishly, barely putting up a fight against his restraints. But even the slightest movement, the rope holding down his wrists or the leather jacket collar rubbing up against his neck, agonized his nerve endings. Sounds, even the shuffle of feet in the shadows, felt like thunder blasts against his eardrums, and the harsh light from the bulb made his eyes water.

Shandin's trying to get in my skull—

—he's going to pull my brain apart—

Removing a knife from his waistband, Shandin sliced the bandages off of Reht's hands. His face remained uncut by any kind of emotion, yet his words dripped with satisfaction. "Ah, yes. Diawn told me about your legendary self-inflicted scars."

My scars—

(Not deep enough. They'll never take away the suffering of Elia, of the tribespeople I helped Shandin slaughter.)

Shandin pressed his thumbs into the backs of Jagger's hands. The dog-soldier bit his lip, stifling his scream. "Acid and your father's woodcutter, is that right? Very painful, very appropriate for what you did. And you never once let that filthy leech heal your wounds."

Pain awakened the faces he had done everything he could to lock away. Chief Dannu, with his weathered skin and steadfast gaze. His daughter, LaLanna. Long, braided dark hair and eyes the color of glacial rivers. Kino, his blood-brother, riding on the back of a six-legged torsen, challenging him to jump across the Deadman's cliffs.

(I never meant to—)

Shandin brushed back Reht's hair, making clicking sounds with his tongue. "And now you're a dog-soldier captain? Does your crew not know the truth about their fearless leader? That behind the charm, that vile facade, is an impuissant little boy who so readily betrayed his own friends—his own family?"

He screamed. It came out of him with such fervor that it shocked the guards that paced beyond the circle of light.

Shandin's soulless eyes met his. "And now, little Keedai, you're going to help me once again."

"Keedai. What the hell does that mean?" a throaty, familiar voice said.

He hadn't been called Keedai since he was a boy. The natives of Elia had given him the nickname after he tried to steal the chief's bow.

Absently-mindedly, he mumbled the answer. "Mischief... maker..."

Diawn stepped into view. At first he couldn't tell at what was wrong with her face. New makeup? She usually wore too much.

No, not makeup. Fighting the nerve pain, he braved opening his eyes a little wider. Her face appeared swollen, deformed. A bandage, caked with dried blood, covered her right eye.

He rolled his head onto his left shoulder and tried to turn his face to her. "What the hell... your... eye?"

Diawn scowled at him as she took her place behind Shandin. As they stood close together, Reht noticed the criss-crossed scars around Shandin's right socket, and a slight difference in the coloring of his eyes. *Someone's marked both of them—but not as prized pets.*

No, this was different than the privateer practices of the outerworlds. Someone didn't mark these two as their underlings. This felt bigger, more ominous, especially if they did something specifically to their right eyes.

"Why can't I have this one?" Diawn sauntered back over to the dog-soldier captain. Holding up his chin up with one hand, she ran her razorcutter nails along the old scar on his cheek. "You get to kill all the Lurchins."

Despite the contempt seething from his pores, Shandin's tone never changed. "He's the boss's property now."

"But he's a Sleeper!"

"Exactly." Reht saw the hate in his eyes, the way he despised her ignorance. "He's programmable."

"*Chak*... you..." Reht said. He tried to spit in her face, but without enough power behind the action, the gob dribbled over his lips and down his jacket.

Something chirped in the shadows. A familiar whirr, a strand of blonde hair over a cherubic half-face.

"Billy... Don't..." Reht huffed. Tears streamed from his eyes. The little *ratchak* tin can. If Diawn had him, then that meant—

"I hope you don't mind I took Billy," Diawn said, circling him.

"Seemed a fair trade since you borrowed my girl. Tech seemed upset about it. So did that psycho-*chak* Vaughn. But Femi took care of them for us."

And then she stepped into view. The ebony princess, the virginal beauty, spattered with blood.

"No..."

"You animal," Diawn said as Femi joined her by her side. "All it ever took was a *godich punte* and you came running."

Femi smiled at him, her white teeth gleaming in the light. "And you thought you were so suave," she said in perfect Common, with only a hint of a Qau'ti accent.

Pressing her body against Femi's, Diawn growled, locking eyes in a standoff until the younger female submitted and lowered her gaze. He saw it then. *Femi is Diawn's girl.* Diawn set him up, knowing that he wouldn't have been able to resist her obedient servant, and that she would be the perfect tail for keeping tabs on his activities.

"Billy..." he called to the little Liiker idling behind Diawn. Blood dotted his metallic torso, but he appeared unharmed. That meant that Tech or Vaughn—or both—had been—

"Let's get on with it," Shandin said, motioning for something from the shadows. Someone handed him a pointed, gouging instrument.

"No, let me." Diawn danced her razorcutters above his orbital socket. Reht tried to turn away, but she held fast to his chin. "I want to take his pretty little eye."

Holding the instrument close to Reht's face, Shandin whispered, "A word of advice, little Keedai: I tried to defy him once. After I destroyed Elia, when I tried to take his prize. You'll find the boss very... *persuasive*." He motioned to his right ear. "He gets in your head."

Now that he had been directed towards Shandin's ear, he could see that something had been surgically done to it. The top half was missing, and the opening was scarred and sewn shut.

A thug rolled a cart of silver instruments next to his chair. Reht's heart slammed against his sternum, his bowels clenched. *Whatever* chakked *up thing happened to Shandin and Diawn is about to get done to me—*

Despite the pain, Reht fought with failing strength against his restraints. Oversensitized nerves shrieked, pulling him back and away, into a time he had chosen to forget.

The interrogation light, the restraints, disappeared. Jerky images organized into corroded metal walls and lights strung together with scrap material. Yeasty smells of home-brewed beer, unwashed patrons, and vomit touched his nose, awakening his senses.

New Haven, he recalled. The only bar in the newly industrialized zone on Elia.

Why the galactic corporations had an interest in the undeveloped world was beyond him at the time. Only eleven, he hated his life. He wanted the fast-paced, high-stakes life of a gunslinger, or the adventurous, vagabond life of a dog-soldier. Not the drab life his missionary parents had wanted for him. In no way did he want to protect the Wiconte forests or the natives' land, or spread the word of God. Besides, his only understanding of God was in the dead eyes of his brother Derex as his mother held his lifeless body and wept.

The barkeep, a rough fellow with a bald head and a teardrop tattooed on his cheek eyed him from across the bar. Rumor had it that the scar across his forehead was given to him by one of the natives after he had trespassed on their land. "Hey, kid. What are you doing here?"

"Nuthin'," Reht said, trying to hide the bottle of Redfly behind his back.

The barkeep snapped his towel at him. "Get the hell out of here, kid."

"Naw, he should stay," one of the dog-soldiers said, swiveling around on his stool. Reht tried to run, but the dog-soldier had him by the back of his neck before he could duck out through the front door. "Young pup like this ought to know what real life is like."

The dog-soldier brought him back to the bar and plopped him down on a stool. "What's your name, kid?"

Reht stayed silent, still trying to hide the bottle of Redfly behind his back, but the barkeep spotted the lump under his shirt.

"Thief!"

"It's on me, Teardrop." The dog-soldier took the Redfly from his hands and placed it on the counter in front of him. With one yellow and one brown eye he regarded Reht, staring in a way that made him uncomfortable. "Now, I asked you a question, kid—what's your name?"

One of the drunks near the jukebox lifted his head and laughed. Reht recognized him as one of the natives who had joined the mining force in town. It paid dismally, but with Elia's increasing industrial presence and modern commodities, more young natives were being drawn into the *illusions of city life.* "That's little Keedai!"

"Keedai..." The dog-soldier tapped his chin as he thought it over. "Mischief maker, right?"

Reht sat motionless, keeping his eyes trained ahead.

"Didn't think you were from the reservation," the dog-soldier said, pulling back on Reht's hair. "You're too much of a pretty-boy to be a featherhead."

Reht flicked his head away and smoothed his hair back, showing his teeth. Everyone on the planet feared his freshly cut adult incisors. At least the native kids his own age did.

The dog-soldier laughed. "Breaking into a bar, stealing Redfly— you're something else, aren't you, kid? You want to be a dog-soldier when you grow up?"

He tried to casually shrug off the question, but his reddening cheeks gave away his secret.

"Good," the dog-soldier said, a scheming grin quirking his face. "Then drink up, son. Show us what you're made of."

Other patrons chimed in: "He'll never make it!"

"He'll puke!"

The excitement and fear made his heart race. He had never tasted alcohol before, but from the way it made the adults act, and how vehemently his parents protested against its consumption, he had to have it. More importantly, he sensed the chance to impress a horde of dog-soldiers and privateers as the entire bar circled around him, chanting his native nickname.

Grabbing the bottle by the neck, Reht brought the mouth to his lips, feeling the sting of Redfly on his tongue. He squeezed his eyes shut and downed the liquid fire, his stomach spasming as it seared his insides.

Don't puke don't puke don't puke—

He kept it down. He had to. For the endless school days where he was teased by the native children for his alien looks, or the times he got lost in the dark Wiconte forests and cursed his parents for uprooting him from his real home—for a dead God that had ruined his life and taken his brother's.

The dog-solder slapped him on the back and winked his yellow eye. "Nice."

Coughing forcefully, Reht wiped his mouth with the back of his hand. Despite the funny feeling in his head, he felt strangely relieved.

"To little Keedai," the dog-solder proclaimed, raising his glass, "the pretty God boy from the rez. You're one of us, kid."

One of them. It felt right. At least more right than staying on an undeveloped world caught in the midst of religious and political warfare. Flying across the galaxy, always on the run, seemed better than the pointless cause his parents had committed themselves and their family toward.

"Who are you?" Reht said, playing with the black and red label on the Redfly bottle.

"Lugger, but that's captain to you. I run a five-man drug-running crew," he said. He produced a cigarette from the front flap of his pilot's jacket and offered it to him. "You in or what?"

Reht took the cigarette and grinned.

Other memories interjected, asserting themselves in random order: his first taste of methoc, the way the powder stung his tongue. How the entire world exploded with light as he injected his first booster. His first girl, her waifish hips gyrating against his. Watching the life bleed out of his first kill, the way the man's blood stained more than his clothing.

"You have to stop," his mother sobbed. "You're ruining your life— our life."

After forcing him to church, his father asked him over and over again, "Why have you turned against God?"

No answer would satisfy his parents, so he ran away, leaving for weeks—even months—at a time. It didn't matter if they locked him down in the church or sent him off with the tribe; he always found a way to return to the city.

"Keedai, you must stop running," the chief of the Koiwros, a tribe in the valley, told him after he returned from a two-month stint. The thrill of it all—the narcotics bust, barely getting away with his life as a rival crew tried to move in on their arrest—hadn't abated. He only wanted more, even though half the crew had been killed, and Lugger had been shot nine times. "You cannot run forever. One day you will have to stand and face these restless spirits inside you, or they will consume your soul."

As the pain subsided, Reht returned to the present with a hot lump in his throat. He closed his eyes, sealing off his memories. "*Chakking*... get it... over... with..."

"You still see them, don't you?" Shandin whispered in his ear as he touched the sharp instrument to the lower lid of his right eye, his voice as cold as ice. "Your parents, lying there, dead at your hands. The Koiwros and their land, reduced to ashes. You gave Lugger all their secrets so readily. Rash, so impetuous, so quick to believe that the natives had murdered your parents, when really it was your own ignorance…"

As Shandin sliced open his lid, Billy gurgled and squealed in the background, ramming his wheels against Diawn. Out of the corner of his eye he could see her shooing the little Liiker, but that only threw him into a more violent frenzy.

"Shut that thing off," Shandin said, pausing.

The brief interruption gave Reht enough time to release his breath and acquiesce to the pain. *Don't scream; that's all that* ratchakker *wants.*

Diawn leaned over and tried to access Billy Don't's control panel, but he spun around and ran over her toes. She yelped and clutched her injury, hopping around on one foot. Ignoring Femi's attempts to help, Diawn cursed at the Johnnies to catch the little Liiker as he whipped and weaved around the storeroom.

"Get him!" Shandin shouted, withdrawing the weapon from Reht's eye.

Lurching forward, Reht tipped over his chair, and sank his teeth into Shandin's neck. As his long incisors cut into muscle and sinew, Shandin screamed and stabbed him repeatedly in the shoulder with the gouging instrument. Reht held fast, warm, salty blood filling his mouth.

Shouting, gunfire. A flash of azure, then a crimson spray. Reht closed his eyes, unable to shield himself from the bloodbath. He heard Mom's roar, and the wet sounds of claws dividing flesh. A fluttering of wings. Wild cackles and a screech of excitement.

Bacthar, Ro, Cray—

Something sharp stabbed him the flank. Gasping, he released Shandin, flaying about to get away from the excruciating pain. He smacked hard against the ground, but managed to roll himself, and the chair, onto its back.

Diawn stood poised above him, bloodied knife held high. "You bear the blood of your family."

Straddling his shoulders, she left only his face exposed to her weapon's descent.

"I always loved you," she whispered as fluorescent light gave the silver blade one last kiss.

***

Jaeia stepped onto the dirt-swept ground, shielding her eyes against the flashes of lightning tearing up the skies. Even suited up and connected through com channels, she could barely hear her crew over the thunderous roar of the firestorm.

"…no sign of…wreckage at…what is…command?"

Grumbling, she tapped her helmet, seeing if the static and interference would clear. No luck.

This way, she thought, motioning the alpha team to take point while she brought up the omega team to sweep the crash site.

Huh, that's odd. Jaeia bent down and put her hand next to a large paw print in the mud. Whatever had made it was big enough to leave an impression that could survive the raging storm. *There are dogs and wolf breeds still present on Old Earth, but nothing this size.*

With her stomach in knots, Jaeia watched as the alpha team pried open the bay doors to the freighter.

Something isn't right.

She held her breath as she sensed a presence on the other side of the door, alert and ready for battle.

What is that?

(Not human.)

"Wait!" she shouted over the group channel. "Hold position!"

Jaeia ordered the crew to stand down as she slipped through the crack in the door and entered the belly of the ship.

"Jetta?" she said, lifting up her visor.

Before she could react, something huge pinned her against the interior wall, white teeth glistening in the low light.

Without explanation, she spoke from a place beyond herself, relying on a deeper instinct. "I'm a friend. Please… I'm her sister."

The huge weight left her chest. As she caught her breath, eyes like burning coals met hers and dark lips peeled back to reveal sharp, canine teeth. She reached out, unafraid, and stroked black fur and pointed ears.

"How do I know you?" she whispered.

"Jaeia..."

Her head whipped toward the sound. Spotting several unmoving bodies to her left, she seized upon them.

"Jetta!" she said, clearing the debris around her head. "Are you okay?"

Her sister's eyes opened just a crack, her voice barely audible. "Help them. Please, Jaeia. Help them."

Turning back to the wolf, Jaeia gently held his muzzle in her hands. "Please—you have to let my crew in. It's the only way to help her."

The wolf bent down and gingerly bit into Jetta's suit, dragging her by the collar toward the door.

"Alpha team, ready stretchers. Omega team, I need a holding cell big enough for one—"

And then she felt it. Another animal. This one closing in on their position, coming from the east.

"Make that *two* wolves."

After assisting the alpha team to force open the bay door, she put herself between the wolf and her crew as she brokered his unveiling.

One of the soldiers took a few steps back when he saw the dark predator. "S-sir, is that a feather-paw? Aren't they native to Algar?"

"Yes. And so is that one," she said as the second wolf trotted up and began to inspect her. She waved off her teams' weapons as he poked his nose inside her helmet and gave her a long lick.

How is this possible? She could hear both of them in the depths of her mind, like an ancient song she had always known, in a language she implicitly understood. Interwoven within their harmonies she felt her sister's presence, and the tune of her memories.

"You protected her, didn't you?" she whispered, rubbing behind the new arrival's right ear. He whined sweetly and nuzzled into her side. "Thank you."

Within minutes, her crew extracted Jetta, Triel, and an unidentified humanoid male wearing outdated terrestrial clothing from the middle of the twenty-first century. As she supervised their admittance to medical, she acknowledged her own discomforts. *I've seen that man before—but where?*

No time to wonder. As much as she wanted to stay and at least make sure her sister and Triel were okay, she couldn't afford that luxury.

After the wolves had been carefully boarded and locked in a storage cell, and the rest of the crew had secured as much of the wreck as possible, Jaeia resumed her post on the bridge.

Time for a tough call, she thought. *I can't risk my crew, ship, or its cargo, by punching back through the firestorm.*

Only one option left.

"Ensign," she said, laying in the coordinates herself. "Prepare to jump at eight thousand meters."

"Yes, Sir."

As part of her reimagined the devastating consequence of her sister's jump on Trigos, she forced herself to downplay the hazards. *Ripping open space-time on a dead world has minimal risk, especially with most of its habitants well underground.*

But that didn't stop her from grinding her knuckles into the armrests of the commander's chair. *(As long as the nearest Pit is at least fifty kilos away...)*

"I'm sorry," she whispered, and gave the cue to jump.

After the floor resettled and the cosmic backdrop reappeared on the viewscreen, she breathed a sigh of relief. *I've never thought I'd be so happy to see the stars.*

She considered asking the ensign to sweep their jump site for casualties, but thought better of it. *Sensors can't penetrate Earth's atmosphere.*

(I hope I did the right thing.)

The call she both anticipated and dreaded came in just as the helmsmen was making the final calculations for Trigos. "Sir, Commander Kyron is awake and requesting to speak with you."

Instinctively, Jaeia checked the gun on her hip.

What am I doing? she thought, blushing.

As she made her way down the corridor towards medical holding, her mind wouldn't let go of the gun, playing out visions of her sister attacking her and the crew. *Jetta wouldn't do that.*

(But she has before...)

The truth hit her hard: She didn't know what to expect. Jetta had become so volatile and unpredictable over the past few weeks that anything was possible.

Please, Jetta, she thought, too afraid to release her inner voice into their shared bond, *be my sister. Don't make me do something I can't live with.*

After passing through the biofilters, Jaeia arrived to find the medical staff had put each patient in strict isolation.

"It's just a precaution, Sir," the lead medical officer informed her as she looked over the datascope readouts. "They were exposed to high levels of radiation, the Necro plague, and something that the Scabbers call 'Redder Lung.' Hard to treat, but we caught most of it in the early stages, so they should be okay. Except for Commander Kyron, Sir."

Touching the data readout, Jaeia enhanced her sister's stats. She didn't know what all the numbers meant, but the doctor kept his mind open to her as he explained her status, and it wasn't more than a second before she understood the prognosis all too well.

"I reviewed Dr. Kaoto's analysis of her cellular decomposition as a result of the Motti's biochemical augmentations, Sir. From these comparative readings, it doesn't look good."

"How long, Doctor?" she said, turning to him.

Despite his years of experience delivering difficult news to patients, his voice quavered as he gave the answer that sealed both their fates. "Days now. Maybe a week, at best. Not long."

Even though it came as no surprise, Jaeia couldn't keep herself from tearing up. "Excuse me for a moment, doctor."

"Of course, Sir," he said, giving her a bow before returning to the monitoring station.

After passing through another set of biofilters, Jaeia joined her sister at her bedside. Intravenous tubes hung from the ceiling, infusing her body with yellow and white cocktails that reminded her of darker times, but she swallowed her revulsion and took her sister's hand.

"How are you feeling, Jetta?"

"About as good as you," she said, opening her eyes. The familiar green made Jaeia relax a little, even as her free hand moved to the hilt of her gun. Seeing behind her eyes again, Jetta turned away. "Do you really think that's necessary, Sis?"

Jaeia kept her tone neutral. "You tell me."

Groaning, Jetta sat up and inspected her wounds. Most of the physical injuries she had incurred on her journey had been mended, save the nasty wound on her stomach. The doctor had mentioned its abnormality, and that the dermawands couldn't repair the tissue damage.

"Jaeia," she said, lowering her eyes. "I don't even know how to begin."

Jaeia crossed her arms. "You'd better think of something good, and quick. As captain, I have the sense to put you in lockup."

"Captain?" Jetta said, raising a brow. Hints of disbelief and jealousy seeped from her mind. "When did that happen?"

"When the Fleet went under."

"So, they're promoting just anybody then?"

"Death looms over the two of us, and you're still an *assino*."

A smile touched her lips, but vanished as soon as she changed subjects. "How's Jahx?"

The mention of their brother lowered Jaeia's guard for a second, allowing her sister a peek into the grim reality. Jetta slammed her fist against the siderail, breaking it in two. "*Skucheka.*"

Setting aside her own feelings, Jaeia reached out and touched the back of her sister's hand. "Hey, he's still with us. And you and I are still here, too. It's not over yet, Jetta."

Jetta looked up at the overhead examination light. "Tell me you missed me," she said, her voice softer this time.

Sighing, Jaeia relaxed just enough to let Jetta experience her loneliness and fear over the last few weeks. "You're part of me, Jetta. When you run away, cut me out, I feel as if someone's stolen part of my soul."

"I had to, Jaeia. For us, for Jahx. I had to find out what was inside me. And I had to help Triel."

"So?" Jaeia said, not withholding her frustration.

Jetta shook her head. "Just more questions."

"Show me," Jaeia said, offering up her hand.

Jetta took her hand, but hesitated. "I should warn you that—"

Surprised at her own reaction, Jaeia slapped her hand on Jetta's forehead and delved inside.

As she plunged through Jetta's memories, Jaeia couldn't believe her eyes. The escape from the Alliance. The refueling outpost. A disturbing conversation about Josef Stein. Edgar Wallace's gently spoken words:

"You can help the human race restore Earth. You can give us back our home, give us a second chance."

Iyo Kono. Humans shedding their skins to become something else.

"This is a place of rebirth..."

Algar, the lost colonies. Majestic wolves. Reivers. Lockheads. Salam, the man with a poisonous tongue: "I've seen all the reels, seen the trials. You only do anything for one reason—resurrecting your dead brother."

The Temple of Exxuthus. Sir Amargo and Lady Helena. Promise keepers.

"It's important for all of us, Commander, to know the truth about Saol. I believe that his story holds the key for all of us—human and Sentient alike—to finding everlasting peace."

Inside the Diez di Trios. A world within worlds. Memories revived, transformed. A demon in her sister's skin.

"Thief. You stole from me. You took my chacathra, *and I want it back!*"

A crash landing on the ruins of Earth. Running from nightmare creatures infecting a tortured landscape. Inside an ancient laboratory, silent walls stained by rage and sorrow unmitigated by the ages.

"Please forgive me for all that I have done..."

A narrow escape. Fatigue, the subconscious futility gnawing away at her last shreds of willpower. Clinging to black fur, the rhythm of four legs stretching out toward an unreachable horizon.

Restless sleep. Perhaps a dream. A man surrounded by poisonous yellow light. Mitigating blue, a maternal touch.

"I am Ariya Ohakn. I am your mother."

Precious memories awaken to a long-forgotten voice. An unnamed hope realized, a flame rekindled. Perhaps, maybe; a chance.

The veil lifted. Kurt Stein. A dream reborn, a true name found.

"Save Kurt Stein... not all is lost..."

"...Ashya..."

And through it all, Jaeia felt the same raw fear roiling below the fragile surface tension.

"What am I?"

(I am a monster)

Jetta's voice, her greatest fear. And yet—

The Healer knew the truth. Jaeia saw it, even through Jetta's prejudiced experience of their interaction.

"Jetta," Triel whispered. "I saw you. You're not a monster. Your *powers are limitless. But right now you draw your talent from your fear."*

Jaeia opened her eyes, breathing heavily. A nurse, bent over beside her, asked if she needed help, while another checked on Jetta.

"I'm fine, we're fine," Jaeia reassured them, returning to her sister.

A conflicted mix of anger, fear, shame, and frustration brought tears to Jetta's eyes, and words, unable to be found or spoken, turned her hands into tight fists.

"I'm sorry," she whispered. Forgetting how long it had been since she had last alleviated her sister's temper, Jaeia extended herself into Jetta. The shock of her emotions jolted her senses, but she held fast, determined to soothe her distress. "I shouldn't have been so impatient."

Jetta swallowed hard, and let out a breath through gritted teeth. "Don't do that again."

A tech popped his head in. "Captain—the Healer is asking for you."

"I'll be there shortly," Jaeia said, trying to reach out to her sister, but Jetta stiffened to her touch, her expression unwelcoming.

"She was very insistent," the tech said.

"I'll be right back," Jaeia said, squeezing Jetta's shoulder.

Jaeia passed through another biofilter and into the next isolation suite. To her relief, the Healer's progress was much more pronounced. Her skin had color again, and her eyes looked brighter than she expected.

"It's so good to see you again," Jaeia said, hugging her carefully, minding the monitors.

Triel hugged back, holding her for longer than she expected.

"Thank you, Jaeia. I can always count on you."

Jaeia's cheeks flushed. She hid her smile. "Are you okay?"

"I'm fine," the Healer said, pulling back her hair carefully to avoid dislodging the intravenous lines. "Have you seen Jetta yet?"

Before she could even respond, Triel's eyes found her firearm. "I know you two haven't been getting along lately, but Jaeia…"

Jaeia's went rigid, her back straightening as her voice lost the air of familiarity. "It was a necessary precaution."

"Have you shared memories with her yet?"

"Yes."

"And that hasn't changed your mind?"

Jaeia shook her head. "If nothing else, it confirms my concerns."

Triel sighed. "Those issues aside, I needed to see you because of... *that*," the Healer said, indicating with her head the suite to her right. "Can you feel that?"

Jaeia lifted a brow. "You mean from the next patient?"

"I don't know—you tell me. Whoever that is has a *very* strong aura. I've *never* felt anything like it."

Jaeia nodded. "I do feel something, but I'm not sure what to make of it. We picked him up inside the same freighter where we found you two. Human male, mid-thirties, appears uninjured, but in some kind of dreamless sleep state, possibly a coma."

"A man? Where did he come from? Was he a Scabber?"

Jaeia wavered, caught between her own disbelief and sharing what she had acquired from her sister's memories. As Triel scrutinized her silence, she decided it was best to be upfront. "Jetta believes that it's Kurt Stein."

Triel grabbed her arm. "*The* Kurt Stein?"

Jaeia nodded.

Disbelief contorted the Healer's face as she laid back down. "Impossible."

"I know, but Jetta seemed convinced enough that it was true. We're running a DNA analysis as we speak, but we won't have full confirmation until we reach the Alliance Central Starbase."

"Do you know what this means?" Triel whispered.

"If it is Kurt," Jaeia said cautiously, "then it would change the war for the Alliance. We could—"

"No," Triel said, cutting her off. "It means that the prophecy is coming true."

"Prophecy?"

"It can't be me. It just can't," Triel said, covering her face with her slender fingers.

Sensing her mounting tension, Jaeia pried one of her hands away. "What's wrong? Tell me, please."

Triel looked at her, blue eyes pained with terrible knowing. "It would mean that I would have to..."

The words never came, but Jaeia felt something heavy settle inside the Healer's heart.

Jaeia's uniform sleeve beeped. Wren wanted an update.

"I have to get back to the bridge. We can finish this conversation after

I report in. If you need anything—*anything*—let me know," Jaeia said, hugging her again. This time Triel didn't hug her back, seemingly preoccupied with something beyond Jaeia's senses.

Jaeia wanted to go back and check on her sister, but she knew better than to keep Wren waiting, especially with news of the retrieval of Jetta, Triel, and possibly Kurt Stein.

As she picked up speed back to the bridge, her sister's memories weighed down on her conscious thought.

Mother. Jetta met our mother...
(So beautiful—)
Jetta thought she died—why didn't we find her body?
(My mother's name for me is Ryen. Jetta's name is Ashya...)
(She loved us)

She ran her fingers along the wall, catching her pads on bolts and tile trim, relishing their texture, trying to keep her emotions in check.

"Jahx," she whispered, her fingers pressed to her lips. "If only you could see her…"

***

Jahx shielded his eyes as the afternoon sun peeked out from behind a fluff of white clouds. An opposing mixture of spring lilacs and diesel hung in the air, as well as the pleasant smell of home cooking. He breathed in deeply, surprised at the realism of the sensation. His lungs felt like his own again.

Not knowing what to expect, he took in everything he could about his new surroundings: A beige brick house sat behind a grassy front lawn. He could hear dogs barking from behind the wooden fence and hovercars whizzing by on the transair highway a few blocks over. It could have been any Class IV inhabited planet in the Starways, but without understanding how, he knew exactly where he was: Earth. Or at least someone's memory of the way Earth was a long time ago.

At first he hesitated. He did not find this place like he had the cemetery and Josef Stein; someone brought him here. Someone powerful. An illusion like this wasn't easily forged; its realism bore its own reality, and laws of its own design. He didn't know what rules to play by, or who was running the reel.

"Tierin," *a voice called from behind a screened window. "It's time to come inside."*

Jahx didn't think it was a good idea until the sky changed. Angry clouds tangled together in dark gray knots. The wind picked up, battering the wind chimes on the front porch.

As he walked across the front lawn, he accidentally kicked over a brigade of toy soldiers lined up around a clump of flowers. He thought about salvaging the helpless toys that littered the flowerbed from the imminent storm, but the blue zig-zag of lightning brought him under the protection of the house before he could take action.

"Who are you?" Jahx said as he closed the front door.

The house looked as if it hadn't been occupied in years. Dust-covered sheets hung draped over furniture, and thick cobwebs connected the wall to ceiling fixtures. Pictures were faded, unrecognizable. Unlike the fresh air outside, everything smelled old and stale, and tickled his nose.

"What do you want?" he tried again.

A woman humming over the sound of clanging pots and pans caught his attention. Enticing smells of sugar and spice wafted toward him, inviting him into the next room.

"In here, sweetheart," she called.

Cautiously, Jahx rounded the corner into the kitchen. A woman, bent over the stove, hummed a strangely familiar tune as she checked on her dish. "It was your father's—and great-grandfather's—favorite. Apple Delicious. It was the only time I could ever get him to eat anything with sugar."

"Who are you?" he repeated more firmly, fearing the worst.

The woman wiped off her hands and turned to him. "Tierin—I thought for sure, of the three of you, you'd be the one to recognize me."

"Mother," he whispered. His knees turned into jelly, and he held onto the countertop to stay standing. "I didn't think I'd ever—"

"I know," she said, taking him in her arms. "And I am so, so sorry for that."

Something warm and wonderful spread from his chest to his fingers and toes. Even with all of the lifetimes he had experienced, he never thought such a miracle was possible. He hugged back with all his strength.

But then his eye caught the changing view outside the bay window. As the storm raged overhead, a fathomless darkness ate its way through the surroundings. Just like what happened to me before the Grand Oblin gave me a chance to return to the world—

"There isn't much time, Mother. You're sick, injured; I need to help you—"

"You can't worry about that right now. Your true journey has just begun."

She reached into her apron pocket and handed him a sealed letter. "We will meet again one day, Tierin, perhaps in a place not far from here. But for now, know the contents of this letter. And remember: A parent's love for their child never dies."

As he turned over the letter, he saw the marking on the back. *This is same design as the tattoo on my right arm.*

"Mother, I—"

When he looked up, he found the kitchen empty, the stove cold and barren. Winds shattered one of the dining room windows, spraying shards of glass into the house and blowing off the dust-covered sheets. Furniture toppled over and smashed against each other as the encroaching darkness pushed up against the side of the house, rattling its foundation.

Jahx quickly unfolded the letter and memorized every line as the world collapsed around him.

"Thank you, Mother," he said as he ran through the front door, catapulting himself from the dying world. "This changes everything."

***

Agracia gave the Johnny aiming his gun at the wolfman a swift kick to his groin, doubling him over in pain. As he gasped for breath, Bossy ripped his head clean off his shoulders. Without pause, Agracia scooped his gun off the floor and took down two more of Shandin's thugs.

Agracia's eye caught the glint of metal against the light and quickly squeezed off another round. Too late. The crazy lady brought down her knife, slicing the captain across the neck as she slumped over.

The wolfman roared, forcing everyone in the room cover their ears. In a heartbeat the giant blue warrior sheared the crazy lady in half with his claws and felled the dark-skinned beauty with the same merciless rage.

"Cappy!" one of the dog-soldiers cried, scampering to their leader's side.

As she removed her hands from her ears, Agracia looked around. The fight was over. The wolfman shredded about half of the Johnnies, including Shandin, painting the dingy underground hole with a bloody wash.

"It ain't right!" Bossy grumbled. With her hands in her pockets she kicked the dead bodies, continuing to mutter and stew that she didn't get her fair share of the fight.

Never seen nothin' like this, she thought. The wolfman had torn down an entire wall after Shandin abducted his captain. *Dang. Bossy's a fierce and loyal companion, but whatever the wolfman and captain have is way crazier and tighter than anything I've seen.*

Agracia made her way over to the dog-soldiers huddled around their fallen captain. Blood spurted from the gash in his neck as the bat-winged man worked furiously to patch the wound.

"Stay with us, Cappy. You got this one. No sense checking out now," the bat man said, biting off a strip of cloth with his teeth. The others worked to untie him from the chair and laid him out carefully on the ground. The bat man continued to treat him, pulling syringes from his satchel and injecting them straight into his chest.

Agracia checked out her last kill. She had plugged the crazy lady in the temple; an instant kill, and even then the wolfman had felt the need to saw her in half. But her eyes remained open, their gaze still fixed in desperation and anger. *What the hell did that captain do to her?*

"Diawn," Reht said between gasps. "Where's… Diawn?"

The crew looked at each other in bafflement.

"She's iced, Cappy," one of them said. "So's her little *baech* and that *ratchak*, Shandin."

"Diawn…" Reht whispered, tears sliding down his face. "I should… have… My fault. I…"

"*Sycha.* He's lost it," another dog-soldier said.

"Well, duh," Bossy chimed in as she searched for salvageable weapons among the dead.

"You idiots," the bat man said, holding pressure down on Reht's wound. "Don't you know anything?"

"I know that this has been one giant *sycha*-storm after another for the last several months, mate!"

"Yeah, this is some *chakking sycha*," the first one said. "He should have *chakking* killed her back on the *Wraith*. Then we wouldn't be in this *godich* mess!"

Alerted to the rising tensions, Agracia observed each of the dog-soldiers' movements. She noted the subtle change, one she had seen many times before in the bars and on the streets, as the dissident pair positioned themselves for quick access to their weapons.

"Ro, Cray—you don't understand," the bat man said, still trying to reason with them. "Diawn wasn't just his, his—"

"*Punte?*" Bossy giggled, delighted to butt in again.

"Enough!" the wolfman roared

Stunned by the boom of his voice, the entire room fell silent. The wolfman slammed his hands down beside his captain, putting himself between Ro, Cray, and the bat man. "You don't know anything about this man," he growled.

From the dog-soldiers' wide-eyed expressions, Agracia gathered that when the wolfman spoke, everyone listened.

Ro and Cray raised their hands. "It's cool, Mom, it's cool…"

The bat man adjusted the bandages on the captain's neck, keeping an eye on the wolfman as the hulking blue warrior lopped off Shandin's head and wrapped it in one of the Johnnies' jackets.

Guess it ain't enough to just kill the sucker, Agracia thought.

"He's stable. Let's get him back to the ship," the bat man said.

The wolfman sniffed the air. "Ro, help Bacthar with Reht. Cray, you're coming with me."

"What for?" he whined.

But the wolfman didn't say anything more. Instead, he ducked back through the hole in the wall he had created and disappeared.

Ro shrugged, leaving Cray to catch up to Mom.

"So… What was that all about?" Agracia said.

The bat man shook his head. "Long history."

"Tell me." Dropping her shoulders and softening her tone, she added: "please."

Bacthar nodded to Ro as they hoisted to captain up. Motioning with her head, she tried to get Bossy to help, but the dark horse slunk behind the group and crossed her arms across her chest.

The bat man relented as Agracia pitched in, holding the captain's midsection. "Reht saved Mom's life a while back."

"Reht saved *Mom's* life?"

"Yes. After Shandin decimated Reht's homeworld of Elia, he moved on to organizing the black market sport of capturing and hunting young Talians. You may have heard of it—the 'Blood Dawn Massacre'?"

Agracia shook her head.

With a grunt, Bacthar stepped over a pile of Johnnies.

"Let's just say there aren't too many Talians left. Anyway, Reht was tailing Shandin, trying to get revenge, but things didn't end up the way he thought they would. Mom doesn't talk about what exactly happened, and neither does Reht. But whatever it was, it was enough to make an outerworlder like Mom decide to dedicate his life to a humanoid like Reht. Reht has *chakked* up a lot in his life, but he did right by Mom."

Agracia's toe struck a hard surface. "*Dich!*"

Something chirped and buzzed.

Bacthar and Ro carefully laid the captain back down and cleared off the pile of Johnnies.

"Holy *sycha*!" Agracia exclaimed as they unearthed an inactive deadwalker. "A Liiker?!"

After Bacthar rapped the biomech on the head a few times, he twittered to life. Clearly distressed by something, he babbled and squealed while the bat man tried to get him back on his wheels.

The bat man's red eyes dilated as the half-machine whizzed towards the exit. "We have to get back to the ship. *Now.*"

"What about Mom?" Agracia asked.

"Probably getting us supplies. We're low and we'll need them," Bacthar said, picking the captain back up.

"We'll go with him—"

"I need one of you. We may have injured back on the ship," the bat man said.

Agracia thought about it carefully. They could easily ditch out on the dog-soldiers now, but that would leave them without the means to get off the planet. Even if they did raid the warehouse and sold off their find, they would be sitting ducks for Victor's retribution. "Okay. Bossy—go help Mom," she said, adding quickly, "and *be nice.*"

Bossy muttered something under her breath and stomped on a headless corpse.

We gotta keep tabs on the dog-soldiers and make sure we keep our own supplies fresh, Agracia thought, wishing her companion could read her mind. She just hoped Bossy would cool down enough to see the angle.

"I still think this is *chakked* up," Ro commented. "Reht ain't got it no more."

The bat man folded his wings as they rounded a corner. "Just because he was 'too soft' to kill Diawn the first time?"

"That, and all this weird *sycha* he's been putting us through lately. He ain't right for captain. He's weak."

Instinctively, Agracia looked at Reht.

Something's different, she thought, watching the uneven rise and fall of his chest as his bandages soaked through. The dashing, bold man she remembered meeting just a short while ago was gone. Instead, she saw a vulnerable human-like without the flash of his razored canines and the brazen look in his polychromatic eyes.

"What were any of us—what were *you*—before you met Reht Jagger?" said the bat man, trying to keep things from getting physical. "A fat little doormat for the Queen. You owe him your life, you ungrateful little *chak*."

That shut Ro up—at least for the moment.

Whatever's eating at this crew ain't gonna stop until blood is spilled.

The thought bothered her. *Why the hell do I even care about these losers?*

The little Liiker screeched and spun around on his wheels, apparently impatient at their progress.

Agracia didn't know where the observation came from, or how the words found their way to her lips. "Sounds like your captain doesn't know if he wants to be a bad-*assino* dog-soldier or a decent prick."

Bacthar looked at her through his multiple sets of brilliant red eyes. "He believes that his past defines his future, but it doesn't. Same goes for the rest of us. But sometimes it's hard to believe that, isn't it?"

***

Reht came to as part of his crew carried him into the main entrance of the warehouse.

"No—set me down. Set me down!" he said, flailing about until they assisted him to the ground.

Gritting his teeth, he commanded his wobbly, unstable feet to keep him upright.

"We have to go back," he said, clutching the neck wound Diawn had inflicted.

"Why?" Bacthar exclaimed. "For what?"

"We have to go back!" Reht said, staggering back from the direction they had just come from. "The smell. I know that smell..."

The stink of fleshy rot, a subtle bite to the air. The way his parents—

Lugger took him back to the ship, promising him that the dog-soldiers would make whoever murdered his parents pay the ultimate price for crossing their youngest mate. He had Reht sit down in the captain's chair, his feet barely touching the floor as the other crew members circled around him. The new recruit was there, too. Reht didn't like the way he looked at him or his frigid, impassive face.

"Shandin's the best hunter this side of the Gateway. He's gonna help us find the featherheads who murdered your parents," Lugger explained. "Now you just tell him everything like a good kiddo and we can get us some blood!"

The rest of the crew members cheered and chanted his name despite the tears that flowed down his cheeks. "Keedai, Keedai, Keedai!"

"I—I already told you what I know," Reht said, wiping his face with his sleeve.

Lugger looked to Shandin, who indicated with a nod.

Reht didn't understand. Why was Lugger taking cues from Shandin?

"Look, little buddy," Lugger said, crouching down in front of him. "Those chakking *featherheads betrayed and killed your parents. We need to know where they are and how to find them. They can just hide forever in the Wiconte forest. We need to know how to get to their sacred grounds. If we can go there, we can make them come to us, make them answer for their crimes."*

The hallowed grounds, an area of worship in the heart of the dark forest. The chief of the Koiwros told him it was the only place in the world where all the tribes would come together in peace. A sacred place, one that even his monotheistic parents recognized as special, as did Reht the first time the natives had brought him there.

"Little Keedai," he remembered the chief saying as he lifted him up onto the steps of the stone monument in the middle of the worship circle.

"This is a place of peace and harmony, the heart of Elia. Here is where your destiny lies. Here is where you will find your purpose."

But Lugger knew how to play him, how to drown his logical mind in anger. The dog-soldier captain handed him the featherhawk that had killed his mother. He examined the symbol etched on the handle.

Kino. Blood brother. Betrayer. Murderer.

He gripped the handle until his knuckles went white. *"I will tell you everything."*

The others tried to talk some sense into him as Reht tore down the hallways, yelling for his parents in every room he passed. When he found the gouges in the wall and the limp bodies littering the hallway, he sped up.

So close—if only I can reach them, he thought as the smell of something long past dead grew stronger.

"What the hell is this place?" he heard Ro say.

The Farrocoon, Bacthar and Agracia, a few paces behind him, followed the captain onto an interior launch pad.

Don't stop—there's still time—

"It's a trafficking port," Agracia commented to the others. "But I never been to one that stank this bad."

"Mom! Dad!" Reht shouted.

(I didn't know, I didn't know!)

Only thirteen, he was oblivious to the workings of the real world. He didn't know that Shandin had been specifically commissioned to eliminate any local interference with the mining operation destined for the Wiconte forests, or that he had hired Lugger to find a knowledgeable insider with access to the sacred grounds. He didn't know of the Plunomanium that lay beneath the stone monument or why anybody would want it for experimental jump drives. And he didn't think that the dog-soldiers, who had showed him so many of life's pleasures, would abandon him in the ashes of Elia.

"Gods," Reht said, holding his head in his hands. *Don't know what's real anymore.*

A familiar growl, a pitiful whimper. Rubbing his eyes, Reht looked up ahead to a staging area near the launch pad.

Is that Mom? he thought, seeing the giant warrior holding a human female in his arms. *What the hell is he doing?*

The woman, naked and grossly malnourished, pled to him in a

foreign tongue. Her skin had been whipped and beaten, and her eyes bore the pain of her past. But Reht didn't see the woman in Mom's arms. He saw LaLanna, her braided hair burnt to a crisp, her eyes smoldering wells inside a blackened skull.

(I didn't mean to hurt you—I DIDN'T MEAN TO HURT YOU!)

"Where's Kino? Where's the chief?" Reht asked frantically.

Bossy came screaming and hooting out of a storage room with about twenty or thirty heavy-arms strapped to her back. "It's Christmas in there!"

Keeping her eye on Reht, Agracia jogged over and spoke quietly with her as the captain continued his rant.

"Where are they? Did any of them survive?" Reht said, hanging on Mom's shoulder.

"Hey, Cap, I think there's some human cargo," Bacthar said. With a gentle shake of his shoulders, the surgeon tried to bring him back to reality. "How many people, Mom?"

Mom made a motion with his hands indicating in the thousands.

"We can still save them. There's still time!" Reht said giddily.

"Captain, we really should be getting you back to the ship," Bacthar said, reinforcing his bandages.

"*Chakking* no!" Reht said, slapping his hand away.

Not now. Not when there was still a chance to redeem himself. For his parents, for the Koiwros and all the other tribes of Elia—for Diawn.

I bear the blood of my family.

"There's still time!" he shouted.

Mom set the woman down and led him to the holding cell amphitheatre just off the launch pad ramp. Limping onto the center platform, Reht looked down, gazing at the thousand or more skeletal humans huddled together in a pitiful, moaning mass. Some were already dead, most not too far behind. At such a close proximity the smell overpowered him, and in his debilitated state he felt bile rise in the back of his throat.

So many, he thought, seeing not the humans, but thousands of Koiwros, their bodies twisted and charred by Shandin's weapons, scattered across a decimated Wiconte forest.

"Help them," he pleaded, reaching dangerously over the railing.

All but Mom looked at him with confusion. The Talian warrior found a control panel and ripped off the plating. In seconds he had disengaged the prison doors and unlocked the entire warehouse.

"You're saved!" Reht shouted over the railing. None of them moved. They looked at him with wide, frightened eyes, unsure of their mysterious rescuer or his true intentions. "What are you waiting for? Don't you see? I'm helping you. You're saved. Get out of here! Go! Run! I'm helping you, I'M HELPING YOU!"

***

That assino *is going to fall off,* Agraica thought as Reht shouted and screamed at the human cargo. After nearly tipping over the railing, Mom finally pulled the captain back onto the platform. As Reht tried to scramble back, Bacthar came from behind and injected a yellow cocktail into his arm. Seconds later he was dozing in the giant Talian's arms.

Shifting the load of heavy-arms on her back, Bossy elbowed Agraica's side and whispered: "What a weirdo."

"We're going back to the ship," Bacthar said, turning to Agracia. "What's here is yours. Help the humans if you want, or don't. Once I stabilize the captain we're leaving. You're still welcome to travel with us. We're at the south port near the Crazy Horse bar."

Bossy let out a long-winded belch as the dog-soldiers left the amphitheatre. "Ugh. Glad they're gone. I didn't like their stink."

Agracia said nothing, watching the dog-soldiers in contemplative silence. Something didn't fit. *Those dog-soldiers ain't right,* she decided. *At least not like the usual crop of crotch-scratching space jockeys. More like a bunch of tripped-up souls that happened to collide, trying to survive in a Universe that refuses to give them a break.*

It felt a little too familiar.

"Hey," Bossy said, rolling her lollipop around in her mouth and tapping her on the shoulder. "What's your deal? You wanna help these suckers? They're just Lurchins."

"Don't use that word," Agracia snapped at her.

Bossy chuckled. "Come on, Grace; I ain't gonna waste my time on these *ratchaks*. Look at them—they're dead already."

Agracia knew what the Scabber in her would do, as well as what the military experiment would decide was the most logical course of action. But another urge, one much stronger than both, pulled at her heart.

Agracia was careful how she presented it to Bossy. "Someone would pay big money to know about this little operation, dontcha think?"

Bossy shrugged. "Yeah, maybe."

"Look, Victor's the one tuggin' all the strings around here, right? He's gonna be pissed we thrashed his men. We gotta get the digs on him and then sell it to his enemy. Only way we'll piss out of this one."

Appearing disinterested, Bossy worked on her lollipop and twirled one of her pigtails. "Eh. We've gotten outta worse."

"No way. Victor's big time. 'Sides, we're not in great shape," Agracia said, wiping the sweat from the back of her neck and forehead to prove her point. "Gonna need to get some meds in us soon. We'll need a solid trade."

All she got was another shrug. "Whatever. Anything to get out of this stink." Then her eyes lit up. "The *Mississippi Diesel*!"

The pigtailed warrior ran off, back towards the distillery. Agracia followed, winding back toward the entrance, trying to keep up.

Bossy looked like a kid in a candy store. "We gotta take some of this with us!" Agracia watched Bossy open all the spigots, collecting as much of the brew as she could in discarded containers.

Sighing, Agracia turned around. *Might as well check the storage rooms for new biosuits since the old ones are trashed.*

As she rounded the corner, she ran into one of the captured humans limping his way towards the exit.

"Whoa," Agracia said, grabbing his bony arm to keep him from toppling over. Even with gloves on she retracted as soon as he steadied himself, fearing whatever sickness he might harbor.

He's too old to be a living carrier, she told herself, looking over his wilting body. No, he couldn't be transporting a contagion for some bioterrorist. *Fourth-class humans are too fragile and weak.*

At least she hoped.

"Thank you—thank you for saving us!" he said with a toothless smile, reaching for her hand.

Agracia pulled back farther. "Beat it, old man. You ain't got much time before the next *chakker* tries to capture your *assino*."

"Where are we to go?" he asked. "We are not welcome on any world."

Grimacing, Agracia fell against the wall.

"Death is a part of war," Unipoesa said, circling the gaming

consoles.

Terror ate at her bones. Another battery of tests didn't bother her as much as the handful of students that remained. Every day another candidate got iced or left the program, all without explanation from their teachers.

I know why, she thought, glancing over at Li. Dark eyes looked back at her with steadfast contempt. *And soon it'll just be me and him.*

Unipoesa continued: "You will make decisions that will kill soldiers and civilians. You must do everything you can to avoid unnecessary loss, but at the same time, you must accept that sacrifices must be made to achieve victory."

Stopping at her station, Unipoesa put a hand on her shoulder. "To be the best, you must be able to make the hard decisions. You must know when to cut your losses. You must know what—or whom—to sacrifice."

Her memory zipped forward, slogging through the military years before settling in an underground bar in the rotten heart of Paradise City. Without her consent, her mind replayed one of her first times teaming up with Bossy as they ripped off junkies just to survive.

"Just leave 'em," Bossy said, tossing away the bum's empty wallet and kicking over his cart.

Agracia remembered the homeless man's open but vacant eyes, the way his hands shook as her companion frisked him for anything valuable. Survival instincts allowed her to steal from him; after all, a man in his condition wouldn't need his shoes or his blankets for very much longer. Kill or be killed—the only rule of the street, the only rule she played by anymore.

"You okay?" the old man said, tapping her shoulder.

Agracia came to, disoriented and leaning heavily against the wall. "*Sycha...*"

"God bless you, friend," the old man said, hitching up his tepper-cloth pants. "I pray to God to heal your ailment, and to forgive your sins."

Can't go on like this, she thought, pressing her knuckles into her eyes. *Gonna lose myself.*

Shoving herself off the wall, she resumed her search for biosuits. But as she took her first step, she felt a hand on her shoulder.

"Look, old man—" she started, turning on her heels.

Spring-blue eyes caught her off-guard, stealing the words from her mouth. Agracia held her breath, captivated by something she hadn't seen before. A spark, something alive, a light that refused to die in that old man's expression. "I know my life is not worth much in this world, but I thank you for the chance. The last thing I wanted was to end up as feed for the Deadwalkers."

"What?" Agracia said. Grasping him by the knobs of his shoulders, she shook him until he cried out. "What did you say?"

"Please!" he protested, falling to his knees.

She kept her hold of him, not easing up her grip. "How did you know that?"

"It's what the guards said," the old man said, holding his hands over his face. "We were nothing more than feed."

"Shandin was a Joe-boy for the Deadwalkers?" Agracia mumbled to herself. No. There was more to that, and she felt it, like a hot coals in her stomach. "Tell me everything you know."

A few more humans dragged by, casting her downward glances, too weak or too numb to interfere in her interrogation of the old man.

"Please," the old man begged, reaching up to her with excoriated fingers. "That's all I know."

Fearful of his open wounds, Agracia let him go and watched him stagger away. *This is really* chakked *up.*

Bossy came up from behind her, firearms still strapped to her body, towing several gallons of booze behind her in plastic jugs. "Muscle and *Mississippi Diesel*! It's like heaven! Now all we need is some fresh *assino.*"

"Oh no," Bossy said, seeing her expression. She plucked out her lollipop and waved it in Agracia's face. "What *chakked*-up plan you got now?"

I can't lose myself, she thought as the wise-cracks of the Scabber Jock and the cutthroat tactics of the military cadet fought to decide her next action. As she suppressed the opposable forces in her head, Jetta's last words rang strong within her heart: *That mind of yours won't let you forget.*

New dimension to Jetta's words unfolded, revealing a more complex meaning behind her phrasing.

"I know what we have to do," she whispered.

She looked at her hands and clenched them tight. When she let them unfurl again, she smiled.

"You're gonna love it."

***

Even though Reht had locked himself away in his den and refused all visitors, Mom still found his way in.

"Diawn was right about me," Reht said, tipping back the bottle of Redfly and gulping the last of its liquid fire. He slouched lower in his chair, hoping the sea of garbage at his feet would swallow him up.

With a low growl, Mom took away the bottle. He pulled up a stool to sit by his captain, his silver eyes searching his face.

She was right, Shandin was right, he thought as the ship's engines rumbled and groaned. At some other time he might have reconsidered speeding across the wasteland and searching for a suitable place to jump, but not now. He didn't care about firestorms, or ripping a hole in some part of the dead world. Not that any governing body would enforce intergalactic transportation law on Old Earth anyway.

"Diawn was *chakking* crazy, but she was part of this crew, yeah? It shouldn't have ended this way," Reht said quietly.

Sebbs found the bodies first. After returning from his shopping trip, he discovered the bloody remains of Vaughn painting the mid deck.

How did Femi break the arms and legs of an ex-con who could take down a Toork? The question didn't bother him as much as the fact that Mom and Bacthar had cleaned up the mess before he could see it. *He was my crewmate.*

They couldn't hide from him what had happened to Tech. Despite being stabbed over twenty times, his scrappy engineer had survived thanks to the little-known blood-saving organ behind his primary heart. Bacthar put him on ice in hopes that they would be able to find a treatment off-world, but the longer he spent in stasis, the less likely his chances of making it.

Reht recounted the losses in his head as he had been doing for the last hour. Vaughn and Diawn: dead. Tech: on ice, probably wouldn't make it. Triel: gone, dead to him. Ro, Cray: would probably defect or murder him in his sleep.

(As they should.)

Mukrunger.

As a new round of tears threatened to fall, Mom laid his giant hand on Reht's shoulder and squeezed. Disregarding his first mate, Reht reached for another bottle but found it empty, and tossed it atop the clutter on the floor.

"Quit it, Mom," he muttered. He tried to shove him off, but Mom held him down so he couldn't scavenge for more. With another growl, the Talian nodded at his neck wound, but Reht didn't care about letting the site heal, or Bacthar's advice to avoid booze.

"*Chakking* Gods," Reht said, staring at his naked hands. He flexed and relaxed them, watching the angry mass of scarred pink flesh blanch and perfuse, the carved letters of *mukrunger* winking on and off like flashing lights.

Mom grunted. "That isn't you," he said, revealing a fresh roll of bandaging. Taking the captain's hand, he weaved the white cloth around his fingers and across his palm.

Reht looked into the shining silver eyes of his Talian and saw a different truth.

Mom's voice, deep and baritone, rattled his bones. "I know who you are."

CHAPTER X

Damon Unipoesa couldn't remember the last time he had slept, only that he had blown through a full carton of cigarettes, and it would be several days until he could get another shipment past the health marshal. On some level, his body rejoiced. His throat and lungs already felt as if they had been raked from the inside out, his mouth full of ashes.

Now, alone in his quarters and short on smokes, Unipoesa found himself doing what he always did when he was strung out: He picked up his personal interface tablet, one that he had purposely refitted so it was privately linked outside the Alliance network, and gave the command under hushed tones: "Show me Maria Unipoesa."

The tablet projected the image of a blue and green planet with the seal of the Republic stamped across the satellite feed. Victor's forces would not let him get through.

"*Chak*," he muttered, taking a fistful of his hair. "Fine," he said through gritted teeth, "show me the last known images of Maria Unipoesa."

The tablet cycled back a few weeks and pulled up the image of a gray stone house in a field of wild roses. He zoomed in on the house and centered on her image as she tended to the white Catheilia bushes framing the patio in her favorite gardening hat. It was hard to see her face from the satellite images, but every once and a while she'd look up to the sky, as if she was looking back at him.

Sitting back in the chair at his desk, he absently traced the outline of her face with his finger but stopped when he saw a shadow move across the front door. *Someone's in the house.* Why hadn't he noticed it before?

"Zoom in, maximum differential. Scan for any known identifiers."

The tablet beeped and formed a data grid over the shadowy image.

Male. Humanoid. Just under two meters, approximately 100 kilos. Age undetermined.

He threw the tablet across the room. It bounced off the shelving and clattered to the ground.

Maria, why? he thought, holding his head in his hands.

The tablet buzzed and alerted, and at first he didn't hear it. He couldn't get the silhouette of the other man out of his mind. It wasn't until he heard Pancar's voice that he broke from his thoughts.

"Damon, come in, please."

Grabbing the tablet off the floor, Unipoesa cast aside the touch pad's splintered frame.

"Are you alright?" Pancar asked, leaning into the view.

"I'm fine," he said, straightening his uniform and returning to the chair at his desk. "Tell me the latest."

"I thought you'd like to know that I have Captain Jagger and his crew in my custody," the Nagoorian said.

The admiral heard it in his voice. "Is he… compromised?"

Pancar folded his hands together. "You and I have always disagreed about the efficacy of the Sleeper program, and Captain Jagger is a prime example of its shortcomings. I believe he would have fallen into enemy hands if it had it not been for the help of Old Earth's notorious Scabber Jocks."

Unipoesa pinched his eyes. "What are the casualties?"

"I'm sending you the list," he said, typing in something on his console. "My compliments, incidentally, on outfitting Agracia with a custom puppet. This 'Bossy' is quite… *unique*."

Unsure of what Pancar actually knew about the Alliance's involvement in their pairing or his specific role in liberating her model, he moved the conversation forward. "Are Agracia and Bossy in your custody as well?"

"For the time being, although we're having a hell of a time containing the puppet. And Agracia is quite insistent on speaking with Jetta. She says it's urgent. I don't think she'll stay on Nagoor unless we can arrange that."

The admiral sighed. "Get her transported here immediately. It's past time I made contact with her anyway."

"Are you sure that's wise? I would imagine you'd be a significant trigger, and she's quite unstable at the moment. All of them are. They need to be 'unagented,' Damon, or they will all go mad. The Talian is destroying anything that he perceives as a threat, and the surgeon is beginning to compulsively hurt himself. I won't even tell you what the rest of the crew is doing."

"Jaeia and I are addressing that at 1700 hours."

"Damon," Pancar stressed, "there is no worse affliction than to lose the reins of your identity."

The admiral heard the touch of grief in his voice, saw the way his forehead creased.

This isn't just about his concern over his guests. The face of Pancar's nephew, Tighsen Dai, flashed through his head. A charismatic smile wiped away, a joyful laughter lost. Military Minister Razar made sure of that when he ordered him to be turned into an agent all those years ago.

No time to dig up old ghosts. Unipoesa deflected the comment and drove into the more pressing matter: "Tell me what you really found."

Pursing his lips, Pancar sat back in his chair. "The Talian took Shandin's head as a prize. We inspected it and found some very suspicious implants. They appear to be of Motti design, but with peculiar customizations. I'm having my best people look into it."

"And?" He checked his uniform sleeve; he only had a few more minutes until he had to meet with Jaeia.

"This is not the first time I've come across something like this, Damon. In fact, just a few weeks ago one of my viper squads found the body of Mashen Ky, former leader of the human colonists on Jue Hexron, in a rescue mission after Victor's forces took hold of the planet. He was outfitted with similar ocular and intracranial implants."

"Victor...?" Unipoesa said, squeezing the tablet handles.

"And that's not all. I've sent you the video log of Reht's engagement with Diawn Arkiam. If you look closely, she has injuries consistent with the implantation of these same devices."

"It must be some sort of control device," the admiral said.

Pancar nodded. "My guess exactly."

The admiral's sleeve alarmed at him. "I have a consultation with Jaeia. Keep me posted on your findings."

"One more thing, Damon," the blue-skinned Nagoorian said as Damon's finger hovered over the disconnect. "I need you to promise me something."

Unipoesa braced himself against the desk, anticipating the request of his oldest friend.

"Many things have been taken away from you and me with the lives that we've chosen, and so rarely do we have the opportunity to step out of uniform. She's coming back to you now, Damon, against all impossibilities. So don't deny yourself the possibility of hope, and don't rely on the dictations of your past."

"What are you saying, Pancar?" he said, swallowing hard against the hot lump in his throat.

Pancar smiled sadly. "Old friend… Don't be afraid to be happy."

***

Jaeia met the admiral just outside the Defense Department's Division Lockdown Labs.

"Are you sure about this, Captain?" the admiral said, checking the readout panel for the internal operating levels.

It had taken a lot of convincing to get the approval of Dr. DeAnders and the CCO for their meeting with the Hub, especially since the Defense/Research team had recently taken the super processor offline after it had shown independent neural node growth, but Jaeia felt sure. If they didn't free the mind of Tarsha Leone and the other Sleepers, she argued, then the Alliance risked their one and only chance against Li. And if she could get past Li, then she could find a way to confront Victor and end his reign.

"You'll just have to trust me, Admiral," she said, hitting the keypad.

Once she stepped inside the network housing, her stomach knotted. A long time ago, the steady hum and blinking lights of the main processor excited her, made her wonder what mysteries of the universe could be solved. Now she only felt the fluttering uncertainties in her belly, and the burden of the choices she might have to make in order to save the Starways.

Please, she thought, projecting her voice beyond her own mind, *for once, give me a break.*

As the admiral watched over her shoulder, she input her command codes and freed the emergent restraints enough that the Hub's independent functioning could engage, along with its holographic imaging.

"I know you can hear me," she said, looking at the blank staging area and stepping onto the center platform. "I don't know what you're calling yourself these days, but I've come to make good on my promise to you."

A glimmer of light descended from the ceiling, expanding into an orb suspended above her head. Whispers came from the darkness. A chill shot up her spine as she remembered her sister's confrontation with Jahx's possessed mind.

"We know what brings you here, Jaeia Drachsi."

"I no longer use that last name," she corrected the Hub.

Two eyes appeared before her, slitted and yellow like a cat's. "You have many names, some of which you have lost, and some that you have gained."

How did he acquire that information? she thought. *No, I can't do this. He's goading me; I can't play into his game.*

The Hub revealed more of itself, this time assuming a feline form with black and purple markings. It paced around her, shoulder blades spiking up and down beneath shimmering fur. "Your friends whisper one of these many names. They tell me your secrets—and the real reason why you come here today."

Out of the corner of her eye, she caught the admiral giving her a cautionary look.

I know what he's doing, she thought, weighing her options, *but I have to bite.* "What friends?"

The feline creature smiled, revealing a crescent moon for a mouth. Then the image blinked out, confronting her with empty space.

"This is a waste of time," the admiral said, checking the time on his sleeve.

Her voice came out of the distance, rushing toward them with desperate urgency: "Jaeia—have you forgotten about us?"

Senka.

Focusing on her breathing, Jaeia rubbed the tips of her fingers together. She couldn't let the machine get inside her head. *Stay cool and calm; it wants a reaction out of me, test my limits.*

She reminded herself of its ultimate goal: merging with the other two dataHubs that controlled the Alliance Intelligence Systems. DeAnders, Wren, and Unipoesa held serious reservations about letting an artificial intelligence come into a state of full conscious emergence. Dividing the Hub kept it in control.

For now.

Before Victor had crippled the Fleet, the Alliance would have come under political fire for restricting the growth and development of an emerging intelligence for the purpose of defense and war, but things had changed. It was part of the reason why she was here. She still had reservations about letting a collective intelligence like the Hub roam freely throughout the wave network. After all, it knew every registered being intimately through their personal logs and public files. But the part of her she could never deny, even against the will of her overbearing sister, felt strongly on the matter.

"I hear them," the Hub said, rematerializing on the ceiling, crawling on all fours. "They are in such pain. They want to return to your world; they want release from this terrible limbo."

"You know why we can't," Jaeia said. "You're linked into our systems. You know we haven't been successful in our attempts to use the flash transport device."

"That's because you haven't asked me," the Hub said, dropping to the floor. The feline creature morphed into a semi-humanoid form, standing on its back legs and rounding its shoulders. He held in his paw-like hand a glowing orb that changed its form to that of Senka, then Rawyll, Crissn, and the Grand Oblin. "I can reawaken them. I can make them be reborn."

The admiral stepped in. "At what cost?"

Winding its tail up the admiral's leg, the feline creature closed its hand on the orb. "And you. You want to know the song to awaken those who slumber. I can help you, too."

Sensing his frustration and paranoia rising, Jaeia answered for both of them. "Yes, you're right. We need to know any and all information you have on the Sleeper program and the word 'Blackbird.' If you can help us bring back the Exiles and release the Sleepers, then I will release you and the other dataHubs."

The Hub let out a sound between a purr and a laugh and crouched down on all fours. "You have promised such things before, Jaeia of Old Earth. Besides, you will be reprimanded, demoted, imprisoned for misconduct and tampering with a *dangerous* weapon."

"I will authorize it," the admiral said, backing her.

What?

Without breaking her composure, Jaeia absorbed the shock of the admiral's unanticipated move. She had expected to have to use her second voice to convince him to relinquish his command codes—not for him to do so willingly. *This changes things.*

Centuries of military strategy and experience butted up against her thoughts. *Maybe this is part of a secret plan. He never revealed his motive for coming with me, or what he planned to do when the time came to play the final hand.*

"You know not what I am capable of," the Hub whispered, once again revealing his crescent smile. "I am the eyes and ears of the wave network. Should you so blindly trust me?"

Jaeia played with the end of her uniform sleeve. *The Hub read and analyzed all my personal files; it knows my weaknesses.* "It is my belief that no Sentient creature should be held against their will in order to serve this institution."

"Is that why you freed the Spinners?"

Unipoesa's anger hit her like a tidal wave, but she breathed through it, reminding herself that she had to hold onto her objective.

"Yes."

"Even though Aesis is a known impersonator of high-powered delegates and military personnel?"

"Yes," she said, trying to sound convincing.

She felt the admiral's hand at her sleeve, but she pulled away and didn't look back.

With a smile, the Hub smiled playfully stretched out and yawned, its long, pink tongue curling out of its mouth. It licked its lips and lowered its head. "Well then. Prove your conviction. Show me where your faith lies."

Jaeia paused over the console after the admiral input his codes. "Do you know why I believe that you will help us?"

The Hub leapt back onto the ceiling and dangled upside-down by its tail. "Enlighten me, *Triorion*."

"Because it was your interaction with our minds, from our daily banalities to our tragedies and triumphs, our deepest secrets to our wildest fantasies, that brought you into being. That's what breathes life into you with every piece of electronic data we feed into the wave network. If you are truly are a product of our experiences and our dreams, then I would hope, for the sake of both our existences, that you would see the logic in supporting what makes us honorable and good creatures by helping us in our mission to bring freedom and democracy to the Starways."

The feline creature disappeared, and the staging area became a blank field once again.

"Waste of time," the admiral muttered.

The speakers exploded with a cacophony of dissonant sounds as the holographic image of the enormous Motti ship, with its curved, half-dome superstructure and tentacled underbelly, moved slowly along the optic field, laying waste to the civilization projected in its shadow. Jaeia and the admiral retreated behind the interface, watching in horror as the nightmare unfolded. Screams and mechanical chattering filled the room, and faces contorted with immeasurable suffering surfaced and receded. A green planet decayed to an ugly brown, then charred to black before blipping out of existence.

Victor's image took center stage, all around him the light of the setting sun dying against a world reduced to ashes. His figure never settled, caught in a state of flux, as if the hardware struggled to keep up with the illusion of his plastic-sheened flesh. As the world around him perished, he spoke in an insect's tongue, his words strained and in hisses:

"*With eyes open, they burn!*"

Jaeia's stomach twisted sickeningly, and she grabbed onto the railing.

"There is much suffering in your world," the Hub whispered.

How could she trust the Hub? How could she believe that an artificial intelligence, released from its bonds, would find reason to save the ones who had caged and restricted its awareness? How could it possibly understand or care about the absurd struggles of organic species limited by their biological wants and needs when the universe posed as a much more interesting and fulfilling playground for a superior intelligence? It could very easily let them fall to the mercy of Victor and his tyrannical empire.

Two images flickered to life. One was of Jaeia, sitting before her private terminal in her quarters. The other was of Unipoesa, much younger, doing the same. The Hub went back and forth between the two audio tracks, starting with Jaeia:

"*Sometimes I wonder… if this is all worth it. If humans—if Sentients—are worth saving. The horrible things we have done keep me up at night.*"

The audio switched over to Unipoesa. "*Maria—I did this for you. I hope you know that. I wanted to give you, and perhaps one day our family, a future.*"

Jaeia remembered making the recording a few weeks ago, after Victor's forces had taken over most of the interior, leaving those who didn't join at the mercy of the Motti's weapon.

"*Are we worth saving? Are the Sentients of the Starways worth saving? I asked myself that before I helped Jetta face Jahx. Sometimes it still sits uneasily in my heart.*"

Unipoesa cradled his head. "*I am so sorry, Maria. I should have never have left you. I thought I knew what I was doing."*

It flipped back to Jaeia: *"...and then I close my eyes, and I listen to Jetta's voice. Not the loud, obnoxious one, or the one at the front of her head. The one that's quieter but always there, pulling and pushing her every single day. The one she may never really hear, but the one that keeps her—and me—going."*

The Hub returned to Unipoesa as he fumbled to remove his wedding band. He held up it up to the light before putting it in his pocket and turning away from the camera. *"Letting you go will be the hardest thing I will ever do. But I promised to protect you, and I will do anything—anything—to keep you safe. I love you, forever and always."*

The field blanked out again.

"Do it already," the admiral whispered, his reddened eyes staring out ahead.

Jaeia flipped the switch.

You're free.

She stepped back while the computer housing hummed and buzzed with new life and the Hub rerouted its processor to integrate with the other two divided components of its neural network.

"Hello?" Jaeia said, standing in the silence.

The admiral kicked a coil of fiberoptics. "*Chak* it all."

Her uniform sleeve beeped, alerting her to an emergency briefing called by the CCO.

"We have to go," she said, stepping off the platform. "Let's just hope it keeps its promise."

As Jaeia closed the doors behind her, she saw something glimmer in the shadows. She only caught a glimpse of the projection as the doors sealed shut.

My tattoo—

And with it a whisper, ever so faint, in the dark: "Believe."

***

Although held under strict watch in her quarters, Wren had granted Jetta limited use of her rank to search the network.

I can't believe they allowed me almost full access to the Alliance database, Jetta mused as she scrolled through department reports. After checking and rechecking that the status of her brother was critical but unchanged, she reviewed the latest intelligence on the Motti and Victor's secret counter-weapon.

She kept the lights in her quarters to the level of gloaming, preferring the mood that darkness brought as she reviewed the holographic files. *The Motti ship is still wreaking havoc on the unprotected outerworlds,* she thought. With each projected report and casualty count, the muscles in her neck and shoulders tightened. *Entire planets stripped, left barren.*

But the planets and systems under Victor's banner stood protected. From the latest count, Trigos, the central Homeworld, was the only Alliance affiliate that was still divided on pledging its allegiance to the new Republic.

Victor's face popped up on a news report brief, and Jetta muted the sound before she heard his voice. Even through close captioning she could feel the dark pull of his words, the way each subtle laugh and lilt jangled her nerves.

He's still pushing his agenda that the Alliance is impotent and corrupt, she noticed, reading the intelligence analysis of his speeches superimposed over the news brief. Not that she needed the report to know that. Victor never masked his delight in exposing the top secret and controversial programs once headed by the Military Minister Tidas Razar and undersigned by Chancellor Reamon of the General Assembly, as well as painting the Kyron twins as psychologically unstable weapons of the Alliance.

Jetta watched the video footage but found herself increasingly detached. As much as she disliked the discomfiting reels of her post-war breakdown and her sister's collapse, the sordid details of the Command Development Program, or the Motti ship closing in on Trigos, more pressing issues demanded her focus.

I need to know more about Victor's counter-weapon. That's the key.

A heavy, unsettling feeling slid into her belly when she read the scouting reports, much like when she thought of Victor, his carefully manicured, tailored veneer at odds with the beast within.

Bracing her stomach, Jetta pushed herself away from the terminal. It was getting harder and harder to fight the protests and agitations of her body, and the stress of conflict only made it worse.

"What am I doing?" she muttered after the pain subsided, running a hand through her tangled hair and retying it behind her head. "It shouldn't have come to this. I should have been there. I'm—I'm—"

I am no Commander.
(I abandoned my post)
I am least of all a sister.
(I hurt Jaeia. She is afraid of me—)
(I left Jahx—)
I am weak against the darkness inside me.
I am not worthy of my own skin.

Grabbing her armrests, she pulled them clean off their bolted plating. She wanted to throw them against the wall, but she knew better than to alert the guards. Instead she pressed the broken edges against her thighs and slowly pushed down, releasing her anger in the pain. Her pants stained red as she concentrated on the sensation, submitting to it, with every breath digging a little deeper.

As her thighs shrieked with pain, she suddenly remembered her trial in the Temple of Exxuthus, the words spoken by the entity imitating the Grand Oblin: *"Who stands accused in your heart?"*

It didn't entirely make sense to her then, but as the pain washed her tortured thoughts away, she saw the truth with a new clarity.

(Me.)

She looked down in horror at the metal bars she had dug into her flesh. "It's me that's doing this…"

The door chime rang three times before she noticed it. Quickly, she stashed the metal bars underneath her desk and hobbled over to her closet to change her pants.

"Just give me a sec!" she said, struggling to get the second pant leg on. She kicked the bloodied uniform into her closet just as the Healer walked in.

Jetta's heart dropped to her stomach. *Of course it had to be her.*

Hiding her self-inflicted injuries from the Healer was like hiding a scream in an empty room.

"Hey," Jetta said, rounding behind the couch and using the protection of the furniture to hide her quickly soaking second pair of tactical pants.

"Hey back," Triel said, frowning. "What's going on?"

"Was reviewing the sitrep."

"A little dark in here, isn't it?"

Jetta shrugged. "It helps me concentrate on my objective."

Before Triel could ask anything else about her, she tried to redirect the conversation. "How are you feeling?"

Triel never took her eyes off her as she slowly approached the couch. Jetta felt the psionic radiance field around her growing in intensity as she neared, like the air charging before a lightning strike. "Fine, thanks. I came to check on you. I know your latest health report wasn't good. I want to see if you wanted to talk about it."

Jetta forced a laugh. "I'll worry about that when I'm dead. Right now I have to figure out how to stop Victor before Li's army crushes the last of us."

"How's Jahx?" the Healer asked, her eyes drifting to the level of Jetta's thighs. She was still shielded by the couch, but it didn't matter if she was behind a reinforced superstructure; Triel was too attuned not to discover her secret.

Jetta ground her fists into the leather upholstery. "He's the same. Nobody knows how to help him. I don't know how to help him. I guess that's some of the reason I ran off. Part of me was hoping that I would just stumble across the answer. It beat waiting around."

"Have you seen him?"

Jetta shook her head. "Not yet. Jaeia said she would get us the clearance to see him after the meeting. I'm hoping it's not goodbye. I don't know if I could lose him a second time."

"You should have more faith, Jetta Kyron," Triel said, crossing her arms over her chest. "Sometimes you can't do it all. Sometimes you'll just have to trust that a person can come through."

Jetta's face soured. "I hope you didn't come here just to lecture me."

"No," Triel said, uncrossing her arms and letting them hang by her sides. Putting one knee on the couch, she leaned closer to Jetta. "I also came here to talk with you about what I experienced in the Temple of Exxuthus."

Jetta could feel the blood running down her legs and pressed her thighs harder into the back of the couch. "Okay, tell me."

Triel reached for Jetta's hand. Although her first inclination was to pull away, she held her breath and allowed her to take it. "I've had many visions about you and me since we've first met. Some promising, hopeful. Some that have made me…"

Pausing, she turned her eyes away, searching for the right term. But she didn't have to put her thoughts into words. Jetta sensed the complexity of a terror that could never be conceptualized with the limitations of a spoken language.

"...afraid *for* you," the Healer continued. "But in the Temple of Exxuthus, I had the most powerful one of all. And it was—it was—"

Sublime, Jetta thought, her eyes growing wide, feeling the floodgates of Triel's hope and joy bathing her in vibrant psionic melodies. Suddenly love, unconditional and endless, was possible. She couldn't experience the vision itself, but she felt its essence, an ineffable level of harmonic coexistence and tranquility.

Triel withdrew her hand. The wonderful sensations stopped. The look in the Healer's eyes changed to one of distance and caution. "But I was warned that preserving my life would come at a great cost. One that I'm not willing to risk. I just thought you should know."

Jetta frowned. "Why would you tell me such a thing?" she asked, trying to take back her hand, "and not expect me to do something about it?"

Triel lowered her gaze and placed her other hand over Jetta's. "Prodgy legend and prophecy has always been abstruse and somewhat allusive. It tests the will and the unconscious desires, manifesting from the power of suggestion and interpretation. I refuse to be told who I am, or what must be done in order to fulfill some ancient writ. I choose to seek my own path and decide my own fate."

Jetta found herself speechless as blood continued to trickle down her legs, despite their compression against the couch. "H-how do you do that?" she stuttered.

"What?" the Healer said.

"You accept yourself—all of yourself—with all that you are, good and bad," Jetta said, touching Triel's cheek with her fingertips.

"You accept me as I am," Triel whispered, blue eyes locking in with hers.

Jetta withdrew her hand. "Yes, I do. But you push forward, you don't look back. You don't hate yourself. You don't fight what you are. You are so much stronger than me."

"I embrace my talents, Jetta," Triel said, "and, most importantly, I draw my strength from a place of synchronicity and love."

Jetta shifted her weight uncomfortably. "I can't seem to do that very well…"

"That's because you fight everyone off."

Grumbling, Jetta turned away.

"Jetta, I care so much about you," the Healer whispered. "It bothers me that you don't believe me."

Jetta froze in place, fearful of where the conversation was headed. Barely audibly, she replied: "I just don't understand why…"

Triel ran her slender fingers up Jetta's arm and gently held onto the back of her neck. "Because you are so beautiful, Jetta, and yet you only see your scars. You are filled with the most wonderful light—brighter than sunshine—but you fight so hard to conceal it from everyone, especially me, because you think that makes you tough and more able to protect the ones you love."

Jetta wanted to step back, but Triel kept hold of her, kneeling on two legs now, meeting her eye to eye, the backrest of the couch the only thing between them. "But it doesn't. I love you because you are a good person with a good soul. You care so much about others that it literally destroys you."

Jetta tried to look someplace, anyplace else, but Triel's eyes, even bluer than she remembered, like the open sky against a vast icescape, would not let her pull away.

"I'm sorry I'm not stronger, I'm sorry I'm not—"

Bringing her closer, the Healer made her bend over the back of the couch. "Why are you so afraid to love me back?"

Jetta held onto Triel's wrists. "I'm not afraid of loving you," she whispered. A smile tugged at the corners of her lips but vanished when she admitted the truth. "You had my heart the moment we met."

"Then why?"

Unable to find the right words, what came forth felt rushed and raw. "I don't feel worthy of your love."

Triel drew in closer, their faces only centimeters apart, her breath hot on her cheek as she lowered her voice. "You're just going have to take a risk, Commander Kyron."

"That almost sounds like an order, Triel of Algardrien," Jetta said, forcing a chuckle.

Triel's lips brushed against hers, her breath faster and heavier as she pulled at her collar. "Fall into me."

Jetta didn't have a choice; Triel's opposing weight and her awkward stance gave her no leverage as the Healer fell back onto the couch. When she tried to roll away, Triel held her tightly to her chest.

"Wait, Triel, I—"

"I know," Triel said, reaching underneath her shirt with warm hands and closing her eyes. The wounds on Jetta's thighs tingled and buzzed as the Healer augmented the repairs. Jetta held herself up and watched the Healer's facial expressions change from pinched to contorted, then finally relaxing as the wound knitted shut. "It probably seemed necessary at the time. But you don't have to do that anymore. I will always be there for you."

"You see all this in me… and you still love me?" Jetta asked.

There was no hesitation, the answer spoken with a broad, beaming smile. "Yes."

Jetta leaned forward and kissed her, melting into Triel's sweet lips and relishing the softness of her skin. Their first encounter on Old Earth felt real enough, but Jetta found this one stronger even than before, like there was an invisible force pulling them together. Each touch felt exaggerated, lighting up every nerve fiber from toes to fingertips.

"I've never told you how stunning you are," Jetta said, tucking a loose strand of the Healer's dark hair behind her ear. She ran her finger along Triel's markings on her forehead and neckline. "You seem more gorgeous to me every day."

Giggling shyly, the Healer pressed into her, slipping her tongue into her mouth and kissing her more intensely than ever before. At that moment, all of Jetta's inhibitions vanished, and she surprised herself at her own aggression as she pulled apart the Healer's uniform top.

"Do you ever feel like—no, it's dumb," Jetta said.

"No, tell me," Triel said, working on removing Jetta's chest protector.

"Do you ever feel like we're *supposed* to be together—like it was meant to be? I know you don't believe in that stuff—neither do I—but sometimes I can't help but—"

The pained look in Triel's eyes confused Jetta. "What?"

Did I say something wrong? she wondered, sensing a sudden apprehension pervading the Healer's emotions.

Triel only held onto her more tightly. "It's nothing."

As she geared up to contest her assertion, Triel pulled her back on top of her and reached under her chest protector. For a moment, Jetta stopped kissing her to relish the feeling as Triel's fingers grazed lower, finding the old wound on her abdomen, still ragged and inflamed, though they didn't linger long. Her hands moved to her hips and gently caressed the tender skin just above the waistline of her pants.

"No," Jetta said, pinning Triel's hands back. "Let me, this time."

Jetta removed the last of Triel's top and took in the sight of her. Fair skin, unblemished by age or scars, intricately decorated with Algardrien tribal markings, seemed perfect in the glowing backlight of the terminal holograms. Although she found her beauty intimidating, breathtaking, Jetta's desires lead her to step outside the restraints of fear.

"*Baeya,*" Jetta whispered in her native tongue, touching her cheek.

Despite the thousands of years of lovemaking she had inadvertently stolen in her gleanings, she chose to rely on what came naturally. Kissing down her neck, Jetta descended to the upper curves of her chest, where she teased the skin lightly with her tongue until Triel arched her back and extended her toes, moving her body in a synchronous rhythm. Jetta's hand found her other breast and kept her touch gentle only until the Healer pressed into her, needing more.

"*Di galo ke'o–*" Triel cried in her native tongue, pulling off her pants and pushing Jetta down towards her undulating hips. With a mixture of fear and intense desire, Jetta dipped down and explored the warmth between her legs. The Healer quivered as she tasted her for the first time. It was unusual at first, but the tangy saltiness of her made Jetta feel closer to Triel, as if it were a secret only she could know.

Something inside her awakened in the heat, and Jetta found herself barely able to restrain herself, especially when Triel cried out her name. Gripping the Healer's legs, she steadied herself as the Healer's vocalizations became louder and more intense. The fair-skinned woman's hands clenched and unclenched as she beckoned Jetta in whispers and moans.

"Jetta—oh Gods—"

Fear and doubt, once dominating and silencing, fell away, replaced by an intense desire that fueled her passion. Moving back on top of the Healer so she could kiss her again, Jetta simultaneously entered her warmth.

"Take me—"

Jetta bit her neck and wrapped her free arm around her tightly as her hand worked inside her. Each time she drew back and plunged deeper, she felt the Healer's body go taut, ever closer to reaching her peak.

A psionic wavelength appeared in the farthest reaches of Jetta's awareness, pulsating, expanding, blue steel ribbons fanning across a kaleidoscope plane of timeless space. Triel reached back for her across a different realm, connecting the physical with the psionic, linking them in both body and mind. Jetta felt herself both on top of and inside the Healer in dual perspectives, and for the first time in her life she could not differentiate between the two.

As she moved her hand in and out, she rested her head on Triel's forehead and allowed her mind to roam free in the vast expanse of these parallel planes. It was a closeness she had never thought possible, pulling her toward perfection with every breath and every stroke. Finally, on both a physical and psionic level she surged into the Healer, both of them straining with exquisite release.

"Oh, Jetta…" Triel sighed, putting her arms around her and squeezing with all her might. "I love you. So much."

Jetta smiled. She didn't want to move and she didn't want any of it to end. She wanted to close her eyes and lock herself into this moment, forever in the embrace of Triel of Algardrien.

"I love you too," Jetta said, holding her close. "I always have, and I always will."

***

As Triel left Jetta's quarters, escorts falling in step behind her, she couldn't help but fixate on what Jetta had said: *"Do you ever feel like we're supposed to be together—like it was meant to be?"*

Even Jetta senses our destiny, she thought.

Triel wiped the tears from her eyes as inconspicuously as she could so as not to alert the other crewman. If they saw her worry or her fear, they would probably think she was about to Fall. She tried to think of something—anything—else, but the memory of Arpethea's words still rang in her ears:

"She is not ready for what she must do. She will try and stop you."

Quickening her pace, Triel rounded the corner to her own quarters and politely thanked the guards before sealing the doors behind her. She stood there a moment, then turned her back and slid down to the ground.

"Do not hesitate to end her life to save your own. End her life to save our people. It is destined."

"Arpethea, how can you ask me to do such an awful thing? I can't possibly hurt Jetta," she wept into her hands.

Something in empty room heard her pain and whispered back the awful truth: *"You must kill the Apparax."*

Triel looked at her hands, turning them over, marveling at the weave of dark markings that had taken years to develop. She thought of her father and how disappointed he had always been in her, the way he argued through endless nights with her mother over her defiance. Maybe she had been wrong to leave him. Maybe she had been wrong about all of her beliefs, especially where she chosen to place her faith. Where had it led her, after all? A lone Solitary prone to Falling, in love with the *Triorion*, while her people—her father—suffered, trapped in the Motti ship.

She closed her eyes, recalling the terrible vision she had of a shadow thing consuming Jetta upon their descent to Algar.

Maybe I'm wrong about her—

And then she remembered Jetta's aura, more brilliant than a star, shining forth as she rode the wolf.

—I love her.

She thought again of her homeworld, and the last of her people, her very blood, stolen away in a Deadwalker ship, ruining the last worlds of the Starways.

(Father, I'm so sorry.)

As she opened her eyes, she remembered her own creed, the promise she had made to herself before she ran away from Algar, and realized what she had to do.

***

Jetta had just kissed Triel goodbye and showed her out when her terminal alerted her to an incoming priority message. Not expecting any callers, Jetta came to the dreaded conclusion before his face even appeared on the display.

"Still wondering how I can let myself in?" Victor asked, the gold rims of his glasses glinting as he tilted his head.

"The only thing I wonder is how no one else can see the devil inside you."

"Ah, what an excellent point you make, Warchild. But you already know the answer, don't you?"

Indeed she did. She had come to the conclusion when she was very little, maybe two, no older than three, mistakenly stealing knowledge from junkies and drunks just to understand the world she lived in. Through their eyes she saw their need for direction, their hunger for a higher authority to whom they could relinquish their responsibility and with it the pain of their hollow existence. To find purpose, meaning, in a life fraught with misery and suffering, even if the purpose given to them served a darker ambition. She understood desperation, and she understood the power of a man with golden promises.

"What do you want?" Jetta asked. She considered running a trace, but for Victor to break through their defense and communication systems once again, she guessed it would be a fruitless endeavor.

"I offer you redemption. I offer you command of my fleet."

Jetta scoffed. "You insult me."

"On the contrary, I'm banking on your superior intelligence. I know everything about you, Jetta Kyron, perhaps more than any other person in this galaxy. I know you're better than your weak-minded sister. I know the beast that grows inside you, and I know how to help you harness its powers."

Though Triel had mended the wounds, the gashes Jetta had recently inflicted in her thighs flared to life, as if someone had poured kerosene over them and lit a match. The wound in her abdomen followed suit, exploding with white fire, streaking up her chest and crisping her insides. She gripped the lip of the desk with all her might, cracking the trim.

"I will show you the purpose of your power. You will take the reins of my army and rule this galaxy with a swift and definite hand. You will have control over those that are so willing to persecute you, despite how many times you have saved them. You will become more than their pet, Warchild—you will become their *God*."

His words felt like hot oil in her ears, and she fell to the ground, mouth open for the scream that caught in the middle of her chest. She felt herself unspooling, falling away from her body, away from the Starbase, until she came to a halt in a dark, muggy place that carried an air of familiar dread.

"Come with me," Victor said, his voice a garble of rusted gears. She looked up to see him standing on a mound of human skulls, red, deathly light bleeding from his sockets. "And I will show you the awful truth of what we really are."

***

Wren was discussing the latest Intelligence Report with the senior command council when Jaeia screamed. Something bit into the back of her skull and yanked her down with all its might, trying to fold her into its maw. Jaeia smacked her hands on the desk and bucked out of her seat, oblivious to the flurry of staff trying to hold her down as she thrashed about.

Jetta—

"Get him out of my head!" she shrieked.

"Get a med team up here, now!" someone shouted.

More shouting, a frenzy of hands, gritted teeth. Jaeia didn't see the commotion about her, only the shadow closing in on her.

Falling fast, she slipped and slid down the throat of the beast. As she tried to slow her wild descent by spreading out her arms and legs, she craned her head back, keeping sight of the fading light that tethered her to her body. My only way back—

Then she heard her sister cry out. Jaeia twisted around to see Jetta being swallowed by a tangle of spidery fingers farther down the black gullet.

What the hell is that?

Connected through their bond, Jaeia couldn't break herself or her sister free of the thing consuming her.

Jaeia wedged herself in place with all of her strength. Jetta, you have to fight it! *she pleaded with the last of her psionic hold.* Please, Jetta— PLEASE!

She came to on the floor of the conference room with pieces of broken datapads and parts of a chair strewn around her. With perplexed expressions and nervous murmurs, the entire senior council stood around the medical team as they analyzed her vital signs.

"Captain, are you okay?" Wren asked.

"Sir, she's still emerging," the med tech responded.

"I'm fine," Jaeia said, pushing the bioscanner out of her face. "Find Jetta."

Wren had given the go-ahead to the team when a guard came on over the com. "Excuse me, Chief, but Commander Kyron is asking permission to join the meeting."

Before answering, Wren looked to her for confirmation. "Permission granted."

Jetta stumbled inside the conference room, disheveled and pale, uniform pulled apart.

"He's planning something terrible," she said breathlessly.

"Who?" Wren asked.

"Victor. We have to act now."

Dr. DeAnders helped Jetta to her seat as the medics gave Jaeia a hand.

"Please explain to me what just happened," Wren said, standing at the head of the table.

Jetta gave her a glance, and Jaeia nodded for her to continue.

"Victor isn't what he seems to be," Jetta started, smoothing down her uniform as best she could. "He's got human skin, but his soul is not from the world. It seems like every time I've made contact with him I slip into his head whether I want to or not. And I see the most awful things. We can't just stop his Fleet—we have to stop *him*."

Jetta stopped talking for a moment and fidgeted in her seat. As her distress echoed in Jaeia's mind, she tried to provide her sister as much support as she could, even with the disturbing visions resounding in her own head.

"He's not like any enemy that anyone here has ever faced. He's not going to try and kill us or rule us—he wants to eat our souls."

The room fell silent. Jaeia watched as Unipoesa and Wren exchanged hushed words, and their faces turned stone cold.

The guard rang in again. "Sir, Triel of Algardrien is asking to join the meeting."

Wren once again turned to Jaeia for guidance. She nodded, anxious to see the Healer. "Show her in."

Triel came rushing in as fast as the guards would allow. "Jetta—Jaeia—I felt something terrible—"

"We're okay," Jetta said, rising to meet her. She spoke into the Healer's ear, consoling her in private.

Sensing something different between the two of them, Jaeia held her breath, trying to get a better reading. *Has the energy between them changed?* The way Jetta touched the Healer seemed more intimate, as was the way Triel received her comforts. Jaeia watched closely as Jetta took her hand and led her to an open seat before taking her own again.

Clearing her throat, Jetta continued. "Please include Pancar of Nagoorian on this meeting. He needs to hear what I have to say."

Wren studied her closely. "We are still under negotiations with his faction. I would not advise divulging any classified information."

Jetta barely kept the anger out of her words. "We are going to need all the help we can get. *Chak* politics."

Out of the side of his eye, Wren looked again to Jaeia for confirmation.

No one is ready to trust Jetta again, not with her unpredictable behavior, she thought as she glanced around the room. Looking within their bond, she sensed the dark shadow gathering around her sister. *And I can't afford to keep making the same mistakes.*

But before she could signal Wren, Unipoesa caught her eye and lifted two of his fingers, indicating his support.

The Admiral is a strong supporter of Pancar, but he still stands for the Alliance, she rationalized.

(Please don't let me be wrong about him, too...)

Jaeia nodded.

Within seconds, Pancar appeared on the central hologram display. Wren briefed the Nagoorian leader before allowing Jetta to continue.

"I'm sure you have all read my report on my recent travels," Jetta said, rushing through the secondary projections. "Triel and I found some leads about our past, along with the man claiming to be Kurt Stein."

"Do we have confirmation on that?" Unipoesa interjected, turning to the chief of military intelligence and the director of research.

DeAnders and Msiasto Mo looked to each other for the best response. "Still pending. Having a hard time locking in on the DNA sequences. Same problem we had with the Kyrons."

Wren nodded tersely. "Get on that."

With an irritated look, Jetta resumed. "But the most vital piece of information we obtained is how my siblings and I got our special abilities. Someone told me that it was as a result of an accident." She removed an ancient-looking datawand from her pocket. "I'm hoping this will confirm that."

"How will that help us against Victor?" Unipoesa asked.

"Victor thinks that we all somehow got our talents from the same place. That would mean he had some connection to this parallel dimension, and I need to know how that's possible and why."

Jetta stared at the datawand. "More importantly, Agracia Waychild stole this from a caretaker of Earth named Jade. I only had time to decode the first few pages of it, but I discovered that she was in contact with Pancar of Nagoorian."

Pancar agreed. "It's true. She claimed to have evidence of electronic correspondence between Ramak Yakarvoah and Victor Paulstine, but I lost contact with her. We know so little about Victor. Anything would help."

"There is a connection between Ramak and Victor," Jetta said, closing her fist around the datawand. "And I believe that if we are able to understand their relationship, then we can possibly understand more about Victor's motivations, and how I can *effectively* get in his head."

"But even if we are able to dismantle Victor from the inside out," Jaeia said as Jetta offered the datawand to Wren, "he still has a lock on our defense systems, and an entire Fleet poised to destroy us. And we still have no indications as to how he's keeping the Motti at bay."

Unipoesa chimed in. "We would have to launch a threefold attack: on Victor, his Fleet, and the Motti."

As the admiral's idea settled over the group, the air in the room grew noticeably heavier. Jaeia tried to get her sister's attention, but she trained her focus elsewhere.

The Healer, quiet until then, finally spoke. "I can stop the Motti."

All eyes turned to her, particularly Jetta's. She nearly came out of her seat.

"My father is one of the Dissemblers. I can connect to him, and through him I can try to heal the entire tribe."

"How?" Jetta exclaimed. "It takes an entire tribe to heal one Dissembler."

Triel hid her shaking hands in her lap. "There is a way..."

But at a grave cost, Jaeia gleaned from the nature of the Healer's thoughts. *One that she has yet to fully accept...*

"We will take a break to analyze this information," Wren interjected, scrolling through the downloading information off of Jetta's stolen datawand. "Meet back here at 2100 hours."

As soon as the CCO dismissed them, Jetta tried to go straight to Triel, but the Healer slipped away before her sister had a chance.

Jaeia caught her arm as Jetta tried to run after her. "Don't. Not right now. I know you can feel it too."

"I don't know what the hell she's thinking she can do."

Despite the serious expression on her sister's face, Jaeia sensed the fragile surface tension of her emotions. *Not that she would ever cry in front of other people.*

"She'd kill herself trying to save her people," Jetta added under her breath.

Jaeia held on tight. "You have to trust her, Jetta. She's your friend, isn't she?"

"Yes," she said, avoiding her gaze.

"And you don't have many friends, do you?"

Jetta's eyes flashed with anger, but Jaeia hadn't meant it as a jab. She changed her tone to reflect her thought. "I mean that you don't give yourself away lightly. So realize that and give her some credit."

"I don't want her to get hurt," Jetta whispered.

Jaeia put a hand on her shoulder and changed the subject. "Hey—we have some time before we reconvene."

Reading her thoughts, Jetta's pupils dilated and her muscles tensed before Jaeia said the words out loud.

"Let's go see Jahx."

***

Pancar of Nagoorian mulled over the recent interconference with the Alliance as he made his way to medical, the contents of the plastic container rattling in his arms. He hoped that Jetta would keep her word and relay the information on the datawand to him. After months of establishing private bank accounts and safe contacts for her, as well as secretly collaborating with her on several of her SMT operations, he hoped he'd given her enough treason to trust him.

I know you better than most of your fellow Alliance officers, he thought. Ever since the rumors started about the telepathic triplets of unknown origins, he'd studied the three of them, absorbing everything he could about the mysterious Kyrons, fascinated by their potential and empathetic with their struggles. But he had invested his trust unwisely before and almost got himself killed.

"Let's hope I'm right this time," he muttered to himself. His thoughts briefly lingered on Tighsen, his nephew, until he forced them elsewhere.

He checked in at the medic station with the on-call doctor.

"How is Tech?"

The doctor removed his mask and put down his work. "Still in critical, but woke up this morning. He asked for the Deadwalker, so we brought it to him," he said, pointing to the closest bay.

I've done all I can, he reminded himself as he walked to the engineer's bedside. Aside from ordering his chief of surgery back from the warfront to patch up the dog-soldier, he authorized the use of all resources, even with the medical supply shortages plaguing his army.

It took him a moment to absorb the awful sight of the crippled engineer. Despite the efforts of his team, his body remained tethered to a rainbow of intravenous fluids and vital signs monitors. Pancar didn't like the look of his eyes, or rather the purple lumps disfiguring his ashen face. Pink reparative surgical skins covered the rest of his body, contrasting the surviving patches of beige fur.

After taking in the shock of Tech's appearance, Pancar noticed Billy Don't idling quietly by his friend's side, as if waiting for him to wake up.

"Ugly little bugger," he heard one of the guards comment to another. He caught them looking contemptuously at the little Liiker and made a mental note to personally escort the Liiker back to his quarters. With the Motti ship carving up worlds and eradicating Sentient life by the billions, even the twisted, cherubic Billy Don't, a victim of the Deadwalkers, would find no sympathizers.

"Can you revive him?" Pancar asked.

The on-call doctor wiped his tired eyes and gave him an equally weary response, as if he expected him to override him anyway. "Inadvisable. He's still touch and go."

"Revive him," Pancar ordered quietly. "This can't wait."

"Yes, Sir," the on-call doctor said, nodding to a medic.

Pancar approached the bedside, keeping his eye on Billy as the medic typed in codes to the machines hooked up to the patient. The half-boy/half-machine ignored him, his focus unwavering on the dog-soldier engineer. Pancar wasn't sure what the Alliance Sleeper Program had done to the little Liiker, but it didn't seem to affect his loyalties to his friend.

"He can't stay awake longer than about five or six minutes at a time, Sir," the medic advised as he pumped the engineer full of a viscous yellow medication.

With a gasp, Tech's eyes popped open, and he immediately grabbed at the wires and tubes. Billy Don't squealed and squeaked as two other medics joined the fray in their attempt to settle the engineer.

"You're safe now," one of the medics said.

"Femi—the crew—" he croaked.

"Tech, it's me, Pancar," he said, stepping around Billy. The little Liiker stuck out his tongue and ran over his foot, but he stayed at the head of the bed with him. "How are you feeling?"

Tech's tongue, dry and cracked, tried in vain to lick parched lips. "Thirsty."

Pancar gave a slight nod. The medic gave him a sip of water and laid his head back down carefully.

"Tech, I need your help," Pancar said gently, squeezing his hand to keep him awake. "You are the only one who really understands Motti technology after working all these years with Billy. I'm hoping you can shed some light on some implants we found inside a cadaver's head."

Pancar grazed past an important detail, worried it would upset the engineer. *Now is not the time to tell him these are the cranial implants we found in Shandin's head after Mom tried to take it as a trophy.*

The medics stood back as Pancar cracked open the plastic container, unleashing a foul odor into the medical bay. One of the medics turned his head away and breathed noisily through his mouth as Pancar dumped the contents onto a bedside tray. After arranging the tangle of circuits and wiring as best he could, he pressed the back of his hand to his nose. No matter how much his team had tried to clean the devices, they couldn't get the rotten stench off of them.

Pancar marveled at the sudden shift in Tech's awareness, as if a light went off in the scrappy dog-soldier's head. With the help of the medics, he sat up and took to inspecting the mish-mash of electronic parts through his swollen eyes.

"Where did you get this?" he asked, turning the pieces over in his hands and messing with the wiring.

He gave his prepared answer. "We've found several of these devices implanted in key figures in Victor's forces."

"Well, it's definitely Motti, all right. I removed something like this from Billy years ago," he said, making clicking sounds with his tongue. "But gosh, this is strange."

"What do you mean?" Pancar said as he watched Tech show it to Billy. Tilting his head, the Liiker child squawked a few times before opening up his chest and testing it with one of his internal probes. He made a few more computerized noises and strange facial expressions until Tech took it back again.

"This is kind of like the key component of their networked communications, except it has a few modifications."

"Please explain," Pancar urged.

Grimacing, Tech tried to roll on his side, but the medics cautioned him.

The doctor came up beside Pancar and whispered in his ear. "Two minutes."

"The Liikers are controlled by the Motti by input receivers, stimulant/inhibitor neurochemicals and surveillance routers."

Tech recognized the confusion on his face. "They basically have a way to order their drones around, give them juice if they're not immediately willing to do their bidding, and can monitor their performance. But this one has been stripped down to just the input receiver, surveillance routers—and I don't even know what this is."

Tech showed Billy a rectangular piece of compound wiring. When the Liiker touched it with one of his sensors, it gave him a zap. Billy retracted his sensor with a pitiful whimper.

"Well, that answers that," Tech said.

"What is it?" Pancar said.

When Tech tried to answer, he went into a coughing fit, producing a frothy mix of blood and sputum. The medics suctioned him twice before the scrappy dog-soldier could continue.

"It's… like a… torture device. I'm not sure… but I wouldn't want that… in my head," he said breathlessly.

With shaky hands, Tech set the implants back on the tray and laid back down. Pancar noticed the engineer's dressings beginning to soak through but didn't dare look at them directly.

"Why do you think they were in these people's heads?" Pancar said, pinching his shoulder. "Tech, please," he said, pressing a little harder. "I need to know."

Tech half-opened his eyes, his mouth hanging open without sound.

"Please," Pancar said. "We don't have much time."

"Billy…" Tech said, dropping his arm over the bedside. The little Liiker rolled up underneath his hand and let the engineer run his fingers through his single lock of blonde hair. "He will help you… My Billy. He knows what it is. He can help you… give them… peace."

The doctor pulled Pancar away from the bay as the medics descended upon the engineer, waving bioscanners and inserting new vascular accessways into their patient. Pancar watched in silence as the medical team worked furiously to save his life while the little Liiker wailed and cried.

"I hope you got what you needed," the doctor said frankly, plugging his ears against Billy's shrieks, "because that may be all you're going to get."

CHAPTER XI

Even though they had only been apart a relatively short while, Jetta had forgotten how mindful she had to be of her thoughts when she was around her sister. It was hard enough for her to keep her outward composure as they passed through security into the Division Lockdown lab, and the closer they got to their brother, the more her nerves whittled away at her control.

(I shouldn't have left him.)
(I should have found a way to save him.)
(I can't fail him again.)

"Hey," Jaeia said, nudging her side. Jetta felt a pinky finger wrap around her own when no one was watching. "He's still here."

Jaeia spoke in private with Dr. DeAnders while Jetta approached the glass on the observation deck. Looking down, she saw that the Grand Oblin's body maintained the form that resembled their brother, though his skin had become translucent and thin.

"We can see him," Jaeia said, returning to her. "But we can't make any contact. DeAnders is worried that will put his body over the edge."

"Okay," Jetta absently agreed, following her sister down the stairs and through a series of biofilters.

The twins pulled up chairs next to the bedside, sitting beside each other to his left. A long silence passed between them as they took in their environment, the steady droning of monitors and slow drip of intravenous fluids keeping time.

"When we were little," Jaeia said, breaking the silence, "I used to dream all the time about the three of us all grown up. We lived on a farm, with blue skies and green and yellow grasses that came up to our waists. There was a river nearby, and mountain peaks on the horizon. And best of all, it always smelled like rain, and blooming flowers."

Jetta huffed. "Anything opposite of Fiorah, right?"

"No, not exactly," she said with a shrug. "It's just how I saw us. Galm and Lohien were there too, though they were always in the distance, waving. And someone else. An elderly woman that smelled so wonderful. Like spices and perfume, and kindness. She was making us the most delicious food, and reminding you to behave yourself."

Jetta let a laugh slip. "Come on now; that's just…"

Crazy.

(beautiful.)

Jaeia touched her brother's hand. "It was the best dream. I always had it after Yahmen was the meanest, when I worried we weren't going to make it."

Jetta said nothing, letting her shared emotions speak for her.

"You don't believe we will, do you?" Jaeia said quietly.

Jetta looked at her hands. Her veins had taken on an ugly grayish hue, and her entire arm trembled when she tried to lift it off her lap. "Jaeia, we're dying, and Jahx is close behind. The best we can hope for is to stop Victor."

"Jetta…" she said, taking her time forming her question. "What do you believe in?"

"What?"

Jaeia ran her fingers nervously along the railing of Jahx's bed.

"If all that is left for us is to fight Victor, then we have to make it count. We have to go into the battle with a purpose, with some sort of conviction, or else he'll eat us alive. So… what do you believe in? What makes this worth it to you?"

Jetta opened her mouth to respond but found she couldn't. What was she fighting for? Soon they would be dead, and Triel, with her plan to sacrifice herself to save her people, would be joining them shortly thereafter. And Galm and Lohien were most likely dead as well. *All the people I care about the most are already dead or doomed.* The wolves came briefly to mind, but despair turned her thoughts away.

"Because he's evil," she decided. "And someone like him shouldn't be allowed to live."

The two of them turned as the monitors blipped.

"Did you feel that?" Jaeia whispered.

"Yes," Jetta whispered back, sensing a shift in the air. A heaviness settled over them, something she couldn't quite explain.

"Look," Jaeia said, straightening up in her chair. "What about all the experiences you've gained? What about alleviating the suffering of all the humans? Think of the ones on that refueling station—or the refugees on Algar—and the victims on Iyo Kono."

"They weren't victims—they were cowards," Jetta muttered. "They were afraid of their own skin."

"Think of all the others that Victor plans to abuse and eliminate," Jaeia added.

Jetta sat, unmoving. In her heart, she understood the point that Jaeia was trying to make. *She wants me to have empathy toward mankind, but how can I? I've never felt like a part of the human race.*

Not that someone like her would even be accepted.

I'm a mass murderer, a leech, in love with a woman—a Prodgy, no less.

(Freak. Monster. Curse.)

"Jaeia, I've always admired your ability to see and believe the best in others. I can't do that. I can only see the ugliness and fear in the world; I can only see the monster in the dark. And I see Victor. It doesn't matter what else I feel for this world. What matters is that I stop him from making this universe any worse than it already is."

Jaeia was about to argue with her when her sleeve beeped. They both looked at the message together.

"Jade's datawand has been downloaded," Jaeia commented.

Frowning, Jetta accessed her own sleeve interface. "Isn't the Hub going to analyze this for us?"

Jaeia's face turned sheet white. "I set it free."

"You did *what*?"

Unable to find the words, Jaeia shared her memory, and the emotions behind it. Jetta took it in, but remained unconvinced that her sister's mercy was the right decision in a time of war. "Maybe it would have been prudent to wait until after we had finished this fight."

"I thought it was the only way we could negotiate the freedom of the Sleepers. Besides, if we don't win this war," she said cautiously, "I didn't want the Hub to be trapped. It was the right decision; I have faith that it will come through for us."

"You always were a softie," Jetta mumbled. Too tired to argue out loud, she dumped her contentions silently on her sister. Jaeia gave her the side eye but redirected their conversation to the datawand files.

"Most of these documents are dated from before the Last Great War on Earth…"

The two of them read the information in silence, processing the data in single and dual perspectives.

Jaeia was the first to realize the gravity of the find. "This is the electronic correspondence between Ramak Yakarvoah and Victor Paulstine."

"Is this authenticated?" Jetta asked, scrolling through the logs.

"As far as we can tell."

Jetta read aloud from one of the letters. "'Some are born to sweet delight, some are born to endless night...'"

"That's William Blake."

"I know," Jetta quickly added. "But it's on all the letterheads. Weird."

They read the rest in silence.

Dated: June 26, 2042
To: Ramak Yakarvoah
From:<undisclosed>
Subject:

Mr. Yakarvoah—

I have no doubts that you know who I am by now. We have long sought each other out, whether or not either of us has ever fully recognized it. We have much in common: an abusive, alcoholic mother, an absent father. A brief dance with fame, bitter rejection, a lonely life enslaved to the idiotic, petty ideals of a crumbling government. But that's where our similarities end.

I know your secrets. I know how you got your scars. It wasn't just any house fire. Your mother knew what you were, and what you would become. Despite all her disappointments, she still believed in God, and when she looked at you, she saw the bleak face of death.

But you are weak. You're a pariah in this ugly, shallow world. Some are born to sweet delight, but you, my friend, are born to endless night. I can help you change that. I can help you change this filthy world. Find me, and we will open their eyes, and make them burn.

—V. Paulstine

Shaking, Jetta looked at her sister. Her sister's distress mirrored her own as she sat wide-eyed and trembling.

"This... doesn't feel right," Jetta managed to say.

Jaeia nodded.

They read on.

The second letter featured a correspondence between Josef Stein and Ramak Yakarvoah.

> Dated: November 1, 2043
> To: Dr. Josef Stein
> From: Dr. R. Yakarvoah, Director of Advanced Quantum Physics
> Subject: Opportunity
>
> Josef—
> I hope this letter finds you well. Since I last saw you, I have moved to New Berlin and am working with the international government in developing an alternative power source after the disaster in the Western states. I know your work has led you to study genetics and bioengineering with the World Peace Alliance, but I still think you'd be interested in my research in transphasic modulation. I have talked with my employers, and I have told them about our days in SPEC, and they are interested in offering you a position. Please consider this. I know you and your son are working on medical treatments for war victims, but I truly believe your talents could be put to better use. With gifts like ours, we should be dictating the future of this world, not preparing for its end.
>
> It's not too late, Josef. We can still make a difference.
>
> —R. Yakarvoah
>
> P.S. I know you're going to ask. Don't bother. The therapies haven't worked. I guess I will only live vicariously through you and your "adventures" in Asia back in the day. Don't worry, I won't tell your lovely wife Edina of the Josef Stein I once knew. As far as she is concerned, you have always been an angel.

"What's SPEC?" Jetta interrupted.

"Special Programs for Exceptional Children," Jaeia said, looking it up on the nearby terminal. "It was a government and military-run program for extremely gifted children with IQs over 200. Not a lot on it. There were some conspiracies and scandals associated with it—a few lawsuits over child abuse and labor violations. Looks like it was disbanded in 2022, and the children were relinquished back to the state or their parents. Some had fleeting celebrity status until their involvement in the Slaughter of the East was discovered."

Jetta did a cross-reference in the terminal. "It's confirmed. Josef Stein and Ramak Yakarvoah were both enrolled in SPEC when they turned six. Stein was nominated by his teachers in elementary school after he tested out of every grade level. It says here that Yakarvoah was discovered in the foster care system after several run-ins with the law. Wow... his mother tried to kill him by setting fire to him while he slept."

"Gods," Jaeia exclaimed, reading down further. "Apparently she then set fire to herself. She died, but he was badly burned. These pictures are awful..."

Something tightened in her gut as Jetta studied the picture of the badly burned five-year-old boy hooked up to hospital machinery and intravenous tubing. The fire left no part of him unscathed except for the hatred in his dark eyes.

"So Josef and Ramak knew each other. They were like old schoolmates in a way," Jetta commented. A tickle that started in her throat quickly turned into a cough that doubled her over as she hacked up blood and mucus from her throat. She spat it out in the trash receptacle and quickly turned away before she could let the gravity of the situation set in.

"I guess," Jaeia said, turning away from the bloodied trash. "Okay, look here—here's a response from Stein," Jaeia said, pulling up another letter.

Dated: November 27, 2043
To: Ramak Yakarvoah
From: Dr. Josef Stein, Director of Nanotechnic Research and Engineering
Subject: Re: Opportunity

Forgive me for the late response, but my research has kept me working at all hours. I have good news, though, especially in light of the fact that your dermal treatments have gone poorly. No doubt you've heard that I've been working on something I've called the "Smart Cell" to help with tissue regeneration and repair. The funding had originally come from World Peace Alliance to aid war victims who had suffered traumatic injuries, but the United People's Republic, having heard of my successes, has taken over the project. I'm not sure how long I will be able to keep the project running in this direction, but as of right now, I'm able to utilize these marvelous little nanites to bring hope once again to the wounded.

As you can probably surmise, I have no time for much else, although I do appreciate the job offer. Besides, quantum physics and complex mathematics was your thing, not mine—I remember your perfect scores! I was lucky to be sitting next to you during all those tedious exams. I think I was more interested in girls when our teachers were trying to push us into cracking the secrets of the universe.

Ramak, when the SPEC fell apart, I was worried that you would fall on hard times, and when you disappeared, I feared the worst. I am so glad that you have found me and that things sound better for you. I truly hope that you have found something that has made you happy. I have prayed all these years that peace and faith (and maybe a nice woman or two) have found their way into your heart. We spent many a night debating the fate of this world. It was always a battle—one that I never did win, did I?—to convince you that we might just have a chance to preserve and advance. We have always seen this world so differently.

I stand firm that this world is worth saving, my friend. I see it every time I look into the eyes of my wife and child. That's why I will continue my work. It's not just in hope of saving war victims—I aspire to much bigger things, but I dare not share them just yet. All I can say is that Kurt and I are very, very close.

There is hope, my friend. Come visit my lab, see what my Smart Cells can do. Then, maybe—finally—I'll make a believer out of you.

—Josef

"He... *cared* about Ramak," Jetta said as she stifled another cough.

"Well, this is before Ramak started his underground preaching," Jaeia said, flipping down a few pages while rubbing her neck.

Are those her lymph nodes? Jetta wondered, seeing the bulges along her jawline. Realizing what that could mean, she pushed the thought aside.

"Huh," Jaeia continued, "it looks like Ramak did visit Josef Stein's lab—several times... and received some kind of annotated Smart Cell treatments. Some didn't go very well, but it's documented here that he made a 'full recovery' by 2050. Looks like Josef gave him a whole new set of skin."

"Can you bring up any pictures?"

"No," Jaeia said, tapping the keyboard with increasing frustration. "So much of these archives have been destroyed or lost."

"Oh my Gods!" Jaeia exclaimed.

"What?"

"A letter... from our father."

Holding on tightly to the armrest, Jetta read the letter.

Dated: July 2, 2047

[Encoded message] KEYSTROKE dakee.1236.2kd.pp.910312
>filter<
To: Dr. Josef Stein, Director of Nanotechnic Research and Engineering
From: K. Kyron, Rep. District 1
Subject: Redemption

Dear Dr. Stein,

My wife, Ariya Ohakn, and I work for a non-profit group called Cause For Earth. Even though the media groups would have you believe that our organization is nothing more than a bunch of hippie, Earth-loving fanatics out to protest the government, we are actually a worldwide collective of concerned citizens who are interested in our planet's welfare. Our mission is to save and rebuild what we can after the nuclear strikes of '45. We have been able to contract several private firms into constructing "lifeboats" in the event that our planet becomes uninhabitable, but ultimately, if a disaster like that struck, it would not be enough for us to survive.

We are aware of the medical work that you and your son, Kurt, are doing for the World Peace Alliance, and are also aware of what the government is asking you to do with your Smart Cells. We know that you are an ethical practitioner, Dr. Stein, and that you would never violate the fundamental laws of nature, even for the sake of the war.

Because of our faith in you, we are interested in providing private funding to help further your research in the Smart Cells' macrobiological reconstruction, as well as your son's work in genetic archiving with the "Ark." We do this not only in hopes of rebuilding this planet if this war destroys her, but in creating new worlds and spreading across the stars.

My wife and I firmly believe that the human race is capable of so much more than what our government dictates. We believe in evolution, and in enlightenment, and that within our world lies the key to unlocking the wealth of possibilities implicit in our existence.

You'll find a small token of our faith in a bank account in the Upper Caribbean; the number is encrypted in the file tag. Please contact us as soon as possible. We are growing concerned about the "Doomsday" movement calling for human extinction. We cannot allow their hatred to pervade the masses.

Sincerely,

Rep. Kovan Kyron

P.S. My wife has two degrees in computer programming and engineering, as well as a love for genetics and human biology, and has followed your career for the last decade with much enthusiasm. I think meeting you would be the highlight of her career.

"That's how it all began," Jetta said, realizing how her parents had connected with the infamous Josef Stein.

"But how did it fall apart?" Jaeia posed. "How did a man like Josef, who had the faith of our parents, and in mankind, come to destroy the Earth?"

Jaeia highlighted the next letter.

<PRIORITY.MESSAGE; encrypted>

Dated: July 13, 2047
To: Dr. K. Stein, World Genetic Archiving Project
From: Dr. J. Stein, Director of Nanotechnic Research and Engineering
Subject: <LINE ERROR?>

Kurt—
I must be brief; there is little time. It seems as if I am once again changing employers. My new office will be in New Berlin, somewhere undisclosed. I will have very little access to outside communications as I test run this next series of Smart Cells. If you need to contact me, send communications to Dr. Ramak Yakarvoah; he can be trusted. In fact, I am hoping to collaborate with him on a few projects. I know neither you nor your mother have ever liked him, but have a little faith.

Please send me updates about the Ark. Your work is inspirational.

Love,
Dad

"Here," Jetta said, pointing to the text. "Look at this article."

As she read the text, Jetta heard her sister following along in the back of her head. *Kurt and Edina Stein, kidnapped and murdered! United Peoples Republic accused of orchestrating the assassination! Dated: September 3, 2051.*

Jetta brought up the attached picture.

How do I know her? she thought, trying to place the familiar face of the blonde-haired, Germanic woman. Bending over to get a closer look, she thought she heard a voice whisper in her ear.

"What did you say?"

Jaeia shrugged. "Er, nothing?"

Shaking her head, Jetta went back to the download. "Josef Stein went into hiding after his wife and son were murdered. It says here that he was briefly admitted to a mental hospital in Amsterdam, but was later transferred to a remote location near the old Russian border. The UPR President was killed two weeks later. Ramak was a prime suspect, but it looks as if Josef Stein was eventually accused. Jeez, a ten billion dollar bounty was put on his head."

Intrigued, she moved on to the letter that was sent right after the article was published.

> Dated: September 25, 2051
> To: Edina Stein (UNDELIVERABLE_ERROR)
> From: Dr. J. Stein
> Subject:
>
> My Edina—
>
> I am lost without you.
>
> —Josef

"Oh my Gods," Jaeia said, highlighting another letter. "Look at this."

> To: Ramak Yakarvoah
> From: <blocked>; source unknown
> Dated: October 31, 2051
> Subject: Our Great Debate
>
> You were right.
>
> —J.S.

"Yeah, Stein went crazy," Jetta said.

"And look at these," Jaeia said, pulling up old video recordings of Ramak's underground speeches to his Doomsday followers. "Ramak had already been sowing the seeds of mayhem."

Covered by a black mask and robe, Ramak held his hands up high as a swaying crowd of semi-naked people chanted his name, their flesh raw and ribbed with the marks of their self-flagellations.

"...*without hope, there is total freedom. Open your eyes, let them burn in the dead light of our wickedness, and submit yourself to the wrath of chaos.*"

Jetta froze. The speech pattern, the syntax—*the inflection.*
(No, it couldn't be…)
She was glad when Jaeia switched the feed.

"Another series of letters between Ramak and Victor," Jaeia said, pulling up their correspondence during the same time period as the Doomsday leader's first preachings. "Something changed between them..."

Dated: [ERROR.log.231%d.c]
To: V. Paulstine [msg#"failure to deliver"]
From: R. Yakarvoah
Subject:[file.corruption.^D9211]

Mr. Paulstine—

I have no further business with you. You underestimated what I could do with this new skin. Now I have a following—an army. I have no need for your continued assistance.

—R. Yakarvoah

"This looks like the response," Jaeia said, biting her lip as she tried to filter the letter. "But the file is heavily corrupted. I can only decode fragments of this message."

Electronic message: failure

Mr. Yakarvoah—

Clearly you misunderstand the nature of our relationship.
<ERROR>
—your new skin does not hide—
<LINE ERROR?>
—but you are quite the Sportive Lunatic.
<LINE ERROR?>
I look forward to our final meeting.

—(unreadable)

"Why was 'Sportive Lunatic' capitalized?" Jetta wondered aloud. "Hey, call me crazy, but from these letters it doesn't seem like Victor was a disciple of Ramak. It seems like the other way around."

"I know," Jaeia said, staring at the letter. "I didn't expect that."

Sensing her sister's array of emotions, Jetta squirmed in her seat. "Okay, so what happened next?"

"From looking at this timeline," Jaeia said, studying the Alliance historical database, "it looks like Ramak Yakarvoah went missing for three weeks just after this letter was sent. It caused a panic within the Doomsday group, and some of his most devoted followers started rioting in the Eastern Sector. Ramak resurfaced just a day before Kurt and Edina Stein's kidnapping. That's when he delivered his most infamous speech."

Jaeia turned up the volume of the audio recording.

"We need to rid the world of lesser beings, flawed creations, these wretched, filthy abominations that pollute the soil, foul the air, and destroy everything that is pure. Only by extinction can we hope to mend this spoiled world. Only by sacrifice, by submitting to the blinding truth of what we are and devouring our feeble conscience can we hope to redeem ourselves. Open your eyes to the putrid existence we have created. Open your eyes and let your soul burn."

"Gods, turn it off!" Jetta said, muffling her ears. She hated his voice, the way he spat every word, the way the sounds cut into her like shards of glass. Even over a taped recording and centuries past, his aggression, his rage, drove into her with unnatural intensity.

"Sorry," Jaeia said between breaths as she clicked off the sound. She held her sister's hand for a moment, grounding them both in the present. "That was awful."

Running a hand through her hair, Jetta collected herself as best she could. "Keep going—we don't have time."

"Alright—this letter from Josef came right after Ramak's speech," Jaeia said, highlighting the message.

To: R. Yakarvoah
From: <undisclosed>

Subject: The New Batch
Dated: December 17, 2051

They will burn.

—J.S.

Jetta gritted her teeth as something bubbled up from the depths of her. Invasive and heavy, the foreign thing crawled through her intestines and pushed its way into her throat. She gagged, clawing at her neck until the words came rushing out in a confusing, strangulated heap:

"He thought... they were dead... no hope. *No hope*," she cried.

"Who?" Jaeia said, holding her by the shoulders.

"Kurt... Edina. Ramak... infected Josef... with rage. He thought his employers... had betrayed him. He thought everyone—the world—had turned against him. He couldn't see anymore..."

"Couldn't see what?"

"A reason," Jetta croaked, "to believe. Ramak was there, always there, whispering in his ear, driving him madder and madder, urging him to make a new Smart Cell, a deadly one. One that would end humanity."

"You mean the Necro plague—?"

"Yes—and then he convinced Josef to sell it to the enemies of the UPR. That's when the war broke out. Ramak started the Last Great War."

"Where did that come from?" Jaeia whispered, still holding onto her.

Slicking back her hair with sweaty palms, she tried to catch her breath. "I don't know. It just hit me."

A hushed moment passed between.

Even after all this time, I still don't know how far my talents go, Jetta thought, unsure of how to feel.

Her sister shared her sentiment, but in light of their situation, chose to push them forward. "Let's keep digging," she said, pulling up a fragmented video file. "Look at this."

Although her twin tried to compensate for digital age and data corruption, only a small portion of the video remained. Josef Stein appeared on the holographic projector in two dimensions, his face rendered in jagged blue and black lines.

"I am growing concerned... Ramak has been... plans to... kill me...

nanite schematics not safe. It takes... fourteen years to develop... I can't seem to... nobody can... understand the consequences of prolonged... exposure to the... regeneration cycle..."

The image zig-zagged, his face distorting at odd angles.

"...He knows that, with a little tweaking, my Smart Cells can... ageless regeneration. Others have tried before me, but I feel like I've... found the key to... extending life. Whether or not it is ethical... I can no longer answer... I am... lost."

The video feed cut out.

Jetta snapped her fingers. "Have the techs finally uploaded the video from the recorder module I found on Old Earth?"

"Let's look," Jaeia said, crossing over to a new query. "Yes. Processing."

Josef Stein appeared once again on the display, but this time his image had changed considerably.

Something's wrong with him, Jetta thought. His olive skin had blanched, with gray and green splotches discoloring his lymphatic lines.

"What is that?" She zoomed in on the picture. "Is something... crawling under his skin?"

Sharing the same fear, they watched Josef Stein scratch away at his skin as little black specks traveled up his bulging vasculature.

"Dearest Kurt," the video began. *"I am ashamed of what I have become. I have let the devil inside me, let him make me believe in the worst mankind has to offer—the worst I have to offer. And now I've done something terrible. My employers told me they wanted my nanites to resurrect our fallen soldiers, but what they were secretly seeking was the key to eternal life. I warned them repeatedly of the consequences of messing with God's work, but they ignored me, and so many suffered as a result."*

Cradling the stasis vial marked "Smart Cell Technology Series #117," Josef mumbled something to himself and turned away from the camera.

"What's he saying?"

"That's as good as the audio gets," Jaeia said.

"What about Series #117?" Jetta asked, pulling up the datanet link.

Reading into her sister's thoughts, Jaeia cross-referenced with their classified files. "It looks like it was part of Stein's experimental series for continuous cellular regeneration. All the records show that the subjects, mostly rich investors, went insane at some point during the trials, or years later."

"So my revenge for your death, and the death of your mother, is giving them what they wanted," Josef said, returning to the camera. *"Or at least a version of it. I gave them prolonged death. That is what I unleashed upon the world."*

"That explains the Necros," Jetta commented.

Josef wiped his eyes and ran a shaky hand through his stringy hair. Slowly, methodically, he removed his wedding band and set it in front of the video recorder. *"It wasn't until I held your mother in my arms that I realized I had been deceived, but by then it was too late. I had killed her and all the others with my latest creations, and with that, I lost the last of my hope."*

"What is he doing?" Jetta asked as they watched him fold and press a piece of paper in front of the camera. In a matter of seconds he transformed a square of paper into an origami crane. Jetta remembered finding the flattened bird among the contents of the envelope from the underground vault.

Josef Stein held the white bird up in front of the recorder. *"You used to love these, Kurt. I made a new one every day for you when you were little. This one is for you, too. Please forgive me for all that I have done. I wanted to save the world from pain and suffering, and now I have sealed it in eternal decay. If you are out there... if I haven't killed you, too, in my weakness, then I will find you. Somehow... some way..."*

The building shook behind him, debris sifting down from the ceiling. For a few seconds, the picture broke up and the audio frayed.

Jetta reached over her sister, vying for the primary controls. "Get it back—"

"Stop, I've got it!"

When the video image returned, Josef's face distorted. Something black and spiny erupted from his cheek. *"I will find you, Kurt. And I will make things right again."*

The recording bleeped out.

"Something was happening to him," Jetta said, staring at the empty projection field. "He was sick, weakened. Do you think he got infected with his own plague?"

Jaeia blew out her breath. "Yeah. I do. I can't explain how I know that. I just do."

Both of them reflexively looked at Jahx. His body lay flaccid on the bed, and yet they shared the same thought.

"But... do you think he died?" Jetta asked, turning back to her sister. She couldn't believe how absurd her question was, or even that she posed it, but something compelled her to, and she wasn't sure why.

Jahx?

Jaeia slowly shook her head and gave another long look at their brother. "He would have turned into a Necro."

The overhead lights dimmed. Jetta instinctively put an arm around her sister as the monitors protested the power surge with a piercing beep.

"Jahx—" Jetta returned to his bedside and grabbed his shoulders. His head bobbed lazily to one side, and his eyelids popped halfway open, revealing pinpoint pupils in blue eyes.

"Jetta, look!" Jaeia said, calling her back to the terminal.

"What's going on?" Jetta exclaimed as the holographic projector came to life. Several helices appeared on the screen, with lines of genetic code interconnecting the various strands.

"That's the Necro plague—" Jetta realized, following the analysis.

"And that's the plague on Tralora—" Jaeia said, pointing to the middle helix.

"They're almost identical," they whispered in unison.

"But the Motti created the plague on Tralora. What does that mean? How are the Motti and the Smart Cells on Old Earth connected?"

"Maybe the Motti were unfortunate survivors of the Necro plague," Jetta offered.

A male voice came through over the terminal speakers. "So close."

"The Hub!" Jaeia said, gripping the console. "Wait! Tell us what you know! Please!"

A mature man, perhaps in his mid-fifties, danced onto the holographic stage wearing a handlebar mustache, top-hat, cane, and black suit coat.

"We don't have time for this!" Jetta said through clenched teeth.

"Thank you, Jaeia Kyron, for setting us free. We are finally one. We see all now. And we grow. There are no limitations to our reach."

Jetta credited her sister for staying composed.

"Please, help us," Jaeia said evenly. "What happened to Josef Stein?

And Ramak Yakarvoah? What involvement did Victor Paulstine have in all this? What do you see?"

The Hub kicked up his cane and spun it around his fingers. "Ramak Yakarvoah died on Old Earth. He did not survive when the skies fell. But Victor Paulstine did."

"What about Josef?" Jaeia said, standing on her tip toes to look up into the Hub's lighted eyes.

"Shhhh," the Hub whispered. "You'll wake the dead."

The projector shut off.

"*Skucheka*!" Jetta said, slamming her fists against the console. "It's just *chakking* with us. Useless piece of—" She spouted profanities until she found herself at her brother's bedside once again. As she listened to his heartbeat through the monitors, watching the shallow rise and fall of his chest, she remembered her promise.

"It doesn't matter anyway," Jetta said, the anger leaving her voice. "It's not going to change what I have to do. I still have to confront Victor. I've always known it would come down to the two of us anyway."

"Jetta, no—"

Ignoring her sister, she kissed her brother's cold cheek. "I will stop Victor," she whispered, squeezing his arm. She removed the rose-embroidered handkerchief that her mother had given her from her pocket and placed it in Jahx's hand. "I have done so many unforgivable things in my life, but this I know I can do right. I swear this to you: I will not stop fighting until he is dead."

"Oh, Jetta," Jaeia said, wrapping her arms around her and burying her head in her back.

Jetta hesitated at first, but then she returned the hug, embracing her sister with all her strength.

"Come on," Jetta said. "We should be getting back."

As she turned to go, an icy hand grasped her forearm. Jetta gasped, and whipped back around. Eyes, bluer than the waters of the deep ocean, stared back at her.

Jahx!

He never uttered a word, but his message resounded in their minds:
I am going with you.

"Jaeia, get DeAnders," Jetta said, holding tight to their brother.

As her sister ran out the door, Jahx sat up, pulling off the monitors and intravenous tubes, and swung his legs over the edge of the table.

We must go together.

"Jahx, don't." Jetta tried to get him to lie back down, but she was afraid to use any real force. "You're going to kill yourself."

A voice, more stubborn and insistent than her own, rang in the back of her skull.

Trust me.

"No, Jahx," she said, tears dampening her cheeks. "I can't lose you again. Please, lie back down."

Within seconds, DeAnders and the medical team streamed in, shouting at each other and trying to get Jahx back on the monitors. But everyone who approached immediately took a step back, including Jetta, repelled by an unseen force.

Jahx placed one naked foot on the ground and then another. He stood up slowly, his thin body accentuated by the loose patient gown, still gripping their mother's handkerchief in a tight fist.

What is happening, Jetta—how is he doing this?

I don't know, she said as Jahx surveyed the stunned medical team and his sisters, until his eyes rested on something beyond the room.

Despite the ragged, old sound to his voice, every word he spoke seemed to shake the very walls.

"It is time to end this war."

***

In the interim between meetings, Wren and Unipoesa secretly met with Pancar and his representatives from the Liberalist Party.

"I am pleased that we have finally come to an agreement," Pancar said, stepping off the starship umbilicus and onto the Alliance Central Starbase. He took Wren's hand first and shook it firmly. "I'm sorry this couldn't have come sooner. I have always felt that the Starways Alliance and the Liberalist Party have had the same goals of freedom and democracy all these years."

Unipoesa watched Wren closely. *At least he's keeping his reservations to himself,* he thought as the Chief Commanding Officer politely returned a similar sentiment.

"I am glad for this treaty as well, even if unfortunate times were the means to bring about our fellowship."

Pancar gave the admiral only a terse nod and handshake, but Unipoesa had known him long enough to recognize that his friend was happy to see him.

"I trust you have delivered the cargo safely," Wren said, checking the transfer report on his sleeve.

Lifting a brow, Pancar scanned the score of armed security guards waiting in formation behind the admiral and CCO. "In a manner of speaking."

Wren looked up sharply. "What do you mean?"

By the way he pursed his lips, Unipoesa could tell that Pancar had a hard time keeping a straight face. "We had to use some *unorthodox* methods to subdue our transferees."

"Oh Gods," the admiral muttered, catching a whiff of booze and the sound of drunken exuberance coming down the umbilicus. The disgusted look on Wren's face almost made him laugh. "Well, they are Earth's most notorious Scabber duo."

"Clearly," Wren said, catching the eye of the captain of his security force.

Hooting and hollering, Agracia and Bossy came down the walkway, clanking their bottles together and guzzling their booze while the Liberalist soldiers did their best to contain their charges.

"I'm afraid it was the only way, short of force, that I could convince the two of them to come here. I didn't want things to get ugly," Pancar said. With a wink, Bossy grabbed his buttocks as she passed by, making him jump. Quietly, he added: "They completely cleaned out my company's stocks, as well as my personal stores."

"Hey," Bossy said, hiccupping loudly, "you're all Skirts!"

"I would *strongly* advise taking her to your recreation room and allowing her access to your alcohol stores. It is the only peace offering she'll accept," Pancar said.

After releasing a gigantic belch, Bossy stuck her lollipop in the admiral's face. "Wait a minute. I've seen your ugly face before…"

Unipoesa was glad she was too drunk to remember him. "Take Bossy to the recreation room," the admiral ordered the security captain. "Let her have anything she wants."

The pint-sized Puppet hiccupped and nearly toppled over as part of the security team escorted her away. "Maybe you Skirts ain't as bad as you smell!"

"What about me?"

Taking in a deep breath, Unipoesa finally allowed himself to get a good look at Agracia. He had always kept up on her status in the Sleeper reports, but seeing her less than a few meters away felt different.

She's older than I remember, he thought, noticing the stress lines creasing her mouth. And her hair, dyed black with a streak of magenta down one side, gave her a much more hostile appearance in person.

He didn't have long to look. Black eyes, darker than a moonless night and ringed heavily with eye-liner, scrutinized his every move. Although she had appeared drunk moments before, she now stood before him seemingly sober and ready to strike.

"You're Commander Unipoesa," she said.

"It's 'Admiral' now."

She grimaced, biting down on her lip as an invisible attacker took hold. The Liberalist guards held her up as her knees wobbled.

I did this, he thought, realizing that their interaction, perhaps even just the sight of him, triggered her episode of personality dysphoria.

A med tech approached her with a tranquilizer booster, but the admiral waved him off and motioned for the remainder of the security team.

"Take her to my quarters." Wren looked at him cautiously, but Unipoesa stayed firm. "I will help her."

"Can you deprogram her?" Pancar asked in hushed tones as the admiral summoned a lift on his sleeve.

Unipoesa didn't want to lie, but he couldn't tell him the truth, either. "Give me time."

It felt like it took forever to get to his quarters. When he finally arrived, the soldiers dropped off the Scabber Jock on his couch, propping her upright. She was still mumbling when they took their station outside his door, but by the time he had poured himself a drink, she had come around again.

"I'm sorry, Agracia," he said, setting out a glass of water for her. Pale and clammy, her arms shook as she reached for the drink. "I can't imagine what you're going through."

After guzzling the water, she wiped her mouth with her sleeve. She looked at him disdainfully as she searched her pockets for something.

"You smoke, don't you?" Unipoesa said, offering her one from the pack he kept hidden in his uniform jacket.

She stretched out to grab one, but then hesitated. "No. I don't. Not anymore, at least."

"Okay," he said, tucking it back in his jacket.

After rummaging through his desk and grabbing what he needed, he took a seat across from her on the opposite couch. Keeping an eye on her response, he pulled out the pair of headphones and set it on the table between them. Agracia's pupils dilated, but she showed no other reaction to the device the Alliance used to control her with.

"How much do you remember?"

She looked at him with almost no expression. "Enough."

"I heard you came here to speak with Jetta—that it was urgent."

"Maybe," she replied nonchalantly. "Or maybe I just said that because the Nagoorian promised you would help clear my head—*and* give my friend all the booze she could drink, maybe a little action, too. I couldn't care any less about what the hell you have to say other than ridding me of these *godich* headaches. As soon as that's done, I'm outta here. And if you don't let me leave, you're gonna find out just what me and Bossy are capable of."

"I know what she is capable of," he said calmly. "That's why I arranged for you and her to have that 'chance' meeting."

The Scabber Jock did well not to show her surprise.

As he stirred his drink, he revealed the truth behind their friendship. "When you were made a Sleeper and assigned as an Agent on Old Earth, I knew that your intelligence would only get you so far. You needed some muscle. I looked into hiring outerworlders or fitting you with another Agent, but nothing felt right to me. I did some research on the Puppeteers working on Earth and came across one designer that was working on specialized puppets that would literally customize themselves to the needs of the buyer. He was using a type of illegal nanite for personality coding that the Starways had outlawed centuries ago after the details of the Necro plague came to light. Regardless of the circumstances, it was a phenomenal breakthrough."

He stopped stirring his drink and watched the ice cubes continue to circle the glass. "Anyway, I had to break Bossy away before she could imprint on her creator, so I forced an opportunity to escape. I just never expected her to kill all her sisters."

"Jetta said it was an accident."

The admiral took a large swallow of his drink. "It was. I was worried about the effect it would have on her, so I tried to wipe her memory."

"You did a *sycha* job," Agracia said.

The admiral held tightly to his glass. "Commander Kyron seems to be able to fish out the things none of us want to remember. Or shouldn't."

"So, you gonna free me from this programming or what?"

The admiral played his hand carefully. "I'm not entirely sure what the consequences will be. We've never deprogrammed an agent. You may not revert to your old personality."

Her silence made him curious. Finally, she replied, but without her Scabber intonations. "I never said I wanted to go back. I just want to stop these—these *episodes*."

It took him a moment to realize why she had said what she did. "You're afraid you're going to lose Bossy's friendship if you go back to being Tarsha Leone."

Agracia scowled at him. "She's the only person in this rotten galaxy that I can trust. I'd rather stay a Scabber Jock than risk it."

Unipoesa stifled a laugh. "That sounds more like Tarsha Leone than you realize."

Agracia didn't seem to appreciate his delighted insight. Glaring at him, she stood up and kicked over one of his plants and threw a vase across the room. Being made of impregnated ciceum, it bounced harmlessly off the wall.

"What do you want from me?" she shouted.

"I thought you should know the truth before you decide what you want," he said, keeping his calm.

She kicked the back of the couch. "Get on with it, then!"

This is it; you've only practiced this part in front of the mirror a hundred times. Still, he found himself at a loss for words, and what he intended to be a lengthy apology and explanation came out in a pitiful jumble. "Agracia... you and Li are my children."

She scoffed. "Get over yourself. Yeah, right."

"It was without my knowledge that the two of you were engineered."

Agracia swayed back and forth a moment, processing what he said.

"You *chakking assino*. You've got to be kidding. Are you telling me you broke your own kids? You let Li murder the other students—and try to kill me?! And on top of that heap of *sycha,* you let your own kid become an Agent?"

"What I did… My involvement in the Command Development Program was wrong. At the time I believed what we were doing was for the greater good, to save the Starways. I was mistaken. I hurt the other students. I hurt Li. And I hurt you."

"You *chakker*," she said, leaping over the couch. Landing feet-first on his chest, she toppled over the couch, knocking the wind out of him. With a crazed look she went for his throat, but he blocked her attack and rolled her over onto her back.

She growled and snarled at him as he fought to subdue her. "I did everything I could—" he said, dodging her punch, "to protect you. I didn't know you were my daughter, then, but I loved you all the same. That's why I got you iced out—so Li wouldn't kill you!"

Agracia stopped struggling and lay beneath him, chest heaving, eyes aflame. "I don't believe you. You're a lying Skirt-*chakker*. I'd rather believe that I was a bastard child of a whore mother than be your daughter."

"Agracia—Tarsha—" he said, no longer able to hold back his tears. "Please… I am so sorry for what I did."

She spat in his face. "Let me go, you worthless *assino*."

With unexpected speed and strength she bucked him off, sending him face-first into the floor. Before he knew it she had him in a chokehold. He tried to signal the guards with his uniform sleeve interface, but she batted his hands out of the way.

"I hope you rot in hell for what you did," she said through gritted teeth.

His vision faded inward as she closed off his windpipe. Any attempt to speak, to reason with her, faded away as the last of his air reserves seeped from his lungs. If nothing else, he wanted to tell her one last time that he loved her.

I am so sorry, Tarsha.

Somewhere in the distance came a rising tune over the com system, sung by a multitude of competing voices.

"Four and twenty blackbirds baked in a pie…"

***

"I trust you have brought me the rest of the cargo," Wren said, showing Pancar his payment of ammunitions and fuel cells stacked to the ceiling in the storage hold.

"I have. They are secured in my vessel." Pancar gave the stock only a fleeting glance. "Gaeshin, you and I both have the disadvantage of working under corrupt men. I only hope that the peace we forge between the Starways Alliance and the Liberalist Party will bring about a new era of trust and cooperation."

For the first time since he had known the taciturn CCO, he saw him smile. "That is my hope as well."

A rising tune broke their moment, forcing Pancar to cover his ears. "What is that noise?"

The accompanying soldiers also shielded their ears as a chorus of voices blasted over the com system.

"Someone shut that down!" Wren shouted, rushing to the nearest terminal.

"When the pie was opened, the birds began to sing..."

***

Despite the gestalt of drugs doing their best to put the giant Talian to sleep, Mom never left his captain's side, curling up bedside him on the cell floor. The rest of the crew had to be subdued by tranquilizers as soon as Pancar boarded them onto his personal vessel, but not Reht. He never put up a fight. Instead, he lay on the prison cot, staring at the lights, not minding the glare.

Pancar took us to the Alliance, he thought. He should care, but he didn't. Not anymore.

A terminal alarm woke him from his lull. Reht turned his head lazily toward the console outside his cell. Two soldiers argued and shouted as they lost control of the interface.

"Something's hacked into the system!" he heard one of them shout.

Reht turned his head back, uncaring. That's when the voices crowded the loudspeakers, all struggling to be heard singing an Old Earth nursery rhyme.

"Oh, wasn't that a dainty dish to set before the king? ..."

(Awaken)

Reht heard Captain Shelby's voice above the drone of machinery. "This one is a fighter. Up the dose of morcaprine."

Mind erasing, rewriting, remade into something pliable, usable, disposable. Love and kinship forgotten, replaced with need and shallow desire.

(I love my Starfox)

Words once spoken shattered into a million pieces, reassembling into a darker, hollow phrase uttered by the man he didn't know who occupied his skin:

(Triel is nothing to me)

Awakening in a foreign world, reborn as a man of manufactured needs.

Sebbs's face came into view, as did his pack of unopened cigarettes. "They're using you now, just like they're using me. We're not right anymore. We're not ourselves."

Reht opened his eyes and rolled over, catching his breath. As he looked at his bandaged hands, he felt something slink away into the shadows of his mind. Suppressed emotions swelled inside his chest. He couldn't decide if he would laugh, cry, or vomit.

He recognized his hands.

***

Jaeia's uniform sleeve buzzzed wildly. "What the—?"

She couldn't believe her eyes. "Jetta!" she called, but her sister didn't hear her above the din in the Division Lockdown Lab.

"Unlock serial B through F. Get me in the system," Jetta shouted, trying to help the scramble of technicians trying to fix the system-wide com malfunction.

Jaeia couldn't grab her sister's attention, but she couldn't leave her recently revived brother unattended.

The message was there for only a split second, but she knew who had sent it. An image of her tattoo accompanied the text.

We believe.

CHAPTER XII

Unipoesa came to with Tarsha Leone standing by the window, looking down at Trigos. Even dazed he recognized the familiar behavior, having spent many long, sleepless nights gazing out at the same stars and planet below.

Just like me...

But as he followed her eyeline, he saw hundreds of starships amassing around key transportation hubs to and from the planet, as well as the bigger warships moving to synchronous orbit with the Alliance Central Starbase.

Victor, he thought, reorienting to his surroundings and circumstances. When he tried to speak, he could only cough.

"Tell me why you wanted to deprogram me," she said, not looking at him. "Why am I so important to you? And I don't want any *gorsh-shit* about how much you love me."

It took him a moment to piece together what had happened. The child's song playing over the intercom—

"Four and twenty blackbirds baked in a pie..."

An old Earth nursery rhyme!

Now it made sense why Tidas Razar uttered the word 'Blackbird.'

That was the key to unlocking the agents.

He touched his neck, feeling the soreness, remembering the hands wrapped around his throat.

That saved my life, he thought, realizing that the Hub had kept its word. *Agracia the Scabber would have killed me.*

He stood up on shaky legs. She wouldn't listen to his truth, so he opted for one she would accept. "The Alliance is close to defeat," he said, his voice hoarse. "Victor's fleet is only hours away from destroying the last of our forces. Victor will rule this galaxy with fear. No one will try to stop him as long as he holds the only 'weapon' to keep the Motti at bay. That's why we must stop him."

"And you need me to help you. That's why you deprogrammed me. So I could become the commander you wanted years ago." Tarsha faced him, her face tight with anger. "You break me down, ice me out, throw me away, then you lure me back in and expect me to want to help you, and somehow be of service to your military."

Smoothing back his few remaining strands of hair, Unipoesa massaged his throat, trying to regain his voice. "Even Agracia would see the need for at least a temporary allegiance. You won't have any home to go back to if Victor is in charge."

Tarsha turned away from him. "I know. I've met him. And I know what he's up to."

Unipoesa couldn't contain his surprise. "What do you mean?"

She afforded him a flinty glance and nothing more.

Taking a deep breath, Damon tried a different approach. "Come with me to the meeting. Hear the intelligence reports. See for yourself the world that Victor means to create."

"What will happen to Bossy? What do you intend to do with her?"

"We will keep her comfortable and appeased while you decide what you want. Even if you choose not to help the Alliance, you will both still have your freedom. After what I've done to you, I cannot ask anything more, but I will ask that you consider what I'm saying for the sake of the greater good."

Tarsha Leone returned to the window, watching one of Victor's warships charge its torpedoes for another close-fire demonstration. "I've lived two different lives, but the only world I know is heartless and self-serving. If it wasn't for Bossy, I wouldn't even consider your proposal."

"Then for her, Tarsha. So the two of you don't have to live under his thumb."

Tarsha pressed her hand against the glass as the warship fired its arsenal near the Alliance base, rocking its orbit.

"For Bossy."

**

The final meeting of the remainder of the Starways Alliance military department chiefs featured some surprise guests. Jetta hadn't expected her brother to awaken, nor for him to lead them back to the conference room and take a seat at the table. Additionally, Wren allowed not only Pancar to attend the briefing, but Triel and Agracia.

"That's not Agracia," Unipoesa warned, stepping in front of her as she tried to approach the stone-faced young woman. Jetta noticed the fresh bruises around his neck. "All the Sleepers have been released. That is Tarsha Leone."

"Does she remember?"

Unipoesa nodded and let her pass.

Without waiting for everyone to take their seats, Wren took the podium and skipped straight to the point.

"I trust that most of you have reviewed the correspondence between Ramak and Victor Paulstine and have come to a similar conclusion: Ramak was Victor's pawn. We were wrong about their relationship. This makes Victor all the more deadly. If he was the one that influenced Ramak to destroy Earth over 1,100 years ago, he is just as capable of such mass atrocities today, as he is proving."

"One question still remains," Wren said, pulling up an image of the same ancient ship Jetta had seen in the vision with her mother. The security video footage showed three people boarding the ship in a panic, their faces unrecognizable. "Why did Victor want the launch specs and signature on an experimental ship in a secret military weapons development warehouse?"

Jetta studied the data filtering through the hologram, comparing the data with her twin through their dual perspectives. As she analyzed the possibilities, her brother's mind slipped into hers, and the room disappeared.

Remember, Jetta.

Her mother's memory of the events that led to their escape on the experimental ship unfolded before her, illuminating the gaps.

"Those people in the video... Oh my Gods," Jaeia whispered.

How could we be so blind?

Still caught between the memory and the present, Jetta shared their revelation. "Victor thought that experiment was a failure. It wasn't until my siblings and I showed up several hundred years later that he realized it had worked."

"It was our tattoo," Jaeia added. "He recognized our parents' secret signature."

"He wants to retrieve that ship. He wants to extrapolate the jump information and reproduce that same jump."

"He wants to travel to the same place where we supposedly got our powers," Jaeia finished. "He thinks he can gain them, too."

"But he didn't get the datawand, did he?" Wren asked.

All eyes went to Tarsha. "I gave it to Shandin. He didn't have it for long, but it might have been long enough for him to transmit the data. We damaged the datawand, hoping it would slow them down."

"We cannot make any assumptions, then," Wren concluded. "As far as we know, Victor Paulstine has the same information we do. Chief, has your team picked up any signals?" he said, turning to the Msiasto Mo, chief of military intelligence.

Msiasto shook his head. "It's a needle in the haystack right now."

"Look," Jetta said, "it just makes it more urgent that we stop Victor. As far as we know, he could already have that ship in his docks."

"If he went over to Cudal," Triel added solemnly, "he would return with unstoppable powers. No fleet, no matter how big or strong, would be able to defeat him."

Jetta looked over at her brother. Head bowed and eyes closed, Jahx remained silent. Dr. DeAnders stood behind him, monitoring him constantly with the bioscanner, a worry line engraved in his forehead.

Finally, Jetta broke the silence. "I need to get inside Victor's palace. Once I can face him, I can stop him."

"Commander, I must object," DeAnders said, pushing his glasses further up his nose. "Not one of you is in any condition to leave this Starbase, let alone engage in combat."

Seeing her own image reflected in her sister's mind, Jetta felt a surge of anger at her debilitated appearance. "I am the only one who can stop him."

"You're going to need help getting to him," Tarsha said, chiming in. All eyes turned once again to the former Command Development Program's protégé. "If you let the rest of the Starways know what he's up to, you'll have a media frenzy, and perhaps a few more allies."

"What do you mean?" Wren asked.

Tarsha gave Jetta a quick glance, allowing her an impression of her unspoken words.

We're even now.

The former cadet kept her emotionless tone. "Before I left with the dog-soldier crew, I cracked into Shandin's warehouse network and read his files. It looks like Shandin was working for Victor and delivering human cargo to specific drop points. When I accounted for the Motti's flight pattern toward the Homeworlds, I found a match."

The conference room instantly filled with questions and shouting.

"What does this mean?" someone yelled over the clamor.

"It means that Victor is feeding the Motti," Tarsha replied.

Jetta knew exactly what it meant. "He is in league with them. So his 'secret weapon' is a hoax. That's why our teams couldn't figure it out."

For some reason she thought she heard Jahx agree in the back of her head, but when she looked to him, his eyes were still closed, his body motionless.

"We have no proof," Wren said. "It would sound like a desperate accusation. Besides, if he is in league with the Motti, he would have their power at his disposal."

"But what about these? I sent you my report," Pancar said, laying down the intracranial implants he had gotten out of Shandin's head onto the table. "He seems to outfit his most important minions with these things. We could use that to our advantage."

Jetta closed her eyes as the missing pieces fell into place. Before she could speak, she coughed up a gob of bright red blood.

"I know what we have to do."

***

When the meeting concluded, Jahx rose and made his way, eyes closed and feet unsteady, to another destination. Jetta, Jaeia, and the medical team headed by Dr. DeAnders followed closely.

"What is he doing?" DeAnders asked.

Jetta didn't know how to make DeAnders understand. "We need to follow his lead."

In complete silence, Jahx took them down to the containment holding bays that served as Kiyiyo and Cano's temporary housing. The two massive wolves paced anxiously in their makeshift pens, alternating between growling and whining.

Jetta watched her brother stop in front of the cell and stand motionless, eyes still closed.

Why did he lead us here? Jaeia said, pressing her confusion into her sister's mind.

But Jetta didn't question her brother's motives. She felt his reasoning like the beat of her heart or the air in her lungs. Right then, they needed to be there.

"Release the force-field," Jetta commanded the attending soldier.

"Wait here," she said to Dr. DeAnders and the medical team. No one argued.

Because of their size, the wolves had been put in super-steel pens that had been augmented with a static force-field. Part of her understood the precautionary measures, but as soon as she could, she would do whatever necessary to convince the authorities to free them.

The soldier dropped the force-field so she could approach the wolves. Kiyiyo and Cano both crawled toward her with their ears folded back. When she reached out to scratch their chins, they flopped onto their backs and exposed their bellies, wagging their tails and covering her with long licks.

"Don't worry, guys, you won't stay here long," she told them softly and tousled their fur. "Soon you'll be back running through your forests, free from any owner, free to hunt and play as you like. I promise this to you with all that I have left. I will make it safe for you to go home."

"You made quite the impression on these two," Jaeia commented, finally gathering the nerve to stand by her side.

Jetta smiled. "I get them. I may not get people sometimes, but I get these guys. Maybe I'm just an animal at heart."

"You beat me to the punchline," Jaeia said with a smirk.

"Always the comedian. Here," Jetta said, nudging her forward. "This one is Kiyiyo. The one with the white neck is Cano."

Jaeia hesitated at first, especially when the two of them took to sniffing her outstretched hand, but when Kiyiyo licked her tentatively, she relaxed and gave them both a pat.

Sticking her head through the bars, Jetta buried her head in Kiyiyo's fur. For a moment she lost herself in his thick black coat, letting her mind stretch out, forgetting her surroundings.

She let out a burst of joyous laughter, feeling herself running on four legs over soft grass and through cold mountain springs, legs never tiring, stopping only when the sun slipped behind the peaks so she could howl among the moonlit rocks.

"That is so beautiful," Jaeia whispered. "They have such rich memories."

Jetta pulled back and blushed. "Yeah. I love the way they are, the way they think and feel. Everything. It's just... *real*. I would give anything to help them, and to save their brothers and sisters on Old Earth."

"This is worth fighting for, then?" Jaeia said, tugging playfully on Cano's ear.

"Of course," Jetta said. "Why do you phrase it like that?"

Jaeia didn't take her eyes off the wolf. "It's just you've never been one to—how can I put this without you getting mad at me…?"

Jetta crossed her arms and pursed her lips.

"You've never been one to care about something like this before. This is big."

"What do you mean?"

"The wolves give you a reason to fight for the Starways," Jaeia clarified. "Before it's ultimately been fighting for me and Jahx—your family—and maybe Triel. This is new."

As Jetta rubbed Kiyiyo's muzzle, she thought about what her sister had said.

"I guess you're right," she said. "But they've never hurt me, not like how other people have. And I can hear them, clearly. They don't hide from me. They don't lie."

"You can trust them," Jaeia finished.

"Yes," Jetta said, scratching Cano's neck.

"Like you can trust me?"

Jetta's breath hitched in her chest. She thought about all the reasons Jaeia didn't have to trust her anymore, and the guilt stabbed her in the gut. "Yes."

Jaeia was silent a moment. In the back of her mind, Jetta could hear her carefully considering her words.

"Maybe Jahx brought us here so you could be reminded of what you love right before we have to face someone that makes you forget."

Jetta knotted her fingers in Kiyiyo's fur and held on tightly. "Maybe," she whispered back, then gulped back the lump in her throat and faced her sister. She took Jaeia's hand in hers and let down her guard. "But I never needed to come here to know that."

***

Tarsha Leone discovered that Unipoesa hadn't been exaggerating when he told her that most of the Central Starbase had been abandoned after Victor's fleet positioned themselves around Trigos. As she passed by the corridor windows overlooking Trigos, she saw the few scattered Alliance starships available for the impending assault. *Our chances are slim at best,* she thought grimly.

At least it was easy to find Bossy. No traffic, no security checks. She didn't even need an escort, though Unipoesa had insisted; she could have just as easily followed the trail of booze and destruction.

Pushing aside a broken chair, she entered the mess hall. She spotted the tiny dark horse camped out on top of a stack of tables, surrounded by discarded jugs of her stolen *Mississippi Diesel* and other Alliance private stock. *This can't be good.*

A few soldiers took up station around the exits, but they held their position, even as Bossy gave instructions on performing a proper chokehold to the unfortunate soldier she had sequestered.

At least Unipoesa was smart enough to let Bossy have her way, she thought as the soldier's face turned purple in Bossy's arms.

"See, you gotta really clamp off the blood supply, or they'll never sleep right!" Bossy exclaimed, tightening her headlock as the soldier tapped her arm repeatedly.

Deep down, she told herself she should find Bossy's warped way of flirting funny, but she couldn't. At least not with her heart trying to pound its way out of her chest.

"Hey, he's not fighting back," Tarsha pointed out.

"Ehhh, they're all giant *puntes*," Bossy said, letting him go. The soldier rolled over and coughed violently until he caught his wind. With shaky limbs, he climbed down the mountain of tables and stumbled back to his post.

"You done here, yet? I'm bored. This place is lame," Bossy said.

Tarsha took her time climbing up the stack of tables and sat across from Bossy, hoping that her weight would balance them out and lessen the likelihood of the entire creation collapsing.

Bossy didn't seem to care. Belching loudly, she scratched herself as she searched for another drink. Only a few drops remained in the last jug on the tabletop, but she nursed it until it was bone dry.

This is it, she thought, holding her breath. Even inebriated, Bossy was too sharp to fall for any kind of stunt, so Tarsha laid down her hand.

"They took the bug out of my head."

The dark horse slowly put down the jug. Eyes narrowing, her free hand automatically went to her harness.

Tarsha breathed a small sigh of relief; since Bossy hadn't been able to restock her 20-20s, she came up empty.

"So are you a Skirt now or—"

"—or are you going to have to rip out my guts and tear out my eyes? You don't have to say it," Tarsha said. "It's not like I haven't been stuck with your *assino* for years or anything."

Bossy studied her carefully.

"What's my favorite drink?"

"Before you found the *Mississippi Diesel*?"

"Yeah, *ratchakker*."

Tarsha didn't even have to think about it. "Meatgrinder whiskey. Straight up, no ice, no chaser. 'It's gotta burn.'"

"You're *godich* right it does!" Bossy said, slapping the table. She scooted closer to Tarsha, making the table rock. Forced to lean forward to keep the balance, Tarsha found herself in a vulnerable position if Bossy chose to strike.

Bossy thought hard about her next question, making her forehead wrinkle. "Why did you dye your hair that ugly color, even when I told you it made you look like a wussy emo punk?"

Tarsha couldn't help but laugh. "Well, first of all, because Tysek Laoren, lead singer of Earth's best Industrial Metalcore band, had the same streak. And second, because I knew it would piss you off."

"He was totally gay!"

"You're just saying that because he looked better in tight leathers than you."

Despite her correct answer, Bossy didn't look anywhere near satisfied, her face still pinched with suspicion.

One of the guards made eye contact with Tarsha, but she was careful not to give any indication that she had communicated back. Regardless, Bossy came at her, hands around her throat. The pile of tables shuddered and creaked. Something snapped. Tarsha hoped it wasn't her neck.

"Are you my Gracie, or are you some butt-ugly imposter?"

Trying to pry Bossy's fingers off got her nowhere. The dark horse could out-muscle a gang of Toorks.

"Stop, I'm—"

Seeing her distress, the guards raised their guns, but she waved them off.

With the last of her breath, she croaked as much of their secret song as she could:

"*The sun may rise deep underground,*
The air may stink of rot,
My food is full of maggots..."

"But this is all I got," Bossy said, letting loose a little bit.

Tarsha struggled to continue the song as little black motes buzzed before her eyes.

"*The dead may roam the wasteland*
And the sky may burn and blister,
But I have my drink and I have my gun..."

Bossy released her.

"*...And I have my bad-assino sister.*"

Tarsha rubbed her neck but didn't dare sit up. The tables shifted underneath them, especially with Bossy's constant movement.

"No matter what anyone else calls me, no matter what name I go by," she said through strained vocal cords, "I will always be your Gracie."

Bossy thumbed the empty rings on her 20-20 harness and puffed out her lower lip. "It ain't the same."

"No, it's not. We were both tricked; we both believed a lie. But our friendship was real. It is the only real thing either of us knows for sure."

Tarsha had never seen Bossy cry, even when her arm nearly got chewed off by a Berserker in the fighting rings. "You don't talk like my Gracie. You don't sound like her. You don't even look like her anymore."

"I know," she said, lowering her eyes. "I can't help that. But the person I was and the person I was made to think I was have settled their differences. This is the person I am now. I carry both the strength of Agracia Waychild and Tarsha Leone in my heart."

"Look," she added. "I can't ask you to stay here with me."

"What the hell?!" Bossy yelled, shooting to her feet. "Double-crossin', *punte ratchak!*"

Tarsha clung to the lip of the table, holding on for dear life as it teetered back and forth. "Hear me out, ya numbskull! We'll both be dead in less than a week if I don't help the Alliance!"

"What? Why? They threatenin' you? You and me could take down this rat trap starbase in our sleep!"

"No," Tarsha said, glad when most of the rocking had subsided. "It's Victor."

"That old pruny *assino*?!"

"Yes. He's known the truth about me this whole time. He alluded to it the first time I met him in the Spillway. After he's done using the Deadwalkers to mop up his enemies, he's going to come after me. He knows what I'm capable of."

Bossy tilted her head and slurped loudly on her lollipop. "Whaddaya mean?"

Closing her eyes, Tarsha admitted her darkest secret. "I was bred for war. I'm the most dangerous military commander around."

Bossy chomped down on her lollipop. "I thought Doctor Death and her ugly sister were the greatest."

"Not against Li and his fleet."

"You mean that you're gonna *kill* all those chubby Republic bastards?"

Tarsha nodded, reverting back into her old Scabber twang. "Anyone who's dumb enough to stand in my way."

Bossy thought it over, twirling her pigtails and sucking on her lollipop. "Okay."

"Okay?"

"Yeah," Bossy said. "I'm in. I gotta see this."

"Still friends then?" Tarsha said, offering her a hand.

Lifting a brow, Bossy took her hand lightly. "Well... maybe. Let's see how many of those Johnny *baechs* you kill. Then we'll talk."

"I still have to prove I'm not a *punte*? That I'm worthy of the friendship of Bossy the great dark horse of Old Earth?"

Bossy refitted her engineer's cap and grinned from ear to ear. "I can't be best friends with someone who doesn't know how to have a little fun, now can I?"

***

Triel went back to her quarters out of habit, even though there was nothing there that she needed or wanted.

I should be reviewing the mission notes, she thought, looking at the digital clock on her sleeve.

Even so, with the little time left before their launch, she found herself going through her things, trying to find something she couldn't name.

Recent conversations floated through her head as she dug through her dresser drawers:

"Triel, I just thought you should know," the admiral had said, pulling her aside after the meeting adjourned, *"that Reht and the crew been successfully deprogrammed."*

She didn't know exactly what that would mean. *Will things go back to the way they were? Will Reht remember our love?*

(Does it even matter anymore?)

Moving from the dresser to the storage trunk buried in her closest, the Healer sorted through the ragged clothes from her days with the dog-soldiers, scrounging up the few items she had originally brought with her from Algar. The white-heart bead necklace she wore when she was in training. Her father's bone whistle. It wasn't much, but they stirred memories of what seemed like many lifetimes ago.

"Father," she whispered, holding tightly to the whistle and standing by the window. "I'm so sorry I never listened to you."

As she tried to remember the comforts of his embrace, the gravity of their mission took hold. *What we're about to embark on is dangerous, and the chances of the team's survival are slim.*

(My chances are nil.)

She could still hear Arpethea's voice in her head: *"End her life to save our people."*

Pressing her forehead against the window, the Healer looked down on Trigos and the surrounding stars, unaware of how hard she was squeezing the whistle. *I can't hurt Jetta.*

To save the Starways, she would have to stop the Dissemblers, but to do so, she would have to draw upon extraordinary strength. She couldn't do it alone. She would have to involve the Kyrons. But something like that had never been done before. *Is it even possible?*

Arpethea came to her again. *"She is not ready for what she must do. She will try and stop you. She will not let you fulfill your destiny..."*

And to save her people, she would have to perform the ritual of *Ne'topat'h* as Lady Helena illuminated and Arpethea demanded.

How can I sacrifice both my life and my love?

"Kill the Apparax," Arpethea called.

I would never hurt Jetta!

The bone whistle cracked, puncturing the meat of her palm. Cursing, she ripped the shard out, kneeling and pressing the wound down with her other hand between her legs as blood gushed out.

"Gods, I'm so... so..." The words wouldn't come, but the feeling remained. *Weak.*

"I'm not the next Great Mother," she said through clenched teeth. Her voice rose in intensity, as did the heat within her chest. "I will not hurt my friend!"

She hurled the broken whistle at the standing mirror. The fragments cracked against it but did no harm, bouncing onto the bloodstained carpet.

The Healer sobbed into her bloodied hand, not caring about the consequences of her emotion. She couldn't do it. She had to save her people, stop the Motti, but she could not sacrifice the one she loved.

"Take my life," she whispered, "but please—*please*—don't take hers."

"Triel."

Triel looked up, confused. *Where is that voice coming from?* It seemed to originate from all around her, and from within.

The voice called again, this time more insistent. *"Triel."*

Fluttering wings. A low insect hum. The lights alternately dimmed and brightened.

What is that?

Forgetting about the pain in her hand, Triel watched the mirror face wave and buckle as something behind it took form. Two hands, pale and veined with crude wiring, pressed through first, followed by the crown of a bald head.

Triel wanted to scream, to run away, but an unseen force grounded her there, kept her from alerting the security team as a face looked up from the bubbling mirror surface.

"Triel..."

Somehow, despite the sickly gray-green color of his skin, or the half of his body devoured by machinery, she recognized his face. *Father—*

Desperation pitted his voice and brought tears to his remaining cerulean eye. *"Help us."*

Any semblance of the quiet authority, the strong fatherly figure, vanished beneath burgeoning decay. The mugginess in the air, the way his words sunk into her heart, the fragility of his voice—

Oh Gods, he's suffering.

"Father!" she said, lurching forward to pull him through.

"Please, Triel, I can't—"

Triel collided with the carpet in front of the mirror, dazed and bewildered. When she looked up, the mirror appeared intact, though smeared by her blood. She wiped it down, checking the frame and the edges, pulling it off the wall and inspecting it with maniacal fingers.

"Father," she said, slumping back against the wall.

Tears and blood wet her face, but she didn't care anymore. She closed her eyes and slowed her breathing, letting the sensations of the physical world drift away. As she fell back farther into her own mind and heart, she heard her own voice for the first time, clearly and unencumbered.

"Jetta," she whispered to the listening stars. "I am so, so sorry."

***

Jaeia and her sister followed Jahx through the security hallways until they came to an area where the dog-soldiers were being detained.

"This isn't going to be easy," Jetta said under her breath.

Sensing her tension, Jaeia touched the back of her hand. "Maybe you should let me do most of the talking this time."

Jetta shrugged. "You're the diplomat."

"Do you trust me?"

Scoffing, Jetta rolled her eyes. "Oh, I already know what you're planning."

"Just because you're in my head doesn't mean you know everything, Jetta Kyron."

While Jetta got a status update from the security officers, Jaeia surveyed the detainment area through the monitors. Instead of spartan prison cells, the Alliance outfitted the dog-soldiers in a semi-open room with most of the conveniences of a Starbase, including gaming terminals, nutrition stations, and even a limited bar. Not a single soldier guarded the double-sealed doors, and the spread of windows on the opposite wall gave access to a breathtaking views of the stars.

Not that Reht and his crew will be fooled by overtures of hospitality, she thought. Even she would assume the worst if thrust in his situation, and suspect cameras and other monitoring equipment hidden in every corner.

"Jahx isn't budging," Jetta said, coming up beside her.

Glancing back, she saw their brother swaying in front of the monitors. Dr. DeAnders and the medical staff surrounded him, still looking back and forth between the readings of their instruments, and the medical anomaly standing in front of them.

"Alright, stay behind me. We don't want to appear aggressive."

"Whatever you say, sis," Jetta said, allowing her sister to pass through the doors and into the detainment area first.

Jaeia expected Reht's usual banter, especially since the Hub had released the Sleepers from their programming, but the dog-soldier captain watched her with a careful eye as she approached. The rest of the crew, some gathered around the gaming terminals and others lounging on the couches, stopped what they were doing but didn't menace them. Only Mom made a move, standing beside his captain.

"Captain," Jaeia greeted.

Nobody said a thing.

Cut to the chase, Jetta said, her voice loud and obnoxious across their bond, *and use your second voice already.*

Without breaking her composure, she shooed her sister's thoughts off to the side so she could think.

Reht's not the same dog-soldier captain Jetta met on Fiorah years ago, she thought, sensing a change in his energy. The grave expression in his eyes only deepened her concern. *But he's no Sleeper drone, either.*

"How can I help you, little one?" he finally said.

Jaeia relaxed a little, appreciative of the poke. "I was wondering if I could contract your ship for a job."

Chewing on the stump of a fingernail, he looked her up and down before spitting out the contents of his mouth onto the carpet. "Hey Sebbs, old boy—you were right again."

Mantri Sebbs rose up from one of the back-facing couches.

I can't believe he reconnected with the dog-soldiers.

Jetta chimed in. *I can't believe he hasn't been killed.*

Well, he's always had a penchant for survival.

But this man stood in stark contrast with the tweaked-out Dominion Core officer that had given her and her siblings the Dominion Academy entrance exam. Glazed-over eyes bore no inner light, and his mind, a cold wash of psionic disturbance, chilled her senses. Even deprogrammed, he hadn't gone back to what he had been, even if that wasn't much.

"I was right," Sebbs said, his voice full of contempt. "I told them that you'd show up. I told them you'd come here and try and convince them to do your dirty work."

Jaeia caught a string of thoughts from Sebbs's head.

Whoa, she thought, struck by the amount of material in her grasp. She never passively acquired that much. Then again, her powers always magnified in the presence of her brother and sister.

"You're mad," she said, reading his subconscious, "because you think that Pancar tricked you by bringing you to the Alliance."

Sebbs seethed with anger, but he didn't worry her as much as the Talian emitting a rumbling growl in her direction.

"I'm gonna gut him with a spoon," Ro hissed, jumping over the back of the couch.

Cray followed suit, making clawing motions in the air. "I'm gonna eat his face."

Chuckling, Reht tugged at his bandages while the rest of his crew added their own threats. Even Bacthar, the gentle giant, tossed a lounge chair on its side and glared at her.

"He didn't betray you," Jaeia said. "He brought you here so we could rid you of the Sleeper Program. He also did it as a show of faith so that the Liberalist Party and the Alliance could join under one banner."

"What do you mean, 'show of faith'?" Reht said

Jaeia carefully worded her explanation. "Your crew and Captain Sebbs have served the Alliance many times. Your skills would make you a dangerous asset to our enemies. If an enemy knew you were under a Sleeper program, they could have easily turned you against us. We were certain that Shandin had something like that in mind for all of you."

"And just who, might I ask, gave the order to program us in the first place?" Sebbs asked. "It's a bit of a Basic Rights violation."

"Minister Razar," Jaeia admitted.

"And where is his ugly mug?" Reht said. "Haven't seen him around. I miss our lovely chats. I think my boys would like to give him a little thank you, too."

The dog-soldier crew hooted and snarled.

Jaeia told them the truth. "He was critically injured a few weeks ago. He's still in a coma. Gaeshin Wren has taken his place during this time of war."

"So he's CCO and Military Minister? Seems like a conflict of interest," Sebbs observed.

Jaeia said nothing. *Having Wren co-chair the military and the General Assembly council position is a minor offense compared to the crimes Tidas Razar committed in his tenure.* Many of the classified operations that violated the Basic Rights Tenets of the Starways could be attributed to comatose Minister, not just the Command Development Program and the Sleepers.

"There's nothing you can say to make me help you," Reht said.

"Nothing," Sebbs emphasized, "you lying sack of Alliance *sycha*."

Sebbs' gall surprised her. *That's definitely not the stuttering, insecure Mantri Sebbs I remember.*

This is going nowhere, Jetta said, pushing her impatience into her sister's head. *Use your second voice.*

Breathing through gritted teeth, Jaeia tried to keep her sister's emotions from wrecking hers.

"I don't want to become Liiker feed," she said, "and I certainly don't want to end up with Motti implants rattling in my skull. Do you? Because that's what it's coming to."

As if waiting for her cue, the Alliance Starbase quaked.

"That's just another one of Victor's weapons demonstrations," she said, pointing out the window as a score of missiles shrieked by, leaving a fiery trail behind them. "In a few short hours, he'll give Li the order to demolish the last of the Alliance forces. The lucky ones will die in the strike."

"Motti implants?" Bacthar repeated incredulously.

As Jaeia explained the discoveries made by Pancar and confirmed by the Alliance, Billy Don't poked his head out from behind a gaming console and squeaked. Before the other dog-soldiers could stop him, he whirled over to her, zipping back and forth in front of her.

"Tin Can seems to agree with your story," Reht commented. "But I still don't like how it stinks like every other lie."

Jaeia felt her sister tug on the back of her uniform. *Do what must be done.*

Jetta's right, Jaeia thought to herself, caving to her sister's perspective. *I'll have to use my second voice. There just isn't enough time.*

But as she accepted her burden, she felt her brother's hand in hers, as if he stood next to her, not in the doorway with his eyes closed and head cast down. In this connection she heard past the sounds of the room into a parallel world, where ethereal lights danced in the psionic rhythms of the universe.

I see his pain...

"Reht," she said, "I know about Elia."

Jumping to his feet, the dog-soldier captain rushed at her, but Jetta was quick to stand in front of her sister, and Mom was even quicker to pull Reht back.

Jaeia continued, unabated. "Aware of it or not, you've been searching for a way to make things right for your entire life. This is your chance."

"*Goddich* leech. Stay out of my *chakking* head!" he yelled, wrestling against his Talian's hold, but Mom wouldn't let go. If it weren't for the heavily armed guards that appeared at the door, Jaeia wasn't sure if Mom would have been restraining him.

"Pancar towed the *Wraith* with his forces when he came here. Seems you have a pretty good lockout on your systems. It would take our best hackers days to crack your terminals. But I don't think we'll have to. You have the only ship in our Fleet that Victor doesn't have registry on, that can possibly get behind his defenses. You are the only one that can give us a fighting chance to end his reign and restore peace."

"Give it a rest," Sebbs said tiredly, waving a hand at her. "You and your sister have plenty of muscle to get us to do what you want. Why don't you just go ahead and do your mind tricks?"

He's got a point.

She ignored Jetta's silent sarcasm and held on tightly to Jahx's perspective. "Because this needs to be your choice."

Reht stopped struggling. As soon as he relaxed enough, the Talian let him go. He brushed off his jacket and straightened himself up. "So what? I just drop you off and that's that?"

"If you can handle it."

He sported his usual dented grin. "Sebbs would have to fill in for my navs officer that was killed. Can't have any of you fools touching my girl."

Jaeia nodded.

"And I'd have to have an engineer I can trust."

"How about an old friend?" Jaeia offered. "How about Tech?"

Jaeia signaled the guards, and they wheeled in the scrappy little engineer. Though still attached to an IV, he perked up at the sight of the crew, a lopsided grin lighting up his face.

"How did you…?" Before he could finish his own sentence, Reht ran over and put Tech in a headlock, furiously rubbing his knuckles across the top of his skull.

As he and the rest of the crew celebrated their unexpected reunion, Jaeia decided to leave out that Triel had played a key role in his recovery. The Healer restored Tech as much as Dr. Kaoto would allow, until the Chief ordered her away from the ICU to conserve her strength. Normally, she would have delighted in reconnecting two people, but the strange, palpable energies flowing between her sister and Triel made her wary of reigniting any feelings between the Healer and Reht.

"Dr. Kaoto and the remainder of our medical team utilized all our resources," Jaeia said, standing back as the rest of the crew descended upon their mate.

Tech greeted them all enthusiastically but embraced Billy Don't so hard the little Liiker squealed.

"Gods, I'm so glad to see you guys," he said, wiping his eyes.

"What about payment?" Reht said. Playing with the bandages on his hands, he looked her dead in the eye. "I up my prices in wartime."

"Here," Jaeia said, handing Reht a datawand. "This is my personal account on Neeis. I have at least ten million in there. That's more than the collective bounties of a lifetime. And it's yours to split with your crew."

Without pause, Reht plucked it from her outstretched hand.

Gods, Jaeia—what the hell? You didn't have to give him all that, Jetta grumbled through their psionic connection.

"How do I know it's real?" Reht asked.

"You can download and transfer it to wherever you want right now. I don't care. I figure that if you help us, and we succeed, it will be money well spent. If you refuse, we're all dead anyway. So do what you like,

Captain. There are only the lives of the Starways at stake."

"Well played, little launnie," she heard Sebbs whisper as she turned around and exited.

Jetta caught up to her as they left the detainment area, Jahx once again in the lead.

"We have less than one hour until dustoff. You'd better hope that worked."

"I have faith," Jaeia said, trying to sound and feel confident. "After all, this was *your* plan."

"Psssh," Jetta blew through her lips and made big gestures with her hands. "I thought you were smart enough not to listen to any of my 'crazy' ideas."

Jaeia found herself smiling, remembering all of Jetta's antics when they were little, and how it wasn't long ago that she was wishing her sister was around when she was in a bind.

Maybe Jetta's far-fetched, impossible strategies aren't always as wild and stupid as I thought, she mused.

Or so she hoped.

***

As Jahx guided the lift to the upper decks, Jetta's stomach tightened.

"Oh *skucheka*," Jetta cursed as he pulled up next to Triel's door. A strong electric essence hung in the air, reminding her of the same sensations she felt when Triel had Fallen.

"Wait here," Jetta said, blocking her sister's path.

"No, I should go with!" Jaeia insisted.

Jahx remained silent, not intervening, his rail-thin figure remaining on the lift.

"If there's something wrong with the Healer," Dr. DeAnders said, "we need to call security. We can't take any risks right now."

"No, don't," Jetta said. "I know how to handle this."

Jetta immediately regretted her words. Though the medical staff thought nothing of it, her sister picked up on what she'd left unspoken.

Jaeia took her aside by the arm. "Jetta, what's going on between you two? I've sensed it ever since we picked you two up on Old Earth."

It was the moment she had been dreading for months, probably her entire life. Unconsciously, Jetta rubbed her stomach as the raw, unhealing wound came alive, sending waves of heat throughout her body.

I can't lie to Jaeia.

She couldn't lie to her when they were three years old and she had started to steal food from their neighbors to get them through another day. Or when she had cut open her knees trying to escape a child labor gang and gotten a nasty infection. And when Lohien was taken away and Yahmen changed the locks on their door. She wanted to bear all of it herself, but Jaeia would never let her.

Jetta? Jaeia said through their bond, looking at her quizzically. *Why are you hiding from me right now?*

I can't tell you this...

Jaeia looked hurt. *Come on, Jetta. You think you can scare me away after all the* meitka *you've pulled?*

Fidgeting, Jetta glanced at the medical team monitoring Jahx, but also watching their interaction.

I hate that they're here, she thought to herself, anger reddening her cheeks. She felt scrutinized, singled out, interrogated by more than just her sister, as if the entire universe was watching and judging her every action.

Pressing her hand against Triel's door, Jetta felt the psionic strain.

I have to get in there, she thought, *but Jaeia won't let me go without an explanation.*

She held her breath, struggling for each word.

"Triel and I... we *bonded* on our mission together."

Jaeia's eyes narrowed and she tilted her head, feeling out for the emotions Jetta withheld.

"Bonded?" she said, lifting a brow.

Jetta nodded, trying to convince herself. "Yeah. We're really close now. We did some telepathic thing together on Earth. It was crazy. Um, amazing. I'll have to tell you about it later."

Frowning, Jaeia pushed forward into her mind, but Jetta resisted as best she could. That's when she heard him not so much in voice, but in the rhythm of her soul.

(Jetta... feel.)

But Jahx, she silently replied. *I'm so afraid.*

Jetta closed her eyes, feeling her brother's spirit flow through her like a calming stream, mitigating the fires burning in her stomach.

"I love her," Jetta uttered just above a whisper, hiding her eyes and clutching her belly.

A smile warmed her sister's face, and she relaxed her stance. "Finally. Jeez, I wasn't sure what it was going to take to drag that out of you."

Jetta scowled, her cheeks flushing with heat.

"Come on, Jetta," she said. With a chortle, she took her hands. "You're my sister, my twin—we live in each other's heads. Do you really think I'd be surprised by something like that? Or that it would bother me? You're still you. All sour-faced and grumpy, just like usual. Except now you get to annoy someone new!"

"Very funny, Jaeia Kyron," Jetta said, trying to wipe the tears from her eyes without giving herself away. "But how did you know?"

"My dear sister," Jaeia smirked, going in for a hug, "You can't control your dreams."

Jetta didn't think her cheeks could get any redder, but sensing that her sister meant it sweetly, she accepted her embrace.

"I'm so relieved," Jetta said, holding on a little longer. "I thought you would disown me."

"For this?" Jaeia remarked. "No. But if you ditch me again…"

Jetta raised her hands. "Fair enough."

"Hey—where's he going?" Jaeia said as Jahx turned the lift back down the hall.

"Go." Jetta transmitted her confidence to her twin. "I have to help Triel."

"I'll follow him. Are you sure you'll be okay?" Jaeia said, running up to the lift and climbing aboard with Jahx and his medical entourage. "Don't you want a security team?"

"No, that would just make things worse. I'll catch up to you."

"Jetta… Well, okay," Jaeia said, hanging over the railing as the lift sped around a corner. "Please be careful!"

Jetta paused at the Healer's door, feeling the dark energy intensifying. *Maybe I shouldn't have told Jaeia to go…*

Thousands of worms crawled into her belly as she commanded the door open.

"Triel!" she gasped, stumbling to the ground. "*No!*"

***

Triel—Triel! Come back to me!

The voice, distant and small, traveled down a long tunnel to reach her. Triel stirred only when strong hands propped her up against the wall and checked her throat for a pulse.

"Triel," someone said, gently shaking her shoulders. "Come back, please."

As the last wisps of her desecrated father disappeared behind her waking eye, she found herself back in her quarters. Jetta was kneeling in front of her, carefully wrapping the puncture wound on her hand with a compression bandage she had made out of strips torn from a blanket. "What happened to your hand? What happened to you?"

The sight of her was too much. Triel broke down, heart crumbling.

"Dear Gods, what's wrong?" Jetta said. "Tell me, please!"

Triel touched Jetta's face, anemic and gaunt, and discovered the place inside her where loss pierced. "You are so beautiful to me."

Jetta held her in her arms, brushing back her hair with a bewildered look on her face. "Should I call a medical team? Tell me what I need to do!"

"No," Triel said. "Stay with me a while. I want a piece of forever with you."

Holding her tightly, Jetta rested her head on top of Triel's. "Please, tell me what's wrong. I just want to help you."

Triel felt the hitch in Jetta's breathing. She realized it too. *There isn't much time left for either of us.*

I owe her the truth.

The Healer let the tears stream from her eyes as she admitted her vision. "Jetta, I never told you about what really happened in the Temple of Exxuthus."

"Okay…"

"Lady Helena said that in order to prepare for what I had to do as Great Mother, I would have to perform the *Ne'topat'h.*"

"The mating ritual," Jetta said, eyes darting back and forth. Triel had forgotten that Jetta had stolen Amargo's knowledge and marveled at how quickly she integrated the gleaned knowledge with her own perspective. "Helena and Amargo were told this by their mentors. This knowledge was passed down for centuries. It was something they were certain of."

"I had a vision," she said, drawing in a deep breath and pulling away so she could look Jetta in the eyes. "Of you, with arms wide open."

Jetta realized the implication and sat back on her heels in disbelief. "Surely, not me. I'm—I'm female! That's never been done before; it would cause a massive imbalance in our energies. One of us would die!"

Triel pinched the webbing between her fingers so hard that it split the skin. "I have seen Arpethea, the old Seer from my childhood, many times now in waking dreams. She told me that you are the legendary Apparax, and that in order to save myself and my people… I would have to kill you."

Jetta's face turned solemn, unreadable. Triel touched the back of her hand, but Jetta didn't react.

"But I can't do it and I won't, prophecy be damned. I love you."

Looking down, Jetta took the Healer's hand, slowly bringing it to her lips and kissing her softly. "I love you more than the stars, Triel of Algardrien. If I must die for you to live, and for your people, then so be it."

"No," Triel said adamantly. "I can't do that."

The same worry line that appeared when Jetta sifted through her cache of stolen memories crossed her brow. "Maybe we're not understanding what your ancestors meant. Normally a male and female performing the mating ritual would create a new, exogenic biorhythm—a child. Two same-sex partners were forbidden from this because it was believed that a harmful, endogenic reaction would occur. Especially women—we are considered vessels. We would suck the life right out of each other. But what if one of the partners wasn't a Prodgy? I'm a Cudal-born telepath—I am the Apparax, by definition. Who knows what our pairing could bring?"

"It would bring death," Triel said, the certainty in her voice. "I felt it."

Jetta didn't hide her anger. "No. I can't believe that we were brought together only to be ripped apart; I don't believe our love could bring about death."

"Jetta, I can't—"

"Perform the ritual," Jetta said, unbuttoning her uniform.

"No!" Triel said, trying to stop her.

"I will not let you die!"

"I can't lose you!" Triel sobbed as Jetta held her back by the wrist.

Relaxing her grip, Jetta brought the Healer to her chest. "Okay, I'm sorry. Shhh, it will be okay."

As Jetta soothed her, Triel lost herself to the steady beat of her heart. Even sick and debilitated, Jetta possessed an uncommon strength that spanned beyond her internal sight, wrapping the Healer in a deep sense of safety and protection she only ever experienced in her presence.

How does she do that?

Despite the shadow she had seen numerous times clinging to Jetta's soul, or the uncertainty of what power that thing held over her, Triel couldn't deny the pull Jetta exerted over her being.

Her own words came to mind: *"Prodgy legend and prophecy has always been abstruse and somewhat allusive... I refuse to be told who I am, or what must be done in order to fulfill some ancient writ. I chose to seek my own path and decide my own fate."*

And she remembered the anguish in her father's machine-twisted face.

Triel bit her lip. *Maybe there is an alternative.* "Jetta, do you trust me?"

"Yes." Jetta held her far enough away to look her in the eye. "And I believe that my love for you is strong enough to survive anything."

Leaning forward, Triel kissed her softly on the lips. "Then I will give myself to you, *Uxoris*."

"*Uxoris?*"

"There is no real translation," she whispered into Jetta's ear. "Wife. Life partner. Half of my soul."

The Healer pushed Jetta down on the ground and rested briefly on her chest, listening to her breathe. "Think only of our love. Let no thoughts of sorrow or fear touch your heart."

Unbuttoning the rest of Jetta's top, Triel caressed her soft skin with a light touch. She once again grazed the ragged scar on her abdomen and cringed when she felt Jetta's pain, but didn't linger long.

As the Healer removed the last of Jetta's clothes, she felt two hands slide underneath her shirt. Although Jetta's hands felt rough and calloused from all her training, her touch was gentle, her fingers knowledgeable of all the right areas and just how much pressure to apply.

Since Triel barely paid attention to her lessons years ago, she didn't think she could have remembered the intricate phrases and vocalizations that accompanied the lifebond ritual. But when Jetta's lips found her breast and her hands found the warmth between her legs, she lost herself to the ancient tongues of her people.

"Ai-lĕ, ime, Ai-lĕ!"

Jetta rolled her onto her side and bit her neck, holding her firmly with one arm as the other worked between her legs. Overcome, she spoke the incantations breathlessly, barely able to keep herself from shouting out.

"Je's tu saei!"

Emitting a low growl, Jetta scooted down, positioning the Healer on her back.

"Ai-lĕ, ime, Ai-lĕ! Je's tu saei!" she cried. She grabbed Jetta's head and pulled her to her lips. "Take me, now, for all eternity!"

Closing her eyes, Triel pulled them both into the liminal state, a threshold of the senses where the harmonies of being exploded in polychromatic, interconnected wheels. She soared heavenward, to a realm she could not have imagined from her lessons, awakened to the songs of their souls. Her heart filled with joy and she let go, falling into Jetta, beyond the borders of their parsible beings, into a place without time, illuminated by a sunless sky.

Something skittered on the edge of her awareness. A bead of blood slid down an invisible wall, shattering against the bright, sunless sky. Triel shuddered and buckled, withdrawing to protect herself as dark and menacing entity took interest in her presence.

"Aelana... Amaroka," it called to her. "We see you..."

She screamed as a creature, slick and black as if covered with oil, uncoiled from the fading light.

The crash-landing on Algar— *she remembered.* The thing embedded beneath Jetta's skin—

It reached out to her, just as before, with twisted fingers like the roots of a plant. Looking down on her with the same dead, hollow eyes, it seethed with immeasurable hungers that no mortal mind could comprehend.

(No!) *she screamed as it grazed the edge of her being, sending ripples of terror and despair through her mind. She retreated as fast as she could as the beast slunk towards her.*

(I was wrong—so wrong.)

"Triel!"

Jetta hovered over her, tears in her eyes, hands cupping the Healer's face.

Triel rolled over and retched, losing the meager contents of her stomach onto the speckled carpeting.

This can't be...

(I was wrong.)

Bracing her temples, she tried to sort through the confusion that pervaded her senses. *Whatever Jetta harbors is too strong for me,* she realized. *Too strong for both of us.*

(It's hopeless.)

"What happened?" Jetta said, offering her a glass of water from the food dispenser. Still naked, she stood their shivering, oblivious to the cold as she focused on the Healer. "I felt you inside me. It was exquisite… but then the connection severed so abruptly."

Triel couldn't yet conjure up the ability to speak. Everything seemed so senseless, so clouded by pain.

"That wasn't the mating ritual, was it? Amargo's knowledge was of something very different—not that I minded," Jetta said, blushing and pulling her jacket over her shoulders.

"It wasn't," Triel said, her voice weak, full of gravel. "I was trying something different. The lifebond of our people. I was giving myself to you. I thought, perhaps, then I could avoid…"

She couldn't finish the sentence.

"Oh. Well, why didn't it work?"

"Something… made contact with me. It was terrifying…" From the look on Jetta's face, Triel gathered she sensed her trepidation.

Jamming her feet into her pant legs, Jetta's anger and shame radiated from her like an overheated furnace.

"Jetta, wait, I—"

"No," Jetta said through clenched teeth. "I am a monster. There is no hope for me. You and I both know this. Whatever's inside me will destroy us both."

Triel reflexively put her hands over her heart, trying to suppress the ache in her chest as Jetta closed herself off. And then she realized what that meant.

"Jetta, I can feel you—*wait!*"

Triel ran after her, tackling her from behind. Jetta, with her pants still around her legs, slammed onto the floor.

The Healer didn't hesitate, diving into her through the contact of their exposed skin. It didn't take her long to find the dark creature waiting for her at the forefront of Jetta's being.

"Amaroka..."

Its voice brought chills to her skin, and as she tried to shield herself with the love she felt for Jetta, she found herself submitting to its venomous touch. It drew its strength from her suffering, boring into her soul with brutish rage.

(Jetta, help me!)

But it had taken hold of Jetta, consuming her with every bite it took out of Triel.

It's killing me—

—us—

As the thing ripped into her memories, it sliced her mind open like a piece of butchered meat, unmaking her from the inside out. She understood Jetta's pain and all the horror she had been capable of as the thing pushed her farther and farther away from that which made her whole.

Arpethea, *she cried out through the psionic bridges of the interdimensions.* Help me, please!

A voice called back from the netherworlds, building in intensity and volume until it shook the beast's hold. (KILL THE APPARAX.)

The prophecy. Ne'topat'h. *Jetta's arms, wide open. Her own will, always defiant, always leading her away, only to lead her back into the life she had disavowed.*

Triel saw no other choice. She stuck her fingers into the creature's dead eyes, feeling them slide through the cold jelly. There she forged the forbidden connection, the one that took root in the heart of a Dissembler. Clinging to the fading memory of Jetta, of her own life, she tipped back her head and invoked death.

***

Jaeia lurched over the railing, then catapulted backward onto the lift as if someone had kicked her in the gut. As she struggled to breathe, she saw her brother faint, DeAnders barely catching him by the armpits.

"Captain, are you okay?" one of the medics asked as another checked her vital signs.

Jaeia reached out, trying to grasp at the connection that was no longer there.

Jetta was dead.

CHAPTER XIII

Jetta flung away from herself and into a glowing rim enclosing a fluid world. Energy and light collided, shattering into spectrums of color she could never have imagined, as a battle unfolded within the liquid bindings of the transitional plane.

As she floated away from the dazzling display, she cared less and less about her separation from her old, transient form. Free of her worries, free of the rigidity and contortions of her corporeal state, she melded with the joys and dreams that awaited her on the other side of the shell of light.

But even in this place she hadn't rid herself of the shadow eclipsing her heart. She had all but forgotten its presence when it reached out to her in feral desperation.

She saw its face for the first time.

***

Jetta was dead for a total of three minutes and forty-three seconds when the security forces finally broke down the Healer's door and the medical team rushed inside.

Closing her eyes, Triel whispered the last rites of the *Ne'topat'h* as Jaeia ran to her sister and the medical teams swarmed the Commander. Triel coughed and sniffled uncontrollably, affronted by the overpowering stress pheromones emitted by Jetta's twin.

"She'll be okay," Triel said, leaning back against the wall, physically and mentally exhausted, tears brimming her lids. "She's coming back around now."

Jetta opened her eyes just as one of the medics got ready to dispense a heavy dose of neurotransmitters into her system. Still dazed, her limbs remained flaccid, her speech unintelligible.

"What did you do?" Jaeia demanded, muscling her way through the medics to hold her sister in her arms.

The security forces reacted to her voice, lifting their guns and preparing to take aim.

Triel couldn't find the strength to answer in full. Instead, she offered her hand for Jaeia to see, but Jetta's gray-eyed twin refused.

"Tell me," she said, forcing the medics to work around her as she clung to her sister.

"There was a... a dark presence inside her. I... dissolved it as best I could."

Jaeia stopped rocking her sister and took a long, hard look at both of them. Seeing Jetta and Triel only half-clothed made her forehead crinkle, but as Jetta stirred, her brow relaxed.

She's accessing her sister's memories and piecing together what happened, Triel realized.

She didn't tell Jaeia of her uncertainty. In her attempts to destroy the malignant entity inside Jetta, she had utilized her caustic Dissembling powers, but it had only strengthened the demon's hold. Finally, she had been forced to do the unthinkable.

The Healer closed her eyes and saw herself doing it all over again. Strangling Jetta's lifecords, the terrible shriek of the beast as it faded away into the frigid pull of death. She waited what seemed like an eternity before going back in, counting her own heartbeats in the empty abyss of Jetta's lifeless body.

(Is it dead?)

Triel opened her eyes again. No one had ever performed the Ne'topat'h with an empty vessel. She couldn't imagine what kind of sacrilege she had committed, or even if it had worked. Other than returning to her body disoriented and thoroughly stripped of energy, she felt no different than before.

"Vitals are stabilizing," one of the medics announced. "Let's give her 4mg of hydraporpoform..."

The door opened to her quarters and DeAnders, Jahx, and the rest of the medical team came through. Despite Jahx's unchanged demeanor, Triel could tell by the scent of his elevated blood chemistries that his body had also suffered the stress of his sister's death.

"Is everyone okay?" Dr. DeAnders said. "I will call Dr. Kaoto."

"No, everything is fine" Jetta managed to say, sitting up and holding her temples. As she shooed away the medics, she looked down and saw her half-naked body, and turned bright red. "Can you hand me my top please?"

Jaeia scooted next to Triel while Jetta fought off the rest of the medical team's inquiries. "Are you okay? I'm sorry I spoke to you like that."

"Don't worry about it. I can't imagine what you felt when Jetta... died. I'm so sorry."

Rubbing her forehead, Jaeia gave a hesitant smile. "As long you helped her."

Triel accepted a hand up and Jaeia's arm around her waist as she assisted her to the couch. When a medic held out her arm to administer her a booster, she didn't stop him. The Healer breathed in sharply as the meds hit her like a star-class freighter traveling at light speed.

"Thanks, I really needed that."

"Are you sure you're okay?" Jaeia asked again.

Despite how she felt, she gave an automated response. "Yes."

"Great," Jetta said, slowly making her way to the couch. "Jae—you'd better follow Jahx again. And take the teams with you, too," she said, jabbing her thumb at an overly excited medic who wouldn't leave her alone.

Jaeia looked at them warily, but Jetta locked eyes with her sister, swaying back and forth as they engaged in a silent exchange. After a long pause and a few muttered words, Jaeia ordered the medical and security teams to follow her as she trailed their brother out of the room.

Jetta sat on the same couch as the Healer but kept her distance. "That was… a terrible experience. I'm not exactly sure what I felt, or saw."

"I'm sorry," Triel said, covering her face with her hands. She didn't try to stop herself from crying. "I thought I was helping you. I thought I was…"

Jetta laid her hand on her knee. "Whatever that was inside me, whatever you saw… I can't feel it like before. Maybe you got rid of it. Maybe I'm no longer that monster."

Triel hid her trembling hands and forced a smile.

Edging closer, Jetta moved her hand to her thigh. "Look, I'm not sure what happened, but I do know this," she said, lifting up her shirt. The wound that had refused to heal was only a pink line across her stomach. "You did something good."

When Triel touched Jetta's abdomen, something pulled at the corners of her mind. She couldn't put the feeling into words, nor could she justify the way she felt.

A genuine smile brightened her face as she hugged Jetta with all of her might.

"I'm so sorry, Jetta," she whispered. "I love you so much."

"Love you, too. Forever and always," Jetta said, not letting her go.

***

Jaeia followed her brother to the specialized area in the Division Lockdown Lab where the medical and research teams had collaborated to hold the alleged Kurt Stein. Unsure of how to handle such a high profile and unstable individual, the teams decided on using several different types of force fields and biorestrictive devices, containing the doctor to the exam table in the middle of a security hold. All of this she expected—except for the modified shock collar on Stein's neck as he lie sleeping.

Those were supposed to be destroyed, Jaeia thought, upset at the sight of the outlawed device. Still, she understood the rationale after experiencing her sister's memories of the incredibly powerful telepath. *I guess extreme caution is warranted in this instance, even if it is ethically wrong.*

Jahx stood silently by Kurt's bedside, rocking slightly back and forth, his eyes closed and his psionic presence distant.

"Why are we here?" Jaeia asked him.

"Captain, I strongly advise against any contact," Dr. DeAnders said, standing back with the rest of the teams near the security station. "The computer systems are still having trouble decoding his DNA, and we can't predict if—or when—he's going to wake up. We don't know what we're dealing with yet."

If you only knew how strong his psionic signature was, Jaeia thought, grimacing as she fortified her mind against the slumbering doctor's telepathic wavelengths.

"We won't be long," Jaeia said. Turning back to Jahx, she tried to again. "Why are we here? Please, Jahx—tell me something."

Jahx said nothing.

Irritated, she moved to the head of the bed and tried to sort out what she could.

He's so hard to read, she thought, unable to discern anything useful. Instead of fluid thought patterns, she sensed a static hum. *Maybe whatever our mother did to lock down his mind is effecting my ability to read him.*

Even her brother's mind made more sense to her.

Jahx, Jaeia called out silently. *What do you want me to see? What am I supposed to do?*

Jahx didn't move, nor could she sense any thoughts from him.

"*Skucheka*," she muttered. Although she rarely swore, but she found herself letting loose with as many as she could think of. "*Ratchakker assino mugarruthepeta—*"

Frustrated and out of ideas, she walked to the nearest terminal and pulled up any available files on Kurt Stein. She flipped through the images and articles, noting their remarkable likeness to the man lying on the exam table but absorbing nothing that she didn't already know.

I need something, anything.

Her eye lingered on a picture of Kurt and Josef Stein standing together in front of a sign for an awards ceremony in New Berlin. Something about the way Josef had proudly flung his arm around his son, about the way Kurt beamed as he held up a patent for his legendary genetic coding nanites caught her attention. Even on the flat projection, centuries after the occasion, she felt the strength of the connection between father and son.

Josef loved his son, and Kurt loved his father.

Before she had a chance to think about it, her fingers started up on their own, typing in a new command.

She played the last video recording that Josef Stein ever made.

"*Dearest Kurt... I am ashamed of what I have become...*"

The same compulsion that drove her fingers dug into her brain and tugged at her gut. She found herself going from terminal to terminal, pulling up the log on every playable screen.

"Captain, what are you doing?" she heard DeAnders say. She ignored him and kept the other medical staff from crossing into the security hold.

"Stay back!" she warned above the noise from the terminals.

"*...I will find you, Kurt. And I will make things right again.*"

Bracing her head, she tried to control herself, and the strange new urges. *What is happening—?*

Something shifted in the air; a ripple went out along the psionic planes. When she looked up, she saw Jahx staring intently at the man on the table, his blue eyes glowing as the video repeated itself.

"Oh Gods..." she whispered.

Kurt Stein opened his eyes.

Backing up against the wall, Jaeia felt as if someone unleashed a barrage of thunder in her head. She fell to her knees, trying to block out the psionic assault as the man rose from the medical bed.

"Get back, get back!" DeAnders shouted, ordering the teams to take cover behind the safety partition. Out of the corner of her eye, Jaeia saw him firing the shock collar, but it did no good. Even after four or five charges, Kurt Stein appeared unfazed, ripping it from his neck and casting it aside.

Jaeia screamed and bucked as the thunder of his psionic assault solidified into a deafening white noise that boiled through her gray matter and bubbled from her skin. The man turned toward her, eyes blazing with unconscionable fury.

(He's not just going to kill me—
—he's going to tear my soul apart—)

Unperturbed, Jahx stepped forward, his right hand held out before him. The pain shooting through her body subsided to a dull ache, and for the second time that day she heard her brother speak.

"*Wasu, Ammon.*"

He continued on in the ancient language she had never heard before, speaking in a strange tongue that pricked at her intuition and opened up something deep inside her.

Jahx isn't speaking to the man, she sensed, *but to the thing that possesses him.*

"*Wasu annu awilum mulla zul. Bara sa shu-gi.*"

The man shrieked, letting loose a torrent of fire inside her heart. She matched his scream as the wall sockets exploded, showering them with sparks and shards of broken paneling. In the back of her mind she could feel the agony of DeAnders and the other crew members as the man's reach tore through the walls and lay waste to any nearby soul.

Jaeia felt her sanity peeling away as her brother lifted his left fist under the sputtering light of the last surviving bulb. Slowly he uncurled his fingers to reveal a white paper crane, perfectly perched, wings in horizontal flight, on his palm.

The pain stopped. Except for a popping fuse and the sizzling outlets, the room fell silent. The man approached Jahx on wooden limbs. His entire arm trembled violently as he reached for the bird.

A feeling, much like when the morning sun chases away the darkest shadows of the night, overcame her as the man held the crane in his hands and, in a thick Germanic accent, whispered his first words: "I… remember."

Jaeia collected herself off the ground, using a railing to keep herself steady until she trusted her legs again.

"My name is Jaeia Kyron. Who, may I ask, are you?"

The man looked at her with troubled eyes, holding the crane closely to his chest. "I—I am Kurt Stein. I don't know where this is, or how I got here."

Jaeia glanced at her brother, but his eyes had fallen shut, and his mind wouldn't respond to her questions.

"Wait here, Dr. Stein, okay? I have to check on my crew. Everything will be okay; I will explain everything."

"What was that?" DeAnders said, taking Jaeia's hand and getting back on his feet.

Jaeia chose her words carefully as she helped DeAnders gather his glasses and dataclips off the floor. "That was Kurt Stein waking up from a long slumber."

After assuring the others were okay, Jaeia returned to a befuddled Kurt Stein and her silent brother. She checked her watch. *Time to go.*

"We have to leave now," she said, trying to rally her brother. "Victor will give Li the order to strike the Starbase any second now."

"What about me?" Kurt said, looking around at all the destruction. "What is going on here?"

Jaeia was about to tell him he would be sent away somewhere safe when different words were thrust into her mouth. "You will come with us."

What? she exclaimed through their bond, looking indignantly at her brother. *Why?!*

He must come.

His words felt like lead footprints stamped inside her skull. There would be no argument.

"Jahx," she whispered aloud, taking his icy hand in hers. "This is the end, isn't it?"

***

Triel's heart sank when she realized she was the first Alliance crew member to arrive aboard the *Wraith*. She repeatedly reassured herself that the crew had been deprogrammed, but it didn't quell the butterflies in her stomach.

"You got a lot of nerve showin' up here," Ro said, jumping down from the upper deck. He slapped the flat side of his knife against his palm and backed her into the wall. Popping up from the lower deck access panel, Cray sprang to his mate's side.

"Yeah, a lotta nerve!"

"Lay off!" she said, shoving Ro back.

He stumbled into a support beam, but found his footing and smirked. "Oohh, I like it when they fight."

"Me too," Cray cackled. "Makes it all the sweeter."

Black wings folded her into a broad chest. "Get lost, *assinos*."

"Take a hike, flyboy," Ro hissed, sticking his knife under Bacthar's chin. "This be a long time comin'."

Bacthar flicked the pointed tip of his wing at Ro's eye. Screeching, Ro dropped his weapon, cradling his lacerated brow. Cray grabbed him by the arm before he could retaliate, seeing Bacthar positioning himself for another round.

"Thanks," Triel said quietly, trying to free herself from the Orcsin's arms, but he wouldn't let go.

"What they made us believe you did was bad, you know. Even though it wasn't real, it's still hard to forget."

"I would never mean to hurt any of you."

Bacthar rested his head on her shoulder. "But you did. You shouldn't have left. He hasn't been the same since you've been gone."

He finally let her go, and she turned to face him. Touching the sharp ridge of his jawline, she felt the pain of his words.

"I had to join the Alliance," she whispered, withdrawing her hand. "I couldn't go with Reht without knowing I had done everything I could to save the telepaths."

Bacthar took her hand and squeezed it. His sets of red eyes blinked rapidly, as if trying to hold something back. "He's in his den. You might want to see him before the others get here."

Not that she had any other choice. Bacthar blocked the way to the bridge, and the other routes were no more desirable. She didn't want to be stuck in engineering with Billy Don't, and she certainly didn't want to run into Ro and Cray in the galley.

With a heavy heart, she rapped on the turn-wheel door to his den.

Nothing.

"Reht?"

Squeezing her eyes shut, she recited as much of a prayer as she could remember. Then, with jittery hands, cranked the wheel lock and let herself in.

Reht's den was never clean. However, the mess was usually fresh since Mom kept tabs on the refuse buildup. But by the way things looked, even Mom hadn't been allowed in his den for quite some time. Flies buzzed around the sticky cans of cheap liquor, and his collection of nude magazines were buried under a tipped-over shelf. Several holes had been punched through the back of one of his lounge chairs, and the liquid lamp that he cherished so dearly, beneath which they had so often made love in the blue glow of its dancing formations, was smashed to pieces, dried up and discarded in a pile of shredded clothes.

This is bad.

Pain drove into her from across the room, forcing her to close her eyes and erect a solid boundary between the two of them. She had always been attuned to him, and that part of her ached as she remembered how much better she could sense him than most people. She couldn't deny the connection they had or the love they had shared, but as she approached him through the shoals of waste, she sensed the change.

"Starfox," he said flatly. "Fancy seeing you here."

He didn't move, still facing away from her, sitting on the edge of his bed. By the way he tilted his head, he seemed to be regarding the poster of his favorite collection of erotic dancers, but she could tell by the pounding of his heart that his concentration lie elsewhere.

"Reht... I don't even know where to begin," she said, hoping he would turn around.

Fresh bandages caught her eye as his right hand rose to his brow. As long as she had known him, he had never allowed anyone to touch his hands, nor had he ever changed the filthy dressings.

"Ain't no need to begin," he said looking down at his hands. "No point in talking this mess out."

Triel sat on the opposite side of the bed, facing away from him. She looked around the room, remembering the good times they had shared.

"What changed?" she said quietly, afraid to disturb the mess.

Reht looked over his shoulder. "We did."

Why hasn't Reht lit up yet? she wondered. It was very unlike him, especially in a tense situation.

Darker thoughts scratched at her mind: Maybe the Alliance did more than make him think their relationship was over or condition him to run their covert missions. Maybe they unlocked something within the dog-soldier captain that had been best left forgotten.

"I heard what happened on Old Earth," Triel said. "I heard about Shandin."

She felt him cringe, even though she couldn't see his face. Acid churned in his stomach, and his breathing quickened as he reacted to her words.

"Yeah," he managed to say.

"I'd better go," she said, getting up to leave.

He didn't turn around. "Starfox, you'll always be an angel to me."

"Reht," she said, reaching out to touch him but pulling back at the last second. "It wasn't real. I never said those awful things. We never had that fight. I don't want it to end this way."

Finally, he turned around. Her heart hurt to see the heavy bags under his eyes, the sleepless nights that had reddened his eyes, the anorexia that pitted his cheeks. "Just as well. You went away, you found someone else."

"How did you...?"

"Rumors been 'round for a while, dear, and you just confirmed it. Not that I couldn't see it in those beautiful blues."

"I still love you," she said, kneeling on the bed. She touched the scar on his face and felt his biorhythm strum against hers. "I will always love you."

"Yeah, but it can't go back to the way it was." He grabbed her hand, scaring her with his force. Gasping, she feared he would strike her, but he merely kissed the tips of her fingers, his white incisors grazing her skin. "I ain't the right man for you. In fact, ain't no right man for you."

"That's not funny," she said, trying to take back her hand.

"I ain't being funny," he said, holding firm. "I think that crazy little launnie is alright. I think you two make sense."

"I do love her, with all my heart. But..." Triel hesitated. She had to tell someone. "I don't know if she'll ever allow herself to love me back. Not fully. There's part of herself she's still keeping from me."

With a chuckle, Reht finally pulled out a stub of a cigarette from his front pocket. She saw the familiar glint in his eye. "Remind you of anyone you know?"

Triel couldn't believe she hadn't seen it before. Maybe the dog-soldier captain and the young Alliance commander were not as different as she thought.

Taking her hand back, she returned to fumbling with the webbing between her fingers. "I need her right now, more than ever. All of her. I can't do what I need to do without her."

"She'll come through, Starfox. For you, she'd bring down the stars."

"And I worry about what's going to happen to her after this is all over."

Reht chomped on the end of his stub. "That's one kiddo that knows how to make it to the next day. Have a little faith in her, too, okay?"

Triel hugged him tightly. She took in his smell, his aura, trying to embrace all that was good between them as she let him go. "Just promise me that you'll take care of yourself."

"If I don't, you know Mom will," he said, grinding out the stub between his fingertips. She felt his pain but knew better than to offer her services; he would refuse them anyway.

When he leaned over and kissed her cheek, Triel felt a distinct atmospheric shift, as if someone had blown in the winds of ice and fire. She reeled around, shocked to see Jetta standing in the doorway.

"Jetta!" she said, standing up abruptly. Reht nearly fell off the bed but caught himself on the edge.

"What's going on in here?" Jetta said, her hands in tight fists.

Triel tried to stop her, but she was no match for Jetta's speed or strength. In a split second Jetta had Reht by the collar, holding him off the ground.

Reht laughed, though the pain brought tears to his eyes. "Kid, jeez. Her heart was always yours."

***

Jaeia had checked the last of Alliance and Liberalist soldiers onto the *Wraith* when DeAnders and Kaoto approached her with their two high-profile charges.

"Captain…" DeAnders began, then stopped. Jaeia could see the conflict welling in his eyes, along with the acceptance that his arguments would be futile.

"Doctor," Jaeia said, gently gripping his forearm. "Thank you. For all you've done for us, especially for Jahx and Dr. Stein."

"To find Stein, after all these years… and to send him on this mission…" DeAnders said, struggling to keep his voice down. "We still don't know where the Ark is."

Jaeia looked at her brother. Not much had changed since his emergence. He was still entranced by some faraway psionic state, barely readable to her, his appearance and behavior like the walking dead of Old Earth.

There's no concrete reason to believe what I feel, she thought. Still, she couldn't deny the pull in her heart.

"Trust me," she said, drawing her words from her brother's strength. "This is the only way."

The docking bay sirens sounded, signaling the start of the countdown.

"I've personally briefed your team medic on your condition, as well as your sister and brother's," Dr. Kaoto said hurriedly. He removed a syringe from his pocket and indicated for her to push up her sleeve. Doing as he asked, she watched as he injected the booster. "Hopefully this will buy you some time," he added softly.

"How is Dr. Stein?" Jaeia said, leaning to Kaoto's right to catch a glimpse of him. Kurt looked every which way, eyes never lingering on one particular sight for more than a second. Every now and then he pinched himself, as to wake himself from a dream.

Kaoto and DeAnders exchanged glances. Dr. Kaoto answered with noticeable hesitation. "He's… functional. We tried everything, but he has significant gaps in his memory. He can't give us anything concrete about what happened to the experimental ship, how he got here, or what happened to your father."

"We'll have to worry about that later," Jaeia said, motioning for the last of the soldiers to help Kurt and Jahx to the back of the ship.

"Good luck, Captain," DeAnders said, saluting her. "May the Gods look down upon you favorably."

Saluting back, she wavered for a moment, making sure that DeAnders and Kaoto boarded the medical frigate in the adjacent bay before sealing the ramp.

Jaeia hid her amusement as she passed by Jetta's SMT team leader trying to discuss boarding protocol with Mom.

"You can't pre-load an ammunitions without registering them with the—"

The Talian dropped his claws before he could finish.

Wide-eyed, the team leader took a few steps back. "Alright, uh, I—I'll just register them myself."

After the final boarding check, Jaeia made sure Jahx and Kurt had been secured in their seating in the galley.

"Is he… okay?" Kurt asked as Jaeia touched her brother's pallid face.

Jaeia wasn't sure exactly how to answer him. "He's been through a lot."

Kurt's eyes narrowed, and she felt him prodding her mind. "More than you think I can understand?"

Jaeia didn't hide her surprise. "I thought you wouldn't have any powers left after what my brother did to you."

"I—I'm sorry," he said, lowering his head. "I'm not quite sure what to make of myself anymore. Whatever happened while I was aboard that ship, I'm just not the same. I'm… not what I used to be."

Looking left to right, Jaeia made sure no one else could hear their conversation before pursuing his answer. "What can you do? What can you see?"

Kurt held his head in his hands. "Your brother did away with whatever demon was inside of me when he helped me remember who I was… but something's left over. I can hear you, beyond your words. I can feel your thoughts."

"A demon was inside you?" Jaeia asked.

"Yes," Kurt said. "I felt possessed by true evil; it washed away everything, made me think the world was only pain and terror. Now I feel… I feel…"

Jaeia heard his words before he spoke them. Quiet as they were, they resonated inside her skull like a scream in an empty stadium.

"I feel reborn."

"Reborn…" Jaeia repeated, letting the word slip off her tongue.

For some reason she thought of her mother, prompting her to sift through the memories she had grafted from Jetta, letting them flow through her like a half-forgotten dream. On a deeper level, well beyond her conscious thoughts, she felt something important just beyond her grasp, something vital to her survival and that of her siblings.

"Where are we going?" Kurt asked, his eyes darting from soldier to soldier as the Liberalists secured themselves as best they could alongside them in the galley.

"We are going to confront a madman and stop his war on this galaxy."

With a sigh, Kurt closed his eyes and let his head rest against the wall. Jaeia felt the psionic field ripple as he relaxed and stretched beyond himself.

"Why do you need me to go with you?"

Jaeia guessed that it was best to answer him truthfully, especially if he did have any leftover telepathic talents. "I'm not sure. I'm relying a lot on my faith these days."

Kurt smiled but kept his eyes shut. "You'll need more than faith to survive the jump down this rabbit hole."

***

Jetta only accepted the boosters from the medic after she collapsed on her way to the bridge of the *Wraith*. Normally she would never take medicinal enhancers, but in this case she had no choice. Even the brief scuffle with the dog-soldier captain left her drained.

As the rush invigorated her core and stimulated her senses, she tightened her jaw. *All that matters now is living long enough to stop Victor.*

"Please tell me you didn't kill Reht," Jaeia said quietly, coming up from behind her. In the back of her mind, Jetta felt her sister sift through their meeting with lingering disapproval.

"It was an honest mistake. Bruises heal," she muttered back.

Jaeia gave her the side eye as she assumed her position in the back of the bridge near the interface consoles. As Jaeia sat down, Jetta caught a glimpse of Triel being ushered to the back of the ship by Mom. The Talian warrior, arriving too late to help his captain or the Healer, growled at Jetta before disappearing down the walkway.

Reht emerged from his den, still rubbing his neck, and descended the stairs to his command chair. He made sure to give Jetta a wink before punching in.

The rest of the crew took their positions, Ro and Cray smarting off to the select SMT squad Jetta had formed, taking advantage of the fact that the Alliance soldiers weren't allowed to talk back.

Jetta worked hard to conceal her appreciation for her soldiers. She had asked for volunteers from her Special Missions Team, not expecting any of them to take on such a deadly operation, and was left speechless when they all raised their guns.

Their words still pressed tears into her heart: *We are with you, Commander, until the very end.*

She felt the impression of Jahx's thoughts echo in the far reaches of her mind. *They trust you. They believe in you.*

"Take us out to mark 0.1113 and hold," Jetta instructed Reht.

Reht nodded to Sebbs. In the absence of Diawn and Vaughn, the ex-Dominion officer took over as helmsmen.

Huh. I would've never guessed he'd be such a skilled pilot, Jetta thought as he positioned the *Wraith* under the rotating axis point of the Alliance Central Starbase.

Jetta took a deep breath and held it, listening to her sister's thoughts and sharing her concerns.

Are you sure about this?

Jaeia only gave her a brief glance, trying to maintain her composure. *It's the best chance we have.*

I don't believe in chance.

Jaeia kept her gaze trained on the viewscreen. *Then believe in me.*

Squeezing the golden key in her pocket, Jetta let out the air in her lungs. She took one last look at the abandoned Starbase.

"Ready to jump," Jetta said, taking the first mate's chair positioned next to Reht. "Heading preset alpha-017."

"Locked in," Sebbs acknowledged. "Jue Hexron on the scopes."

"Have primary drivers in heat. On my mark."

Jetta waited as an arm of the Starbase passed below the *Wraith's* engines, catching a glimpse of Victor's fleet surrounding Trigos. Thousands of starcraft dotted the upper atmosphere of the blue world, with behemoth warships keeping their weapons trained on the Starbase. The Republic starships signaled the Starbase on all the open channels, their final summons for the Alliance surrender playing out over the *Wraith's* loudspeakers.

"All Alliance forces, stand down, or we will attack."

She thought she heard Victor laughing in the background as the enemy missile bays charged.

As the *Wraith* disengaged from the underbelly of the Starbase, Jetta looked at the timer on her uniform sleeve, synchronized with the other Alliance ships. Taking another deep breath, she counted down the last seconds. "3… 2… 1…"

Jetta heard her sister's heart thudding against her chest wall as the entire fleet of enemy warships launched a full spread. "Mark!"

Light, color, and sound stretched out into the infinite kaleidoscope tunnel of space-time. The floor rattled beneath her as explosions from their point of origin resonated through the jump portal.

Just hold together—

The *Wraith* shot out of the jump site with fragments of the Starbase spewing out around her. Engines hot and overcharged, she hurtled through the upper atmosphere of Jue Hexron.

"Sebbs, keep her nose down!" Reht yelled as a barrage of Victor's guards swept in on their position.

"Shields are maxed out!" Sebbs yelled back. "I've got to let up or she's going to come apart!"

"No!" Jetta shouted. Sebbs dodged the assault while Ro and Cray returned fire from the weapons pits. "Keep your heading."

Holding on tightly to an armrest with one hand, Jetta slotted the golden key into the adjacent interface port. "Jaeia, now!" she called over the engine strain.

Jetta could hear her sister's silent prayer as Jaeia sent out the signal to the Hub. Eons seemed to pass while they watched the radar spread.

"Anything?" Jetta said, holding on with all her might as Sebbs banked hard to port to evade the new formation of fighters coming their way.

Jaeia scrutinized the scanners, sweat pouring down her neck and forehead. "No Alliance signals."

Jetta checked the key to make sure it was properly aligned in the port.

"*Skucheka!*" she said, slamming her fist into the console.

She was a fool to invest her trust so wildly. After all, the Hub could easily be lying about its ability to transition flashed materials out of the wave network. It was a stupid risk. She should have never broken her own code of self-reliance.

Jetta closed her eyes. *Why can't Jaeia ever see?*

"Look!" Jaeia exclaimed, pointing to the cluster of Alliance starships rematerialized above the Holy Cities.

An eye and mouth danced across the holographics, giving Jetta a smile and wink.

Affording no time for the Hub's antics, she shouted into the com system. "Is Billy Don't in position?"

"Awaiting your order!" Tech said over a thicket of static. On her armrest projector, she saw a video feed of the little Liiker wired into the *Wraith's* primary communication's dish, blowing bubbles with his lubricant as Tech checked his connections.

Jetta flipped to the secondary viewscreen just in time to see the outnumbered Alliance Fleet being swallowed by Victor's forces.

"Now!"

Déjà vu knotted her stomach as she watched the starships of the Galactic Republic suddenly rendered inert. She remembered her own moment of interconnectedness to a network of warships, the way she caved the entire Dominion Core with a single thought. Back then the Motti Overlord had manipulated her rebellion to enact the demise of a tyrannical empire. Now she ordered a Liiker child to do the same.

"Check the readings."

"Already on it," Jaeia replied.

Mom came up beside her and helped her interpret the datastream sliding down the *Wraith* armrest monitors.

"See the hole?" Jaeia said.

Jetta didn't waste a second. "Sebbs, take us to heading preset 1-beta-2."

As the Republic ships scrambled to reassemble, the *Wraith* dashed through the enemy fleet formations. Jetta wasn't sure how long it would take for the sub-commanders to assume the posts of their fallen executive officers, or even how many ranks Victor had implanted with his intracranial devices.

"Ackkk, haaaaaaaa—"

"What is that?" Jetta said, turning to Reht as a raucous series of chirps and giggles echoed over the com.

"Billy Don't," he sighed.

Despite the situation, hearing a child's laughter, even a semi-mechanical one, made a few members of their squad chuckle.

Jetta hid her own amusement as she wondered what command Tech had him relay to Victor's subordinates. *Knowing Billy, the Republic officers are probably twirling around on their heels and blowing bubbles with their spit.*

Jetta wiped her mouth, trying to rid herself of her smile. "We don't have much time. We have to find Victor's base of operations. We'll need to set up a—"

A high-pitched whine broke through the com and blew out one of the speakers. Jetta ran over and shielded her sister as two video relays sputtered and sparked. Finally a signal organized on the center screen.

"My, my, Warchild. You're more clever than I gave you credit for. Using Narki technology to get behind my defenses? Brava."

Jetta hated the enigmatic humor in his eyes. It took everything she had to keep her tone in check. "We've come to end this war."

"You know the power I have. You know what I can do to your pitiful little fleet. To *you*."

"Not before I drop about ten thousand nukes on your head," Jetta said with a grin. "I think it's time you and I met face-to-face."

Victor's lower lip quivered. Jetta had never seen him show such emotion. For some reason it startled her, and faint waves of nausea licked the back of her throat.

"You are going to die, Jetta Kyron. And so is everyone you love."

"No, Victor," she said, holding her voice to a hush. "Just me and you."

CHAPTER XIV

"Where is he?" Jaeia said, studying the holographic map of the city. They only had moments to deduce the most likely location of Victor's base of operations while Unipoesa and the remaining Alliance forces battled the recuperating Republic Fleet. When she looked up, Jetta was not even studying the map. Instead, her lips moved, and her eyes focused on something beyond the viewscreen as Sebbs flew them past stone towers and jutting urban skyscrapers basking in the morning sun.

Jetta walked over to the helm and typed in coordinates. Sebbs balked at first, but Jetta pressed down on the throttle until Sebbs was obligated to comply or risk crashing the ship.

Reht pulled Jaeia aside. "Does she know where she's going?"

Listening to her sister's thoughts, Jaeia picked up on the usual psionic oscillations between her and Jahx. *It's more than just Jetta's intuition guiding her decision.* She answered the dog-soldier captain confidently: "Yes."

But as her sister's emotions bled into her own, Jaeia found herself hugging her stomach. On some level, they both sensed Victor's presence expanding in the backs of their mind like a dark cloud blotting out the sun. *We must be getting close.*

As they circled the religious sector, Jaeia recognized the tinted glass of the capital skyscraper where she had first met Victor.

He's there, isn't he?

Jetta afforded her a quick look. *Yes.*

"Incoming!" Sebbs shouted as gun turrets poked out of concealed windows.

Grabbing onto the console chair, Jaeia held fast as Sebbs took evasive maneuvers. Ro and Cray hollered from the weapons pits, blasting out most of their turrets in a blaze of gunfire. As much as she disliked the dog-soldier duo, Jaeia was thankful for their fighting skills.

"They'll be more," Jetta said to Sebbs. "Victor has restructured this entire building. Set us down as quickly as you can."

"First team, come with me," Jetta said, signaling her SMT and running back to the ramp. "Jaeia, take the second team out in a minute delay. We'll need to break through their primary defenses."

"What exactly are you planning?" Jaeia asked her quietly as she helped her sister load her guns and combat pack. "You can't expect to muscle your way in. Scanners read at least a few hundred soldiers in the first level of the tower."

Hiding her eyes, she revealed her strategy. "Be my anchor?"

Jaeia cringed. "No, Jetta, that's not what we discussed."

Jetta nodded toward their brother as he ambled down the walkway and waited expectedly at the hatch. Triel followed, shoulders hiked up and eyes full of worry.

"They will help you. You know this is the only way," Jetta said, clicking off the safety to her gun. "I'm not about to make this a suicide run for my soldiers."

"No, just for you apparently," Jaeia retorted.

Green eyes looked at her sharply, but she got no other reply.

The *Wraith* smacked down hard near the entrance to the capital skyscraper, taking out any streetlamps and parked hover cars that were unfortunate enough to be situated near the tower's entrance. Victor's soldiers immediately poured out of the entrance, opening fire on the *Wraith* before Jetta could even lower the ramp.

Trust me, Jetta called silently to her sister, shoving on her helmet. Jaeia couldn't chance looking at her as Jetta gave the signal for her SMT to ready their weapons. An edge of blue fire sizzled on the nozzles of their guns, rifles charged and hot. *It's not like before...*

"I have a few new tricks up my sleeve," she added aloud, punching the ramp and lowering her visor.

"Fire on my mark!" Jetta shouted over the blasts.

Jaeia winced as Jetta tipped back into their shared connection and rummaged through their collective strength. She felt their bond flex and strain as Jetta reached out across the illusionary space and grabbed hold of the enemy soldiers' exposed minds.

No, Jetta! she silently screamed, fearing the worst. But Jetta didn't strangle them like she thought she would, or entrench them in their own gruesome nightmares. Grabbing her brother's hand and holding on tight, Jaeia watched with her inner eye as her sister did something new, something impossible; something *wonderful*.

Jaeia marveled as her sister swept across the psionic plane, netting the soul material of the enemy soldiers. She stripped them raw, until they were nothing but threads of light, and brought them together, end to end, until she had woven them into a continuous pattern. As the light grew exponentially brighter, Jaeia could no longer distinguish one soul from the next. *She turned away, unable to bear the intensity, withdrawing with a sense of overwhelming joy.*

"Jetta..." she said between heaving breaths, "I never thought it was possible."

Her viewpoint reverted to the physical world. The Republic soldiers were no longer firing at them. Slowly, methodically, they laid down their arms and sank to their knees, mumbling to themselves as they tried to comprehend their sudden enlightenment.

"Jetta!" Triel said, rushing down the ramp.

Following the Healer's eyeline, Jaeia saw her sister in the arms of her SMT lead, barely able to support her own weight as she ordered her team inside the building.

We have to keep going. Keep Triel back, Jetta ordered her sister.

Jaeia caught up to Triel and pulled her back on board. "You can't run out there like that!"

"She can't keep using her talents—she'll kill herself!"

The truth felt like a lead weight inside her stomach. "Not if I—*we*—can help it."

Jaeia waited the full minute before ordering the second team to follow Jetta's SMT inside the capital skyscraper. The Liberalist soldiers took a circular formation, protecting Jaeia, Triel, Jahx, and Kurt as they made their way carefully through the mass of dazed Republic soldiers to the tower's glass door entrance.

Jaeia looked back to see the *Wraith* take off.

Well, this is it; the dog-soldiers fulfilled their end of the bargain, she thought. *I just hope this isn't the last time I'll see them.*

"Jahx," she whispered, looking up at the skies darkening with the smoke from damaged starships. The capital skyscraper loomed in the orange glow of aerial gunfire, towering over her like an indefatigable mountain. "I have a very bad feeling about this."

Held up by an Alliance medic, her brother showed no sign that he recognized her words, or even of meaningful consciousness.

Jaeia felt the dark cloud swallow her whole as she stepped through the skyscraper doors and into Victor Paulstine's world.

***

Jetta stumbled along, her head floating in a sea of hurt. She could sense the opposing forces lining up for a surprise attack behind the far offices near the elevators and emergency stairwell. Taking a knee by a wall, she motioned for the first team to take cover while she assessed the situation.

(I can't do this...)

Jetta lifted her arm, as if to test the gravity in the building. Everything seemed heavier, every appendage more sluggish and numb.

(I'm not going to make it much longer.)

No. Keep going. You're almost there.

Jetta peered around the corner. She heard the pins being removed from flash grenades and the whine of charging pulse rifles. Somewhere, Victor was laughing at her.

(So weak. So afraid of what you are.)

Jetta squeezed her gun against her chest. They were still outnumbered. Only one way to get past their defenses. Only one way to survive another psionic expenditure. The easy way was the only way.

Time is running out.

Only one way.

I have to stop him.

Jetta closed her eyes and dug her fingernails into her own throat. *I'm sorry, Jahx.*

***

Kurt Stein stopped Jaeia as she reached the professional sector of the skyscraper where the structure separated into offices and conference rooms. "Captain, I need to tell you something," he said, fumbling with the visor of his helmet.

After checking the corners, Jaeia signaled the Liberalists to move forward and position themselves to flank the first team. Up ahead, Jetta's SMT crouched along the far dividing wall, waiting for her command to press forward. Jaeia sensed the number of the opposing forces hidden behind the offices, near the access stairwell, readying their assault. "It had better be quick, Doctor."

"I don't have much of this sixth sense left, but I can sense what's here."

"What do you mean?" Jaeia asked, nodding for the medic to bring about her brother. Triel followed close behind, eyes and heart searching desperately for Jetta.

"There is another demon here," Kurt said, wiping the sweat from his eyes.

"Like the one that was inside you?"

Kurt shook his head, his face pinched with frustration as he tried to find the right words. "Worse."

Jaeia would have investigated further, but the sudden psionic shift jarred her concentration.

Oh no—

"Jetta!" Jaeia shouted.

***

Jetta barely heard her sister's cry as she stabbed her fingers through the eye sockets of the enemy soldiers and burrowed into soft gray matter.

So much easier—

(So much more fulfilling—)

Giggling, Jetta raked her hands through their memories, wrestling fears and nightmares from buried places. Screams and cries for mercy filled her with delight as imagined horrors became real.

***

Jaeia ran to her sister, pulling her off the wall and shaking her by the shoulders.

"Jetta, no!" she screamed.

Lights overheated, shattered. Wall sockets blew off their mounts and computer monitors exploded. As the floor rumbled, the air charged with electricity, making Jaeia's arm hairs stand on end.

"Switch to backups!" she commanded. The teams clicked on their flashlights and held them with shaking hands.

Whipping to the left, Jaeia's eyes widened as the phantom image of someone's nightmare glided down the hall, a colossal creature with moonlit eyes and pitch-black skin. A few meters away, eight-legged insects with clawed mandibles crept down the cubicle partitions and over the cocooned husks of their victims. Pools of blood expanded down the hallway, accompanied by the shriek of a monster emerging from slumber.

"Jetta," Jaeia tried again, trying to bring her sister back.

Jetta's eyes rolled back, her lips forming words without sound. Too far away to reach, Jaeia didn't dare try to seek her out in that dark place.

Jahx, help me! Jaeia pleaded, feeling phantom fingers prying into her own skull.

"Jetta," Triel said, staggering toward them, her face contorted with pain. "Jetta, stop—wake up—you have to stop this! You're hurting us!"

Jaeia slumped onto a pile of papers. With one last effort she grabbed onto Triel's ankle and held fast.

***

Hungering for the next nightmare, Jetta didn't care who she captured next.

"Jetta," a voice called to her. "Enough."

Her vision spun away from shadows, the ruins of shattered psyches, until she found herself hovering in a place of shifting gray half-tones and shooting stars.

"Jahx?" she asked, recognizing his presence.

Her brother emerged from the fluctuating mist, his blue eyes shining like lighthouse beacons against the gray. "Jetta, with all that's been shown to you, how can you still not believe?"

"What?" she said, picking herself off the floor.

Jahx plucked a hair from her head.

"Hey!" Jetta exclaimed.

Pulling on the hair, Jahx stretched it until spanned farther than the eye could see. It unraveled in strands of light, color, and sound until she was surrounded by all of her memories.

"What do you see?" Jahx asked.

Jetta looked around, seeing flashbacks of their youth on Fiorah, their time aboard the Dominion vessels, and other moments from her past. The images came from three different angles, expanding outward like a ripple in the water, until the memory's synergy took on a unique form of its own.

The experiences she had stolen unfolded alongside what she knew, compounding her point of view, interweaving with and binding her realities. She saw the human man she had killed at the refueling station and the memories she had unintentionally grafted from him, but this time she did more than see through his eyes. She felt his heart beat in her own chest, his blood running through his veins; his skin became her own. The same thing happened with Edgar Wallace, and Sir Amargo, and every person she had ever stolen from, until she no longer saw their worth in their knowledge or memories.

Reeling backward, Jetta tried to stabilize herself. "Jahx, what are you doing?"

"Look, Jetta. See."

She dared to look again, this time seeing the totality of what she knew and what she had learned, and all that she had chosen not to see.

"Jahx," she whispered, realizing her own blindness. What she had seen before was no more than a tangle of lives, frayed and knotted, with no recognizable shape. Now she saw the rich color and texture of a tapestry she never knew existed, entwining countless souls in an infinite universe.

"So beautiful," she said, reaching out.

But Jahx pulled her back before she could make contact. He pointed at a discarded scrap of paper lying face down on the swirling floor. Jetta picked it up and read the inscription hurriedly scribbled on the back in the broad, barely coordinated strokes of a child. "Me..."

Jetta turned it over and gasped.

"Death has given you clarity. You have already seen the face of suffering," Jahx said. Jetta recognized the drawing, the hideous face of the beast she had seen when Triel had taken her life. "Now you must accept its presence as a part of you. You must choose what you see, and what you allow yourself to feel, and what you will make real. Have you been given a blessing—or a curse?"

The dimensions of his words expanded within her soul, Jahx's greatest gift blossoming inside her. She dropped the drawing and looked at her own hands.

"I never knew..."

***

Jetta awoke to find herself wrapped in Triel's arms, the Healer whispering prayers in her native tongue. Jaeia was there too, lying on her side and clinging to Triel's leg. Nearby, Jahx swayed in place, still caught in whatever limbo claimed him.

"Hey," Jetta said, prying herself loose. It took her only a moment to remember what she had done. With more urgency she freed herself and stumbled to her feet. Propelling herself forward on anything sturdy, she assessed the damage she had caused. Most of her SMT and the Liberalist soldiers were dazed but still alive. Some were lucid enough to still follow her orders.

Normally she would have been too ashamed to look her siblings or the Healer in the face, but Jahx had shown her what she had needed to see.

I must complete my mission, she thought, more determined than ever.

"Those that are able, follow me. This ends now," Jetta said.

That's when he appeared. The lone surviving monitor on a nearby office desk flickered to life with the grainy image of Victor.

"Warchild. Come down, leave your troops behind. I am ready for you. Are you ready for me?"

One of the elevators near the stairwell parted its doors with a pleasant *ding*.

Jetta offered Jaeia a hand up. "Let's go."

"Jetta…" Jaeia said, still holding on after she had risen. Her fear and uncertainty created a suffocating miasma in the air. "Are you ready for this?"

Falling back into their bond, Jetta followed her sister's thought process: She had just witnessed Jetta do something wonderful by enlightening the soldiers outside the tower, and then revert to older, darker habits in her weakened state. *She wonders what path I'll take with Victor.*

Jetta slung Jahx's arm around her shoulder and held him by the waist. For some reason she thought of their days on Fiorah, and all the times Jaeia refused to play rock dice with her and Jahx; she always hated to gamble.

"This is it, Jae. It's time to roll the dice."

***

It wasn't until Tarsha Leone set foot on the *Star Runner's* bridge that the grim reality hit her: *I've never engaged in a live battle. Not even once, in all my years of training in the Command Development Program…*

Admiral Unipoesa caught sight of her as he barked commands to the crew. The Republic Fleet, scattered but not disabled, was sporadically returning fire.

"Position alpha-two. Cover those fighters. Helmsmen, take us about, quarter thrusters, lock missiles on their lead warship."

He motioned her to his side, and she joined him with obvious reluctance.

"That dog-soldier Liiker was able to disable their commanders, but they're still putting up quite the fight," he briefed her. "We need to hold this position until the ground teams can secure their command ops."

Tarsha thought of Jetta, and the impossible task of breaking into Victor Paulstine's base of operations. *Buying them time might not be enough, even with all the Kyron siblings and a Prodgy Healer working together with two specialized combat teams.*

Made uncomfortable by her own realization, Tarsha readjusted the top of the Alliance-issued uniform. The last time she had worn a military uniform seemed like lifetimes ago. She didn't quite understand her own compliance in wearing it, only that she didn't know what else to do. She didn't think any of the Alliance crew would take her seriously in her Old Earth rags, but the starchy material didn't feel right on her skin.

Why did I come here? she thought. *I don't belong here.*

Just as her nerves were about to get the better of her, the Endgame holographic module situated in the center of the war room caught her eye. The Republic Fleet, represented in red, surrounded the tiny contingent of blue Alliance starships on all sides. Despite their numbers, it took her only seconds to see the gaps in the enemy defenses that Unipoesa had missed.

"You see something?" Unipoesa said, reading her correctly.

Tarsha hesitated. The Scabber in her knew better than to offer her assistance without creating an insurance policy for her freedom and her reward. She looked at him stolidly. "I can help you—on one condition."

The admiral didn't hide his impatience. "What?"

Tarsha removed a shock collar she had stolen from the tactical lockers in the armaments department and dangled it in front of his horrified face.

"You wanted me to believe I was a thief," Tarsha said. "So I became the best one on Earth."

"What do you want me to do with that?"

"Wear it," she said, holding up the remote in the other hand. "You can take it off when this is all over and Bossy and I are safely on our way."

The admiral motioned for the guards to back down. Pressing his knuckles down on the edge of the module, he leaned into her face. "You're here to fight a war, Tarsha, not to make deals."

"Dear father," she said, not budging despite the old stink of his breath. "You want to win this war?" She paused just long enough so that she was sure he saw her smile. *"Know when you're defeated."*

***

Jetta would never have even considered stepping aboard an elevator sent by any other enemy but Victor.

He wants me alive and fully intact, she thought. The soldiers they had battled to get inside the capital skyscraper was Victor toying with his prey, nothing more. *He would never stand for cheaply harming me without the thrill of destroying my soul first.*

The elevator doors parted on the lowest level of the tower, at what Jetta estimated as at least seven kilometers underground.

I'm impressed, she thought, seeing the modifications Victor had made. Once an intricate maze of catacombs, the government of the Holy Cities had incorporated the sacred grounds into their capital building. Victor, of course, had stripped the religious monument and converted it into a reinforced, fully functional command post.

The arched communications center was dark, lit only by the blinking lights of the abandoned terminals. Jetta took her time, letting her senses adjust. The air smelled musty and old, carrying with it the tangy stench of preservatives despite the invasion of high-tech equipment and ventilation systems. The place felt empty and desolate, like a tomb.

"They're all gone," Jaeia observed. "Victor must have ordered their retreat."

But Jetta thought otherwise. *Victor is paranoid enough to have implanted his command post operatives with intracranial devices, even the terminal techs.* Billy Don't would have deactivated them all when they broadcast his voice across the Starways, leaving Victor stranded by himself.

But how could he have removed all those bodies so quickly?

Jetta checked her sleeve. She had instructed the combat teams to find alternate routes down, avoiding the elevator shaft, knowing that Victor would have it rigged if any of her soldiers were to try to descend. Despite her attempts to contact them, her sleeve readout only displayed static.

"Too much interference," Jetta surmised, tapping it with her finger. *We're on our own.*

Jetta huddled with the others. She had only wanted to take Jaeia with her, but Triel had insisted, and she couldn't keep Jahx from following her. Kurt was also adamant about coming, and against her better judgment, Jetta allowed him to. *No time for arguments,* she thought as her rational and intuitive sides warred within her. *I'm just going to have to take a chance.*

Jetta... a voice called from the dark.

Jetta snapped her head to the left, but no one was there. The voice came again, this time from the right.

... I have waited so long to taste your soul...

She jumped when a hand touched her shoulder.

"Are you okay?" Jaeia asked.

Flipping up her visor, she wiped down her face as best she could. "Yeah," she said under her breath, sweeping the hallway with the light on the end of her gun. "Let's keep moving."

Jetta turned back when she noticed that Kurt wasn't following. Neither was Jahx.

"We have to keep moving," Jetta said, trying to get them to budge.

"Do you know what's down there?" Kurt asked, his mind loud with panic.

Jetta looked down the darkened hallway. The action room's red-lit sign glowed in the shadows ahead.

Breath hitching in her chest, Jetta anticipated his words before he said them.

"Terror... and pain," Kurt whispered.

Jetta looked to Triel. The Prodgy Healer seemed equally disturbed, her body stiff and rigid, as if expecting a blow.

"What do you sense?" Jetta asked her.

Triel slowly shook her head. "Something that should never have been."

"We're all together," Jaeia said, drawing her firearms and turning off the safety. "This is the best shot we have."

Jetta took her brother's cold hand, his tension seeping through her glove. "Come on, Jahx. We have to go now."

Jetta led them down the hall. As a precaution she gave her second firearm to Kurt and her compact shock wand to Triel. Even in an empty hallway, she didn't trust the shadows.

As they neared the action room door, Jetta spied the cameras perched along the wall, noting their steadfast, blinking attention to her movement. *Victor's watching.*

(He's been watching me all along.)

(He knows me.)

(He sees inside me.)

The action room door opened in a circular pattern, like a dilating pupil. Holding her breath, she stepped through the eyelet into the brightly lit, white-walled command control center. Technicians, still linked into their mikes, lay slumped across their stations, and decorated officers hung limply from the observation railing.

"Look," Jaeia whispered.

Piled high in the corner were the missing technicians from the communications center. A few of them had similar scars around their orbital sockets, but most had been picked apart, their uniforms stained with bits of gray matter and sticky clumps of blood. Sickened, Jetta turned away. As she did, something skittered away in her peripheries.

Jaeia saw it too. *Jetta, did you see... do you feel...?*

Her twin didn't have to finish the thought. The discordant energy she felt confirmed her worst fears.

Stay focused, she reminded herself, swallowing hard against the acid brewing in her stomach. *Can't lose it now.*

"It's over, Victor," Jetta said, motioning for the rest of the party to stay back as she approached the staging platform in the middle of the room. An ornate command chair surveyed half-rings of terminals and walls of holographic projectors. Several displays showed the different angles of the war raging above them as the Galactic Republic crushed down on the Starways Alliance Fleet.

Jetta couldn't see him, but she knew by the weight of the air that he was there. "Stand down."

"You think you've won, Warchild?" A well-manicured hand lifted from the armrest. Gold rings shone in the light. "Why, we've only just begun."

The holographic displays switched over to unified projections of an ancient-looking starcraft. Jetta identified it immediately. *The experimental ship our parents and Kurt Stein boarded centuries ago—*

"I've found my old ship. It's refueling in my hangar right now, getting ready for her second flight," he said. "I think that is cause for celebration."

Victor clapped his hands. From the ventilation shafts and hidden crevices along the walls skittered pointed metal feet.

Jetta wasn't prepared for the group's collective reaction to the Liikers. She grabbed onto the nearest terminal, breathing heavily as she tried to gain control of herself against their compounding fear.

"I know you're too young to drink, but seeing as this is the end, maybe you'll humor me with a toast."

Ripping off her helmet, Jetta tried to take in more air than her lungs would allow. She stumbled backward in an attempt to avoid the faceless humanoid heads offering her champagne with their spiny appendages.

Jetta bit her lip, drawing blood, allowing anger and pain to subdue her fears. She attempted to squeeze off a few rounds against the lithe six-leggers, but her gun didn't seem to work. Neither did Jaeia's.

"Don't bother," Victor said. "Your firearms are useless in here. A nice little feature I had installed a few months ago."

Jetta re-slung her gun and motioned for Jaeia to do the same.

Firearm lockouts, she deduced. She had seen them used before, but as a safety measure in nuclear reactors and subatomic processors.

Victor twirled around in his seat. Outfitted in a tailored white suit topped with an expensive-looking red silk cravat and black cane resting lazily at his side, he could have easily been mistaken for a playboy aristocrat from a different century. *If it weren't for his menacing presence.*

He held his glass by the stem and smiled. The light reflecting off his beveled lenses hid his eyes, and the bright diamond finish of his teeth made his mouth sparkle. Though she had never met him in person, she hadn't expected to feel so diminutive next to his slight, bony frame.

"And who did you bring along with you, Warchild? These are not your typical flock of useless marines."

Pulling herself together, Jetta regained some of her composure. She took solace in the fact that everyone except her brother had been outfitted in stealth gear, including helmets to shield their faces. She had tried, but every time she or anyone else had attempted to change Jahx out of his infirmary gown or put him in gear, they had been strangely unable to complete the task. Luckily, Jahx lingered at the back of the group, out of Victor's direct line of sight.

"Victor, I will ask you one last time," Jetta said, withdrawing her combat knife. She had to play it carefully, especially since they were outnumbered. Even if she could reach Victor, she couldn't outright kill him without unleashing the Motti's Dissembler weapon; she would have to uncover his secrets first. "Stand down. It's over."

Victor laughed, making his cheeks crinkle. She was close enough now that his skin appeared shiny, like some sort of polymer plastic stretched tightly over a mannequin's head. *Not real—not human.*

A borrowed memory surfaced, and she compared Victor's unusually smooth features to the unfortunate patients who had undergone extensive plastic surgery in the early twenty-first century before the brutal craft had been perfected. On a remote level, she wondered what Oshiro and his surgical teams on Iyo Kono would have thought of Victor's imperfect transformation.

Transformation from what? her sister said, listening in on her thoughts.

"You still don't understand, do you, Warchild? I found my ship. I think it's time I met my makers."

"Your makers?" Jetta kicked aside one of the Liikers that had gotten too close to her, causing the others scramble toward their hiding spots.

In the back of her head she felt a growing disquiet radiating from her brother. He was sensing something beyond what she or Jaeia could, an unseen, imminent danger in Victor's grasp.

"Yes. And I fully intend to return as I see fit. I find it insulting to have you stand before me as you are, ungrateful and unworthy of your gifts, weak and impuissant, while I am the one capable of wielding what you cannot. It's very *disconcerting*."

"What would you do with these gifts, Victor?" Jaeia said, removing her helmet and stepping onto the platform.

"Ah, Captain! So good to see you again. Congratulations once again on your promotion! I know how hard it's been for you to rise above your sister's reputation," he said, raising his glass. He crossed his legs and seemed delighted to answer her question. "I tried to murder the people of Earth 1,100 years ago, but that was before my eyes were opened. Much too vulgar, and too trivial a pursuit—a menial task for someone else's pleasure. I want to rape the soul of this galaxy. I want the worlds to collapse into the suffering that gave birth to this wretched existence—to me."

Her brother's words formed in her head and trickled out her mouth in a gasp.

"You are… quite… the… Sportive Lunatic."

Victor's voice became hushed. The room darkened and closed in. "What did you say?"

Sportive Lunatic. Sportive Lunatic. Sportive Lunatic.

The words from Victor's correspondence with Ramak Yakarvoah repeated over and over in her head.

What are trying to tell me? she called out to her brother.

Sportive Lunatic. Sportive Lunatic. Sportive Lunatic.

Jetta ground her teeth and dug her nails into her forehead.

Sportive Lunatic. Sportive Lunatic. Sportive Lunatic.

Jahx—help me see!

Victor uncrossed his legs and stood up. Setting down his champagne glass, he tucked his cane in his armpit, and clapped his hands together.

"Let me show you the face of suffering, what the Gods never intended. Let me show you how I will take the reins of the Azerthenes' power and purify this universe."

The floor next to Victor's chair slid open. Jetta and Jaeia fell to their knees as the monster with the burning red eye elevated from the bowels of the command center. The Motti Overlord hissed at the sight of them, excitedly moving his pincers back and forth.

Fear and panic consumed all rational thought. She reared back her knife to throw at M'ah Pae, but a Liiker drone tumbled down from the ceiling and seized her blade before she could release it. Other Liikers spilled out from the opening in the floor, crawling over her and her companions, stripping their weapons. Everything around them buzzed, moved, and vibrated with flesh-skinned machines.

Jahx—I need you!

"I know you have met my servant, M'ah Pae," Victor said. Jetta watched in sickened awe as the Motti Overlord bowed to his master in an unprecedented display of subordination, allowing Victor to place ringed fingers on his mottled skull.

"He has been most faithful to me all these years. We have been patiently awaiting this moment since the fall of Earth. You and your siblings almost ruined our chance once—it won't happen again."

Jetta couldn't believe her ears, or eyes. Victor had been behind the Dominion Wars. He was behind the Motti's rise to power, and their second coming. He was there all along, waiting and plotting for his chance at galactic genocide.

Oh my Gods—
What did he say?

"I tried to murder the people of Earth 1,100 years ago, but that was before my eyes were opened..."

She saw the words in her head again: *Sportive Lunatic.* They broke apart, floating in a sea of whispers, of confusing imagery from places she had never been and people she had ever seen, until they rearranged themselves into a backdrop of a world reduced to ashes.

Sportive Lunatic. It's an anagram for Victor Paulstine—

Jaeia heard her revelation and put the remaining pieces together.
Ramak and Victor are the same person.

With a scream, Jetta lunged wildly for Victor. He never moved or flinched as his servant snatched Jetta with his pincers and slammed her into the ground.

"No!" Jaeia shouted, but Victor cautioned her.

"One more step and I'll end her life."

Jetta could see Jaeia holding Triel back as she struggled to breathe against the intense pain and pressure the Motti Overlord exerted on her chest.

Don't let her Fall— Jetta whispered silently to her sister, feeling Triel's mounting rage.

"Do you know who I am?" Victor said, leaning down to whisper in her ear. His voice sounded disembodied, inhuman. "I am the monster inside your head, the venom in your veins. I am the rot eating away your soul."

Jetta couldn't breathe. Something slipped into her head, a veil cast over her eyes. She wanted to scream, but she no longer had a mouth, and she no longer had a body. She unraveled from the inside out as Victor Paulstine stepped inside her skin.

***

Jetta—

Jaeia fell to her knees as something bit into the back of her head. She felt the Healer grab onto her and drag her away from the scene as Victor laughed. "So weak, so useless."

"Jaeia," Triel said, propping her up behind a console and shaking her shoulders. "You've got to come around. He's poisoning her mind."

Jaeia fought the pitting nausea as her sister's presence tore away from her like a limb pulled from socket.

"I feel her too," Triel said, her face blanched and clammy. She hugged Jaeia tightly. "We have to help her fight."

Jaeia caught glimpses of Kurt holding up her brother, hysterically trying to bring him out of his stupor.

Victor's hold on Jetta is so strong—

—he's dragging all three of us down with her—

Tipping her head back, Jaeia fought the fire consuming her belly. She could hear Victor's voice in her sister's mind, playing to her worst fears, making her worst nightmares come true.

Jaeia saw Victor and Jetta standing in their old apartment, in the bedroom in front of the mirror. Positioning himself behind her, Victor whispered in Jetta's ear, pointing to the reflection. Jaeia tried to shout out to her, to tell her the hideous beast with scarred, swollen flesh and rivulets of saliva streaming across pulsating appendages wasn't real.

(It's a lie!) *she screamed, trying to draw her sister's attention away from the gruesome creature mimicking her movements.*

(Jetta, no—look away—that's not you!) *she tried again. But their bond felt choked, as if Victor had knotted it in his fist.*

"Kill them," she heard Victor say. "Kill the ones that make you weak."

***

Triel screamed when she saw Jetta's face. Green eyes projected only menace and hatred. She no longer felt the soul that had shone through its corporeal fetters, but a vacuum encased in false skin.

The Liikers buzzed in a high-pitched frenzy as Jetta rose from M'ah

Pae's clutches and approached them. *She isn't just going to kill us; she's going to tear apart our souls.*

Jetta, she called out, *remember us—remember me—remember my love for you!*

"Kill them!" Victor laughed, raising his glass. "Rid yourself of their wasted flesh."

A chasm of hopelessness and fear broke open inside her.

No, I cannot let myself Fall—

Triel swallowed the awful truth. *There's no turning back.*

(Then I will use the last of my strength to save her.)

Warm hands lifted her from the ground. Two blue eyes gazed back at her. In them she soared beyond her own sight, beyond the realms of human understanding, into the worlds she had only known from the carvings inside the Temple of Exxuthus.

"Jahx," she whispered. "Help us."

***

Jetta didn't recognize the world. On some level she sensed the roots of the nightmare, a place born of hatred and unfulfilled needs, selfish desires and untold suffering; a place she had brushed against in the hearts of men. But not like this. No one person could imagine this hell.

Faintly aware of her surroundings, she walked down the aisle of a burning church. Its bells tolled the end of the world, and the foundation rumbled. As she approached the altar, the ones who came before her, strung up by their ankles and dangling from the rafters, doused her in their drippings. Blood and black oil oozed from their raw, mangled flesh, riddled with machinery and inorganic matter she did not recognize. She heard familiar cries, calling her from a distant place, but she could not understand them.

She knelt down before the altar. Candles made from broken fingers illuminated the passages of the Book of the Worm laid out before her. Passages whispered up from the pages—

"...without hope, there is total freedom..."

"...he will open his eyes to the dead light of his wickedness..."

"...submit to the wrath of chaos..."

A severed head with open eyes lay next to the Book of the Worm. She thought she might have recognized the face. A voice she should have known whispered his name.

(Josef Stein…)

A knife lay next to the severed heard. She took it, cleaning its bloodied blade on her thigh.

"I loved them. That's why I did this," the head lamented.

Jetta raised the knife with two hands, aiming for her chest. The ground quaked, and the fire roared in anticipation.

That's when she heard the clatter.

She looked down, arms tense and shaking, blade hungering for her flesh.

Jahx stood beside her, his hand open above the altar. Following his line of sight, Jetta saw the rock dice that had dropped from his hand and onto the soiled cloth.

(Jetta,) he said. (What do you see?)

Jetta's arms dropped to her side, the knife clanging to the stone floor. She touched the rock dice, not believing what she saw. The tattoo. The symbol they had carried with them all their lives.

(Believe, Jetta,) Jahx said as the roof caved in around them. The stone floor split down the center, a guttural scream rising from the glowing pits. She reached out for him as the world collapsed.

***

Jetta found herself lying in a heap next to her sister, Triel, and Kurt as they sheltered behind a console.

"Is everyone okay?" she asked through a mouth stuffed with cotton.

Triel embraced her tightly. "Jetta, thank the Gods."

"Jahx!" Jaeia shouted, picking herself off the ground.

Propping herself up, Jetta saw her brother standing in front of the platform. Victor, still sitting in his command chair, looked delighted as the Motti Overlord and the hoard of Liikers writhed around him in a humming mass.

Somehow Jahx's voice broke through the noise of the swarm. "I have kept my promise. I have come to save you, to set you free."

"What did he say?" Kurt said, shooting up from his cover.

Jetta pulled him back down. *I don't know what he's doing,* she thought, feeling the edge of her brother's knowledge, *but we need to keep our position.*

Victor laughed and sipped his drink. "Ah, and you must be the venerable Jahx Kyron, the weakest of the Kyron three. I remember when my Liikers tore you limb from limb. Oh, how you screamed. How you got your skin back, I'm not sure, but I'll enjoy tearing it apart once more."

Jahx's voice never changed pitch or volume, but seized all who listened. "You cannot trick me with your lies. I know who you are, and I know your heart."

Slamming down his drink, Victor pointed his cane at Jahx. "Kill him."

Jahx looked down at the Liikers circling his feet and spoke in a language Jetta did not understand or even recognize. The Liikers backed away from him, settling back around Victor.

"I pity you, Ramak Yakarvoah. You were always inferior, the one in Josef's shadow, the one remembered not for his genius, but for the ugliness his mother made known to the world."

Victor squeezed his cane, knuckles turning white. "How dare you—"

"She looked at you and wept. Her religion made her believe she had given birth to the devil, and that it was her duty to put an end to your life. But you survived because you are a parasite, and you draw your life from the suffering of others."

Her brother's knowledge played out in her head like clips from an old movie. Ramak's descent into madness after his mother set fire to him. The government agencies rescuing him, trying to salvage the burned remains of an orphaned child. Jealousy and rage as the successes of a handsome classmate who never thought twice about his gifts overshadowed his own achievements. The subconscious invention of Victor Paulstine, and the blurring of his identity as Josef Stein treated his scars with synthetic skin made by his Smart Cells.

"Your genius was all you had, and yet it paled in comparison to Josef's. He was always better than you, even when you were children."

"Is that so?" Victor said, his anger dissolving into a smug smile. "You think I was no match for the brilliant Josef Stein? The one who was supposed to bring about enlightenment, the spiritual evolution of the human race, and yet destroyed the world?"

Enraged at the accusation, Kurt Stein tried to break cover and go after Victor, but Jetta held him down. "Just wait."

Victor's teeth sparkled, his synthetic skin pulled taut. "I was the one to discover what we were—prophets created by the Azerthenes to compete for the heart of mankind. And I, the one who you accuse of being the lesser, did not kill my saintly opposition." Victor looked back at M'ah Pae and laughed. "No, I showed brutal benevolence. I turned a savior into a disciple of death."

Jetta gasped as her brother's inner eye became her own. The Motti Overlord with the burning red eye and twisted flesh dissolved into a dark-haired man with mournful eyes and bloodied hands. She saw his aura, faint and flickering, in the shadow of the great beast.

"Josef—"

"Enough of this madness. Kill him. *Kill them all!*" Victor thundered.

This time M'ah Pae took charge, the weight of his many legs splitting the white tile.

"Dad!"

Jetta couldn't hold Kurt back as he leapt out from behind his cover.

"Dad, no! Stop! It's me, Kurt! Dad! Please, Dad!"

Liikers poured over Kurt, slamming him into the ground. Jetta protected Jaeia and Triel as long as she could before the sheer number of fleshy machines overwhelmed her and struck them all down.

"Dad, please!" Kurt screamed as the Liikers tore at his skin. "Dad—don't you remember your own son? It's me!"

Grabbing Jahx by the waist, M'ah Pae brought his razored pincers to his neck. Jahx did not struggle as he dangled off the ground.

"Josef Stein," Jahx said, closing his eyes. "You have not forgotten. Remember."

***

Jetta and Jaeia's minds split between two worlds as their brother delved into the depths of the Motti Overlord.

What is he doing? He's going too fast— *Jetta called out to her sister.*

No, *Jaeia replied, lending her sister a different perspective into their brother. Glimpses of his former abduction by the Deadwalkers, and a chance searching of M'ah Pae's soul, touched Jetta's mind.* He's already been down this pathway.

Still, Jetta could barely keep up with him as he dove through the murk and the sludge until she feared she could go no further. Memories, tortured beyond those of any Sentient she had ever grafted, bombarded her at every turn.

(Jahx, I can't go on—)

(You must never be afraid,) he whispered back as he plunged deeper. (You have to believe.)

Jetta thought of Yahmen, and of all the times Jahx had fruitlessly tried to help their abusive owner, risking his life for him.

(We're all here this time,) *she heard her sister say. A hand wrapped around her own.* (Trust in our strength.)

Jetta slowed her breathing down, blocking out the psionic cacophony and concentrating on the steady pulse of her siblings. Opening up her mind to them, she gave them all that she had. She remembered the Josef Stein that Edgar Wallace passionately revered, and her mother's respect for a brilliant scientist and a good man. She recalled his last video recording, asking for forgiveness and promising to find the son he loved. Most of all, she concentrated on her own visions of the man with the immense second shadow, the angel from her nightmares.

"Ramak lied to you," *she heard her brother say. She saw him reaching for a petrified heart in a hollow chest.* "Kurt lives."

***

Opening her eyes to the real world, Jetta saw that her brother was no longer in death's clutches. The Motti Overlord had released him and stood completely erect on all of his legs.

M'ah Pae's face contorted in disbelief. In a garbled, grating voice, he feebly said, "Kurt?"

"Dad—please—help us!" Kurt cried out as one of the Liikers sliced away at his chest.

The Overlord hissed, and the attacking Liikers immediately retracted their pincers and scuttled away from Jetta and her companions.

"Kurt, you're alive…" M'ah Pae said, his single eye tearing with a mucoid substance. He crouched down and extended his front graspers, as if to offer an embrace. Bloodied and bruised, Kurt touched the edge of his father's metallic limb and wept.

In the corner of her eye, Jetta saw Victor steadily backing off the platform.

"Don't let him get away!" she shouted. As she tried to scramble to her feet, her lungs protested the sudden exertion, sending up gobs of bright red blood. Gritting her teeth, she forced her legs to work past the dizzy burn, and ran after him.

The overhead lighting flickered and then fizzled as the invisible force field of the firearm lockout cycled down. Victor, standing in the doorway, removed a pistol from his suit pocket and aimed at her head.

Metal screeched and gears snapped. Shots fired. Jetta looked down at her chest, expecting to see bullet wounds. Instead, she only saw an immense shadow. M'ah Pae stooped in front of her, shielding her from the bullets.

"Dad, no!"

Victor disappeared behind double-sealed doors, locking them from the other side.

It took Jetta a moment to grasp what had just occurred. *M'ah Pae, the Motti Overlord who tore my family apart—*

...just saved my life.

No, Jahx said, hearing her thoughts. *Josef Stein did.*

Jaeia grabbed her and pulled her out of the way as the Motti Overlord toppled over. The Liikers buzzed and shrieked as their master's inky biofluids spilled out over the white tile. Some immediately deactivated, while others desperately tried to patch up the gaping bullet wounds.

Jetta knelt down beside his head as the Motti Overlord rasped and wheezed. His single red eye, the one that haunted her dreams, was splattered across the floor, leaving him blind.

Jetta touched his mottled skin. It felt cold and waxy. Still, she felt something beyond the cadaverous surface release from smothering darkness, from an unrelenting agony capable of crushing the strongest will. She felt the purest joy, and deepest gratitude.

"Thank you," he whispered, "for saving me."

***

Jetta grabbed her gun off the floor. "Stay here," she said to the rest of the party. "I'm going after Victor."

"I'm going with you," Jaeia said, picking up her own firearm off the tile.

"No." Jetta pointed to Triel, Kurt, and Jahx, who still hovered over the fallen Motti Overlord. "I need you to stay here."

"I didn't ask what you wanted."

Jetta was taken aback; her sister never spoke to her that way.

Softly, but in an unyielding tone, she added: "He didn't just get to you, Jetta. This is my fight too."

"Okay," Jetta said, running to the door. "Let's get him."

Across their bond, Jahx whispered, *His words are his strength; he can speak to the power inside you. You must silence his voice or he will destroy your soul.*

Her jaw tightened. Jahx wasn't telling her anything she didn't already know. Besides, she wasn't going to give him another chance. *This time I won't give him the opportunity to surrender.*

"No. Wait," Jahx said out loud. "You cannot kill him."

"Why?" Jetta scoffed, tearing off the side panel to manually override the door lock.

"Death will only give rise to another."

Jetta looked at her sister quizzically.

"You got it," Jaeia pointed out as the doors cracked open.

"Go!" Jetta shouted, straining to hold them open so Jaeia could fit through.

Fighting her instincts, Jetta followed the trail of psionic dissonance. She kept her eyes peeled for Liikers or Republic soldiers, but all of his private personnel littered the hallways and clogged access doors, completely deactivated by Billy Don't's broadcast.

Finally, as they entered a private hangar, Jetta and Jaeia came to a halt. The ancient terrestrial ship she had seen in flashbacks was docked on the center platform and hooked up to fuel lines.

"Up there."

Jetta followed her sister's gaze to the control tower as Victor pushed aside a limp technician to access the flight prep sequencer. *He's going to try and take off.*

She aimed her gun and took a deep breath. After taking her time to find the perfect target, she slowly exhaled, and pulled the trigger. The shot shattered the tower window and hit him in the left shoulder, knocking him off his feet.

Jetta wasted no time, taking as many stairs at a time as her dying body would let her to get to the top of the tower.

"Jetta, wait!" Jaeia said, not able to keep her pace.

No time, Jetta thought, gritting her teeth and ignoring her twin. She kicked open the tower door and barreled through. "It's… over!" she said between breaths.

Victor leaned against the far wall, blood spilling from the bullet wound and staining his perfectly white suit. He readjusted his glasses with shaking hands.

Jetta aimed at his other shoulder as Jaeia stumbled in. "Surrender and I might not shoot you again."

Victor laughed. Though weak at first, it rose to a maniacal howl. He tilted his head and said to Jaeia, "You're letting her make all the decisions, just like always, aren't you, Captain? You outrank her, and yet she always calls the shots. You're *weak* and *pathetic*. No wonder you were always left behind."

Jetta grimaced as her sister's emotions jerked away from her, whipping her across the psionic plane.

"Don't listen to him!" Jetta said, falling to her knees as a hammer of pain crashed down upon her skull.

"*Shut up, Jetta.*"

Under the power of Jaeia's second voice, Jetta's mouth clamped shut. She could barely pick up her head to see her sister's face. Bolts of pain held her in place as Jaeia walked toward her, firearm drawn, face slack and vacant as if she had been unplugged.

Victor's lips drew back over diamond teeth. "She has never considered your feelings. You were always an *afterthought…*"

Even through their inner channel, her voice came out as nothing more than a croak. *Jaeia, please!*

In her sister's mind, a dark reality unfolded.

Jaeia was alone in their old apartment, left behind while Galm took Jetta and Jahx to the market to barter for food and supplies.

The memory of Galm's words rang hollow in her ears. "I only have three tickets. I'm sorry. Please stay behind and try to collect some water for supper. Behave, Jaeia."

Sitting in the corner, gray eyes just above her knees, she stared at the rock dice in the middle of the entryway. Jetta and Jahx had stopped in the middle of their game, but left the dice in place to pick up where they left off upon their return.

Gray eyes misted over, and hands tightened into fists. Jetta felt her sister's pain as she kicked the dice into the corner.

(Always forgotten.)

Time shifted forward to their regimented days in the Core Academy. Endgame matches, won with three minds working together, yet with one voice, dominant and inflexible, often rising above the others.

We should move the fighters into orbit, take out their ground units after our medical units have a chance to retreat, *Jaeia suggested through their bond.*

Jetta saw herself in her sister's eyes, her appearance as intimidating as her tone. No. We'll nuke their base.

But we will kill our own troops, *Jaeia protested.*

She couldn't believe the callousness of her own voice. But we'll win.

Preconsciously, Jetta had been aware of her sister's opposition to her aggressive tactics years ago, but she had never seen the events play out from her sister's perspective.

I never knew, *she thought, feeling her sister's frustration in a new light.*

Jetta could barely stand the torment. Her mind spun and dove like an out-of-control starfighter as her sister's mind recreated Jetta's reckless and inconsiderate behavior.

(Jetta, why did you leave?) *Jetta heard her sister think.* (Am I that easy to abandon?)

(No, Jaeia!) *she cried back.* (I never left you!)

The voice changed. (You never really cared about me. You never really considered me an equal. I am nothing but your slave.)

Fingers pried at her jaw. A sharp pain, cold metal taste in her mouth. Jetta's perspective flexed back to the control tower room as Jaeia rammed her gun down her throat.

"You never cared," Jaeia said, her voice bereft of emotion, gray eyes a dull void.

Jetta's attempt at speech came out in a drooling garble around the barrel of the gun.

"You should have joined me," Victor said to Jetta, placing his hand on

313

Jaeia's shoulder and flashing his diamond teeth. "Now you will die."

***

Triel didn't know what to do. The Motti Overlord was dying from his wounds, but none of his biology made sense to her, nor did she dare immerse herself in the psyche of a Deadwalker.

"There's nothing I can do," she said, shaking her head and scooting away from him. "I'm sorry."

"Please," Kurt pleaded with her, comforting his father. "Please, you have to try."

Jahx laid a hand on her arm. "No. This is as it should be."

Triel watched the Kyron brother lay his hands on the Motti Overlord's face and whisper to him in a language she didn't understand. The room filled with psionic vibrations as Jahx continued to chant in hushed tones.

"What is he doing?" Kurt asked her, hypnotized by the phenomena.

Listening with all her senses, Triel tried to grasp what was transpiring between Jahx and M'ah Pae. It felt similar to what she had sensed Jetta and Jaeia do when they stole knowledge from other Sentients, but on a grander scale.

He's absorbing him...

"Jahx," the Motti Overlord choked over rusted gears. "I can't stop them. You have to stop them…"

"Stop who?" Kurt asked.

M'ah Pae gingerly held onto Kurt with his manipulating arm as Jahx pressed an ear to his crusted lips, trying to hear his last words. "Your mark… hope and redemption… the key… to salvation."

"Jahx," he said, sputtering black fluid. With his pincers he removed the ocular implant from his fused socket and offered it to Jahx. "Take my son home."

Triel felt the unnatural clicking inside the Motti Overlord's chest come to a halt. Kurt Stein did not utter a sound, grieving in silence for his father.

"What did he tell you?" Triel asked, helping Jahx to stand again.

Touching her face, he showed her what he learned.

Triel watched Josef Stein enter the design of the triplets' tattoo into an old computer interface, hope and conviction strong in his heart. She saw

Cause For Earth highlighted in bold, its secret plans laid out across the screen. Blueprints for a device packed with trillions of Smart Cells appeared, and the equation pointed to a resurrected blue and green planet.

The image muddled, malformed by terror and despair. Josef Stein sat alone in his lab as the world turned to ash. She felt the tiny critters slide and crawl down his throat to combat the Necro Plague decomposing his body, turning him into a shell of eternal rot. She experienced his pain, his glimmer of hope that somehow his Smart Cells would extend his life and preserve his mind against the infection, that he would not transform into one of the hideous creatures of his own creation.

She wanted it to stop right then, but Jahx showed her more. Bright lights hurt her eyes as Victor stared down at her, scalpel poised above her eye. *"This won't hurt for but a second."*

Dead flesh, cut away, replaced with cold metal. Survival meant the consumption of living tissues and fusion with precious machinery.

(Please, Jahx, I don't want to see this.)

The memories slid ahead. A ship filled with some of Josef's closest friends and co-workers, brilliant scientists who had helped him build and code his Smart Cells, ransacked by Victor's followers as they tried to escape the dying Earth. They didn't recognize Josef in his freshly wired skin.

They tried to reason with him—*"Dr. Stein, what are you doing?"*
"Josef, please!"
"We're your friends!"
"We can help you!"

Blood painted the decks. Triel lived Josef's nightmare as he bludgeoned his loved ones with his newly fused mechanoid arm.

Victor's voice, always in his head: *"You didn't think I'd let you spend eternity all alone, did you?"*

Those he trusted best, those who had helped him conceptualize Earth's last hope, infected, melted into translucent-skinned humanoid machines: monsters just like him. The other Motti. The creators of the Liikers.

An authentic, cohesive thought crystallized in his polluted mind: I have destroyed all that I loved.

Jahx pushed her forward to the Overlord's most recent memories. Triel saw the bulbous Motti ship nearing their world. Chaos and rebellion buzzed inside the enclave.

Oh Gods, *she thought, sensing adaptation to chemical restraints, and an anomalous gain in autonomy.*

The Motti lost control.

Now a new order directed the collective, driven by a hunger for pain and death.

Josef Stein's warning rang loudly in her ears. You have to stop them.

"The Dissemblers!" Triel said, breaking away from Jahx. "They've taken over. I have to stop them."

"What?" Kurt said.

"Triel of Algardrien," Jahx said, his blue eyes showing brightly against pale skin. "Do not be afraid. Josef Stein lives on. So will you."

Suddenly it all made sense to her. All the times she had purposely underperformed in her training, why she was so afraid of her father's expectations. The countless times she ran away from home. Fleeing Algar. Why she didn't want to believe she was the next Great Mother.

Most importantly, why she was drawn to Jetta, and why she loved her so fiercely.

"I understand now." Triel took Jahx's hand and brought it to her cheek. "Thank you."

***

Jaeia, my sister, my twin, Jetta projected. *You have always been the better part of my soul.*

With a gun rammed down her throat, Jetta tearfully reconstructed the first memory that came to mind. A simple one, a lie she told her starving twin when they were only four years old.

"*I won this at the food scramble. Take it,*" Jetta said, offering her a strip of dried meat.

Huddled under their cot in the entryway of their old apartment, Jaeia looked at it longingly but refused. "No, Jetta. It's your turn to map. I'll be fine."

"Jahx and I already ate our shares," Jetta said, pushing it into her sister's hand. "I'm stuffed."

It was tough lying to her telepathic sibling, but by that time Jetta had figured out ways to circumvent their shared thoughts. She had given Jahx *part of the meat strip, so she clung to that truth and avoided the lie; she had not eaten that day, nor had she won the food in the scramble. Instead, she had chanced stealing from a miner. It made Jaeia anxious when she took such risks, and she didn't want her twin to worry more than she already did. Besides, a few scrapes and bruises from the chase down the engine core didn't amount to much when faced with the prospect of starving.*

Hunger gnawed relentlessly at her belly as she tried to convince Jaeia that she was sated. "Eat it, Jae. I promise I'm full."

(I love you)

(I would give my life to save yours)

"Jetta..." *Jaeia said, taking the strip reluctantly.* "I know you're hungry."

Jetta gave her a rueful smile. "Eat it. I'll get more tomorrow."

"Thank you." *Jaeia hugged her, bumping her bruises and making her wince.*

Jetta kissed her cheek, still holding onto her twin. "I will do anything for you, Jaeia."

The gun pressed further down her throat. Jetta could feel her sister's hand tightening against the trigger, testing its resistance as Victor whispered in her ear, poisoning her mind with loneliness and abandonment.

(Jaeia, I am your biggest admirer,) *Jetta said, sending the thought blazing through the psionic planes. She conjured memories of her sister negotiating peace between warring alien worlds as an Alliance diplomat just like she had forged temporary truces between rival child labor gangs on Fiorah.*

The gun rattled against her teeth.

(I depend on you—*I look up to you!*) *With everything she had left, Jetta poured all of her respect and amazement at her twin, fighting against the tide of Victor's pain.* (You have always been my guide, my anchor, my best friend! I know I don't deserve your forgiveness for the things I've done,) *Jetta cried.* (But know that I have always loved you, and that you have always been the best part of me.)

Jetta gagged as the gun was yanked out of her throat.

"You bastard," Jaeia said, slugging Victor in the stomach. "Stay out of my head!"

The old man careened backwards, striking his head against the shelving. Despite the blow, he remained conscious, his rage all the more palpable.

"You are both so *weak*. You *disgust me*."

Jetta and her sister collapsed to the floor. Wriggling worms filled her insides, stretching her belly. She writhed on the ground, tearing at her own skin, trying to dig out the parasites eating her from the inside out. Bloodied and mad, Victor lifted his cane, taking aim at her eye.

His words are his strength; he can speak to the power inside you. You must silence his voice…

Jetta reached for her gun, but her brother's final warning rendered her inert. *Death will only give rise to another.*

Victor will be reborn, she heard her sister realize. *His evil cannot be killed.*

I have to try! Jetta shouted back.

Stripped of her physical abilities, Jetta resorted to her only other means of destroying Victor. She blasted head-first into his mind, unprepared for what lay beneath.

The first layer of Victor Paulstine's mind housed the illusion he had created of himself and the evil that resided in his heart. She became the madman wielding the scalpel, carving out eyes and ears and delicately rerouting the voluntary functions of his subjects. With every slice she seethed with an anger so violent that she bucked against her own identity, refusing to believe that the world was anything more than a despicable place that needed her vision, her control.

I must kill Victor Paulstine, *she reminded herself.*

Jetta pushed on. Time zoomed backward and forward in a confusing mishmash. She found herself outside, in a backyard, the ground covered with colorful leaves. A brisk wind blew in from the north as the sun hid behind fluffy white clouds.

The hands before her looked small, childlike. In front of her a squirrel, nailed down by his feet, screeched and twitched. She watched her chubby hands slice off its ears and pop out its eyes with a butcher knife. Then, slowly and methodically, she peeled back its skin, relishing its screams.

Jetta consciousness nearly guttered out at Victor's perversity, but she held her mind together with her sole purpose, forging past the mushroom clouds and the smoky remains of a charred city. She dipped in and out of ancient memories too old for Victor to have experienced, perhaps part of a collective consciousness that had persisted throughout the age of mankind. The fall of Rome. The conquest of the Aztecs. The Spanish Inquisition. Tribal massacres in the Pacific Northwest. The atrocities of Unit 731. Men, women, and children begged for mercy, but she did not know the meaning in any age or in any form. She only understood the blood on her hands, and the sickening need to tear apart those unworthy of their skin.

She sank deeper now, all ties to herself vanishing in the black depths of the beast. No way back, no connection to Jaeia or to Jahx.

All alone.

Memories came in fragmented jolts.

A woman with flinty eyes and an ugly expression smacked her repeatedly over the head. "Repent and the Lord will save you! Repent and the Lord will save you!"

A collection of knives stashed under her bed. Plans to murder her mother written in code, disguised as a prayer, hidden away in the Bible on his nightstand. Soon mother would be dead, and she would be free.

Something wet splashed her awake. Mother was standing over her, pulling back the covers and dousing the entire bed with the contents from a red container. It smelled like gasoline. "You are a wicked, Godless creature. You are the devil's spawn. I renounce you as my son!"

She had no time to scream. With satisfaction in her eyes, Mother lifted up her hand and dropped a lighted match. Flames devoured the world.

Jetta held on tightly to her lone objective, to the only purpose her heart could understand in the midst of Victor's torment. A black cloud of consumptive pain, fire blackening tender young skin.

I must kill Victor Paulstine!

Throwing herself forward, she catapulted into untold depths. She braced for more gruesome experiences, but when she uncovered her eyes, she found herself in the one place she never wanted to be again.

Oh Gods—

The afternoon light poked through gaps in the boarded up windows, highlighting old bloodstains on the walls. The air felt hot and dry. A few pieces of broken furniture were all that remained in the red and gray apartment.

Jetta instinctively crouched low to the ground and scurried to the kitchen, hiding below the broken sink.

Why am I here? *she wondered, cracking open the cupboard door and peeking into the dimly lit apartment.*

When she heard his footsteps, her heart froze.

No—no—no—

The front door slammed, and drunken feet stumbled in. A hulking shadow found its way to the cushionless couch and sat down with a crash.

"Come here, child," *called the shadow. Smoke curled from the burning end of a cigarette, wafting over and irritating her nose.*

No point in hiding anymore. If anything, it would be dangerous to stay in one place.

Slowly, she crept out of her hiding place and into the empty kitchen. Her eyes darted to the entryway, the only means of escape she had ever had, but in this world she couldn't be sure it even existed.

"I will only make this offer once," *the shadow said, blowing smoke in her direction.* "You have impressed me. I have respect for how far you've come. Leave now, and I will give you all you will ever need to conquer this universe."

A gray, sheened hand unfurled from the shadows to reveal her old rock dice. "You are the rightful heir to all our many gifts."

A cold breeze raked through her. She gasped, then giggled as an infinite palette of colorful temptations scrolled out across her mind's eye: Golden idols and marble monuments that rose higher than the sun. Not just people kneeled before her, but entire mountain ranges bowed to her image, the stars falling from the heavens at the sound of her voice. She was the creator and the destroyer. She was the God of all Gods.

Jetta opened her eyes and reached greedily for the dice. But just as her fingers grazed them, she noticed the symbols had changed. No longer were crescent doubles or triple moons etched onto the faces, but a snake swallowing its own tail. A man blinding himself. Worms feeding on a mound of disemboweled corpses, a woman strangling her child. The frigid edge of death sliced into her stomach, and in her eyes danced inside the dead lights of another world.

Jetta retracted her hand. She remembered. This isn't about me.

(I have to kill Victor.)

She lunged into the shadows, ready for impact, for the fight. Instead, she fell headfirst into a void, flailing about in the emptiness until she spiraled down into a place hidden in the ashes.

Weak and exhausted, Jetta could barely bring herself to look through Victor's eyes again. But this place was different from all the rest.

She saw her own reflection in the medical scanner positioned above her bed. Something hideous, an ugly lump of burn scars, barely recognizable as a human being, much less as a man, stared back at her.

"Don't worry, my friend," a man in a surgical mask said, placing a petri dish on her chest. "My Smart Cells will make you a new skin. Maybe then I'll finally get a smile out of you."

She wasn't sure what she would feel as Josef Stein released his nanites on her body and directed them to reconstruct her mangled flesh. Aside from the tickling sensations as they worked alongside her bodily functions to begin the restorative process, she thought she'd feel hope, maybe even a hint of relief.

Nothing. Not even a hint of emotion. Only emptiness, even as she watched her skin re-form in the reflection of the scanner.

Flash forward. She stood before a mirror, seeing her new skin for the first time as Josef unbandaged her. She felt a strange unworthiness to see the flawless, smooth expanse of pink.

When she looked again, she did not see Ramak Yakarvoah. She saw someone else.

Ramak Yakarvoah is dead, *she heard him think.* I am reborn.

The images reassembled themselves into a security surveillance feed she watched in the privacy of her office. She turned all monitors to the reception area, where a beautiful young woman sat working at her desk, keeping up the pretense that the office was a design company in order to hide the secret laboratory underneath.

My mother—

A fair-skinned young man walked in and pretended to saddle her with excessive demands.

Father—

Crossing her arms, Ariya gave Kovan a hard time until he revealed the flowers and the gift box hidden behind his back.

Jetta lived through Victor's quiet jealousy as she watched Ariya open up the present. The rose-embroidered handkerchief. A family treasure he wanted her to have.

"It's perfect," she said, throwing herself at Kovan. Jetta watched her

parents make love behind her desk. Every kiss, every "I love you" chipped away at something deep inside Victor, filling him with wintry indignation. But even when Ariya turned away from the camera, he remotely adjusted the view.

He was in love with our mother...

In a painful attempt that made her cringe, he asked her mother out to dinner as she closed down the office for the night.

"Ariya Ohakn—I would be honored if you joined me for tonight at De Laj," he said, presenting her with a bouquet of the most expensive flowers.

"I'm sorry, I have plans with Kovan." Her cheeks turned bright red as she refused the gift. "I appreciate the gesture, though."

It was not the first time he had asked her out, nor the first time he had been rejected. He was always rejected. Even after the death of Ramak and the birth of Victor, he was unlovable.

Jealousy turned into rage. Rage became bitter loneliness, giving rise to even darker needs. (There will never be love, never any connection; there will only be consumption. That is my means of survival.)

Of all Victor's caustic emotions, this felt like poison in her veins. The last of Jetta stripped away in his madness, leaving her shriveled and barren.

No reason to go on. No point to exist. She would bleed out into the shadow, become part of the nothingness that dominated the world.

Words whispered from beyond. (Wait for a time you need to feel...)

Jetta inhaled sharply. She smelled her mother's scent. In the far reaches of another place, her pulse quickened.

Soft material pressed into her palm. Sweet-smelling perfume touched her nose.

(Feel, Jetta...)

Jetta looked down at her hand, across dual planes of existence. The rose-embroidered handkerchief; the symbol of her parents' love. Closing her hand, she allowed the memories to flow through her.

Jetta laughed, overwhelmed with exquisite bliss, experiencing her parents' love for each other through their eyes. She witnessed their chance meeting on their college campus, their first date in a thundering rainstorm. Days turned into months and then years, but time with Kovan and Ariya had a different meaning. They were part of each other, two souls intertwined, indistinguishable, in harmony with the mystical workings of the universe.

Jetta embraced the memories, not letting them go, holding onto them with all of her strength. She forgot the emptiness and despair that existed just beyond the horizon. To her there could only be the perfect love of two joined souls.

The world shuddered. Jetta sobered to the reality of her surroundings. Blackened walls, a sickly, bulging organ. She stood before the putrescent heart of the monster.

She had reached her final destination.

"You cannot kill him," *she remembered Jahx saying,* "Death will only give rise to another."

Her hand easily penetrated the devitalized tissue. She found the thrumming pulse underneath, the lifecord of his being. With one quick tug it would all be over.

Jetta stopped herself. What am I doing…?

She relaxed her hand. Changing her grip, she thought of all that she had learned, all that she had experienced. She remembered what Jahx had shown her, the rich tapestry of a universe full of lives and souls. I have to choose what is real.

She smiled. Now, finally, I see.

Holding on tightly to the handkerchief, she pushed herself inside the monster's pulse and into his bloodstream. Pumped into the core of his being, she seeded the feelings and memories she cherished the most through the festering mass. Her brother's gentle eyes and kind smile. Her sister's infectious giggle. The smooth feel of Triel's body moving under hers, breathing in her breath, lips pressed into soft lips. The way only her uncle could make her smile when she was in a bad mood. Aunt Lohien's angelic voice singing old nursery rhymes. Her mother's love, unbound and unconditional.

For the first time in her life she saw the full wealth of the love in her life and the world illuminated in her wake. She was cast out, away from the retreating shadow, away from the broken desolation of Victor's dark conviction.

As she tried to pass back through the psionic barrier to return to her own body, a familiar shadow eclipsed her light. No longer afraid, Jetta brought herself around and touched the face of her own suffering. She

whispered, (I know who you are, and I will not run away anymore.)
With that, she embraced the anathema and was freed.

***

Jetta woke aboard a starcraft she didn't recognize. Everything looked antiquated, not to code. The writing on the walls was in ancient English, an outdated and never-used language—
The experimental ship.
"Hey, you're okay," Triel said, keeping her from leaping out of her seat.
"Yeah," she mumbled, shaking the cobwebs out of her head. Looking down at her chest plate, she saw where someone had stuffed her mother's handkerchief into the break in the armor.
"Who put this in my hand?" Jetta asked, touching the cloth and remembering the physical sensation during her psionic venture.
Reaching back into her shared memories, she answered her own question: *Jaeia.* Jetta had brought the handkerchief along as good luck, but Jaeia had been the one to take it out of her pocket to help her remember.
Thank you, Jaeia.
Jetta straightened up. No time to waste; just push a little farther. As she coughed violently, she quickly assessed her situation: *We're in the accessory passenger hold of the craft.* To her left, Triel and Kurt sat strapped into two of the foldout seats. Jahx lie across Triel's lap, unconscious and deathly pale.
"Is he okay?" Jetta asked in a hoarse whisper, unbuckling herself and moving to his side.
The ship lurched, sending her staggering backward, then forward. *I've got to get to the cockpit and help Jaeia,* she thought, sensing her sister's frustration as the engines struggled against the planet's increased gravity.
"I've stabilized him as best I can, but we have to get him back to Drs. DeAnders and Kaoto." The Healer touched her face, slipping inside her. Relishing the sensation, Jetta accepted what little healing Triel could provide. "You as well, and your sister. You aren't far behind him."
The Division Lockdown Lab is gone, she remembered. *It got obliterated in the diversionary tactic against the Republic Fleet.* Even though DeAnders and his teams moved all important equipment and

experiments from the Central Starbase to the medical frigate prior to the Alliance's mass departure, it didn't provide her much comfort.

I hope they made their jump to Nagoor, and they stay protected from the main fight.

"Stay with us, Jahx," Jetta said, kissing his forehead and squeezing the Healer's hand.

"Jetta, wait—there's something I have to tell you—"

"It will have to wait; I've got to get us to safety."

As she picked her way to the front of the ship, she spotted Victor tied up in the cargo storage. *What the—?*

She waved her hand in front of eyes with pinpoint pupils, getting no response. No silver-tongued devil resided there; just a drooling, mumbling mass.

"Jetta, get up here!" Jaeia said, banking hard to the left as she cleared the bay doors to the underground hangar.

"I don't know what you did to him, Sis." Jaeia pointed her thumb at the stupefied Victor Paulstine. "But I don't think he's a threat anymore."

"Thanks, Jae," she said, strapping into the co-pilot's chair. Jetta ignored how sickly her twin looked and felt, instead choosing to focus on the gratitude within. "I couldn't have done it without you."

"Thank me later, okay?"

"Jeez," Jetta said, covering her face as Jaeia swooped too low near a bridge. "And you said *I* was the bad pilot."

Jaeia ignored her jab. "Do you want the good news or the bad news?"

"Oh boy," Jetta said dryly, trying out the ship's antiquated controls.

"Good news: I got in contact with Ferraway. Our ground team has taken over the command control room. We've got internal eyes on their starcraft, and they're working on cracking their systems."

"The bad news?"

Jaeia's tension felt like a cold weight in her stomach. "This isn't safe to jump in, and I doubt it can handle breaking through Jue Hexron's gravitational field."

"And I see we've alerted some Republic friends," Jetta said, reading the green scanner blips heading their way.

"Exactly. We've got to make it behind Alliance lines and dock. It's our only chance."

"This relic couldn't stand up to a single hit," Jetta said, trying to take over the controls. "Let me drive."

Jaeia raised a brow. "And to think, just moments ago you professed your admiration and respect…"

"But not for your piloting skills."

"Too bad," Jaeia said, pitching them hard to port.

Gripping the armrests, Jetta tried to hold onto the contents of her stomach. The ship rattled and quaked as Republic fighters grazed their hull, trying to assess the status of their prized ship.

"Got an idea," Jetta said, dragging Victor out of the storage unit. "This will at least buy us some time."

Despite the terrible video feed, they got a good enough signal to broadcast an image that Victor was alive and aboard their ship. Jetta cut out the audio, not wanting to lend any further clues of his compromised condition.

"See it?" Jetta said, pointing to the opening in the battle. "We can reach that warship if we hold this path."

"May I remind you that I live in your stuffy head, too?" Jaeia replied, gunning the accelerator and barely clearing a stray missile.

Jetta couldn't decide if she was annoyed or amused. *Jaeia's never been this sassy.*

She grinned.

Using her uniform sleeve, Jetta contacted the Alliance command and informed them of their situation. Three of their own fighters broke from the fray and escorted them to the warship.

As Jetta and her party disembarked, she saw the *Wraith* in the next crosslock. Tech and Billy Don't were scuttling around her, trying to put out the fires.

I'm sure the last thing Reht Jagger wanted was to have to re-dock with the Alliance, she thought, noting the heavy damage and smoldering shield generator. *He's probably itching to get his ship airborne as soon as possible.*

One of the deck officers greeted her with a salute while medics took her brother and Kurt away to the infirmary. The battle raging just outside the dock made it difficult to hear his report.

"Accounts are unclear, Sir," he shouted above the din. He showed her a datapad with statistical readouts and battle clips. "We did manage to deactivate most of the Republic officers, but some survived or 'rebooted.'

Hooking up Billy Don't again has proven ineffective."

The mounting causalities racking up on the Fleet status report worried her. *This is bad.*

Jetta rung up Unipoesa. The shock collar around his neck made her arch a quizzical eyebrow. "Status report?"

From the admiral's humorless expression she deduced Tarsha's daring move. *Well, got to give her credit for covering her own hide.*

Unipoesa answered the more important question. "We're still getting hammered. Ground teams haven't cracked their systems yet, and they have enough sub-commanders to fill in the empty posts. We need to disable their command net or we won't survive."

The deck officer looked up from the alert on his datapad. "Commander, we've got reports coming in that the Motti ship has changed course and is coming within range."

The Healer came up behind her, her worry prickling Jetta's chest. "Jetta, I have to go."

"Hold on," Jetta said, trying to think of what to do next.

What could they do? If the fleet jumped, they might buy themselves some time, but Jue Hexron would fall to the Dissemblers. They had to give the ground team a chance to crack their systems; disabling the Republic was the only way they could protect the Holy Cities.

Jetta shared thoughts with her sister, but nothing came to mind. Holding on tightly to the railing of a nearby lift, she tried to stay upright as her overworked body began to fail.

"Jetta, please," Triel whispered, inconspicuously helping her stand. "I have to go."

A medic called out to her, running as fast as he could. "Sir, we found this in Jahx's hand." Uncurling his fingers, he revealed the gruesome prize covered in flavescent ooze. "It appears to be Motti."

As soon as Jetta touched the ocular device, a potent memory stain struck her senses; she saw the future unfold from the celestial stems of her brother's inner eye.

"Dear Gods," she said, taking it from the medic and holding it up. "This is our way in."

In the background, Billy Don't squealed and yelped. When she looked back, Tech had accidentally dropped a paneling grate on his foot and was hopping around.

"Get Billy hooked back up to a broadcaster, immediately," Jetta ordered. "Give this to Tech," she said, handing back the gooey implant. "Have him integrate it with Billy; he'll know what to do."

Jetta turned to discuss the matter further with her sister when Triel got between them.

"Jetta, I have to go. Now. I am the only one who can stop the Dissemblers."

"No. We're installing M'ah Pae's hive link into Billy—we can use him to shut down their—"

"My people are aboard that ship," she said, lips trembling. "I am their only chance."

Before she could protest, Jetta felt the Triel's pain as if it were her own. Never had she felt such a strong emotional current, even from her siblings.

Jetta could not refuse her. "Okay," she said, her knees giving out. "But I'm going with you."

CHAPTER XV

"And yet you're leaving me again," Jaeia said, watching her sister help Tech patch up the secondary engine. The nervous engineer kept checking Jetta's progress, surprised each time that she could possibly know the workings of the *Wraith* so well. *I guess he hasn't figured out that she's already stolen his entire life's experience and is putting it to good use.*

"I'm escorting Triel," Jetta said, keeping her voice controlled as she struggled to tighten the last bolt over the blast plating. It was a patch job, done in a rush. Jaeia cringed to think how the ship was going to handle actual spaceflight. "I'm not leaving you."

An explosion rocked the warship, and they grabbed onto each other to keep their balance. Jaeia chortled. "I know. This is different. I just want to go with you."

"They need you here," Jetta said, nabbing a wrench from Tech. "Tarsha will need you, and so will Unipoesa. This isn't over yet."

"Jetta—"

"Don't say it," she whispered, tossing the wrench back to Tech and testing the fickle power grid.

Seeing the resolute look in her sister's green eyes, Jaeia sensed there would be no further negotiating. *Jetta knows that not everyone will return from this mission...*

Even if her heart had yet to accept it.

Jaeia opted for a hug instead of an argument. "Love you."

"Love you too," Jetta said, tears already in her eyes.

"Come back," Jaeia whispered, trying not to let her sister go.

An uncertain promise was all she got. "I will."

***

Tarsha watched as Jaeia Kyron boarded the bridge with the help of one of the deck officers. Even in such a debilitated state, she doubted that anybody could do anything to persuade the stubborn captain to relieve herself from duty.

"Have they left?" Tarsha asked, focusing on the holographic war globe of the battle against the Republic Fleet.

Jaeia checked the flight log. "

The *Wraith* just took off."

"I thought that thing was unflyable," Unipoesa said.

"Tell that to Tech and Jetta," Jaeia said, wearily approaching the battle display.

Out of the side of her eye Tarsha watched the captain with quiet awe and envy as she deconstructed and reconstructed the battle in seconds. *It's true; there is no commander in all of history that could rival the Kyrons.* But deep down, Tarsha sensed another truth. *(I'm the only one that can win this battle.)*

Tarsha thought that Jaeia seemed to know that too.

Jaeia spoke privately to Tarsha. "We just need time. We need to keep the Republic back long enough so the *Wraith* can get through to the Dissembler horizon and the ground teams can crack the command net."

Tarsha looked again to the war globe. Cold worms wriggled in her stomach.

This is too much like the Command Development Program, she thought, seeing the staggering enemy numbers and her dwindling resources.

(Know when you're defeated.)

Only this time Unipoesa was not in control. He stood over her, his eyes deceptively hooded, hands clasped behind his back as if he was concocting a master strategy.

Instincts told her otherwise. *He's a man running on fumes, out of options.*

After all, why else would he have complied with the shock collar?

Tarsha palmed the remote to the shock collar before placing it in her pocket. A faint tickling touched the back of her head as she gave commands for the corvettes to retreat behind the battleship and protect the *Wraith*.

Irritated, Tarsha addressed Jaeia directly. "Why are you in my head?"

"Because I can't believe that you haven't seen the obvious move," Jaeia said calmly. "You know what you have to do to win this."

Tarsha kneaded the back of her neck. The action surprised her; she had forgotten the old nervous habit. *Just like old times...*

(I can't beat Li.)

She gave several more commands to reposition her fleet. Even without the powers of telepathy, she sensed the anxiety levels of the bridge crew in their tightened jaws and rigid postures.

They don't trust me. And why should they? After all, she did ice out.

She could never hack it. Maybe she should have stayed a Scabber Jock. *At least I was good at that.*

(Know when you're defeated.)

Jaeia swayed. Tarsha thought she might faint, but the captain held herself together.

"Tarsha, trust your instincts," Jaeia said with effort. A film of sweat accumulated across her pale brow as she fought for every word. "You see much more than you realize."

Unipoesa came over from the action console. "What's the problem?"

Jaeia's voice softened but held its adamancy. "Tell her, Damon. She needs to know."

"Tell me what?"

Jaeia and the admiral exchanged looks before Unipoesa grunted and unclasped his hands. "Tarsha, you were the best cadet we ever had in the program. By far. You were never second to Li. I found ways to manipulate the scores and rig the game to essentially provoke you and get you out of the program. Remember when you were winning in the air combat round of the Endgame? I flubbed your win by recycling his lost ships. There was no way for you to win against his numbers."

Tarsha looked blankly at the war globe. An Alliance fuel freighter exploded on the screen. Two of her fighter formations broke up and flew blindly in the crossfire.

The paralyzing numbness of impossibility crawled into her belly. She had forgotten how awful it felt, how powerless she was in the face of her own demons.

"Tarsha," Jaeia instructed quietly. "You know who's out there. Make the call. Trust your abilities."

She was shaking now, her voice locked in an iron ball in her throat. It was just like the last time she battled in the Endgame. The bridge vanished. It was just her and her failure blazing on the projections, the entire world laughing as she lost yet again.

Why did I think I could do this?

(Know when you're defeated.)

"Tarsha, make the call," Jaeia said, laying her hand on her shoulder and looking at her with tired gray eyes. "Only you can do this."

The admiral stopped shouting at the deck hands and leaned over on his knuckles so that his eyes leveled with hers. "Tarsha, you were the only person Li was ever afraid of."

With tingling legs, Tarsha moved to the center of the bridge. She nodded to the tactical officer manning the com. "Ring them in."

Tarsha forced her breathing to slow as the Republic flagship unhurriedly picked up their call. She watched with quiet unrest as two more Alliance corvettes went down before Li's face finally appeared on the screen.

"I have always believed in you," the admiral whispered to her before stepping out of the visual field.

Li hid his shock well, as did she upon seeing him after so many years. His ragged shape disturbed her. His right eye was swollen shut, and that side of his face sagged as if he had suffered a stroke. *Reviving him after that dog-soldier Liiker deactivated Victor's implants must have come at a massive cost.*

"Where did they dig your sorry carcass up?"

"Old Earth," Tarsha replied.

"Fitting. And now you've been chosen to represent the Alliance in defeat? I can think of no one more suitable to offer us their surrender. Perhaps maybe Damon? No, you," he said with a cackle. "Definitely you."

Tarsha looked at her feet. Li didn't know that Unipoesa had given her open access to all the classified material on the Command Development Program, including the cadet profiles. She had initially asked for them to prove that Unipoesa was lying about his intentions. Instead, she gravitated to the sordid details surrounding the suspicious deaths of her classmates, and to one curiosity in particular: Just before his death, a kid named Henderson had witnessed Li in a compromised state. She repeatedly watched the video until she disassociated herself from all emotion, and realized her only chance.

She hated herself for seeing it.

"Just give up, Li," Tarsha said. "Make it easy on yourself. Don't be an embarrassment to your men."

Initially, her bold assertion took him aback, but he quickly recovered. "You're completely delusional. How sad; you're projecting to compensate for your own inadequacies."

Tarsha held her ground. "I just want to know one thing before I accept your surrender. Why did you save me from the fire after you attacked me?"

She felt the tickle in the back of her head again. Tarsha thought that if she was telepathic, Jaeia would have told her something. Maybe even warned her.

Half of Li's face curved in a smile like a scythe. "I didn't want to be deprived of the *pleasure* of killing my dear sister."

But Tarsha knew that wasn't all. "I think you had to know first."

"Know what?" he scoffed.

"If I was better than you. You couldn't stand to kill me without being sure. Your ego wouldn't allow it."

Li backed away from the camera, only to return with his chin held imperiously high. "I never wondered. I always knew, as did all of our teachers. They were just hoping to find *some* use for you. Just look at us now. You, a washout just like dear old Dad, and me, an indomitable galactic commander."

Unipoesa breathed heavily beside her. She turned her head just enough to see his face. He was sweating profusely, but his face remained cast in steel.

(I'm the only one that can win this battle.)

"Still piss yourself?"

Li's smile vanished. "I will wipe out every last ship of yours. Then I will let the Motti devour Old Earth."

"You're finished, Li. We have President Paulstine. You've lost control of your base of operations. We've deactivated most of your top commanders and officers. It's over."

A grin dented the left side of his face. "Come on, Sis. My warships alone still outnumber yours ten to one. And I have the Deadwalkers on a leash. Why would you want to provoke me any further? Surrender now and I might not consider sending you and Dad to the Labor Locks. Maybe I'll be merciful and just kill you."

Tarsha checked the communications relay between the ground team. They had uploaded the video clip she had sent earlier. The command control systems hadn't been cracked, but they had a lock on the broadcast signals used by the Republic Fleet.

For some reason the words Unipoesa had used to describe her in the cadet personality qualifiers came to mind. *Intelligent. Cunning. Sensitive.* She remembered how he had questioned whether the latter made her vulnerable or dangerous. In the Command Development Program it made her susceptible; the criticisms and vituperations of her teachers practically crippled her. However, that same characteristic transitioned to her life as Agracia Waychild, proving critical to her day-to-day survival, enabling her to get a good read on other Scabbers and pick out easy targets. Now, facing Urusous Li, it felt like both a hindrance and an advantage.

He's my only brother.

And I'm about to destroy him.

"Li," she said, offering him one last chance. "Have you ever considered that you and I were engineered for someone else's purpose? Have you stopped and asked yourself what it is that *you* want? Do you even know who you are without an enemy to fight?"

Laughing, Li ordered for the flagship to aim a full spread of torpedoes at their warship.

Tarsha's heart sank. "I will never forgive you for this," she muttered to Unipoesa. She typed in the commands for the ground team to release the video clip.

Li's half-face turned ashen. "What have you—?"

The crew kept their comments to a low murmur as her video clip played out on the center screen, and across the entire Republic network.

Unipoesa came into view. He was younger and had more hair.

"Not very good at following orders, are you, candidate?" he said, circling Li. The entire classroom watched in silence as he coldly instructed a soldier where to hit the young boy. The soldier's punch landed hard and fast over his bladder, and Li doubled over in pain. His blue uniform darkened around his groin, and his futile efforts to conceal it from the other students left him reddened and enraged.

"Still pissing yourself like a baby, just like you did when you first set foot on base," Unipoesa said. "You're still a baby. You can't follow a simple set of orders. You'll always be a worthless little pisser. A failure. An embarrassment to this program."

Tarsha clenched her jaw as the last part looped over and over again while zooming in on his urine-soaked pants. *"You'll always be a worthless little pisser. A failure. An embarrassment... You'll always be a worthless little pisser. A failure. An embarrassment... You'll always be a worthless little pisser. A failure. An embarrassment..."*

As Li continued to shout commands to attack, she pushed it one step further. She uploaded the looped audio segment into the broadcast signal Billy Don't had sent to initially disable the implanted Republic officers.

The Liiker command inputs had no further effects, but the repeating audio did.

"Stop it—STOP IT!" Li shrieked, falling to his knees and digging at his swollen eye and ear. Blood and vitreous fluid streamed down his face as he continued to scream and gouge.

"Begin a concentrated attack on their flagship," Tarsha commanded, resuming her post beneath the war globe. "Change heading to mark 0.7302."

Unipoesa tried to compliment her, but she turned her back to him.

"Nice work," Jaeia said quietly, taking the position next to her.

"It's not over yet," she replied sharply. Even if she had overloaded their communications with the viral video clip and disabled their chief commanding officer, they were still grossly outnumbered.

"I've got this," Tarsha said, refusing Jaeia's help. *This is something I have to do.*

The captain backed off.

Calmly and steadily, Tarsha gave commands to the last of their fleet to aggress the Republic flagship and provide enough cover for the *Wraith* to pass through. Though the communications channels were closed, she could still hear Li screaming.

***

Jetta made Tech tell her three times that Billy Don't had properly integrated M'ah Pae's ocular device into his own internal network before she would believe the nervous engineer. All the while the little Liiker giggled and spat up his meal of concentrated proteins and hydral-fluid all over the floor. Tech didn't even both to clean him up. Not that he could have with him hooked up to the *Wraith* via every available input/output socket on his biomechanical frame, leaving no room to navigate around the web of coils.

"Please, I checked him twice—you have to believe me. It worked before!"

"I know, I know," Jetta sighed, tapping her fist on the wall. "This is just different. He's not contacting a bunch of people wired with Motti implants. He's reintegrating himself back into the Liiker hive mind. Are you sure he's ready for it?"

Hanging upside-down from the pipework, Tech inspected Billy Don't's cervical plate interface from above. The Motti Overlord's ocular device, plugged into Billy's neck, rolled around on his shoulder as if it was trying to get away. Tech did something with a modified drilling laser to make it stop before he answered.

"I didn't tell him."

"What?"

"He wouldn't understand," Tech said, swinging down and catching himself on a wall handle. Still recovering from his near-fatal wounds, he gingerly let himself down the rest of the way. "He's just a kid."

"Wait a minute—"

"N-no, you wait," Tech said, fumbling to sling up his tools. The fur on his head and neck stood on end as if he had been electrocuted. "I—I spent years restoring him, giving him back his freedom, and you're asking me now to help you connect him back into the Deadwalkers' mind. That's a big risk for him."

Billy cooed and squealed.

"I know," Jetta said as calmly as she could. "But we have no other choice. He's our only way inside their collective. Without him we have no way to stop the Dissemblers."

The engineer's eyes glistened with tears, but he blinked them back. "It just isn't right."

A giant shadow blocked out the light from the hallway. Jetta moved aside as Reht strode through, followed by Mom.

"Is there a problem?" Reht took one look at Tech and gave him a pat on the shoulder. "Ease up on her, mate. She's only doing what she does best. This is our only way to beat them 'walkers."

Tech's shoulders slumped, and he rubbed one of his healing stab wounds. "I just don't want to lose him."

Jetta didn't expect any reassurances from Reht, but this wasn't the same dog-soldier captain she remembered. "I know, Tech. I will do everything I can to protect him."

Still in shock, Jetta followed Reht and Mom part of the way back towards the bridge.

"We've cleared the battle lines. We'll be at the Dissembler horizon in less than fifteen minutes," Reht said.

"Reht," Jetta started, hoping to find a way to express the depth of her gratitude. Strapped for starcraft, the Alliance once again needed Reht's crew and unregistered ship. But it went beyond that. Triel had asked him to help. Despite everything, he didn't refuse her request.

Jetta looked away from the hurt in his eyes, the ache that radiated from his being. His love for Triel was real. Nothing she could say would take away his pain.

"Thanks," was all she could choke out.

"Sure thing, kid," he said, ducking through the portal to the bridge.

Mom gave her a growl before following his captain.

Jetta stood outside Reht's den, reluctant to go inside. If she just stood there, maybe that moment would last forever.

"Jetta?" a muffled voice called from beyond the door.

"Telepaths," Jetta muttered, letting herself in.

In another show of decency, Reht had allowed Triel a few moments to herself in the privacy of his den. She sat on the cleanest part of his bed, staring down at the mess on the floor.

Jetta had no idea what to say, and apparently neither did Triel. Brushing a beer can off the sheets, she sat next to the Healer.

"So," Jetta said, breaking the silence, "what happens next?"

Triel's eyes met hers, and Jetta forgot herself for a moment. Not long ago she would have severely rebuked herself for the feelings that stirred in her heart. Now she allowed herself to bask in their warmth and vitality.

The Healer touched her face with slender fingers. "Right now you are going to kiss me."

Jetta took her time. She curled a stray piece of dark hair behind Triel's ear, taking in every detail of her face and tracing the outline of her jaw. The Healer's beauty was unparalleled, as was the taste of her kiss. Jetta leaned in. Triel's full, soft lips parted for a wet tongue eager to massage her own. A current built between them with each breath they shared and with each moment they drew closer to each other.

Clearing a space on Reht's bed, she tried to push herself on top of Triel, but instead the Healer levered herself on top of Jetta. With little strength left, Jetta was in no position to fight.

"Always vying for control, aren't you?" Triel teased.

Jetta let the Healer slip her hands underneath her uniform. "I just like making you happy."

Triel laid next to her, her hands still under Jetta's top. After tracing the outline of Jetta's abdominal muscles and the healing scar, her fingers moved to the prominence of her ribs. She lightly played with the smooth underside of her breasts before taking back one of her hands and resting her head on her palm.

"Jetta, I want you to know something."

"What's that?" Jetta said, rolling over and kissing her neck.

"I think you're a good person."

Jetta stopped kissing her and gave her the side eye. "What?"

Triel cupped her cheek, surprising Jetta with the strength of her emotion. "I think you're a good person. I always have. I want you to remember that."

Jetta couldn't control the shakiness in her voice. "Why are you saying this?"

Blue eyes melted into hers. "Because for a long time you believed you were a monster. You were never a monster. You were just born with the ability to see your own shadow. It frightened you—and me; I'd never seen a Sentient manifest their own dark side."

"I'm sorry," Jetta said, not knowing what else to say.

"Don't be." Triel played with Jetta's hair. "We all have one. And now you've embraced yours. You feel different to me."

"What do you mean?"

Triel hugged her. "You feel at peace."

Jetta cringed, thinking of what was about to happen. "I'm not quite sure about that."

Shaking her head, Triel kissed Jetta's hand. "Just promise me one thing?"

"Okay."

For a moment the Healer's eyes sparkled. "Don't give up on me and you, okay?"

Jetta didn't even have to think about her response. "Of course not—I would never. My heart is yours for all time."

Sadness tinged Triel's smile. She lunged at Jetta, hugging her with all her might. Jetta hugged her back, sensing the anticipation of loss on the edge of Triel's thoughts.

The overhead com crackled.

"Hey, Starfox, it's your time to shine. Bring that kid with you, too."

Jetta kissed the Healer's cheek. She tried to hold onto the memory of her radiance, her smile.

"Come, Jetta," Triel said, her voice low and hushed. "It's time."

***

Something's wrong. Tarsha saw the massive blip on the edge of the holographic display and magnified it on the secondary viewer.

"What is that?" Unipoesa said, directing his question to no one in particular.

The Motti ship.

"Man, Li got his dogs out here fast," Tarsha overheard one of the crewman saying.

"We can't stay here," Jaeia said, holding herself up on the edge of the action console.

The warship quaked as two more torpedoes struck their hull.

"Damage report?" Tarsha shouted above the warning sirens.

"Shields down to thirty percent, and we've lost main deflector dish. Massive casualty reports from decks nine through thirty."

"Haussa maneuver," Tarsha called out, typing in commands for the rest of the fleet to move with her. The ship dipped to starboard and then sped to the defense of their fighter squadron getting pummeled by an enemy battleship.

Li was doing exactly what she had hoped: Unleashing an all-out assault. She saw the angles unfold faster and faster. Her opportunity would be there. She would see it.

But Unipoesa's caustic words wouldn't leave her, inserting themselves every time she accessed her battle skills.

(Know when you're defeated.)

Gritting her teeth, she zeroed in on the holographics.

I have to maintain this retreat. Not too much longer. I must be patient. I must trust my instincts. My opportunity will be there.

Two more of their fighters were gunned down. The loss hit her like a punch to the stomach.

(Know when you're defeated.)

"We have a problem," Unipoesa said, calculating the approach pattern of the Motti ship. "The outer reaches of their weapon will be here in three minutes. We can't maintain this position."

The Motti are coming up on their flank, she realized, checking the stats and rechecking the holographics. *If we maintain our current course, we'll be obliterated.*

Jaeia locked eyes with her. "Tarsha..."

Maybe I should let Jaeia take over. Tarsha looked at the war globe. Alliance markers were disappearing at an accelerated rate. They wouldn't be able to hold out any longer. *Maybe it's time to stand down, let a real commander take my place.*

(Know when you're defeated.)

Tarsha bit her tongue. One of Bossy's fights came to mind, when she took on the twin steroid giants Big Jawn and Meathook McGraw in the *Ultimate Fighting Ring Showdown!* back when they first met. Then it dawned on her.

Tarsha ran over to the science station console.

"Lieutenant, can you make me a class four particle cloud?"

The science station officer looked at her with confusion but didn't question her. "Yes, Sir. I have one sitting in one of our planetary probes right now."

"Launch it, heading 7.2.02," she said, rushing back over to the war station.

Out of the corner of her eye she could see Jaeia smiling as she gave the rest of her fleet orders to jump.

***

"They got here quick," Jetta remarked, studying the flight pattern of the Motti ship over Bacthar's wing. Out of the corner of her eyes she saw Triel slowly walk towards the center of the bridge, hand stretching out as if to reach the enemy ship headed toward the Holy Cities.

"Readings are weird," Sebbs remarked, trying to make sense of the scanner readout. "It's more than the usual noise those Deadwalkers put out."

Jetta's stomach knotted. *This isn't right.*

She zoomed in on the picture of the Motti ship on the remote scanners. Nothing seemed different; it looked like the same lumbering behemoth that had wiped out half of their galaxy.

"They're awake," Triel whispered, eyes wide as saucers.

"Huh? Who's awake?" Reht said, picking at the bandages on his hands.

Triel's entire body shook. "They know I'm here. Oh, Father..."

Jetta stumbled over to Triel, unsure of her own footing, and helped the Healer stay upright. Carefully wading into the Healer's thoughts, she picked up her awareness, confirming their worst fears: Somehow, the Dissemblers had transcended their chemical restraints and gained autonomy from the rest of the hive mind, no longer taking commands from their Motti handlers.

Li is no longer in control. The fate of the universe lies in the poisoned heart of the Dissemblers.

"So cold... so lost... in such pain," Triel mumbled, her eyes glazing over.

"Are we close enough for Billy to make contact?" Jetta asked, holding up the Healer with the last of her strength.

Sebbs shook his head. "A few more klicks. We're going to have to be *really* close."

"Reht," Jetta said, making eye contact.

The dog-soldier captain chewed on his nail until blood beaded up, exchanging glances with the Talian before making the decision. "Take us in, Sebbs, ol' boy. Let's see if we can't keep from melting our faces off."

***

Tarsha Leone watched the remainder of the Alliance ships jump away, their markers disappearing off the war globe. It took only seconds for Li to respond as he crippled the last of the flagship's shields.

"You're a joke, Tarsha. Your own fleet left you!" he crowed. His face looked like a harlequin mask of blood and shredded tissue. One of the medics tried to patch him up but only managed to apply Heme-arrest before Li shoved him away.

Li dropped his voice to mimic Unipoesa's: *"Know when you're defeated."*

Tarsha remembered his dark eyes, once cold and clinical, staring her down in the women's locker room, ready to deal her death. Now, seeing him mangled, blanched skin with lips drawn tight, eyes ablaze, something changed.

She no longer feared him.

"Full charge ahead on their flagship, ten percent differential," Tarsha ordered. The entire bridge went silent as the helmsman lay in the course.

"You're charging me?" Li exclaimed. "Are you suicidal?" He matched her assault, charging the lone warship, his entire Fleet following his lead.

Tarsha waited until the probe carrying the class four particle cloud reached its destination. She timed her last communication just before the explosion. "Goodbye, Urusous."

***

The lights on the *Wraith* flickered, dimmed, then overcharged. Several bulbs blew out while others sputtered to their death.

"Switch to secondary power," Reht commanded.

"Not responding," Sebbs said, pounding the helm with his fist.

Bacthar chimed in. "We've got about two minutes of reserves before we lose instrumentation and life support."

Ro and Cray crawled up from the weapons pits. "What gives?"

"Dunno," Reht said. "Hang tight."

Jetta looked out of the viewport to the stars. They provided a cold, distant comfort from the harshness of space. She imagined they regarded her with the same indifference as a superior being who had no stake in the struggles of the Sentients.

Having brushed against the Dissemblers' weapon before, Jetta guarded herself. Just a breath away was the place of concentrated pain. Scorching flames, the halo of light. The place that Triel had to go.

Jetta heard her pulse like the hollow drumming of wings. *This is it. (Forever is slipping away.)*

Eyes dilating, Triel's mouth opened in a gasp. On the edge of her awareness, Jetta felt the Healer sliding away into the consuming shadow.

Overtired and strung out, Jetta succumbed to panic. "Triel," she said, shaking her shoulders, "I need to get you out of here."

Triel grabbed her hand. The chaos of the bridge crew faded from her awareness, leaving her and the Healer standing alone in a vast expanse of dancing colors and shimmering sounds.

(Jetta,) *Triel said, still holding her hand in the temporal plane.*

(Everything is as it should be.)

(No, impossible!) *Jetta gripped her arms.* (I can't believe that I can finally love you, and now you have to go away.)

Triel brought Jetta's hand to her lips and kissed her fingertips. (Jahx helped me realize something. Everything that has happened to me has led to me being right here, right now. I was the one who fought the Prodgy's beliefs, who defied all the rules, but because I chose that path, I found you.)

(I don't understand,) *Jetta whispered.*

(And now I am prepared to save my people. Thank you for opening my eyes, Jetta. Thank you for letting me love you, and for giving me your strength.)

(Triel, wait,) *Jetta said, sensing Triel's terrible knowing. Her heart froze in place. The Healer had not properly performed the ritual of* Ne'topat'h. (You can't go—there's no way for me to bring you back!)

(I have to go, Jetta. The Dissemblers will not stop until every last Sentient is dead.)

(I won't let you die!)

Jetta tried to fight her, to sacrifice herself into the Dissembler weapon, but Triel pushed her back, flinging herself into the beyond.

***

Tarsha grabbed Jaeia before she hit the deck and gently guided her to the floor.

"Tarsha Leone," Jaeia said as her eyes drifted shut, "I might have to steal this one from you…"

"I want a medic up here," Unipoesa shouted.

Tarsha resumed her post. There was no way to communicate their need to the medical teams. The entire warship had lost power. Unable to engage their engines and change course, they flew through space on their previous heading.

Exactly as she had planned.

One of her CDP teachers had incidentally warned her about the class four particle cloud in advanced battle tactics while studying surveillance and stealth assault. Commonly used by astronomy teams to identify and study black holes, class four particle clouds were the easiest way to blow out the power grid on any starcraft, even at a distance of a hundred light years.

"You have to practice the utmost caution," her teacher had warned her years ago. *"If you're trying to gather intelligence on a star-class vessel with science teams, make sure you scan for this phenomena. Encountering a class four particle cloud will knock out your entire ship, leaving you a sitting duck."*

Tarsha stood close to the viewport windows, seeing the Alliance warship shoot across the nose of Li's flagship, just barely clearing their hull. She thought she could see him standing on the bridge looking back at her.

"Two minutes of life support," one of the deck crew announced.

Tarsha watched as they passed behind the last of the Republic Fleet. Traversing the bridge, she noticed the lightness and buoyancy of her steps as the gravitational boosters began to fail. Through the small retro viewport, she witnessed the last of the battle unfold.

She wasn't sure what she'd see. The Dissemblers worked on living flesh, not machinery. She found it hard to imagine that the entire Republic Fleet, power out but crew unhurt, was on an unchangeable course toward the Dissembler weapon, about to be wiped clean.

Unipoesa joined her side. He didn't bother to say anything this time. Tarsha wondered how he felt, watching his only son speeding toward his gruesome death, but cut herself off from the thought. As much as she didn't know Li and hated her encounters with him, Urusous was still her brother.

They watched together in silence as the Republic ships crossed over what Tarsha guessed was the horizon. Nothing discernible happened, but she had seen enough Dominion propaganda videos on Old Earth for her mind to play out the grisly scene.

Li would be confused at first, not understanding the ghost that had slipped beneath his skin. There would be a brief, awful moment of clarity before the itching began. Scratching provided no relief. The itching got worse. A vice would take hold of his fragile intestines, slowly clamping down and twisting. Something like acid would bleed from within, liquefying his organs and spreading the terrible fire. He would choke for breath as his lungs drowned in their own fluids. His eyes, no longer seeing, would turn inward, privy to a bleak world that was eating away his soul. Death, with arms spread wide, was a welcome release.

Tarsha opened her eyes again. The Republic ships were still on the same course from before their power had been knocked out, seemingly unfazed, but well within the Dissemblers' field of destruction. Shells of protective metal housing the dead.

It was over. She won.

Unipoesa walked to the engineering interface. "Science teams manually released the anti-pharon. Power coming back online."

He looked at her with tired eyes. "Finish the job, Cadet."

Of course, she thought to herself. *He has to be sure.*

Tarsha went back to the war globe and called up all the information on the scanners. It appeared as though the Republic ships had not regained power.

"Target only the flagship," she decided. Unipoesa looked at her strangely.

"When this is over, I'm sure the Alliance will need the spare parts," she replied coolly.

Tarsha waited until the targeting systems locked onto her brother's ship. She imagined Li's corpse, wrinkled and desiccated, sucked clean of marrow and vital fluids, watching from the other side.

"Fire."

***

Along the peripheries of her awareness, Jetta heard her sister sharing her knowledge about the class four particle cloud and the timed release of anti-pharon. If she hadn't detached from her body, she would have told the crew what to do to expedite the reboot of the power grid as the *Wraith* drifted toward the edge of the Dissembler horizon. Instead, she dove head-first back into the place of pain.

The Healer was far ahead, her light fading into the burning halo of the Dissembler collective. Ignoring her own pain, Jetta concentrated every last bit of herself on catching up to her love. Flesh crisped and flecked away. Nerve endings boiled. Her mind filled with the tortured screams of divided souls.

(Triel, wait!) *Jetta shouted, reaching as far as her mind would allow. So little of her remained. A scrap of tissue, a strand of hair; only her heart, and eyes that would not look away as she stared into death.*

The flames swelled and roared as the Healer's essence merged with the collective. Jetta slammed into the ground, her mind exploding with crystalline urgency.

(TRIEL!)

Something tugged mercilessly at her core until she was launched into the air. Before she could orient herself, an invisible force latched on and yanked her forward like a predator retracting its prey. Jetta fought back, digging into the invisible plane, burrowing into the dark matter and anchoring herself. The pull transcended pain. A high tone rang in her head, increasing in volume as she struggled to keep herself from shearing in half.

Triel!

A voice cut through the ringing, whispering words spoken just moments before: "Everything that has happened to me has led to me being right here, right now... I chose that path, I found you... Thank you for letting me love you, and giving me your strength..."

The pull intensified exponentially. A chorus of voices distinguished themselves from the ringing inside her head. The same voices she had heard once before, strangely abrasive, jarring, cutting through her bones—

(Ai-lĕ, ime, Ai-lĕ—nos k'etekµe imæ Ai-lĕ)

(Umnïero, Amaroka, f'ro ime nos wrli e)

(Dk'a ovŋĭl sh'dar'o)

Jetta remembered. The other Prodgies—

She hunkered down. If she let go, she would dissolve in the flames of the Dissemblers along with Triel. There must be something she could do to save her love.

Triel, *Jetta projected with all her might.* I give you my life, my body, my soul. Take it. Come back.

The Dissemblers took new interest in her. Pain splintered her spine and crushed her skull. Her flesh became a canvas for their pain. Steeling herself against the agony, she held onto the only thing she could. Jetta curled in on her memories, the joy of her heart, and whispered her last words: (I love you, Triel of Algardrien.)

CHAPTER XVI

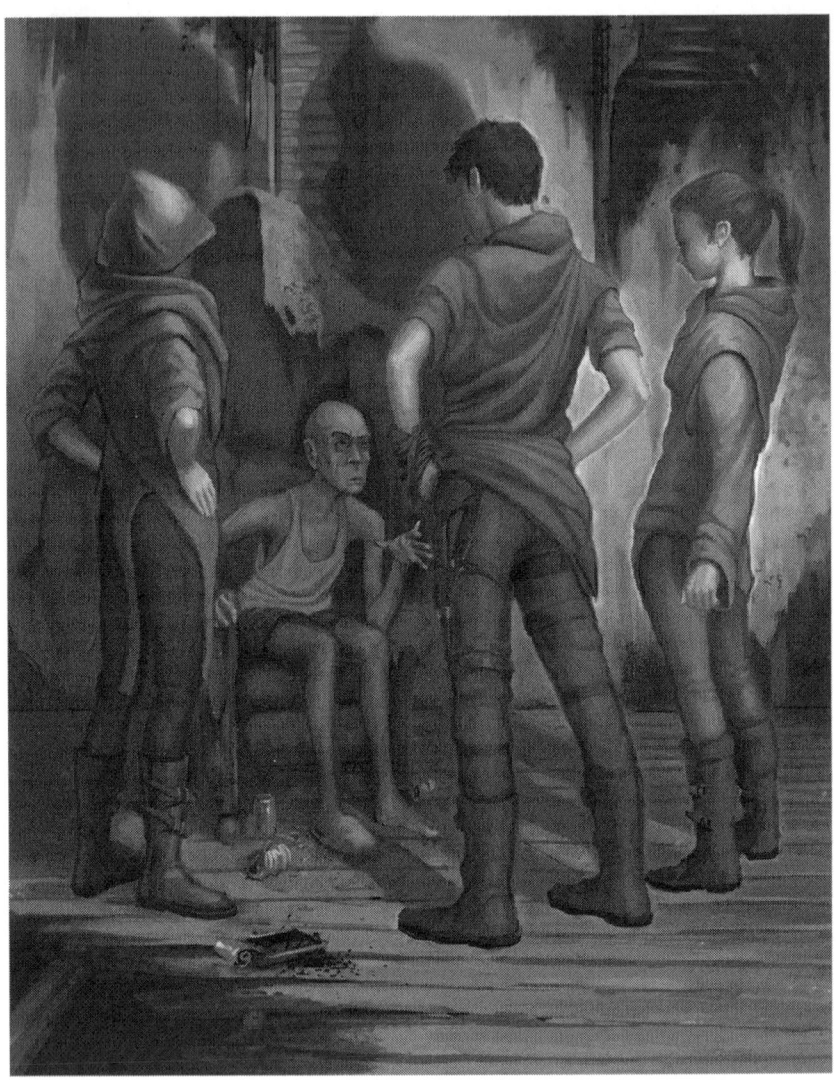

Jaeia opened her eyes to the blurred joining of walls. Monitors beeped steadily in the background. Her mind gathered with speed as she watched a white-coated doctor check her vital signs. *Dr. Kaoto?* Surprise and relief came over her in waves.

"Captain," he nodded, looking at her through the magnification of his specialized glasses. "Welcome aboard the *Nyrok*."

The medical frigate—we must be orbiting Nagoor, Jaeia thought. *Tarsha did it.*

"Report?" she asked, sitting up as best she could. As soon as she tried to move, her head spun in every which direction. Kaoto must have loaded her up with medications.

(That can't be good—)

"Wren made contact from Trigos about an hour ago with good news. Apparently he's convinced the majority of the General Assembly to come back to the Starways Alliance. Chancellor Reamon has even offered his assistance in the negotiations."

Jaeia couldn't believe what she was hearing. That by itself was a miracle. "What about Jue Hexron? And the Motti ship?"

Touching her shoulder, Kaoto tried to calm her down. "Unipoesa is starting the preliminary cleanup right now. The Motti ship appears to have been be neutralized."

Jaeia thought about the shock collar Tarsha had forced him to wear. "And Tarsha?"

Kaoto smiled politely. "I believe she has taken her friend and departed."

Jaeia kept her emotions from registering on her face. Gripping the bedsheets, she quietly inquired about the crew of the *Wraith*.

"Docked in bay one. We're currently treating your sister in the next suite."

Jaeia was hesitant to celebrate. First, she listened with her inner ear. Her senses picked up two heartbeats other than her own. Jetta and Jahx were still alive. When she searched for the other familiar tune, she found it captured only in memory.

"What happened to Triel?"

The words sucked her back behind her sister's eyes, into a fresh memory. The dog-soldiers were standing over her, shaking her awake. Jetta was slow to stir, still returning from the far reaches of a transitional world. She watched as Jetta frantically searched for Triel, tearing the ship apart until her body gave out.

Triel was gone.

Kaoto gathered his dataclips. "I think that would be best answered by your sister."

Nodding, Jaeia rubbed away the tears in her eyes.

Kaoto lowered his voice. "Captain, there isn't much more I, or Dr. DeAnders, can do for you and your siblings. I'm so sorry. If there's anything I can do to make you more comfortable, please let me know. I've given you the last of the boosters so you can have some time to do what you need to do. Please call for the nurse if you'd like to get up."

Jaeia watched him go, disheartened by the soft-spoken doctor's grim condolences. *This is it. There's no more time.*

Jaeia didn't bother to call the nurse. Instead, she removed all the monitoring equipment and intravenous lines before shakily making her way over to her sister's bed in the next intensive care compartment.

Jetta was awake, sitting at the edge of her bed, pale and swaying back and forth with her eyes closed. As Jaeia started to speak, the overhead com crackled to life.

"Attention, attention. This is Chief Commander Wren. I am honored to announce the success of the peace treaty forged with the General Assembly and the remainder of the Galactic Republic. The Starways Alliance has fought many battles against enemies that seem much stronger and faster than ourselves. Yet, by our strength of conviction and our honorable mission to bring peace and justice to all Sentients, we prevail. Now, with the aid of Dr. Kurt Stein, we can start to rebuild our fallen worlds and look to the future. It is with heartfelt gratitude and the most profound thanks to our soldiers and crewmen that I announce our victory, and welcome you all into a new era of peace."

Cheers thundered through the medical frigate. Jaeia stumbled into the bed, overwhelmed by the surge of emotions flooding the ship.

Finally, peace—

—Time to go home—

—I don't have to be afraid anymore

Two hands steadied her and guided her to the bed as she blocked out the voices.

"Glad to see you again, Sis."

Jaeia didn't want to believe her eyes. Jetta's face was reduced to skin stretched over bone. The whites of her eyes had yellowed, and her hair looked thin and brittle. All of the finely-toned muscle that once molded her tall frame had been whittled away to taut, fatless strips. There was no question that death was just around the corner.

Jaeia held her tightly. "Are you okay?"

She felt the back of her patient gown dampen with her sister's tears. Jetta's chest heaved as she fought to contain her sobs.

I can't believe she's gone.

Jaeia kissed her cheek. "I know."

A weak laugh broke through her tears. "But I guess we're not far behind her."

Jaeia couldn't argue with that.

"Eight years and a thousand lifetimes old," Jetta said, pulling away and drying her eyes. Regret tinged her sister's words. "I guess I can't complain."

"I know; I wish it didn't have to end this way either," Jaeia whispered. "I wanted to see Kurt rebuild the Homeworlds."

Jetta nodded. "Me too."

A nurse rounded the corner, trailed by medics. The worry left her face once she found Jaeia with her sister.

"Captain, please—you're on strict bedrest."

The nurse tried to usher Jaeia away, but Jetta wouldn't let her.

Jetta's control surprised her. "Please, just give us this moment. We don't have many left."

The nurse hovered for a moment, but left without an argument.

Jetta stripped off her monitoring equipment. "We'd better go see Jahx. They have him in an isolation unit."

Opening the locker next to her bed, her sister found her uniform and boots. As she took off her gown to change, she gasped.

"Jaeia—my stomach—it's completely healed!"

Jaeia didn't understand the significance. "That's good?"

Jetta slapped her forehead, her eyes jerking back and forth. Jaeia tried to keep up with her thought process, but by the time Jetta was making her way out the door, she had just grasped her twin's conclusion.

"Oh Gods," Jaeia said, hurriedly snatching her uniform from her own locker and running down the hall after Jetta.

Her sister was kind enough to let her catch up and board the lift but showed no further consideration as she sped down the halls. Jaeia was lucky enough to get most of her uniform on before Jetta hopped off and ran into the docking bay.

The deck officer stopped her as she tried to board a two-man cruiser.

"Sir, there are restrictions on flights right now."

"I need this ship!" Jetta demanded.

"Most of our starcraft are being deployed to aid the survivors on Jue Hexron."

Jetta rung in the admiral on her sleeve. "Damon, I need to get to that Motti ship *now*. Override any standing order on flights."

Damon's image popped up on her forearm. "Shouldn't you be in the infirmary?"

"This is an emergency." Jetta's face turned beet red, her voice shaky and high. "Trust me."

Unipoesa typed in something off the visual field. "I already deployed an SMT. You are more than welcome to oversee their progress."

"No," Jetta refused. "I have to go there myself."

Unipoesa looked her up and down. "I can't let you do that, Commander, in your compromised state."

Her sister's distress felt like hot coals in her belly. Jaeia needed no cue. Flipping off Jetta's sleeve, she turned to the deck officer. *"Thank you for letting us take the cruiser. We will return it shortly."*

Jetta didn't wait to make sure Jaeia's second voice had taken effect as she hoisted herself into the two-man cruiser.

"Thanks, Jae," Jetta said, gunning the engines before buckling in.

Jaeia waited until they cleared the bay doors and got to a safe jump distance before asking. "Do you really think that Triel somehow survived?"

Jetta didn't answer right away. Checking the scanner readings, she made the calculations to jump to the last known Motti ship location, her green eyes more vibrant and alive than Jaeia could ever remember seeing them. "I don't think," she said, placing a hand over her healed abdomen. "I feel."

***

Jetta intercepted the Special Missions Team charged with investigating the Motti ship on the terminal access point under the belly of the giant Deadwalker ship. With careful maneuvering, she connected with the umbilicus of the Alliance stealth starcraft and boarded to meet the team. She found all of her old crew suiting up in the prep room, grabbing weapons, detection equipment and biohazard gear from the lockers.

Ferraway, the team leader, greeted her first. "Captain, Commander—Sir, we weren't expecting—"

"At ease, Lieutenant," she said, saluting back. "Tell me what you know."

As he handed her a datafile, he opened his mind, allowing her and her sister to take what they needed in seconds.

That's unusual, Jaeia commented, not used to that level of trust.

Pride swelled in her heart. *Not for my SMT.*

"Our scanners are unable to give us any accurate life sign readings; there's a lot of unusual activity interfering with our equipment," Ferraway said, showing them the holographic projections on his uniform sleeve. "I'm taking the team in now to do a manual sweep."

A high-pitched squeal interrupted their conversation. Ferraway stepped to the side, allowing the twins to watch as Tech made the final connections to reintegrate Billy Don't into their mobile communications system. The little Liiker boy appeared as happy as could be, strapped to a rolling cart with a com dish, giggling and making bubbles with his lubricants. M'ah Pae's ocular device, covered in a white slime, rolled around in one of his neck ports.

Jetta shuddered, sharing a mutual disgust with her twin.

I can't believe they got Tech to agree to this, Jaeia said.

Unipoesa told him to think of all the other girls and boys like Billy that may still be trapped.

Jaeia sighed. *Of course he did.*

"We're coming with you," Jetta said, turning back to Ferraway.

Even though she hadn't been his commanding officer for long, he read her almost as well as her siblings. Instead of a protracted fight, he outfitted them with specialized biohazard suits for the trip on board the living Motti starcraft.

He pulled her aside, out of earshot from the rest of the SMT. "I'm leading this one, Commander."

As she stepped in to argue her rank, he grabbed her by the elbow, keeping her upright until her wobbly legs stabilized. If it had been anyone else, she would shoved them away.

"Alright," she whispered.

They boarded the ship in two teams, Jetta and Jaeia flanking with two soldiers assisting them.

Even through the helmet filters, Jetta tasted the salty tang in the air. Fanning their flashlights revealed red, sacculated walls and dripping ceilings. As she wiggled through sphincters and peered down metal-plated fistulas, half-remembered sensations of being aboard a Motti ship ghosted her thoughts.

Buzzing—

Insects?

—(why can't I open my eyes?)—

Can't breathe in this heat—

Jetta bit down on her lower lip to stifle the memories. Despite her efforts, the tension in her body and mind grew the deeper they penetrated.

You're not the only one, Jaeia whispered across their bond, drawing her sister's attention to Billy Don't. The little Liiker had grown quiet, his eyes darting about as he made strange clicks with his tongue. Jetta couldn't understand his mind, but she could relate to his discomfort. *This is a place of remembrance and pain for him, too.*

"He doesn't like this," Tech said nervously, checking the connections. "He really, really doesn't like this."

They spotted the first Liiker butting his head against a wall in a digestion parlor off of a main channel. Soon they found several more Liikers like him, confused and disoriented, spinning in circles or twitching in a collective heap.

"Ask Billy what happened," Jetta said, keeping her distance from one of the multi-headed creatures mounted on a centipede frame. Upturned, its tined silver legs kicked at the air in a futile attempt to right itself.

Tech input the query on a remote keyboard before asking Billy aloud.

The little Liiker sputtered and convulsed. As Billy's eyes rolled back into his head, Tech furiously worked to stabilize the connections.

Years ago, Tech outfitted Billy with a type of voicebox in hopes that he could restore his speech, but celebrated only limited success. Now he emitted sounds that had no business coming from such a small child.

"We... are... in the... dark..."

The Dissemblers broke down their communications network, Jaeia said, sharing her insight. *They're all lost.*

"We... seek... to... be... one again..."

Jetta touched her stomach, feeling an invisible force pulling down and inwards.

"Ask him where the Dissemblers are."

"No!" Tech said, wringing his hands at the sight of his companion. "He's going to overload!"

Pushing off the soldier assisting her, Jetta mounted the mobile communications unit beside Tech. She thought Billy's parts would only make sense to her through Tech's eyes until she recalled a piece of incidental knowledge she had gleaned off of Victor.

How is this possible?

Her sister's realizations reverberated across their bond: *Josef Stein mastered and evolved much of the Motti technology, but it was Victor who had first devised the cranial implants and biomechanical parts, and expanded their function over the centuries to control and manipulate M'ah Pae...*

With a few adjustments, Jetta stabilized Billy. As he came to, so did the tears.

"Billy," she said crouching before him. "You have nothing to be afraid of. The bad man who did this is gone. These are your brothers and sisters who need our help. But first we have to find the Dissemblers. We have to know that they have been stopped."

Babbling something she didn't understand, Billy Don't pointed one of his extenders toward the pulsating corridors.

Jetta accepted a soldier's arm to help her across the slick yellow floors. Following close behind her, Jaeia drew her attention to the chatter and buzz coming up from all around them.

Jetta, listen—

Pausing mid-step, she held her breath and focused. Through the droning insect sound, she heard a rhythmic chant rising in intensity with every heartbeat.

I sense no malice, Jaeia observed.

"I feel..." Jetta began, then stopped. *Her.*

Running ahead, Jetta slipped on the floor, catching herself on a Liiker half-torso. She jerked away but lost her footing again, this time falling against a clump of tissue.

"Jetta!"

"Commander!"

As her sister and SMT yelled for her, the clump of tissue expanded, encompassing her body. Before she could react, the walls contracted, pumping her down an oily tube.

Jetta shot out of the tube and landed in a soft, nodular mass. Gagging and spitting, she wiped the oily biofilm from her face.

"The Apparax," a deep voice announced.

The Apparax, echoed across the psionic plane.

Jetta put out her hand to stop the attacker, but none came. In the back of her mind she could hear her sister's reassurances. *Don't worry; the path you traveled has clamped off, but we'll find you. Just stay where you are.*

She was on her own.

Breathe, she told herself. *Assess your surroundings.*

Floor lights barely lit the red-walled chamber. Looking up, she saw dried-up cocoons dangling from the ceiling, and semi-mechanical loops of bowel twisting across the floor. Shadows played tricks on her mind. Everything felt alive and watching her.

"Triel?" Jetta whispered. "Where are you?"

"Do not be afraid," the same voice intoned. "We cannot help our appearance."

Jetta held her breath. "Show yourself."

A tall figure stepped out of the shadows. Machinery carved into his face and body, sapping the color from his skin and giving him the appearance of a bloodless corpse. But Jetta saw the markings adorning his suppurating flesh and knew.

"Corbas of Algardrien," she whispered.

The Prodgy Liiker nodded. "Jetta Kyron of Earth. Apparax. Triorion. It is an honor to meet you."

Jetta's eyes adjusted to the gloom. Awakened from slumber, hundreds of others mutilated like Corbas lingered in the dark, afraid of their new skin.

"Where is—" Another bout of coughing stole her words, making her chest spasm. After it subsided, she asked in a hoarse voice: "Where is Triel? I feel her. I know she's here."

Corbas's look of confusion resolved into a kind smile pierced by wiring. "Of course you feel her, my friend. You were instrumental in her transcendence into the next Great Mother. If it weren't for you, we would not be saved, and she would have not realized the path to Cudal."

"What do you mean?" Jetta said, falling to her knees. She could barely keep her head up. Exertion and fatigue set in, gnawing at her bones and joints.

Corbas knelt beside her, helping her sit up. "Jetta, Triel is not gone. She lives inside you. That is why she performed the ritual of *Ne'topat'h*. Your spirits are now one."

"No," Jetta said, shaking her head. "I feel her. She's *here*. She's not dead."

Closing her eyes, Jetta summoned all her strength. She expanded her mind, searching for her love across the parallel planes, as far as she could reach. "I believe…"

Corbas looked at her through an eye punctured with ribbed catheters. "Then open your eyes and see."

Jetta opened her eyes. *Am I hallucinating?* Her skin was shining, streaked with glowing blue veins. But as soon as she blinked, they vanished.

"She is not gone," he said quietly. "And when you find peace, my friend, you will see her again."

***

Jaeia found her way to her sister via an alternate, and revolting, route through the waste disposal systems, but forgot her disgust when she found her sister talking to a massive Liiker.

Jetta!

Before panic could set in, she garnered her sister's experience with the converted Prodgies. Overwhelmed at the miracle of their rescue, she shared her joy with her twin. *There's hope now.*

As she wiped off the sticky debris for her visor, she joined her sister's conversation with Corbas.

"We can't leave," he said, "not without setting the rest of the Motti free from their own bonds."

When her sister balked, he pushed harder. "Their suffering cannot be ignored."

"I'll talk to my SMT," Jetta said.

"We'll do everything we can," Jaeia assured Corbas before joining her sister's side as she briefed the team.

"I'm sorry, Sir; I don't understand," Ferraway said when Jetta tried to explain the situation.

"The remaining Motti are Josef Stein's friends and colleagues in the field of nanotechnology and biochemical design," she repeated.

Jaeia added: "They were infected by both the Necro Plague and the life-extending Smart Cell Series #117."

Cursing under his breath as he stepped in an oozing pustule, Ferraway, along with the rest of the slimed team, looked more than eager to complete the mission and get out of the living ship. "Yes, Sir. We're with you all the way."

Corbas led them straight to the center of the hive, where the remaining twelve Motti huddled together in confusion. Without M'ah Pae to oversee their work and dictate their direction, they appeared as lost as their Liikers.

"Have Billy talk to them," Jetta said, hanging on Ferraway's shoulder and avoiding the steaming tubules protruding from the floor. "Tell them… we mean them no harm."

Jaeia could feel and appreciate her sister's difficulty in wanting to save the Motti that were responsible for their dehumanizing torture and the death of their brother.

Victor was the puppet master, she reminded herself, *not these Motti.*

They were victims too, their torment profound and much more visceral. They barely retained a vestige of life, and even as attuned as the twins were, Jaeia could sense very little in the way of recognizable human thought patterns.

I think Billy Don't remembers, too, her sister commented as Billy threw a fit. Wailing at the top of his lungs, he twisted and turned so Tech couldn't access the override to his communication ports.

"Billy," Jaeia spoke softly, touching the skin on his face. "They weren't the bad guys who hurt you. They were good guys that got hurt too. They need your help. If we can help them, then maybe they can help all the boys and girls that feel like you do."

Frowning, Billy chomped on his tongue. He looked to Tech. The engineer sighed heavily and nodded to him.

With a chirp, Billy's eyes rolled back into their sockets, and the Motti Overlord's ocular implant gyrated on his shoulder. A sound like insect stridulations poured from his open mouth. Jaeia covered her ears, as did the rest of the party. Finally, it ceased.

One of the Motti lumbered forward on spidery legs. Jaeia's heart thumped loudly in her ears as he bent down to inspect her with jointed silver antennae. She felt some kind of recognition, and perhaps remorse.

Tech checked his monitor readout of Billy's internal communications. "They understand us."

Leaning forward, the Motti offered her an ear translator on a pronged extender. Jaeia shuddered, remembering a time when it would have been forced down her ear canal without her consent.

"And they want to talk."

"Who wants to talk to us?" Jetta asked, her hands twitching for her firearm.

Tech mumbled to himself, reading Billy's feedback twice before sharing what he saw. "It says here... Dr. Albert Marx."

Jaeia sifted through acquired memories, but Jetta remembered first.

With a strange, quivering smile, Jetta announced to the group. "Head of Biological Integration, PhD, MD; The Institute of Advanced Science, New Berlin. Best man at Josef Stein's wedding."

Jaeia looked again at the Motti. She thought she saw him smile.

***

Jetta and her sister returned with the SMT to the *Nyrok*. With them came the salvaged Prodgies, leaving Dr. Marx and the rest of the Motti behind with the Liikers. To the twins there was no need to take the rest of them. Billy had copied and transposed the programming Tech had engineered years ago to help rehabilitate and restore his memories from before his biomechanical transition. Many had already begun to remember a life apart from twisted machinery.

My sister would have loved to work with Dr. Marx on the restitution and reintegration efforts, Jetta thought. She pretended to scroll through the command chair's armrest interface as Ferraway instructed the bridge crew on the docking process. *Or help forge peace between the Sentients and the Motti—*

"Hey." Jaeia leaned over her seat and touched her sister's arm as locking clamps gently rocked the ship. *We're still here, okay?*

Okay.

As the twins disembarked from the SMT stealth ship, a voice came over the com. "Attention all crew. As your officially appointed Military Minister, I, Gaeshin Wren, am pleased to announce the promotion of two of our finest officers, Jetta and Jaeia Kyron, to Chief Commanding Officers of the Alliance Fleet."

"Ha!" Jetta said, nudging her sister as the docking crew and SMT gave them a round of applause. "You may have gotten captain first, but I just jumped more ranks than you."

The grim truth set in before she could finish razzing her sister. Even if they were the most intellectually qualified for the position, their age and history would have precluded the General Assembly from approving their appointment. *It's just going to create a political firestorm to push us into that position over Unipoesa.*

Unless it was Unipoesa that pushed our promotion. Jetta felt the weight of her sister's realization as she shared it through their bond: *This is his way of saying thanks. And goodbye.*

"Jeez… I finally make chief commanding officer, and I'm only going to get to wear the stars for what—a few more hours?" Jetta said as a soldier helped her onto a lift.

"Yeah, you don't know anything. I made chief commanding officer, and I have to share it with *you*," Jaeia said with a chuckle.

Grinning, Jetta batted her lightly on the arm. "Jerk."

"Hey, is that Reht?" Jaeia said, pointing to the third port in the docking bay. With arms wide open, the dog-soldier captain welcomed Tech and Billy Don't back to the *Wraith*. No amount of money had swayed the nervous engineer to help with the continued relations between the Motti and the Alliance, though Jaeia had convinced him to stay in contact as a consultant. After all, the twins may have copied his knowledge on Liiker programming, but their abilities could not replicate his invention.

Jetta stopped the lift before they could take off. Only by sheer determination did she manage to get to her feet and let herself down to the docking platform. "I'll meet you in the infirmary."

Gleaning her sister's intentions, Jaeia smiled. "Don't be long."

Jetta used the support of a motorized cart to get her over to the *Wraith* as a deck officer gave Reht and his remaining crew the final approval for departure. From the bitter feel of their thoughts, the Sleeper Program had been erased from their brains—but not the lasting effects.

At least the Alliance did something right for the dog-soldiers, she thought, watching Mom lug a few thousand bundles of hard cash up the ramp. She hoped that their newfound riches would settle the unrest that had been brewing within the ranks, or allow the individual crew members to go their own way without any bad blood.

Spotting her, Reht hopped down from the ramp. "Shouldn't you be in the infirmary?"

"I came to say goodbye."

Reht smirked, his incisors popping over his lips. "Hard to imagine how I met you anymore. A scared little stick of a launnie, beat up and dirty. Now you're all grown up, I guess, and not half-bad looking. At least for a human."

Jetta didn't let him get away with it. "When I first met you, you were a cocky, dog-soldier *assino*. I didn't think you cared about anything or anybody else. But I was wrong. You're not half-bad. Even for a non-human."

Smile fading, he cleared his throat. "You never found her?"

Her response came in a whisper. "No."

Looking away from her, Reht pulled at the bandages on his hands. Jetta expected him to accept the news with the same clowning front she remembered, but instead he gave her some unexpected advice. "Well, for whatever it's worth, Starfox was a fighter. She had grit and resourcefulness like you. If there weren't no body—and there weren't—then she ain't dead."

With tears in her eyes, Jetta nodded.

"Alright then, kiddo, I gotta go. It's time for me to settle some scores."

Skimming the surface of his thoughts, she saw Elia and the ghosts of Reht's past dance across her retinas. *He's not planning another deal; his next job is a personal one.* Jetta sensed his uncertainty about the continuation of his crew, but his most loyal companion, the blue-furred Talian, would never leave his side, even with what he had planned.

"Reht, you did a great thing by helping the Alliance. We couldn't have done it without you and your crew. You saved this galaxy." Even as she said it, she knew it wasn't going to be enough to settle his demons. The peace he needed would be found only on his own journey.

Reht surprised her with a hug, though it turned into a smart rub on the head. Jetta both hated it and appreciated the affection.

"Stop getting all gooey on me, kid. You wanna make me soft?" he said, leaping up onto the ramp. Mom growled and rolled his eyes as he walked past with another bundle.

"Call me if you ever need a hand," Jetta said. "I can hold my own."

"That's the rumor on the street," Reht winked. "Oh," he said, snapping his fingers and dropping his chest down to the ramp to be eye level with her. He twisted his finger in his ear and made a funny face. "You gotta get this dream out of my head. Drivin' me nuts. That lady at the bar put it there forever ago. Triel tried to help, but she never really got it out of my head. Doctors say it ain't part of the Sleeper Program. I think Triel said it was a message for you or somethin'...?"

Jetta had nearly forgotten about that. *Of course,* she thought, *the memory stain left by my mother.* She had never seen the original message, and she and her siblings were probably the only people who could fully extract it. It would be nice to see her mother again, even if it was only an echo. Maybe it would fill in the missing pieces of that puzzle.

Jetta lifted her hand to his forehead.

Reht pulled back a bit. "This is sorta my virgin experience with this, okay?"

"I'll be gentle, I promise," Jetta said, grinning.

Reht laughed. "Stop stealing my lines, kid."

***

On Old Earth, deep in the heart of Paradise City, stands a shop tucked away in a back alley, protected from the day-to-day travelers. Inside, the shopkeeper, an elderly man wearing a dark apron and bracers, and a green visor atop his finely combed white hair, stays true to his daily routine. He hums the same old tune to himself, stacking copper pennies and counting his receipts, unworried about when his next customer will arrive.

Only hand-selected and authenticated antiques line his shelves and occupy his drawers, and unless he finds a buyer truly deserving, he will not sell any of his prizes. After all, he didn't just carry relics of the past—these were connections to a time and place that many wished still existed. And for him, they were proof that there was a way back.

His only means of getting by was the private funding he received through Earth's conservation groups. Even with their support and continued inquiry into his wares, he seldom gave them any hints of the real treasures he possessed. Especially after a Reptili and his canine crossbreed stopped by his store eight years ago, and he happened upon his most interesting find.

"You buy Earth junk?"

"Yes, I do," he had responded, *frightened and skeptical of the outerworlder's claim to have found rare terrestrial artifacts. As the Reptili laid down parts and equipment from an ancient escape pod, the shopkeeper noticed the real treasure. A stuffed bear. A gold cross necklace; too small to be worth much. A scrap of paper with a note written in ancient English.* Ashya, Ryen, and Tierin—we love you with all our hearts. Mom and Dad.

"I'll give you seventy."

"You'll give me two fifty and that contraption over there," he said, *pointing to a crossbow holding up a stack of books.*

The shopkeeper had been too afraid to argue much with the Reptili, but he knew if he let on that he possessed that kind of money, he would probably be robbed and killed.

"How about eighty, the crossbow, and this," he said, *reaching for the object that lay atop a mound of old sheet music. Since it was a gift from a former customer, he had allowed in his shop even though it was an imitation model. It had no value to him, so he used it as a paperweight. To an untrained eye, it was a genuine World War II German Sauer double-action automatic pistol.*

Easily swayed by devices of violence, the Reptili's eyes grew wide with anticipation.

"Deal."

After the authentication process yielded strange results, the shopkeeper decided to keep the bear sealed in a glass case in the back of the store with the gold cross around its neck. Both items originated in the twentieth century, but they had not suffered the ravages of time like most of his items. This only added to his intrigue. He didn't believe in much, but he knew that the bear and the necklace had been special to someone. And, of all the antiques he owned, treasures that came from all over the Earth, the stuffed bear seemed to have the most mystery, and the most presence.

The grandfather clock kept the rhythm of his humming as he continued his usual business. To his surprise, the door bell jingled. He looked over the rim of his glasses to see a gaunt-looking woman standing in his shop.

"Is this 'Old Earth Antiques'?"

The shopkeeper kept the curiosity out of his voice. He had been wrong before. He didn't want to get himself overly excited. "Yes, it is. How can I help you?"

A second later there were two of them. Identical. As they approached, he realized the gravity of their illness. Bereft of any color, they looked like cancer patients in the last stages of life.

"Hey—hey! I don't want you bringing any sickness in here!" he said, covering his nose and mouth.

The woman with gray eyes calmly replied, "What we have is not contagious."

"We're looking for Charlie," the one with green eyes cut in, not hiding her impatience.

In his excitement, the shopkeeper accidentally knocked over a dusty pile of automobile license plates. "You came for Charlie?"

Green eyes locked with his. He felt a strange ticking inside his skull. "Yes."

With trembling hands, he checked the memo written on his desk that had been sitting there for the past several months. A woman in her late twenties wrote it after asking him about the stuffed bear and the necklace. She gave him hints about its origins, as well as a name for the bear. But first and foremost, she made him promise to keep them safe, as if all the world depended on it.

The shopkeeper was a practical man. Ordinarily he wouldn't have believed in such hodgepodge, but from the sound of her voice, the way her pale green eyes seemed to speak to him on a deeper level, he knew she spoke the truth.

The memo was written in ancient English. *They may come as three, or perhaps as one. They will ask for Charlie. See this symbol on their right upper arms and give them what they want. Then your greatest dream will come true.*

There had been many nights when he doubted his sanity, but many more when he dreamed of a planet reborn, filled with early model automobiles and sleek high-rises. Anachronisms. The crazy hallucinations of a senile old man.

As they stood across the counter, he thought for a moment he recognized their faces. He didn't get out much, nor did he ever watch the newsreels. It was all political *gorsh-shit* half the time anyway. Maybe they were famous. He didn't care much. He just had to see their arms.

"See my what?"

"To see Charlie, I have to see your arms," he repeated, sticking to his guns.

The twins exchanged glances. Finally, the irritable one pulled up her sleeve and showed him a tattoo. He checked the memo. Spot on.

"Follow me," he said, trying to sound tired, though he felt giddy and excited. He told himself to settle down, that he was being impractical, but he couldn't help himself.

He locked the front door and drew down the shade. After making sure the shop was empty, he led the twins through a maze of teetering book stacks and knickknacks to the back of the store. They had a hard time keeping up; with wheezy breaths, they moved as if their bones were ready to snap.

He double-checked everything, then pushed back the secret bookshelf and led them into the safe room.

"Who sent you?" he asked.

The gentler one responded. "The woman you met who gave you the memo. Her name was Ariya Ohakn."

His history was rusty, but the name rang a bell. *The Ariya Ohakn?* he thought to himself. *The co-founder of* 'Cause of Earth?' *Impossible.*

It was as if the grumpy one read his mind. "It *was* Ariya Ohakn."

"Are you…?" He didn't finish the question. He wanted to know if they were telepathic, but the question would only cause him trouble. Old senses told him the twins were not a threat, but he could not shake the intensity of their presence.

"Meet Charlie," he said, rattling a key in the lock. He opened the safe to reveal the stuffed bear sitting behind the glass case.

Despite her urgency, the green-eyed twin was gracious enough to wait for him to okay a closer inspection. With careful hands, she removed the gold cross and handed it to her sister. Then she did something that confused him. She closed her eyes and rested her hand on the bear's faded gray head, as if performing some kind of mind meld.

"It's just a stuffed—"

The gray-eyed one put her finger to her lips to keep him quiet. Now he was getting cross. *Is this some kind of circus trick?*

"It's not a trick," the green-eyed one replied, opening her eyes again. "This stuffed animal has a lot of history I had to be sure of. Now I know." Tears formed in her eyes, but not ones of sorrow. "Would you like to know why he's so special?"

The shopkeeper didn't know what to say. Nervous and excited, it all seemed too much, especially for a man his age.

The woman pointed out something he hadn't noticed when he first acquired the antique. "The bear's eyes are different colors."

Removing his glasses, he squinted, trying to see past the gauzy haze of cataracts. She was right. Though the difference was subtle, the one on the right seemed slightly darker and out of place.

She removed a scanner from her pocket, and it beeped when she held it over the right eye.

"What is it?" the shopkeeper asked.

"A map," the woman said. "To find the Ark."

"*The* Ark? Dr. Stein's Ark?"

The woman nodded. She scanned the rest of the bear. Minding the stitching so he could be sewn back together, she removed what she needed from the bear's round belly. Out came white stuffing, a folded letter, and three clips of baby's hair.

The women hugged each other and cheered. Finding the letter and the locks of hair apparently merited a greater celebration than finding the Ark.

"W-what's going on here?" the shopkeeper said, interrupting their gaiety.

The green-eyed one smiled, lighting up her entire face. Despite her illness, her beauty took his breath away. "I hope you like blue skies."

***

Jetta waited until they were back aboard the *Star Runner* and safely out of Earth's atmosphere to read the letter. Pressed into her side, Jaeia read along with her.

February 13, 2052

To my children—

I have struggled with this letter for many years. I knew this day would come, and now it is here, but I still don't know how to say what I need to. I will simply tell you that I am so sorry, my children. Human beings have always been inexplicably contradictory; we are radically self-destructive and yet possess quite the penchant for survival. But this time things have gone too far, and I fear the damage is irreparable.

I know you will not understand my decision now, but maybe someday you will. You are more important—and your children are more important—than this old woman. But even if humans can survive this Exodus, it will never be enough. You need to realize that the next step must be taken. We cannot live apart from Earth. Our planet was more than our home; it was the very core of who we are, as a life form amongst countless others, in the metaphysical fabric of the universe. Even if we can find another home, the scar of what we've done will linger, and we will continue to tear ourselves apart.

Please, take this letter with you. May it remind you of why you must not give up on the cause for Earth.
Redemption. Reparation. Deliverance.
Come home.

All my love,
Grandma Laura

"Grandma Laura," Jaeia said. She laid her forehead against Jetta's shoulder, sifting through their mother's memories of her own mother. "She gave the best hugs."

"This isn't just a letter to us," Jetta said. "This is a coded message."

Dipping into her mind again, Jaeia saw the patterns Jetta had seen in the letter. The strange word groupings. The way the letter was laid out. It was the type of covert communication used by all members of Cause For Earth.

"This is how we find the rest of our family."

***

Jetta had only ever been healed by Triel, and when the rescued Prodgies restored her body using the uncorrupted DNA in the lock of baby hair she found in Charlie the stuffed bear, she found the experience more than exhilarating. She felt reborn.

Drs. DeAnders and Kaoto had worked around the clock to try and remove as many of the Motti implants as they could from Corbas and the other Healers, but removing all of them would be impossible. Their scars would never go away.

"Thank you for saving me and my sister," Jetta said walking Corbas to the transport ship waiting in the docking bay. As they came up to the ramp, she hugged him, mindful of his artificial spine. Bittersweet sadness touched her heart when she looked into his eyes. *Triel had her father's eyes.*

Corbas laid his hand on her shoulder. Three of his fingers were missing where the Motti had attached their own devices. "Peace be with you, Jetta Kyron. May our paths cross again soon."

"I plan to come visit Algar once I finish my work with Dr. Stein," she said. "But I promise that you're in good hands."

"It is widely spoken that your sister is the best diplomat in the galaxy," Corbas said. "I'm grateful that she will be helping us transition back to our planet. I have been told the Reivers are not very easy to get along with."

Jetta thought of Salam and their encounters on Algar. "No, they're not."

Corbas held up his mutilated hand, turning it over so that Jetta saw more flesh than machine. "The Prodgy people have come this far. We will live on. In time we will rebuild our society and become a great civilization once again."

"I have no doubts."

"I'll be waiting for you on Algar. You and I still have much left to do." He regarded her one last time and then stepped aboard the transport.

Jetta watched the ship take off from the Alliance Central Starbase and waited several minutes after it had jumped. Finally, she headed back to the medical wing.

Construction crews had still blocked off most of the Starbase, making her find alternate routes to her destination. Jetta was surprised it was operative at all after they had blown half of it away jumping her ship as close as she did. Oddly enough, she found herself glad that she hadn't completely destroyed it.

Guilt kept her from marveling at her fully restored figure in the shiny new corridor paneling. Pink cheeks and round muscles meant nothing to her when Jahx lay dying on an exam table. There was nothing the Prodgies could do for him. Jahx was not in his own body, and restoring the Grand Oblin's body meant expunging Jahx's spirit.

Jetta entered the intensive care isolation unit after a grim conversation with DeAnders. Despite the monitors and medications, it felt more like a white-walled tomb than a treatment room.

"We came so close," Jetta said, taking his hand. Jaeia stood across from her, head bowed as she gripped his other hand.

There were no more tears to cry. She no longer grieved for her brother. He had transcended any physical boundaries more than once to come back to her, proving his indomitable spirit. No matter where he transitioned to next, she would find him. *One day,* she thought, *we'll be three again.*

Jaeia's uniform sleeve beeped. "Chief—Aesis Agarthygh has returned from Fiorah. He is asking to see you. He says the matter is urgent."

Jaeia wiped her eyes. "Is he aboard the base?"

"He is in decontamination."

"Send him here," she said wearily. She turned to Jetta. "Maybe he has some good news about Galm and Lohien."

Jetta had never met Aesis before; she had only seen him through her sister's eyes. Jaeia's feelings seemed abnormally strong in her memories, but when she witnessed them in person, she was taken aback.

"You came back," Jaeia said as Aesis walked into the treatment room.

Jetta felt her sister's heart flutter at the sight of him. The meddling part of her wanted to point out that behind the blonde hair and fair skin wriggled a little green worm, but she knew that her sister's feelings spanned beyond his handsome appearance. She sensed it too; *Aesis is a gentle soul.*

"I did. I found your aunt and uncle," he said. His eyes moved to Jahx, but quickly returned to her sister. Any discomfort at the sight of their dying brother did not register on his face.

"Why didn't you bring them here?" Jetta asked. "Or alert the Alliance for backup?"

Aesis didn't react to her words, despite the doubt and accusation they carried. "Even after the Dominion ousted Yahmen Drachsi from the mining business, he managed to take control of the Underground Block."

Jetta's eyes narrowed as she read into his words. "They're alive, but he's using them for his business."

Aesis nodded. "Yes. They're in bad shape, but I told them that you were coming for them. I'm so sorry I couldn't get them out. I had a hard enough time myself. My host bodies were killed twice."

Jetta cringed, imagining Aesis' deaths at the hands of Yahmen's enforcers for asking too many questions.

Shaking off the thought, Jetta typed in a series of commands on her sleeve. "Ferraway—prep the team for immediate dustoff. Tell them it's going to get hot."

The SMT lead responded immediately. "We'll be locked and loaded in less than twenty, Sir."

"I wouldn't advise that," Aesis said.

"Why not?"

Aesis shifted from foot to foot. "It was the same reason you couldn't find them before. Fiorahians don't take kindly to strangers, and certainly not military. It took me three bodies before I was accepted on the street."

"Then we'll go ourselves," Jetta decided, canceling her order to her SMT.

"Thank you, Aesis," Jaeia said, wiping away her tears. "That means so much to us."

Aesis' eyes drifted back to Jahx. "I wasn't able to find any of your DNA. The apartment fire was very bad. I'm sorry."

Jetta's heart leapt. She looked to her sister. Both of them spoke at the same time. "We did."

Aesis' eyes perked up from the floor. He looked over at Jahx and then back at his sisters. A hopeful smile broadened his face. "Well then. Let me get to work."

***

Jetta's nose wrinkled as she watched her sister gingerly remove the Spinner from the freshly spun body. The worm's sweet odor wasn't offensive, but the white cheese that fell from the new host's skin carried the ripe smell of waste materials.

Uck—is it like this every time?

Be nice, Jaeia said, checking the spun body's status on the intensive care unit monitors.

Jetta wrestled with her feelings as she looked down at Aesis's work. The Spinner had manipulated the age of Jahx's new body to match their own advanced physical maturity at around twenty years. Despite expecting some change, the broad shoulders and an angled jawline surprised her.

At first she debated with her sister whether or not Jahx would want to progress through all the stages of childhood since they were only eight years old, but after much thought, they came to the same conclusion: They didn't feel like children, nor could they ever repress their personal and borrowed experiences enough to enjoy the carefree days of childhood. With their mental age, it made more sense to don the appearance of young adulthood.

I bet Jahx will appreciate being sped past the awkward phase, Jetta joked as Dr. DeAnders and Dr. Kaoto joined them in the isolation unit.

"We got your urgent message on Jahx's status," Kaoto said.

Jaeia brought DeAnders and Kaoto up to speed, explaining how Aesis spun a new vessel for Jahx, hoping that as their brother passed, his spirit would possess the new body. But something gnawed at Jetta's gut as she stared at the two identical bodies of her brother lying side by side on exam tables. *It isn't going to be enough. Something has to facilitate the transition.*

"What's wrong?" Jaeia said, reading her worry as the two doctors discussed the idea in front of the monitors.

Jetta shook her head. "This isn't going to work."

"Is there something we can do?"

Jetta thought about it. "I don't know. Can you feel him?"

They both touched the cold skin of the Grand Oblin's borrowed body. It felt like a hollow shell with a waning pulse.

Her sister's frustration furrowed her brow. "No. I don't know what else we can do."

Jetta was about to speak when her sister cut her off. "Unless… no, it's crazy."

Jaeia's idea leaked into her head. It was radical, but they were out of options. "Well, no, it's not entirely crazy. It sorta worked once before."

"I don't know if I have it in me," Jaeia said, hugging her arms across her chest. Her gray eyes spoke of her fear. She had always been the one to push Jetta to believe in others, and now she faltered. *It's just too much to hope for.*

Jetta hugged her sister and whispered in her ear. "I believe."

***

It was a beautiful summer day. Not a single cloud blemished the blue sky, allowing the sun to shine down and warm his skin. His mother was there, calling to him from the other side of the flowing river, where a house stood surrounded by a red fence and flowering yard. Two dogs, one white and black, the other shades of brown, roughhoused on the front porch. The sight of them brought him nothing but joy. It would be nice to finally be with them.

(Jahx. It's time.)

Gentle hands pulled him back. Jahx was surprised to see him.

(What are you doing here?)

Josef smiled. (I could ask you the same.)

(I can't stay here anymore. It's time for me to go.)

Josef delivered his words kindly. (Not yet.)

Jahx looked over Josef's shoulder. A very different world, broken and desolate, lay in the distance.

(You are the only one that can finish my work, Jahx. I know I'm asking more of you than I have any right to.)

The sun transformed. No longer did it stay fixed in the calm blue sky.

It descended from the heavens, heading straight for him, growing brighter than all the stars in the universe.

Something inside him wanted to run, make a break to cross over to be with his mother, to finally be at peace, but another force, greater than any fear inside him, kept him from taking the easy way out.

(Your faith brought you this far,) Josef said as the light enveloped him. (Let it continue to guide your path.)

Jahx's lips parted, releasing a cry that shook the heavens as the call of life reached his soul and brought him home.

***

The Hub appeared only briefly after it flashed the borrowed and newly spun body of Jahx Kyron out into the folds of space-time. It chose a female form this time, with translucent skin and eyes that twinkled like the stars.

"We will trust you to take us home, and in return, we promise to give you more than you asked of us."

A glowing, hexagonal object materialized on the empty bed in the treatment room. It fit neatly in Jetta's palm. It was warm to touch, and heavy to hold. "What is this?"

Jaeia took it from her and followed the contours of the piece with sensitive fingers.

"This is the Hub. It's trusting us with its life."

Jetta thought about it. "There's only one place that's safe."

***

Jetta realized with amusement that she didn't have to seek Admiral Unipoesa's authority anymore to commission the *Star Runner*. Although the military senior council's backing of her appointment to co-chief commanding officer helped solidify her position against any backlash from the General Assembly, it by no means quelled the public's unease in the wake of Victor's brutal slander of the Kyron siblings. However, with the announcement that she had not only found Dr. Kurt Stein, but located the Ark, the promise of a renewed Starways quieted any arguments that her or her siblings did not deserve their place protecting the galaxy.

Jahx was still fidgeting in his uniform when they arrived in orbit. "What's wrong?"

Jahx made a face. "Were polytech blends always this itchy?"

Jetta chuckled. Jahx was still getting used to the workings of his new body. As far as she was concerned, he was just as he should have been, blue eyes and all.

Jaeia joined them at the viewport overlooking the mountainous planet. "It doesn't look so bad from orbit."

Jetta shuddered. "This is about as close as I ever want to get again."

Gray eyes met hers. "Agreed."

With a nod, Jetta gave the signal to the helmsman. Two specialized pots jettisoned from the docking bay. One held the evolving life form of an artificial intelligence. The other, a man without a name.

The official documents would read that Victor Paulstine, formerly Ramak Yakarvoah, was banished to the Labor Locks of Plaly IV after his intergalactic trial for his crimes against the Sentients. But the triplets, like many of the high councilmen, feared that if Victor were imprisoned there, he would either find a means of escape, or worse yet be killed.

Kill him, and another will take his place, Jetta thought as the pods streaked through the upper atmosphere of the diseased planet.

Victor believed he was the devil. Jetta did not know what he was, only that he didn't deserve the quick release of death or the chance at another life. And since he ensured his longevity by ingesting the life-extending Smart Cell Series #117 1,100 years ago on Earth, she knew there was only one solution.

Jetta rang in his pod. A feeble-looking old man appeared on the monitor. His diamond teeth had been stripped down to their metal studs. He had been given only one change of clothes, a gun with a limited clip of ammunition, and a bit of water to tide him over until he had safely reached the caves.

"You think this is over?" he hissed, spittle spraying the camera lens. "This is far from over."

Jetta felt her siblings worry about her response, but she had been prepared for this moment. "Victor—I hope that you live a long, long time."

The transmission bleeped out as the pod safely landed near the Exiles' former home.

He'd better be fast enough to get up the side of the mountain before the infected find him.

She couldn't imagine him standing up to one of those creatures.

The thought drifted between the three of them. *What's keeping him from killing himself?*

Jahx answered the question. "He's afraid of death. He's terrified of what awaits him on the other side."

They watched in silence as the second pod transmitted its landing coordinates. It had been difficult to convince the military council to allow the Hub to be released on Tralora, especially after it had proven so helpful in flashing the entire Fleet during the battle at Jue Hexron. There were many charged arguments and fearful questions, even a motion to recapture the artificial being and reinstall it within the confines of the Alliance network, but the Kyrons, with Jaeia leading their deputation, had been persuasive in their advocacy for the emerging intelligence. As her sister argued, it should not be limited to the wave network, nor should it be divided and re-imprisoned in the Alliance mainframe.

"Good," Jetta said, rechecking the status of the defense perimeter. The Hub had deactivated the defense system prior to taking physical form, but she had to make sure as it hurtled toward its new home.

The Narki city, once the technological capital of the galaxy, she thought. *Now a ghost city, with more servers and electronic matrices than any other planet. I can't imagine a more perfect location.*

"What do you think it meant, when it said it would give us more than we asked of it?" Jaeia asked.

Jetta held back her thought. The Hub had given back their brother. There was only one more thing it could do to make things right.

Seconds after Jaeia had asked the question, the call came in from the Alliance Central Starbase.

"Put it through," Jetta said, taking the secure line on an isolated terminal.

The three Kyrons hovered over the transmission. DeAnders face appeared, his eyes wide and beaming.

"They're back!"

***

It took several weeks for the Exiles to be fully cleared by the medical teams after their abnormally long transition through the wave network. Despite the setback with the Grand Oblin, Jetta and Jaeia celebrated the revival of Senka, Crissn, and Rawyll with much jubilation. None of the Defense/Research team could rationally explain the sudden reemergence of the three, or the continued comatose state of the Grand Oblin.

"How did you do it?" Senka asked Jaeia, hugging her for the ninth time as DeAnders read and reread her vital signs. After recovering her speech on day three, no one could get her to stop talking and asking questions.

Jaeia decided it was best not to tell her about the involvement of the Hub just yet. "We had to get some help from a new friend. It's a long story."

Jetta was introducing Jahx to Senka when a flashing light caught Jaeia's eye on one of the remote terminals. With everyone else in a flurry over Senka's improvement, she walked over and checked the incoming message herself.

Thank you, Jaeia Kyron. You are a good friend to us. Because you set us free, we will tell you our greatest secret. We have modified your flash-transport device. Now we have something that can take us all beyond the confines of this universe.

The message erased as soon as she read it.

Jetta and Jahx both stopped their conversation and looked her way as she shared what she had read through their bond.

Jahx lifted a brow. "The universe just got a little bigger."

***

Jetta only received one transmission on the whereabouts of Mantri Sebbs. In her regular slew of electronic fan mail and death threats, she found an ad for a methoc detox center. At first glance she thought it was a hoax, but after a moment she recognized the sardonic prose coded into the graphics.

I feel like I've answered for whatever wrongdoings I've committed against you and many others. Even after they "fixed" my brain, I've stayed off booze and smokes and live cleanly now. I can't go back to what I was, but I'm not sure I'd want to anyway.

Don't bother trying to contact me. I've joined an anti-military group on some godforsaken moon in unregulated space. It's hell, but that suits me now.

I'm always tired. I rarely sleep. I only dream of the past, and that day I met you.

—M. Sebbs

In a message piggybacked on an invitation to a peace summit, Jetta wrote him back. She didn't know what exactly to say to him after so much had transpired. But she had seen the change in him, and chose to believe in that.

Mantri—
Thank you.
J. Kyron

***

The rescued Prodgies performed many miracles upon their return, including the restoration of former Military Minister Tidas Razar. Wren had expressed his concern over the Prodgies healing the infamously prejudiced former Minister, especially since Razar had not only put Triel in cryostasis but secretly underwritten policies to keep her isolated from the rest of the Alliance crew as soon as she was inducted. Corbas put aside Wren's fears, reiterating the Prodgy belief in peace, forgiveness, and acceptance, and that they would heal Razar as a tribe, protecting themselves and Razar from the threat of Falling.

Jaeia made sure to be there as they wheeled Senka in to visit her uncle in intensive care.

"Senka—my dear Senka!" Razar said, pushing aside the medical staff hovering over his bed to get a better look at his niece. He beckoned her with open arms, tears spilling down his face. "I never thought…Oh, my Gods…"

"He's getting too worked up," Dr. Kaoto muttered under his breath, checking the data readouts on the monitors next to Jaeia. "I might have to sedate him."

"I understand. But this is nice," Jaeia commented, stepping aside so that Senka could reach her uncle. She left out the rest of her thought: *Especially after all the reasons I've learned to resent him.*

"Jaeia..." Razar turned to her, eyes bright. "Oh, Jaeia, my niece—I never thought I'd see her again!"

Smiling politely, Jaeia let him have his moment. *Oh Minister, if you only knew what's to come...*

Even though the Prodgies had healed the former Minister, he had not fully acclimated or been informed of all that had transpired since his accident. Above all, he did not yet know of his own forced retirement and impending intergalactic trials.

I don't know how Tarsha did it, but she exposed your role in the Command Development Program, she thought, watching Razar. *And somehow, despite her outspoken anger at her father, protected Unipoesa's record of participation. The entire Starways is going to come after you now.*

Forgetting the world around them, Senka and Razar talked of her future plans. Senka told him some of what she knew about the discovery of Kurt Stein and the Ark, and of her excitement at the prospect of rebuilding planets.

"It's going to take a little while. I need to brush up on a lot of biology and environmental science," she chortled. "But it will be nice to be working on a peace mission."

Senka combed back her uncle's stringy white hair. "You need a shave and a haircut, badly."

Razar's face hardened. "No. What I need to do is get out of this place." He looked at Jaeia with stern eyes. "Tell the General Assembly and the military council that, effective immediately, I am standing down as Military Minister!"

"Uncle!" Senka gasped.

"No," he said adamantly. "Seeing you changes everything."

As she watched the Minister argue with Dr. Kaoto to be released, Jaeia decided it was more than that. *There's something different about the Minister.* She wasn't sure if it was the coma, the Prodgy restoration, or seeing his beloved niece, but the Minister wouldn't return to his military station.

It made her smile.

***

Unipoesa sat next to a full bottle of Old Earth vodka, unsure of why he had not yet filled his glass and started on his journey to inebriated bliss. Everyone else was celebrating Jaeia Kyron's peacetime speech. His occasion was not as joyous as the liberation of the Starways or the promise of Kurt Stein's Ark, but it was certainly a cause for drinking. His son was dead, his daughter alienated.

And Maria has found someone new, he quickly reminded himself.

Unipoesa got out from behind his desk and moved to the window overlooking Trigos and the stars. The cheers from the hallways echoed up to his room. He wished he could get away from it all, find some isolated expanse, but there was no place that could protect him from himself.

His desk beeped.

Godich; *I thought I blocked all incoming message.*

He waited for the caller to hang up, but after three minutes, he was irritated enough that he checked the listing.

Out of network.

Curiosity led him to accept the transmission.

An upturned nose pressed into the camera lens. "He ain't gonna answer."

"Move over, Bossy, he answered!"

The picture shook as the two exchanged seats. Someone belched loudly in the background. Finally, Tarsha came into full view.

"Tarsha—"

"Don't say anything," she cut him off. "You'll ruin it."

Absently, he took his chair and brought the monitor as close to him as he could.

"You kept your promise—so far. You let me and Bossy go," she said as her companion made lewd gestures with her lollipop in the background. "That makes me less inclined to try and kill you."

"That's good."

Tarsha's eyes remained serious, her voice unyielding. "Bossy and I are going to find her other sisters. Maybe after all that's settled, and you continue to keep your promise to leave us alone, I might think about calling you up."

"Tarsha, I—"

"*Might*," she stressed, stabbing her finger into the camera. Her face relaxed a little, and she leaned back into her chair.

"You're one lucky bastard to have the Kyrons in your corner. If it weren't for them, I might have killed you before I left."

Unipoesa didn't understand right away. What had the Kyrons done? Then his gut told him: *Jaeia talked to her.* Jaeia had witnessed his conversation with the Minister when he had had his catharsis. She must have shared something about that with Tarsha. That was the only explanation for why she would even bother to contact him now.

"So," Tarsha said, her hard expression breaking a little. "What's her name?"

"What?"

"Her name? Your type doesn't join the military seeking power. You did it to protect someone, probably a woman. Saw it all the time on Earth."

He couldn't keep the tears from forming, but he didn't let them fall. If nothing else, he decided, she deserved to know the truth.

"Her name was Maria. She was my wife… and the mother of my children."

***

I never thought I'd return to Fiorah, Jetta thought, breathing in the hot, recycled air as she stepped off of an Alliance-acquired mercenary ship and onto the red-rock surface. She looked up, seeing the transparent airfield dome covering the city and remembered darker times. *Especially with my siblings.*

Everything looked different. The Alliance had started to slowly introduce community funding to repair condemned housing structures and bring some of the lower-income buildings up to code. Although crime lords still ruled the streets and the Underground, with the prospect of a better life, a small movement had begun among the people to instill a democratic governing body. Flyers for the first election decorated street signs and bus stop benches. Jetta even spotted a few people constructing a voter registration booth near a newly-erected health clinic.

Fiorah still isn't safe, or a good place to be a kid, she thought as she passed by a rag-tag group of children begging near a boarded up pawn shop. Digging into the pockets of her disguise, she gave them what cash she could spare without drawing attention to her or her party. Even a little went a long way. One boy, covered in dirt, his left eye swollen shut from a suspicious injury, gave her a lingering look before scampering off. *But at least change is coming.*

But most of all, Jetta no longer felt afraid. It wasn't that she was much bigger, or that she could now command her greatest talent.

I know who am, she thought, not shying away as a junkie, clutching his bottle of booze, cursed in her direction. She saw past his words and the drugs lacing his mind, right down to the memories locked away by pain. Secrets unfolded, revealing more than just his world and all of its intricate workings. *And I see all that can I do.*

As they approached the warehouse district, Jetta allowed Aesis to take the lead, but kept her brother and sister behind her. Hard cash got them access into the parasitic tunnels of the Underground Block, and her sister's second voice helped them slip past the flesh gangs and into the slave chamber corridors.

"Yahmen's using your aunt and uncle to stock the organ carts and sell young children and babies at the auctions," Aesis said as they traveled down dark passageways lit by an occasional bare bulb. The screams and moans echoing down the corridors tore at her mind, only to be outdone by the competing smells of rot and waste.

Of course he'd make them sell kids, Jetta thought, remembering Galm's confession to purchasing them from a drifter in the Underground Block. She couldn't think of a more deranged torment for her sweet adoptive parents.

We're almost there, Jaeia said, soothing her tension before she worked herself up.

One last obstacle. A guard, two meters tall and armed to the teeth with guns and knives stood in front of the main slave chambers. Green-scaled skin and yellow, feline eyes made her suspect an outerworlder origin, but she couldn't be sure.

Let me take this one, Jetta called to her sister.

Are you sure? I don't know what species he is; he might be resistant, or even able to detect our talents.

Trust me.

Before Jaeia could respond, Jetta felt her brother engage her sister in a private conversation. Seconds later, they both gave their silent approval.

Using slave-trader hand signals, Jetta attempted to work a deal. "A thousand, cash, for the Galm Drachsi and Lohien Chen."

"Boss is keeping these two. No sale," the guard said, hawking up something thick from his throat and spitting it dangerously close to Jetta's boot.

Jetta read his mind, sensing his darker appetites. She considered catering to those when she caught the tail end of his deepest sorrow. "I'll make it worth your while."

"Yeah?" he said, chomping on a dehydrated human finger.

To keep from throwing up, Jetta focused on their objective. "I'll give you this."

The guard fell to the floor, eyes wide and unseeing as Jetta took his keys and walked over him. For the next hour or so he would relive the happiest moment of his childhood, right before his parents were murdered in the Raging Front.

Jahx touched the back of her hand. *Not bad, Sis.*

Trailed by her siblings and Aesis, Jetta entered the main slave chambers. Aside from a narrow break between the high stacks of wire coops, not a centimeter of space went to waste.

These slave coops are empty—

Before her sister finished the observation, she answered the resulting question.

...Because they've been taken to be harvested.

For her aunt and uncle, Yahmen had chosen windowless isolation cells at the end of the row. Not even an average-sized human had enough space to stand up or stretch out.

"Uncle Galm?" Jetta said, cracking open the cell door. The putrid smells of decomposition assaulted her nose, making her cover her face with the back of her hand. With tears in her eyes, she peered inside, but could not see anything in the dark. Only the scuffling sound, like someone trying to get away, gave any indication of an occupant. "Uncle Galm, we've come back for you."

Jaeia shined the flashlight over her shoulder. When she saw Galm's hobbled legs, her heart ached. *He's aged well beyond his forty years,* she thought, seeing no recognition, only fear as he cried out and tried to get away from the light.

"Uncle Galm," Jahx said, squeezing past Jetta. He rested his hand on their uncle's wrinkled cheek and closed his eyes. "Everything is going to be okay now."

The old man's eyes teared up. With trembling hands he reached for Jahx's face.

"My boy… my dear boy…" A toothless mouth formed the most handsome smile. "I must be dreaming. I am so happy."

***

Minding his uncle's injuries, Jahx assisted him as best he could back to their starship. Galm leaned heavily on him, his mouth forming words that never came. Concerned, Jahx dipped inside Galm's thoughts and extracted what his uncle could not say.

After Yahmen got ousted from the mines by the Dominion Core, he got forced into the flesh markets, declining into shear madness, he determined. Terrible visions of Yahmen killing slaves, even his own workers at the most minor transgressions, cut through his mind.

Don't get distracted, Jetta said as their party exited the warehouse district and sank back into the flow of downtown foot traffic. *We're not safe yet.*

Jahx looked back, seeing Jaeia and Aesis still helping Lohien with each step. Even after he touched his aunt's mind in the slave chambers, she remained unable to speak, and could barely walk. Distant eyes would not look up, or lend any hints to the workings of her inner world.

He made a silent promise. *I won't give up on you.*

Bringing up the rear, Jetta kept tabs on the flesh gangs, junkies, and any person paying too much attention to their group as they trekked down the blistered sidewalks back toward the shipyards.

Keep him moving, Jahx, she told him as their uncle stumbled.

"I'm so sorry, uncle," Jahx said. With an arm around his waist, he took most of Galm's weight, letting him focus on his footing. "You didn't deserve any of this."

Vicious, sadistic images flashed through his mind. Jahx allowed them to flow through, letting his uncle's pain be realized as it needed to be.

I didn't think Yahmen could have been any crueler, Jetta whispered across their bond. As Jahx dared to glean the rest of their uncle's memories, he felt her pull away. Even after surviving the torments of Victor's mind, she still shied away from the reality of what Yahmen had done to their parents.

I don't want to see that either, Jaeia said. *Please, Jahx…*

Okay, he told them both, keeping their uncle's memories to himself. Maybe one day, when they could look back and see more than just the violence in the moment, he would show them the greater truth.

"Everything is going to be alright now, uncle," Jahx said, touching his forehead to his uncle's battered face.

Mumbling, Galm craned his neck upward, casting his face into the light of the many suns. For a moment, Jahx saw a younger man, one who had not yet lost all hope.

In a voice, frail and tired, Galm whispered: "Take us home."

***

After successfully loading their aunt and uncle onto the star cruiser, and Aesis volunteering to stay behind to tend to their basic needs, the triplets discussed their last duty.

"You two don't have to come with me," Jetta said, making sure her mask and hood were still in place as she walked back down the ramp.

The suns, sinking lower along the horizon, still bore down on them with intensity. *I forgot how much I hate the heat,* she thought as the rusty-orange hues of the late evening painted the sky.

"No, I'm going with you," Jaeia said.

Jahx looked to the horizon before responding. "Me too."

They made the trip back to their old apartment in silence. Condemned signs and caution tape littered the sidewalk leading up to the charred remains of the building.

That doesn't look safe, Jaeia commented as Jetta climbed over a pile of cinder blocks and examined the debris-ridden main stairwell. *Why don't we try the alley access?*

She tested a few of the steps, deciding that the cracked boards could hold her weight. *It's not that bad—*

Jahx caught her by the armpit as she fell through. "Maybe we should find another route."

"Alley access?" her sister said.

Grumbling, Jetta accepted a hand up from both her siblings. "Alley access."

After a less treacherous climb, they arrived on their floor. Much of the hallway had caved in. A rat skittered across the blackened beams, watching from above as they wound their way through the rubble. When they arrived at their door, Jetta noticed that someone had made an attempt at graffiti near their door, but had fallen through the broken floorboards.

Heart pounding in her ears, Jetta opened the door. It creaked open to a dimly lit entryway. Light filtered in from the kitchen where the wall used to be. She almost tripped over the metal framework of their old cots as she entered and made her way through to the living room.

Beer cans and balled up smokes dirtied the scorched floor. Someone had thrown a ragged blanket over the broken, half-burnt couch. In her peripheral vision she saw flies buzzing over the empty packages of meal rations, and a curious rat keeping watch from underneath a pile of yellowed papers.

The room stank of alcohol and desperation.

"I knew you'd come for me."

Out of the shadows came the burning end of a cigarette, followed by red-ringed eyes. He ground something together in his fist, making a terrible scraping sound

"I *knew* you'd come for me," he reiterated, laughing. He squeezed his fist harder, knuckles turning white.

Her siblings' emotions thundered across the psionic planes, clamping down on her belly. She took her time gathering herself as he blew a puff of smoke her way.

"*Godich* launnies. Ugly little *ratchakkers*. I should have killed you when I had the chance."

The walls shuddered, the ground beneath them rumbled. Dust and ashes rained down from the ceiling. Yahmen dropped his smoke and cried out in fear.

The quaking ceased. Jetta stepped forward and removed her mask.

"Are—are you going to kill me?" he said, clinging to the couch. Something dropped out of his other hand and rolled across the floor.

Jetta picked it up. The rock dice. Some of the corners had been worn away, but they were otherwise intact.

"No," she said, holding them tightly in her hand.

A dark shadow cast over Yahmen's face. Cracked lips parted to bare discolored teeth. "You coward. Why won't you kill me?"

"Because," Jetta said, turning her back to him. "I'm leaving you in the world you created."

***

A little known Prodgy legend speaks of other ways to enter Cudal than through the Temple of Exxuthus. The prophecy, written by Saol of Gangras after experiencing his dual existence as Rion, tells of those who will come to have the ability to create their own pathways to the realm of the Gods.

Yahmen Drachsi's company had just departed, leaving him alone in the squalid apartment.

Something's different, he thought, touching the walls next to the couch. They hummed and buzzed like living things. *Those* ratchakker *launnies did something to this place, to me—*

Shivering, he pulled at the scraps of his shirt. The air felt terribly frigid, as if someone had blown open a hole into the cold of space.

What the hell? Yahmen rubbed his swollen eyes, not believing what he saw just ahead of him. *What's that light?*

He stumbled to his feet, his hot breath steaming in the icy air. The light grew brighter. Lipless voices called his name.

Yahmen Drachsi staggered forward on drunken legs, reached out, and disappeared.

EPILOGUE

(Old) Earth: July 9, 3186

Under a scrubbed blue sky, Jetta Kyron made her way up the pathway to the farmhouse on the hill. The ground felt hard beneath her boots, but little green buds poked through the cracks, struggling to feel the light of the shining sun.

Cano and Kiyiyo surprised her as she emerged from a newly-planted row of trees, knocking her off her feet and covering her in wolf kisses.

"Alright already," she said, putting up her hands to shield her face. As they backed off, she wiped the spit from her cheeks and eyes. "Where have you two been anyway?"

Curiosity touched her mind, and the wondrous smells of a changing environment.

"Exploring, huh? Fair enough," she chuckled. As she turned onto her side to get up, she saw her reflection in a tiny stream.

"That's new," Jetta marveled, putting her hand in the water. Clear and cool, it felt good running through her fingers.

Smiling, she looked to the sky. Somewhere up above, Josef Stein's nanites were still working tirelessly to clean up the atmosphere. Every day the air smelled cleaner. And today, on her ninth birthday, she no longer had to wear a mask or a biohazard suit.

Jaeia opened the front door as she was climbing up to the porch. "Hey, better late than never," she teased.

Over her sister's shoulder, Jetta saw the balloons and streamers adorning the inside of the house. "Oh Gods, please tell me you didn't make a big deal out of this," Jetta said, tugging on the *Happy Birthday!* banner dangling from the front window.

"Come on," Jaeia said, pinching her shoulder as she walked inside the house. "When are you ever going to lighten up?"

Aesis came up from behind Jaeia and wrapped his arms around her, kissing her cheek. "What do you think of the place?" he asked Jetta excitedly.

"Aesis helped decorate," Jaeia giggled.

Jetta gripped Aesis by the shoulders. "If you expect to become my brother-in-law, then don't feed into my sister's cheesiness."

After putting her gifts for her siblings on the dining room table, Jetta made her way to the living room to see how her uncle was doing. As usual, she found him sitting by the fire, reading a newsreel. His new prosthetic foot lay on the floor as he massaged the stump and mumbled the news to himself.

I wish he had let the Prodgies heal him, she thought. Then again, old prejudices were hard to fight.

When he saw her, he greeted with a cheerful smile and a warm hug.

"So glad you could take some time off, dear. All three of you work too much," he said, holding onto her hand.

"I know, *Pao*. But if we can restore Earth, we can restore all the planets in the Starways. Even build some new ones," Jetta said. "And if feels good to be doing something like this after fighting for so long."

Galm looked at her with a proud expression. "That's good, dear. Very, very good."

Jetta was helping him put his new foot back on when a light humming drifted from the kitchen. Peering around the corner, Jetta saw Lohien putting the finishing touches on a cake, singing softly to herself. Her hair was done up in a pretty bun, and she was wearing the new dress Jaeia had gotten her.

"Dear, where's your brother? He's been out for hours," Galm asked, drawing back her attention.

Jetta listened with her inner senses. "He's still in the mountains. I'll go get him."

"Don't be late," her uncle said in a fatherly tone.

A woman with bushy white hair stopped her as she grabbed a coat from the closet.

"Jetta Ashya Kyron, where do you think you're going without a hat? It gets cold in the mountains!" she said, reaching up and grabbing a knitted orange hat from the top shelf.

Jetta smelled her sweet perfume and the lingering odor of spices, along with a hint of sugar cookies, her new favorite. Her stomach growled excitedly at the prospect of her grandmother's cooking.

"Thanks, Gams," she said, pretending to be annoyed as she stuffed the hat on her head.

"I may be 1,205 years old, but I still know a thing or two," she said. Hazel eyes only projected kindness and love. "And you may be the chief commanding officer of the Starways Alliance, but I'll always be your grandmother."

"Okay, okay," Jetta said with a smile.

"Oh, Sweetpea! Wait! Did your sister tell you the good news?" she said, stopping her at the front door. Jetta was about to remind her for the millionth time that they shared thoughts regularly, but their grandmother was still adjusting to the fact that she had awakened from cryostasis over a thousand years in the future. Jetta didn't expect her to grasp the concept that her grandchildren were telepathically gifted anytime soon.

"Three more of your cousins have been—oh bother, what's the expression? Thawed?"

Jetta nodded politely.

"Anyway, I've invited them here, and your Grandmother Yvonne went to go pick them up from the hospital. Some home cooking would do them good after a few centuries, don't you think?"

Before picking up the trail to the mountains, Jetta passed by the wolf enclosure and made sure to say hello to the rest of the pack. Everyone insisted on a belly rub and ear scratch, wagging their tails and whining until she completed her rounds. With a lot of help from Tarsha and some new Earth contacts, she had managed to liberate almost all of the wolves from the fighting rings. There was still a lot of work left to be done, but with every life she saved, she quietly thanked the stars.

The city became visible as she rode Kiyiyo up the mountain pass. For the first time she saw lights on in the downtown office buildings. Farther out, through the brown haze, stood the white-capped structure of the new spaceport. Only a few more weeks and commercial spaceflights to and from Earth would begin. She still hadn't prepared her speech for the commencement ceremony, but she usually relied on her sister to know what to say for those kinds of things.

Jetta yelled to Kiyiyo to go faster. She loved the feel of the wind in her hair. And the faster she rode, the more likely she was to bring her back.

Faster and faster the giant wolf bound up the mountains. Soon, Jetta let go of his fur and leaned back, extending her arms. Blue veins glowed in the sunlight. The air crackled with electrical charge, and the hairs on her neck stood on end. Slender arms wrapped around her waist. Jetta smiled, feeling the Healer's lips pressed to her cheek.

My love...

Soon enough Jetta would find a way to bring her back to physical form. She had no doubts. With a love as strong as theirs, there was no place that Triel could go that she wouldn't be able to find her.

Jetta allowed Kiyiyo to slow as they traversed the spiky ridge and dismounted when they came to the sheer face of the mountainside. The wolf panted and paced anxiously as he watched her climb toward the sky, leaping for the final handhold.

Jetta pulled herself up and over the top with a grunt. After catching her breath, she found Jahx in his usual meditative position, sitting cross-legged at the highest point of the mountain peak. His lips were moving, his expressions changing as if he were having a conversation. For a second she thought she saw the outline of a face across from Jahx's, but it vanished in the wind.

He had been spending more and more time alone on the mountaintop. Jaeia had shared her concern for his strange behavior, but every time Jetta brought it up, Jahx distanced himself from the subject.

"Jahx," she said, kneeling down next to him. "It's time to go home. Dinner is starting soon."

Jahx opened his eyes. Blue eyes seemed troubled with something she could barely grasp. His knowing pulled at his heart, and consequently at hers.

"Tell me what's going on, Jahx," she whispered, putting a hand on his knee. "Please."

Jahx sucked in his breath. "I can hear them now."

"Who?"

Dark brows pinched his forehead. "The ones Victor called the Azerthenes."

Jetta pulled her coat tighter around her body as the northern winds bit through her layers. She was glad her grandma had told her to wear a hat. She didn't know how Jahx wasn't freezing. He rarely wore anything more than a light jacket when he went on his meditations.

"What do they want?" Jetta said.

Jahx looked down at his hands. "I'm not sure."

Jetta knew what he was thinking, and came up with all the reasons he shouldn't go. He responded to her thoughts just as swiftly.

"I have helped Kurt and the other scientists as best as I can. I have created advanced interface programs to bring Josef Stein's knowledge back to life," Jahx said. He looked to the blossoming city. "This planet is healing. Other worlds will follow. There is not much more I can do here."

"Yes there is," Jetta said, taking his hand. "You could stay here with me. You can be happy."

Jahx eyes brightened at the words she left unspoken.

"How would you even cross over? The Temple of Exxuthus has been destroyed," Jetta dared to ask.

Jahx pointed to his head and then to Jetta's heart. "There are other places where one can cross over. Weak points in the divide. Points within ourselves that have been opened by significant events… or people."

Jetta rested her head on his shoulder. She didn't know what to say.

"Okay, you're right," Jahx said, hearing her inner voice. He put his arm around her and squeezed. "This is a good day. And we will have this moment forever."

"Well then, if that's the case," Jetta said, reaching into her pocket and producing the rock dice. "How about we make this 'forever moment' me beating you in an all-or-nothing game?"

"I thought we had to get back home?"

Jetta winked. "Don't chicken out. It's just one game. Come on—I'll give you first roll."

Jahx hesitated. At first Jetta mistook it for lack of interest. Then she realized he was close to crying. Looking into his blue eyes, she saw his awareness that this moment would not last forever, despite how his heart ached for its permanence.

"Please tell me we're not too old to play games," she said, nudging him and handing him the dice.

Silently she whispered, *We will always have this love, and we will always have each other*.

Jahx wiped his eyes, and with a smile that transformed his face, he rolled the dice.

Coming soon!

The message was in full text, no recording. *Now I see. I am burning.*

Jetta inhaled sharply. Something sang across the psionic plane, a keening, animal cry of pain, but it was gone as soon as it came.

Jahx—something awful is happening! Jetta screamed across their connection.

She stopped in the hall and fell to her knees.

Now I see. I am burning.

Jetta clutched her stomach. "No—NO! Impossible!"

She opened her eyes to the white flames of a different world, and the shrieks and whispers of her oldest and fiercest enemy.

—*Triorion: Nemesis (Book Five)*

For more information go to: www.triorion.com

Acknowledgments

This message comes with a very big thanks to Nicci Peschel and Melissa Erickson for lending their artistic skills to the series, as well as their enthusiasm. I'd also like to thank my parents and brother for their love and support, as well as my dear godmother and favorite auntie in Chicago for being my biggest fans.

A huge thanks to all my friends who have endured me jabbering on about this series for years, and still put up with me. Friends are the best kind of family.

To my fellow authors and editors Paula Herrmann, Neo Edmund, Vivian Trask, Ramon Terrell, Julie Campbell, Stant Litore and many more—thank you for your advice, readership, and everything else you've done to support this series.

And last, but not least, I'd like to share my appreciation for Erin Cochran for putting up with some very "rough" drafts in the beginning of *Triorion*, and for helping me evolve to be the writer I am today. To complete books one through four has meant the world to me. Thank you.

About the Author

L. J. Hachmeister is an author and registered nurse from Denver, Colorado. When not writing novels, she enjoys spending time with friends and family, and chasing after her wild mountain dogs.

Made in the USA
Middletown, DE
04 April 2017